C000002134

Robert Mawson was born in Londo.. ..
at Westminster. A journalist and copywriter, he also spent
ten years working in the aviation industry as a commercial
pilot. He lives near Aldeburgh in Suffolk where, as well as
writing, he is a partner in a design and communications
consultancy. *A Ship Called Hope* is his first novel.

A SHIP
CALLED
HOPE

Robert Mawson

WARNER BOOKS

A *Warner* Book

First published in Great Britain by
Warner in 1994

Copyright © Robert Mawson 1994

John Clare's poem 'I Am' is reproduced by permission of
Curtis Brown Ltd., London. Copyright © Eric Robinson 1984.

The moral right of the author has been asserted.

All characters in this publication are fictitious and
any resemblance to real persons, living or dead, is purely
coincidental.

All rights reserved.
No part of this publication may be reproduced,
stored in a retrieval system, or transmitted, in
any form or by any means without the prior permission
in writing of the publisher, nor be otherwise circulated
in any form of binding or cover other than that in which
it is published and without a similar condition including
this condition being imposed on the subsequent purchaser.

A CIP catalogue for this book
is available from the British Library.

ISBN 0 7515 0985 X

Typeset by Solidus (Bristol) Limited
Printed and bound in Great Britain by Clays Ltd, St. Ives PLC

Warner Books
A Division of
Little, Brown and Company (UK) Limited
Brettenham House
Lancaster Place
London WC2E 7EN

To Christopher, Jonathan and Victoria
with love

PROLOGUE

Her hand reached out, stopped, then reached out again and knocked. She stepped back quickly as though the whole shed might collapse in front of her. Nothing. She waited a full minute, head down, hugging the cardigan tighter around her shoulders against the chill, nervously flicking a thumbnail against her teeth. Eventually she shivered, blew a misted sigh into the clear night sky, reached out once more and lifted the catch.

The door seemed to be stuck. She pushed harder and it gave suddenly, scattering pieces of folded newspaper that had been jammed around the inside of the doorframe. Peering into the darkness, she hesitated before stepping gingerly inside. The smell struck her immediately. Warm, rank and powerful, garden shed smells mixed with men's body odour and wood smoke from the pot-bellied stove.

At first she couldn't see anything: the single overhead light was off. But the computer was on, sitting on the workbench to the right, screen covered in text, cursor flashing patiently at the bottom. As her eyes grew accustomed to the gloom, its luminous glow cast green shadows around the far end of the shed. Books and papers scattered across the bench. Piles of magazines stacked on the floor, haphazardly arranged pictures taped to the walls. A slumped body lying on a worn out leather armchair by the stove.

'Hello?' she whispered fearfully. 'It's Emma.' She stepped closer. He looked like a dead tramp, hunched on the chair, scruffy and unmoving, his head hanging limply sideways onto his chest. A blanket lay on the floor at his feet, lengths of cotton wool protruded from his ears. Wide-eyed she stared down at the motionless form, heart pounding in her chest. Then she heard his breathing, dry, rasping and shallow, saw the tell-tale glint of a bottle poking from the crook of his arm.

'Are you awake?' She knelt beside him and touched a hand to his cheek, but he didn't stir. She ran the back of her fingers down the untidy growth of beard, brushed unkempt jet-black hair from his eyes. His face was slack, almost relaxed; and youthful. Despite the beard, suddenly he looked no more than ten or twelve, a worn out little boy asleep on an armchair. Tears welled in her eyes again, only this time they were for him. She leaned forward and pulled his head gently against her. 'My God,' she gasped, the tears running freely. 'My God, my God, my God.'

She stayed, rocking gently as she hugged him to her. She stayed until his hair grew damp from the fall of her tears. Until his breathing steadied and deepened into real sleep. Until the soft glow of moonlight shone on the grass beyond the doorway.

Then she kissed him once more on the forehead, lifted the blanket back around his chin and went back to the house.

CHAPTER

1

Peter placed the teacup carefully on the table beside his wife's head, flicked on the clock radio, then turned to study his naked form in the wardrobe mirror.

'Wake up sleepy head,' he said absently, twisting sideways to the mirror and running a hand critically down the flat and darkly matted smoothness of his stomach. He stuck his tongue out, fingering the closely cropped black hair at the nape of his neck. 'Must get a trim,' he muttered.

Emma stirred, reaching for the cup. He drew back the bedroom curtains and studied the August morning sky above rows of terraced houses opposite. Faint milky swirls of dissipating vapour trails high in the airspace above the London control zone, otherwise flawless. 'Fabulous,' he announced, breathing deeply. 'Severe clear. All day.'

'You'll be arrested,' she said, hoisting herself to a sitting position. He left the window and pulled on underpants and socks, carefully selecting a suit and shirt from the neat rows suspended in the wardrobe and laying them on the bed.

'Where's my tie? The blue Simpsons one with little white dots?'

'Dry cleaners.'

He frowned, hesitated then discarded the shirt in a heap onto a chair, pulling a different one from the wardrobe.

'There's a PTA meeting at Jamie's school next Tuesday six thirty,' said Emma. 'Do you want to go?'

'Yes. I think we should; we missed the last one.' His mind raced ahead. Probably not. Tuesday, bit inconvenient, weekly sales team brainstorm in the pub. 'Can you cover if I get tied up at the office?'

She shook her head as she sipped. 'You know I'm at the agency most Tuesdays.'

'Ah, yes.' He opened the little leather box he'd bought in Morocco and poked around among the gold and silver, digging past the dull gleam of his wedding ring, until he fished a pair of gold oval cufflinks. 'Are you planning to go back to work? Full-time that is.'

She answered casually, but watched him closely. 'Would you mind? There's nothing much for me to do here; Mrs Newton takes care of it all and what with the children at school a lot—'

'Not to mention the nanny.'

'Meaning?'

'Nothing.' He held up his hands – don't shoot. The cost. They were spending a lot. Far too much probably, and he'd lost track, hadn't really had time to sit down and balance the books. Maybe at the weekend. He picked up his jacket, glancing at his Rolex as it slipped over his hand. 'Must dash. What are you up to today?' He walked quickly around the bed and bent to kiss her.

She lifted her chin automatically, sighed. 'Oh, lunch with Amanda, check out Cezanne at the Tate, probably stop in at Dylan's. Would you?'

He was already at the door. 'Hmm?'

'Would you mind if I went back to work? Always assuming I could find work to go back to that is?'

He hesitated at the door. Not now. 'Um, yes, no, I hadn't really thought about it. Look could we talk about it later Em? I really have to run – sales director's coming in early – board meeting last night apparently. We will discuss it, I promise.' He turned back to the door. 'Say goodbye to the kids for me.'

She listened as his footfall receded briskly down the stairs, a moment later she heard the front door slam.

Peter Deacon first realised that something was not quite right as he drove up the hill towards the factory entrance. Unusually, a stationary queue of traffic was waiting to turn left into the gates; it extended all the way back to the main road and at least a hundred yards down the hill. A grim-faced policeman gesticulated energetically, struggling to liberate passing motorists from the line waiting to enter the factory.

Deacon assumed that the disruption had something to do with security, a change in procedure or a new replacement for Bill on the barrier. He sat patiently, listening to the radio, craning his neck to check the straightness of his tie in the rear-view mirror. Eventually he reached the entrance and swung the Rover through the gates. There was a hold up at the security hut all right, normally Bill waved everyone through as soon as he recognised them, but today every car was being stopped. And apart from Bill there were two other men at the barrier. Not in uniform, business suits, one carrying a clipboard, the other a large cardboard box.

Eventually he reached the barrier. 'Morning Bill, what's up?' The security man shrugged, said nothing. He looked bemused, uncomfortable. The man with the clipboard squatted at the window.

'Name please.'

'Peter Deacon.'

He checked the name off, the second man flicked through

3

the contents of his box and withdrew an envelope.

'May we suggest that you park the vehicle over there in the manager's car-park. You can leave the keys in the ignition.' The barrier swung up; he was waved through. Three minutes later he left the lift at the fourth floor and walked down the corridor to his office.

'Hello Nick, what the blazes is going on?' A lean, balding man in spectacles sat behind the second desk in the small office. He had his jacket off, tie loosened, the top button of his shirt undone. His feet were on the desk, chair tilted back precariously, hands clasped behind his head. He raised his eyebrows.

'Haven't read it yet then?'

'Do I want to?' Deacon dumped his briefcase on the desk, took out the envelope, slit it with a brass letter opener, read for a minute. 'Christ,' he murmured. He perched on the corner of his desk, read again. Nick picked his letter up and studied it.

'Longest six lines I ever read,' he said quietly. 'What do you think Pete? They'll need to keep on some sales and marketing people won't they?'

'Who knows.' He replaced the letter in its envelope and stared out of the window. 'I expect we'll find out at eleven.'

'Good-morning everyone. My name is Jonathan Isaacs. By now I trust you will have seen my letter to you. I am here to explain more fully the contents of that letter, and answer questions of a general nature. I am quite sure that all of you will be anxious to find out how this situation affects you as individuals. As you can see, my staff are on hand, they will be happy to answer all your questions at the end of this announcement.'

The factory floor was packed. Nearly three hundred employees gathered in a huge semicircle at one end. Shop-

4

floor workers in white overalls rubbed shoulders with office clerks and typists; draughtsmen side by side with canteen staff; stress analysts and aerodynamicists grouped incongruously alongside accountants and salesmen. For the first time that he could ever recall, Deacon saw the entire human fabric of the company assembled under one roof. There was an air of bewilderment. Some sought support or explanation, murmuring to each other in low tones. Others turned away. One or two wept. There was shock in some eyes, bitterness or resignation in others. But most wore expressions of wide-eyed disbelief, as though half expecting Isaacs to announce that it was all a terrible mistake.

'At eight thirty last night, the board of directors of United Aerospace Systems appointed my company as official receiver. I am not here to explain the circumstances leading up to that decision, a full announcement will be made by the board to employees and shareholders in due course.' Isaacs stood on a large shipping case, speaking through a loud-hailer, an assistant at his side, carefully and publicly transcribing his every word onto a notepad. His amplified voice echoed around the factory, confident and relaxed. As he spoke, he swung slowly from side to side, swivelling smoothly like a garden sprinkler, calmly drizzling platitudes on the upturned faces of his congregation. The text was as familiar to him as the mute and anxious expressions ranged before him. It was a speech he had made on countless factory floors, in shops and offices, small family businesses and multinational corporations. He felt no pity, just a sense of order and control.

'With effect from eight thirty last night, the management of UAS passed into the hands of the receiver. I should emphasise right away that this means that the board have relinquished all control of the company. In effect the receiver now manages this business and I am therefore your managing director.' He paused to allow this news to soak through. 'It is the receiver's task to act on behalf of this company's secured creditors to recover as much of their investment as possible. Amongst other things, this entails stopping all further expenditure, and therefore I have to tell you that with effect from noon today, United Aerospace Systems will cease trading.'

There was more. After the heartfelt groan had subsided and the little pockets of muttering had died down, Isaacs continued with the details. He pointed to a long row of newly erected trestle tables down one wall of the factory. Behind the tables his staff sat patiently beneath large signs displaying letters of the alphabet. They watched impassively like emigration officials waiting to process the next plane load of travellers; exit visas for all. Isaacs' voice was calm and fluent like a radio newsreader's, droning on about redundancy letters and the distribution of information packs explaining employees' statutory rights. With the exception of one or two accounts and administration staff, the entire workforce were to be laid off immediately, a regrettable but necessary decision, he said. One not taken lightly, best interests at heart, any queries at all please don't hesitate and so on.

Deacon waited to collect his pack with the other D to Fs. As he queued, the girl in front turned and looked up at him, her eyes filling with tears. It was Sandra Everly, the fun loving redhead from the typing pool. He remembered reading about her months ago in the house journal. She'd done a sponsored parachute jump for charity. He had worked with her for years, perhaps even the entire nine years of his service with the company, yet he hardly knew her.

'Oh Mr Deacon, it can't be true, it isn't true is it?' He shrugged, trying to smile, but he could say nothing. Her tears sprang; he hesitated, embarrassed. She stood with her head hanging, her hands at her sides, alone as though in disgrace. Her eyes were awash with muddy, mascara-stained tears. Others in the queue looked away. He drew her to him, held her awkwardly, a strangers' embrace, feeling the little shudders against his chest as they moved slowly with the queue.

All about them, staff were making their way slowly back to workplaces, or standing alone in corners studying the contents of their packs. Some stood around in groups talking quietly as the full implications settled like fall out. Suddenly anxious to separate himself from the mêlée, he collected their documents and set off with her across the factory floor. Eventually he found Sandra's department head.

'This may seem like the end of the world,' he said as they parted, 'but you are a very clever and loyal girl and I know you will be just fine.' Empty cheer, but it was the best he could do.

She forced her flushed cheeks into a wry smile. 'Thank you.' She was led into a corridor. After a few yards she stopped and turned, calling after him over the heads. 'And you'll be fine too Mr Deacon. I know you will.'

The rest of the day passed in a blur of phone calls and telefaxes to customers, a confused sorting of correspondence and filing, and a final clearing out of desks. At lunchtime the dozen or so members of the sales and marketing middle management team fled to a wine bar some distance from the factory. They were not allowed to take their cars off the premises and had to phone for a minibus. There was bemusement at the security gate when they were stopped, relieved of their company credit cards and politely reminded that they were no longer to book any expenses to account.

Over bottles of Soave and Beaujolais the conversation ebbed and flowed. One minute the executive management came under bitter attack for their incompetent handling of the company's business affairs, the next moment the talk, less strident, was of job markets, headhunters and contacts, the decline of the defence industry, their own chances. Money.

Deacon said little but drank steadily. He disliked the kangaroo court atmosphere and the mutual absolution of responsibility. 'It wasn't our fault, it was the sodding design staff. God, if half the systems worked as they were supposed to . . .' There was an uneasiness about the buckpassing. They were all aware that as the department responsible for selling the company's wares to the world's armed forces, their role in its downfall was being perceived by many as fundamental. Already several of them had been on the receiving end of vicious recriminations from staff. Deacon had taken two anonymous phone calls at his desk during the morning, both he assumed from people he had previously regarded as colleagues. One calmly enquired whether he and his 'fellow playboys' were satisfied with themselves. The second, a coarse and abrasive voice he knew but couldn't put a name to, quickly launched into a seamless torrent of foul abuse. He had put the phone down on both without speaking.

After lunch he sat at his desk, drinking Scotch with Nick and sorting his personal possessions into a box. After nine years there were surprisingly few. A framed photograph of Emma and the children, some small gifts and ornaments' from customers, souvenirs of innumerable visits abroad. He threw away a drawerful of matchbooks collected from hotels, clubs and restaurants. Some had names and telephone numbers scribbled inside. Gloria from Taipei, Sam from Sydney, Maxine from Sacramento. He could recall none of them.

He tried phoning Emma but she was out. He considered leaving a message on the answerphone, a forewarning, but he rejected the idea, better face to face.

Finally, at about six he raised his glass to Nick, wished him well, promised to stay in touch. Then he walked down the corridor to the lift, shaking hands and kissing cheeks. He pressed the button and waited. There was a long list of people he knew he should say goodbye to, but suddenly he just wanted to get away, quickly. He took the lift to the ground floor, left the building by a side door and slipped out through the gates unnoticed. The sky was still clear, the early evening sunshine bright and warm. Carrying his box under one arm and his briefcase in the other, he plodded down the steep hill towards the railway station. And he didn't look back.

'You're late!' Emma hissed as he let himself in. She was standing outside the closed door of the sitting room, one oven-gloved hand holding a dish of cocktail sausages, the other resting on the door handle. She was wearing a short black dress, her hair tied back, face made-up. Oh God, the dinner party.

'Em, Jesus, sorry. Something came up at work . . .'

'Well you should have bloody well called, left a message. Everybody's here. We're sitting down in five minutes.' She disappeared into the room, cutting off the crescendo of voices as she closed the door behind her. He checked his watch. Eight fifteen. Jesus.

He'd had to wait for a through train, then catch a cab across town. It was an awful journey, the first time he'd ever done it other than by car. When the train finally arrived, it was packed and he had to stand. Then there was a queue at the taxi rank, and the traffic across London had been terrible. He was exhausted, filthy and hungover from the day's drink. But there was nothing for it. Five minutes later, face washed, wearing a fresh shirt and halfway into a large Scotch and soda, he swung into the sitting room.

'So sorry everyone,' he grinned as they turned, 'spot of bother at the farm.'

They were eight for dinner. They sat at a pine table in the kitchen. It was warm enough to leave the French windows open. Peter turned off the kitchen lights, switching on floodlights in the tiny garden, candles flickered on the table. He slotted a Fleetwood Mac compilation CD into a portable player on the sideboard. As Emma ladled gaspacho, he walked around the table, chatting, pouring Sancerre and unscrewing bottles of Perrier, resting a hand on a shoulder, or nibbling an ear mischievously as he leaned in to fill glasses. Finally he drew his chair in at one end of the table, catching Emma's eye across the candlelight as he sat. It was not yet fully defrosted. Like the gaspacho.

Michelle Mitchell forked a mouthful of salmon, then reached under the table to pat his knee. 'Okay, Peto?' He turned to focus on her, head cocked, quizzical. He'd drunk nearly a bottle by himself. 'How's things in the surveillance radar business?'

He hesitated. If it had just been the Mitchells for dinner, just Dan and Mitch, he could have spilled the beans, discussed it openly; he would have liked to. But now was not the time, not with all these others here. 'Oh you know Mitch,' he began. But she was already nodding, her index finger painting little circles in the air.

'Round and round, who'd have guessed.' She smiled. They had been friends since before he and Dan had left the Air Force to seek fortunes in the civil sector. Dan had gone into advertising, Peter into defence equipment.

'Any more globetrotting on the agenda?'

'Not in the immediate future, I would say.'

They had succeeded, up to a point. Peter was thirty-five, Dan a little older. In ten years they had achieved individual success. Dan was an account manager with one of the bigger London agencies, Peter had risen through the ranks to the post of marketing manager with UAS. They could both reasonably expect directorships before too long. Well, Dan anyway.

'How're the kids?' she asked.

'Fine, fine. Well Jamie is definitely making good progress nowadays. Sal is just a party animal. Into everything, wicked sense of humour.' He had forgotten to look in on them.

'So what's up then flyboy?' She watched him closely. He smiled at her, small crows feet appearing at the corners of his dark eyes. There were tiny flecks of grey at the sides of his black, militarily short hair. He held her eyes for a moment then winked before turning away to refill the glass of a large-breasted blonde sitting to his other side.

'Julia, my love,' he said, replacing the bottle on the table. He reached out towards the cleavage, hands grasping, fingers flexed. 'Let me steady them for you while you eat your peas.' The girl shrieked; Deacon clapped his hands to his ears and recoiled, rocking back on the chair which tilted, teetered, then crashed to the floor. The others roared, he disappeared beneath the table. A moment later Julia screamed again as his hands appeared from below, swimming. His head surfaced above the table in front of her, eyes wide, cheeks bulging like fish. She beat at his head with a napkin, but he swam on up the body until his cheek rested against her bosom. There he stopped, sucking his thumb and rolling his eyes, oblivious to the half-hearted swatting. Everyone was shouting. Dan banged a pepper pot on the table like a gavel, 'Order!' the girls shrieked, fanning themselves and dabbing at the corners of their eyes with

11

their napkins. He glimpsed Emma, laughing as she feigned disapproval, her eyes alight.

Everyone stayed late. After dinner Peter produced liqueurs. He and Dan Mitchell drank Kummel from the freezer. Despite his own drunkenness, Dan noticed there was something about Peter's drinking, an edge, a sense of purpose. Later Michelle caught Dan's eye. After a couple of minutes they rose to leave, the others followed. Emma saw them out. Peter remained down, head back, eyes closed, caked onto an armchair. He listened as the party dissipated on the doorstep, timing his struggle back into awareness.

'I'm not going to touch any of this.' Emma flopped into a chair opposite, surveying the wreckage of empty glasses, overflowing ashtrays and coffee cups. 'Mrs Newton can do it in the morning. What did you think of the salmon? She helped me do it you know. Well I helped her really, passed her the ingredients, made fatuous comments.' She snorted.

'Em.'

'David and Julia are good fun. I'm not having the damn Dunwoodies again though. She's a bigot and he has got to be the dullest dinner partner in history, all divorce and dandruff.'

'Emma, we have to talk.' He lifted his head with an effort, watching her. She sat on the white armchair, steadily swinging one dark stockinged leg as it rested across the other. Around the room her collection of contemporary abstract prints and framed graphic posters adorned peach coloured walls. Books and magazines on design, colour and form littered the coffee table. She flicked at the heel of one black patent pump with the toe of the other until they both fell to the floor.

'God I'm tired. The children were murder tonight. Sally refused to go to bed and Jamie wouldn't allow Pippa to bath him. Mind you she's not really up to it. Bit dippy that one.

I'll contact the agency in the morning.'
  'Emma for Christ's sake!'
  'What happened to the car Peter?'

The next morning he awoke early as usual. It was light outside, and still quiet. An electric milkfloat was making its way down the street towards the house; click hum click rattle click hum. He heard it most mornings; it was a part of his routine.

He lay on his back listening to the ticking of the clock and Emma's steady breathing, then slid out of bed, carefully rearranging the covers behind him before padding blearily across the room and into their bathroom. His body reminded him of the previous night's abuses. But he ignored the throbbing head, the bloated feeling and dizziness and turned on the shower, drinking alka seltzer as he stood under the jets. Too much alcohol, not enough sleep. Air Force prescription. Squadron folklore was founded on the formula. Stay up most of the night partying, rise with the lark, strap a flying machine securely to your rear end and launch into the clear azure to gambol among the gods before winging home like a pigeon for breakfast. *Per ardua ad astra*. Simple and splendid. But it had been easier then, he had been ten years younger.

He had given her the facts last night, at her insistence. She wanted it all, from the beginning. 'Start when you arrived at work . . .' Wearily he ran the story, but it was like screening a B movie: he'd seen it all before and somehow it didn't bear any relevance any more. He edited as he went, selectively omitting certain scenes: the abusive phone calls, the whiskey, Sandra Everly. Emma leaned forward in the armchair, alert and attentive, pouncing on non-sequiturs; 'What do you mean the board weren't there . . .?'

After he finished, she looked thoughtful, flicking a thumbnail against her teeth, her body making little rocking motions. Then she looked over at him, face softening. 'My poor love. It must have been dreadful.' She came over to him, curled onto his lap, resting her head on his shoulder and stroking his neck. 'We'll manage,' she murmured. 'You'll be snapped up. If not' – she twirled a finger into the short hair at the back of his neck – 'you'll just have to put me out on the street.' She squirmed on his lap, he ran his hand slowly up her thigh to the stocking top, then back to the dimples of her knee. If not?

After showering he shaved and dressed then went downstairs to the carnage. He wanted to begin right away, spread himself out on the dining-room table, construct a strategy. Most of the living space on the ground floor of the house was open plan, the dining area forming one end of the main room. The table was littered with bottles and glasses, dishes of nuts and ashtrays. He began clearing, working from the far end of the sitting room, shuttling backwards and forwards to the kitchen. On the fourth rotation, he re-entered the sitting room to find his three-year-old daughter clutching a blanket in one hand and a grease congealed cocktail sausage in the other.

'Hallo my daddy.' He knelt, arms wide. Coyly she shuffled to him, bestowed an oily kiss on his cheek, went back to the table, smearing the back of her hand across loose coils of long blonde hair. She clambered onto a chair, reaching for a glass of port dregs. He intercepted her, stacking the remaining plates and glasses onto the tray.

'I did have some wine,' she said in passing, then: 'Saturday today.' She pronounced it Sattaday.

'Friday Sally, Saturday tomorrow.'

'Sattaday.'

'Friday, and you've got to get dressed, you've got school today.'

'Sattaday.'

'Sally, why do you keep saying it's Saturday?'

'Because my daddy is here when I did get up in the morning today.'

And breakfast was a confusion. Everybody was unsettled by the intruder dislocating their routine. Emma sat at one end of the refectory table in jeans and sweatshirt, steadying her hands around a coffee cup. The children munched cornflakes in silence, studying the interloper, watching, calculating. Sally seemed quite pleased to see him. Jamie, six, openly hostile.

'What's he doing here?' He glared at his father, but sought explanation from Emma. She glanced at Peter, measuring her words.

'Daddy is having a short holiday while he changes his job. For another one.' They digested in silence. Then Sally popped the question.

'Why?'

Emma looked at him, shrugged. Your ball. He shifted in the Windsor armchair, cleared his throat, lowering his head to their level.

'Well, the thing is, unfortunately Daddy's work –'

'United Aerospace Systems,' said Jamie quickly.

'That's right.'

'Night air spale scissors,' said Sally.

'Uh huh. Well it has, closed. And so I am going to get a new job. In the meantime I get to stay at home and spend more time with you two.'

'You mean you got the sack.'

'Jamie! He did not get the sack. He just told you, his work has closed down and now he is going to, choose another job.'

The subject remained closed until it was time for school. Sally stood by the front door: summer dress, pink socks, red

15

sandals, swinging a Snoopy school bag against the wall. Emma was searching for her car keys. They were late; Jamie had disappeared.

'Jamie? Jamie!' She called up the stairs. 'Where is that child? Peter go and get him for God's sake, I can't find the keys to the Golf.'

He doubled up the stairs to the second floor. Jamie was in his room, lying on his back, fiddling with a Transformer. He did not look up.

'Jamie, what are you doing? Come on it's school time.'

'I'm not going.'

'What do you mean, not going?'

'I'm closing it down, choosing another one. In the meantime I get to stay at home.' He squirmed onto his side, turning his face to the wall.

After Emma had left with the children, he had most of the day to himself. She was going shopping and then had a lunch appointment. The battle of wills with Jamie was brief but unpleasant. In the end, with Emma calling impatiently from the hall and reason patently failing, he resorted to bullying and led the tearful child downstairs firmly by the wrist. 'But why Daddy?' 'Because I say so.'

Mrs Newton bustled in at about nine, bade him good-morning, brewed coffee for him but made absolutely no comment on his presence. Before she left at lunchtime however, she tapped lightly on the living-room door and asked if she might have 'a very quick word'.

'I did remind her again yesterday Mr Deacon, but I don't like to nag.'

'Of course Mrs Newton. Please accept our apologies. Let me just find my cheque-book.'

Mrs Newton was owed two hundred pounds. He was stunned. He couldn't find their joint cheque-book; it wasn't in the drawer of the Georgian bureau. He wrote out one of his, calculating as he scribbled. God she must be months behind. But it was only two weeks, twenty hours a week at four pounds an hour. 'Emma did ask me to stay on and do a little extra ironing this week.' He wrote the cheque quickly, gave it to her with a smile and another apology. After she had gone he checked the house over, it was immaculate. She did it all. Made the beds, tidied the clothes – including his and Emma's, cleaned the bathroom. She had loaded, programmed and unloaded the dishwasher, the washing machine, clothes dryer. Dashed off some ironing, vacuumed the carpets. All of it. She even left a toad-in-the-hole in the oven for him. No wonder Emma called her a treasure.

He'd already received one unpleasant surprise that morning. After emptying his briefcase and the contents of the cardboard box from work onto the dining-room table, he began sorting into piles. One pile was for job hunting: three books of business cards and his office address book. Between them these volumes contained names, addresses and telephone numbers of hundreds of industry contacts all over the world and dating back to his Royal Air Force days and beyond. The next pile consisted of the letters and information pack from the official receiver. The staff had been briefed that there would be a quantity of further communication and that it was in their interests to keep careful track of it.

The third pile was finance. He was dimly aware that he had only the vaguest idea as to the state of the Deacon treasury. He also knew that he neglected to keep proper track of household expenditure, he left it to Emma. They ran three bank accounts: his, Emma's and a joint one for standing orders and domestic expenses. He couldn't remember the last time he had seen a statement of Emma's account, yet alone the joint account. Each month he had transferred fixed sums into each, blithely assuming that she would alert him to any problems.

Returning to the bureau, he pulled open the 'finance' drawer. It was stuffed to overflowing with letters and statements, bills, invoices, receipts. Many envelopes were unopened; some were marked urgent. He dug deep into the mess, withdrew a handful at random. Two empty cheque-books, the stubs mostly blank, or marked with meaningless scribbles; a phone number, a name, an undated entry for seventeen pounds fifty. Or was it a hundred and seventy-five pounds? There was an unopened bank statement from six months ago. A discarded leaflet on the new water charges, and a letter from their builder threatening legal action for an outstanding account. It was three weeks old. Had it been paid? He had no idea. There was no way of telling. He carried the letter to the telephone in the kitchen and rang the builder. It had not, emphatically. He wrote a cheque, noting its number and date of payment on the letter before returning it to the drawer. He surveyed the contents gloomily, estimating two or three days work to sort it all out. Next he telephoned his bank manager.

'Peter, thank you for calling. So very sorry to hear your news. Saw it in the FT. Must have come as a dreadful shock.'

'Bolt from the blue John.' Thank you for calling?

'Did you have any warning?'

'Virtually none. Suspicions of course. It's hard to keep a hundred and fifty million pounds of debt under wraps indefinitely, but the board were very bullish, a transitory hiccup they called it.'

'Some hiccup. Any plans?'

'Irons hotting up in the fire as we speak. Might take a little while though.'

'Hmm.' There was silence on the line for a second as the

banker called up Peter's account details onto his screen. 'Any idea how long?'

How long? What kind of a question was that? 'No. Is there a problem?'

'Not immediately. But as I said in my last letter, we were looking for suggestions from you as to how a ... rationalisation of your situation might be put into effect. You know, convert the various overdrafts into a single loan facility, monthly instalments and so on.'

Letter? Probably in the finance drawer, somewhere. 'Indeed. But since my circumstances have changed, we'll have to put all that on ice. Temporarily, and I am going to need an extended line of credit.'

'Absolutely Peter. What did you have in mind?'

'Well a couple of thousand to be going on with.' His mind was still on the drawer. 'We've got a few short-term expenses to sort out.'

The bank manager kept his tone even. 'That's two thousand over and above the four thousand odd currently outstanding on the three accounts is it?' Four thousand! Jesus.

'Ah yes, I think so. For the moment anyway.'

'And the five thousand deferred repayment loan you took out in April.'

'Uh huh.' Good God the holiday in Thailand. His mind reeled. He had completely forgotten, had no idea things were this bad.

'Peter, you must forgive me, and I do appreciate your situation, believe me, but in order to extend credit totalling well in excess of ten thousand, I'll need some security.'

'What about the house?'

'The house carries a hundred thousand pound mortgage, Peter.'

'Yes but it's worth twice that.' He couldn't believe he was

having this conversation. Yesterday he earned fifty thousand a year basic, ran an expense account, flew business class all over the world, was wealthy, making it. Twenty-four hours later he was into pawnshop bartering with his bank manager, just to raise a few pounds to live on. He needed time to think, gather his wits. Deal with this.

'Look Peter, don't worry about it today, you've enough on your plate. I'll cover you for the moment and we can talk it over next week. Come and have some lunch.'

'Yes fine. John, I appreciate it.'

'No problem. Just one thing. Any likelihood of seeing last month's salary arrears?'

Last month? It was now a week into this month. There had been rumours of late pay cheques again at work, but he'd ignored them; it happened so often. He rubbed his forehead with his free hand; his head ached, he felt numb, shocked. He said he'd look into it, thanked him again, hung up gratefully.

He ate Mrs Newton's toad-in-the-hole at the dining-room table, surrounded by his three original mounds of papers and several smaller heaps awaiting sorting. Normally he rarely drank at lunchtime, but there was half a bottle of Fleurie left over from the previous night and his nerves needed soothing.

As he ate he drew up a prioritised action plan on a foolscap pad using the same three headings. Under finance he listed the first priority as 'Damage Assessment'. He needed to establish urgently the complete financial picture. Once that was known he could prepare a case for the bank with a view to securing the vital credit extension.

Beneath that entry, he wrote 'Economies.' There would have to be a certain amount of cutting back on luxury items. Mrs Newton for one – she would simply have to work fewer hours. And the nanny. He and Emma would compile a domestic expenditure list later. The third heading on the list under finance was headed 'Fund Raising'. They might have to look at ways of realising short-term cash if there was any delay in securing a new job.

His receivership pile required little attention. He knew nothing of his statutory rights, nor of the processes of administration, receivership and liquidation and their effects on ex-employees. But the situation was out of his hands: it was low priority, little immediate action required. He scribbled 'study leaflets, etc.' on the page and moved onto job hunting.

Following the revelations of the morning, the urge to begin telephoning friends and contacts, almost at random, was overpowering. But he resisted. He was thirty-five. His employment record was impressive, enviable in his field, unbroken. He must disregard short-term financial exigencies and structure a well-ordered campaign. A hasty or ill-considered decision at this stage was certain to be regretted later.

As he jotted on his pad, it occurred to him that there were two routes for applications. Solicited and unsolicited. It was unlikely that there would be a great many opportunities via the former route, the kind of positions he was qualified for did not crop up often. However he made a note to monitor the defence and aviation trade journals, as well as specialist appointment pages in the bigger national newspapers.

It was far more probable, he reasoned, that the position sought would be obtained by submitting a direct application to the company of his choice, probably through an intermediary such as one of his many contacts, or a specialist recruitment agency. An updated curriculum vitae was essential; his was years behind.

He allowed his mind to ponder the possibilities. A directorship, perhaps. Yes, marketing director of a small but growing engineering business in the aerospace industry. With excellent prospects of advancement to chief executive level within, say five years. Before he was forty. Or at the other end of the scale, management of a European sales team for a multinational, perhaps even a Boeing or Lockheed. Or Antonov – there were excellent opportunities opening up all over Eastern Europe.

One month should do it; he was confident. A week to prepare a hit list and produce a comprehensive curriculum vitae. Another week to propel it to the desks of selected targets, and a fortnight to set up and attend interviews. By the end of four weeks, the offers should be starting to hit the mat. He could afford to allow another week or two to make a decision. Take Emma off for a few days before taking up the new post.

By mid afternoon the situation was well in hand. But his head ached and he felt a need for fresh air. He swallowed two aspirins and walked down to Bishop's Park. The afternoon was pleasantly mild, early autumnal. The park was busy but not crowded; schoolchildren were conducting supervised sports on the playing fields. He stopped to watch a class of nine- and ten-year-old boys playing soccer. He couldn't believe how adept some of them were at ball control. At one point the ball was driven into touch near him. He fielded it neatly, turned on it, flicked it up into the hands of the waiting thrower who rewarded him with a grin.

Later he sat near the embankment and watched the passage of river traffic. Pleasure cruisers, trash barges and rowing sculls and eights from the Putney clubs. Thin trade for a river once the commercial artery to the heart of a nation, but at least there was activity, a bit of bustle. Overhead an unbroken stream of noise, as a procession of gleaming, thundering jets passed by, undercarriage doors yawning, wings glinting in the sunlight as they descended at minimum separation into Heathrow.

Emma and the children were back by the time he returned

to the house. He greeted Jamie warmly but the boy responded with a muted 'Hi, Dad' before plodding upstairs to his room. Sally threw her arms around his legs and refused to let go until, at Emma's prompt, he asked to see what she had made at school. She ran off, reappearing a minute later with a large painting comprised mostly of green and yellow hand prints. He made a fuss, went on too long about it; she lost interest and wandered off. Emma piled shopping bags onto the kitchen table. A Knightsbridge shoe shop, a famous book store and Harrods.

'Had a busy day?' He hadn't meant to tilt his head at the shopping.

'Pretty bloody. Kensington was a nightmare.'

'How was lunch?'

'Some Italian in the Old Brompton Road. Good. Expensive. Celia sends her love and . . .' she waved her hand, plucked grapes from the fruit bowl, '. . . you know.'

'Commiserations?'

'Hmm. How about you? Been out seeing someone?'

'No, just went for a walk.'

'Oh.' She turned away, began filling the kettle.

'Been busy though. Got a lot of sorting out done, groundwork.'

'Sounds highly organised. Did you contact anyone?'

'Not yet Em. It's only day one.'

'Of course. I just wondered.' She began gathering her shopping together, made for the door.

He couldn't stop himself. 'I did speak to John Bishop.' She turned, blank look. He prompted. 'At the bank?'

'Oh, God, him. Let me guess: hello Peter, threat threat threat, let's have lunch, bye for now.' She stood in the doorway with her arms laden with shopping and smirked at him. 'Right?'

He had to laugh. 'Right.'

23

CHAPTER

2

'Next Thursday looks light Dan, early evening is best. I've got the school shuttle at three thirty, kids' tea, I can probably escape around five, meet you at the squash club half-past. Do you want me to book a court?'

'I'll get it. But are you sure you can fit me in? I wouldn't want to mess up your schedule, bugger up an important stroll in the park . . .'

'Well it is something of an inconvenience, bit more notice next time Mitchell. Perhaps you could liaise with my secretary.'

'That good-looking blonde, you mean, with the sticky fingers?'

'That's her. Want a quick word?' There was the sound of whispering and clunking of the receiver, then heavy breathing as Sally came on the line.

'Uncle Dan, Mummy says I've got to go to the doctor because my leg does hurt.'

'Hello sweetheart, what have you done to your leg?'

'No yesterday. Are you coming to see me now?' She left before he could reply. Peter came on again.

'You can't get the staff you know.'

'She makes more sense than my secretary. How's it going Pete?'

Peter leaned back in his chair and looked around the room. There were neat stacks of papers arranged in an arc on the floor around him. Other heaps on the top of the bureau itself beside the telephone, an answering machine and a desk lamp. His word processor sat within easy reach at his side, perched on a table next to the bureau together with two electronic calculators, a personal organiser, an assortment of pens and pencils and the framed photograph of Emma and the children. The walls were covered in odd pages cut from stacks of magazines and newspapers arranged on the bed. Mostly product advertisements torn from trade journals. Pratt and Whitney, United Technologies, British Aerospace. A large cork noticeboard littered with pinned yellow notes, hung on the wall in place of a Michael Potter watercolour now residing under the bed. His portable compact-disc player sat on the floor in the corner.

'Well Em's not too thrilled about me turning the spare room into an office – missile testing centre she calls it, but it was hopeless trying to work downstairs. Apart from that, I guess you could say that we have control.'

'Any leads?'

'Not yet. Got a couple of headhunters onto it, and I'm following up several possibles of my own. Shouldn't be too long.'

'Need anything?'

A momentary hesitation. 'Need twenty, no better make it twenty-five thousand things.'

'Ouch.'

'Don't worry, I've got the bastards where I want them.'

'You will call if you need a sub?'

'Thanks Dan.' They hung up.

It was two weeks since he had been made redundant. Peter was amazed at how quickly the time had passed. The first few days had been spent in the dining room. Sorting and preparation he called it. The piles of paper had quickly grown up around him, his radius of operations widening by the day. He was constantly having to warn the children away and Emma complained at the mess, said he was carrying on like a triffid: 'It gets bigger every day and it looks awful when people come round. And what if we want to use the dining-room table?' He tried telling her it was strictly a temporary arrangement, but agreed it was unsatisfactory, and it was a major inconvenience having to get up and trot through to the kitchen every time he needed to use the phone, which was often.

One afternoon when Emma was out he de-camped to the spare bedroom. He rearranged all the furniture, shoving the bed up against the wall and carrying the dressing table into the box room. He ran a telephone extension lead from the socket in their bedroom out, along the landing floor and into the spare room. Next he disassembled the bureau, carried the components upstairs and reconstituted them against the wall, placing a glass-topped drinks table borrowed from the sitting room at right angles to it, creating an L-shaped work station. He brought the Windsor chair up from the kitchen to sit on.

Using a four-way mains multiplier, he was able to power his word processor which he placed on the glass-topped table, and its printer which fitted neatly on the shelf below. Also an anglepoise desk light and finally the telephone answering machine which he re-programmed with a new message, erasing the old jokey one that Emma had recorded years ago when they had first bought the device:

'Hello this is Peter Deacon. I am temporarily away from my desk. Please leave your name and telephone number. I will return your call very shortly.' It took three attempts before he was satisfied with the quality of the delivery, the right amount of emphasis on the word 'will'.

Later that afternoon, when Emma had returned from collecting the children, she walked into the spare room while he was sticking a full page Marconi advertisement on the wall. She stood at the door and looked around the room, tight-lipped. Sally barged in past her legs brandishing a biscuit tin.

'Daddy!' she said, clapping a hand to her mouth.

'Precisely,' Emma said and walked out.

Within a few days he established a daily schedule that quickly settled into routine. He liked to rise early; he was accustomed to it and found that he missed the hour or so of his own company that he used to spend planning his day during the drive to work. He slipped quietly out of bed at six, pulled on a tracksuit and trainers and jogged to the park and back, returning in time to lay breakfast, take a cup of tea to Emma, and rouse the children. He showered and dressed; they all breakfasted together.

Jamie's tantrums became a regular feature at school time. One morning he locked himself in the bathroom and refused to come out. Peter tried to negotiate from outside but after ten minutes lost all patience and terrified the boy into opening the door by threatening to call the police. Emma said she couldn't handle this nonsense every morning, so Peter drove Jamie to school himself that day, watching in the rear-view mirror while the slight and tearful form stared miserably through the window. Thereafter he always took Jamie to school, sustaining an uneasy truce based on veiled threats and bribes. Peter disliked the situation intensely, belligerent wills locked in opposition, particularly as Jamie was in a no-win situation. He hoped it was a phase which would pass with his return to work.

Sally went to a private pre-school three days a week and Peter dropped her off after Jamie. Completely unlike her brother in every way, she would never dream of questioning the need for her to attend such an establishment; in any case the place would fall apart without her. But then Sally, though naturally inquisitive, was not given to worry. She assumed, as she did with most that occurred about her, that its very existence was largely for her benefit. She went to school because the teachers and the other children were waiting for her. Yet she was also ruthlessly unsentimental. One morning the school phoned to say that they were closing for a few days because of an outbreak of whooping cough. Emma broke the news gently but Sally just shrugged her coat onto the floor and headed for the playroom. 'Typical,' she said, switching on the television.

Sometimes Emma stayed at home with Peter, working downstairs on her drawing board, helping Mrs Newton, or reading out in the little garden. Once or twice, early on, they took advantage of their time alone together and the unaccustomed freedom from interruption. She prepared a cold lunch, antipasta, salads. They ate in the kitchen, by the French windows, or outside if the weather was pleasant, drinking wine and chatting. Then they retired upstairs to bed, dozing and making love until it was time for her to go and collect the children.

Most days however, she went out. Much as he enjoyed the lunches in the garden, and the lazy bedroom assignations, Peter was secretly grateful. Her presence distracted him from his work and although she rarely came into the spare room, he found her presence in the house a distraction. He could hear her moving about, running a shower next door, listening to pop music on the kitchen radio, picking up the phone downstairs while he was using it. She had an

28

annoying habit, when that happened, of interrupting his conversation and his train of thought with irritating and unnecessary asides: 'So sorry darling. Peter could you let me know as soon as you're off the phone, I have to call Adele as soon as possible . . .'

She kept in touch with many of her old work friends and contacts in the graphic art and design world. She regularly visited the West End advertising agency where she used to work before she fell pregnant with Jamie. Occasionally they commissioned small design jobs for her to do on the premises or at home. She usually lunched once a week with Mitch; sometimes she drove down to Sussex for the day to see her mother.

Apart from a break for lunch Peter generally worked all day at his desk, dividing his time between the three categories of activity he had identified on the first day. The job hunt was first priority and he devoted all of each morning to the task. The remainder of the day was split between finance and what he now called 'any other business'.

Within a few days he was forced to acknowledge that his initial estimate of a month out of employment was unrealistic. There was simply too much work involved in preparing the ground. He had contacted three management recruitment agencies that he knew of via third parties. They were all extremely helpful and encouraging but none wanted to see him right away. They asked him to send his CV, and they said they would be in touch the moment anything suitable came up.

'Don't you contact potential employers on an applicant's behalf then?' he enquired of one, a plummy voiced female with an address in Lower Regent Street.

'Very rarely.' She sounded offended at the suggestion. 'This is a highly professional recruitment consultancy Mr Deacon, not a High Street job agency. We operate almost

29

exclusively on behalf of the employer. He has a human resources requirement, we use our applicant database to fill it.'

'I see. So an applicant may have to wait some time, on your database, until you put him forward to an employer.'

'Well naturally if I have an applicant, somebody of really exceptional ability and experience' – from her tone he knew he didn't qualify – 'whose credentials and personality profile strongly match a particular company or corporation's recruitment preferences, then I might put him or her forward.'

'Even if they don't have a vacancy.'

'In exceptional circumstances, yes.' It was obviously a word she was fond of. 'But in answer to your question, Mr Deacon, it is certainly not unusual for applicants to remain on my books for periods of several months, or more. You see most of them are already in employment.'

The direct approach produced similar results. Once the hit list was complete, he began ringing some of his contacts. This produced a great deal of encouragement and where not already known, the names of key personnel within each company to whom he should target his applications. It also took up a great deal of time, as each contact he called was keen to know and, by virtue of their support, entitled to hear the full details of the UAS demise. He quickly grew sick of reciting the saga and began shortening it, adjusting the content according to his perceived return on time invested.

One contact, a middle-grade technical sales manager at British Aerospace whom he did not know well, and who he would normally consider his subordinate, received the full and unabridged version. His company had recently acquired a radar subdivision and Peter needed to know where it was to be located, what investment was to be made in it and who was in charge. Conversely, another, an old acquaintance from the RAF, received short shrift when he told Peter that the optical equipment manufacturer he worked for was also going out of business.

It was nearly a week before the CV was ready. It ran to four pages and was a comprehensive account of his life. It detailed his education at Wellington, his seven year short service commission as a pilot in the Royal Air Force and an in depth resume of his career at UAS. While he polished it on the word processor he began telephoning his target recipients, reasoning that a brief introductory conversation might encourage an open-minded approach to his application.

Those that he was able to speak to directly were invariably supportive although non-committal. But most had secretaries who intercepted and filtered incoming telephone calls, polite but insistent: 'Yes, but may I ask what your call is in connection with Mr Deacon?' Once he told them they generally fobbed him off with the name of the personnel manager.

'Now?' He turned at his desk, Emma's head was poking around the door, eyebrows raised. He looked at his watch; it was late, dark outside.

'Good a time as any.' She walked into the room, one hand resting on her hips which she swung provocatively, the other, fingers stretched, supported a tray. Two tumblers, a bottle of Bells and a soda siphon.

'I see you've brought provisions.' He turned his chair round, facing the room.

'Nobody in their right mind stays sober at an economic summit.' She poured.

'Kids down?'

'Out for the count. Pippa's gone home.'

'I'm worried about Jamie. Do you think we should speak to the specialist again?'

She handed him the glass then went over to sit on the bed, treading carefully to avoid his heaps. 'Perhaps. I don't know. It's never been as bad as this before. Miss Richardson says he is very withdrawn at school, and . . .' She hesitated.

'And what?'

'Well he can be disruptive sometimes. Tantrums.'

'When did she say this?' He took a drink, kept it matter of fact; there was much to confront.

Emma shrugged. 'Oh, I don't know, the other day.'

'I'll drop in and see her.' Change the subject. Get to the point. 'Anyway . . .' he said pointedly, tilting his head back towards the desk behind him.

'What's the damage?'

Working the two hours each afternoon allocated to matters monetary, it had taken him nearly a week to get to the bottom of the bureau drawer and complete a financial picture. Having found most of the bank statements and put them in order he was able to reconcile the three chequing accounts. These, as he had already been told by his bank manager, were badly overdrawn. His was in particularly dire shape owing to the non-payment of his previous month's salary.

But what even the bank was unaware of was the total outstandings: cheques written but not yet banked, unpaid bills, subscriptions, Sally's school fees, credit and store cards and so on. In all, another three-and-a-half thousand pounds. Most of it seriously overdue.

'Have a guess.'

She looked sheepish. She had no idea. 'Maybe two?' He turned and picked up a single sheet from the desk, held it at arm's length between finger and thumb. Toxic waste.

'And the bottom line is –' She sang it like a game show hostess, but her eyes were nervous.

'In round figures?'

'Come on Peter.'

'Twelve and a half. Give or take.'

Hesitation, shock, open mouthed shock, just a second then up like a cat. 'Give me that.' She took it back to the bed, scattering a heap. He drained his glass, slowly. Poured them both another, she held her hand out for it without looking up.

'You never told me you'd taken out a five thousand pound loan.'

'Bangkok. Remember?'

She remembered. 'But it doesn't require immediate repayment. We can pay it off in instalments.'

'What with?' He had to say it. In a correspondence file in the now tidy finance drawer was a letter from John Bishop received that morning. Peter had not been in touch with his bank manager since the first day. The letter was short, Bishop requested that he contact him 'as a matter of urgency'.

'I'll go back to work.'

'I thought I was doing that.'

She started to say something, changed her mind. 'Well just until you get fixed up.'

'I am getting fixed up Em.' He looked at her, auburn hair fresh from the hairdresser, cut neatly, turning in at the shoulders – a bob? It was beautiful, shiny like polished mahogany. But the brown eyes looked doubtful. 'It's going to take some time though.'

'And in the meantime?'

'One or two economies for a start.'

'Such as?' She was glaring now.

'I don't know! The usual, less fillet, more rump, one Scotch instead of two, a little restraint on the shopping front . . .'

'Ah, so that's what this is about.'

33

'Partly, yes. But it's just one piece of the puzzle.' He began counting off on his fingers. 'Mrs Newton has been costing us a hundred a week lately, and Pippa is damn nearly the same. We spend too much on booze, petrol, eating out, dry cleaning, you name it.' He paused to allow the news to sink in. Outside a police car raced by wailing, flashes of blue ricocheting off the curtains, siren note dipping in Doppler shift. She drained her glass, eyes thoughtful. There was pink in her cheeks. Suddenly she brightened.

'So it's humble pie and never mind the trimmings from now on is it?' She grinned.

He laughed, relieved. 'Something like that. Only for a few weeks, couple of months tops. I've made an appointment to see John Bishop tomorrow, tell him how hard we're reining in, sort out a loan.'

She came over, bent and kissed him hard on the mouth. 'Peto, it'll be okay,' she said softly. 'We can beat this thing. I just know we can.'

He left the house mid morning and walked to the Broadway. He was looking for a cab, then thought better of it and took the tube to Aldgate instead. He was back in a suit for the first time since UAS. It felt curious, oddly reassuring yet somehow unreal, as though it was another person's smartly turned out reflection he was watching in the window of the train. It was a uniform. All his life he'd worn them; collecting the rugby prize on speech day at Wellington; dinners in the officers' mess at Coltishall; presentations to prospective customers at trade shows. Or an interview with his bank manager. As the train clattered around the Circle Line he studied his fellow travellers, suddenly struck by an uneasy sense of falsehood, as though they were all just elements of an elaborate simulation. A charade. Actors donning costumes and playing parts, delivering the lines.

Word perfect, every move, every gesture in character. But who were they performing for? And why?

'You see my problem Peter,' Bishop said thoughtfully. Peter could, clear as day. They sat in a sparsely furnished interview room backstage at the bank in ridiculously low seats like steel and plastic deck chairs. There was a chrome and glass coffee-table, block mounted sepia tone views of Victorian London on the walls, potted palms. They drank coffee; he'd declined something stronger, medium sherry probably. He squirmed forward on the deck chair and withdrew the cashflow projection from his briefcase. A single sheet, meticulously prepared; it itemised standard monthly cash expenditure, the absolute minimum required to stay afloat.

The mortgages on the house, including insurance, totalled fourteen hundred pounds a month. Then there were hire purchase agreements on Emma's car and some of the furnishings at Fulham, another four hundred. Mrs Newton, thin lipped as she'd heard the news of her cutback to ten hours a week, still a hundred and seventy five a month; Sally's school, four hundred a term averaged out at a hundred a month and so on. The list was interminable, and sobering.

Last night, after the economic summit, they'd gone to bed, made love in a whiskey soaked damn-the-rest-of-the-world, desperate sort of way, and dropped exhausted into post-coital slumber. But he had awoken within an hour, mind racing like a runaway racehorse. In the near darkness, a sodium street glow penetrating chinks in the curtains, and Emma sleeping steadily beside him, he lay on his back grimly pondering the full implications of their situation, sweating coldly as his imagination took wing. Soon he became uncertain of some of the figures, so he pulled on a dressing gown and padded through to the spare room. He went through it all again. There were errors and omissions: he'd forgotten road tax and insurance on the car, miscalculated the monthly telephone costs.

His mind was cruising in overdrive, wonderfully concentrated. He made a pot of coffee and carried it up to the spare room, played George Benson very quietly on the compact-disc player and worked on. While he was awake and on the problem, dealing with it, the situation did not seem so bad. In no time he had recalculated and obtained the full unexpurgated story. He made more coffee and ran off the cashflow projection on the word processor. While he was at it he tweaked his CV and prepared four more job applications with covering letters ready for posting in the morning. He updated the filing and read through, really studied the stuff sent through by the receivers. There was money to be had from the State, income support, unemployment benefit. No idea how much, but he'd get on to it.

Suddenly it was light outside, gone five. He dressed in his running gear but walked instead, for an hour. When he returned Sally was up, standing on a chair by the kitchen sink drinking neat Ribena, huge tell-tale blackcurrant clown's grin. They embraced warmly then she left for the playroom; he took up Emma's tea.

'Twenty-three hundred a month is a great deal of money, Peter.' Bishop was studying the sheet. Deacon drained his coffee, said nothing. 'Is there something, any assets we can use as security?'

He ducked the question. 'What happens if the mortgage payments stop?'

'They are stopped. Since last month.'

'Well thanks John, with bank managers like you . . .'

Bishop dropped the sheet on the table. 'Now look, I don't have to tell you this, but I'm already right out on a limb here. Your indebtedness now totals more than twelve thousand pounds apparently, and you say you need another two right away plus twenty-three hundred a month for the duration. Yet you have not offered me any suggestions as to how you intend to service this debt, let alone pay it off, and not a scrap of security.'

'There's the house.'

'I can't touch the house Peter, we've already been through this!'

'Not that house, the other one, a cottage. In Suffolk.'

'You own a cottage in Suffolk?'

'Yes.'

'Outright?'

'Outright.'

It was lunchtime. He walked back down Leadenhall Street and into a bar in the market. It was busy, full of insurance brokers carrying radio pagers and cell phones; he was completely inconspicuous, in uniform. Ordering a large Scotch he managed to lever himself onto a bar stool in one corner. The place did standard city fare, pie and chips, tongue and coleslaw, sandwiches to order. He hadn't eaten since breakfast, not really since last night, but he wasn't hungry.

Bishop had bought it. Provisionally. He hadn't exactly agreed to extend the loan, just cover his cheques for a few more days while they worked out something on the cottage. Emma's cottage. Somewhere deep inside him he knew he was out of line. But there had been no choice.

When Emma's father had died two years ago, he left her a modest cash inheritance. At the time, having just bought Fulham, Peter and Emma would have cheerfully used it all to make a substantial reduction on the mortgage, zero all the overdrafts and credit cards, take a couple of expensive holidays and pay for the redecoration of the new house. But this practical and on the whole sensible use of the money would have been in conflict with the spirit, if not the letter of her father's will. It indicated that the sum 'was to be wisely and separately invested to provide enjoyment and security for the Deacons and their children'. Although not a specific pre-condition, there was also tacit understanding that Emma's mother would have to rubber stamp her approval on the chosen expenditure.

The answer presented itself one Sunday morning as they lay in bed reading the papers and playing with the children. Peter spotted it in the property pages of the *Sunday Telegraph*.

'Bedingham, near Ipswich, Suffolk. Three bedroom detached cottage in pleasant village location, garden, outhouses. There you go Em, and look at the price. Cheap at twice the price.' He hadn't been serious, but Emma was captivated. She rang the agents the next morning and made an appointment to drive down and view the place. Peter was due to fly to Hong Kong so she took her mother. By the time he returned at the end of the week, the cottage was theirs. Hers.

'You'll love it Peto. We'll do it up and use it in the summer and weekends. It's perfect for the children and the village is incredible, like stepping into the middle of *Akenfield*.' He wouldn't know, he hadn't read it.

They hadn't used it much though. It wasn't equipped for the winter so there had been just the one summer season. He'd been down twice, Emma once or twice more. It was very basic, no central heating, no telephone, rather run-down and in need of repair. Peter disliked the place, thought it damp and uncomfortable; privately he hoped Emma would become disenchanted with it and sell up.

Eventually he caught the eye of the barmaid who refilled his tumbler. The bar was beginning to empty, lunch break over. He moved from the stool to a bench seat by the window. Through the glass he could see the rest of the enclosed market, open fronted shops displaying fish on marble slabs, whole sides of meat and strings of unplucked game birds. Fruit and veg, a whole shop selling cheese. Whistling boys in butcher's aprons weaved delivery bicycles around fast walking brokers from Lloyds, while above and beyond the ornate iron columns and glass of the market, the pre-stressed steel-reinforced concrete and dark tinted glass blocks of the foreign banks and insurance companies squatted like unwelcome giants, as reflections of the autumn sky slid slowly across their mirrored façades.

The cumulative effects of whiskey on an empty stomach, the sleepless night and the less than cordial interview with Bishop (no mention of lunch this time), had left him drained and weary. He finished his drink and left the bar, pausing at the door to pull his tie off and undo the top button of his shirt before setting off back down Leadenhall Street.

'Your father called. I said you'd ring back. You look shattered; how did you get on with Bishop?'

Peter dropped his briefcase onto the kitchen table and fell into a chair. 'Got him right where we want him.'

'At our throats?'

'Lower.'

'Short and curlies?'

He laughed, guffawed. God she was wonderful. He spread a palm on the table and jabbed his thumb into it. 'Right there girl.'

'Oh yeah? What's the deal?'

'I'll explain later. Any other messages?' Job offer perhaps, interview even.

'Nothing. Explain what Peto.' There was the bump bump of a three-year-old bottom on the stairs. It was her preferred method when she was in a hurry. Strangled sobbing accompanied each thud. 'Uh oh.'

Sally ran into the kitchen, red-faced, eyes awash. 'Jamie did hurt my arm Daddy!' He hauled her onto his knee, glanced at Emma.

'I was about to tell you. Miss Richardson rang at lunchtime. I had to go and collect him.'

He rubbed Sally's shoulder. 'Not there Daddy.' She sniffed. 'This other arm, here look!' He looked, saw nothing, just a slight redness perhaps.

'Why did Jamie hit you sweetheart?'

'Because I didn't play with his train set anyway.'

'Did you go in his room?'

'Sometimes.'

She stopped sobbing, slipped a thumb in her mouth, leaned back against his chest. They would have to be more careful. He hadn't hurt her, not for a year or more. But his moods lately . . . and they'd sacked the nanny this morning.

'What happened?'

'Threw a total fit apparently, right in the middle of lunch. Flung his plate across the table, lay on the floor. Similar to last time.'

'Did he, you know hurt himself?'

'Knuckle biting. Not too bad. He was quiet when I got there.'

'Not the head thing?'

She shook hers. 'I was going to give him a pill, but he was so quiet, went straight to his room. I thought he was asleep.'

He went up. Jamie was on his bed, hunched on his side, facing the wall. Peter sat down beside him and stroked the dark hair, looking round the walls at the paintings of ships and animals. He had his mother's talent for drawing, an eye for detail. Great sensitivity and tremendous patience when

40

he was working. It didn't seem fair.

They first noticed it when he was two. They had taken him to Peter's parents for Christmas; his mother had rung with a summons thinly disguised as an invitation. Since there were no other plans – Emma's parents were away for Christmas – they agreed it would be churlish to refuse. The holiday had passed uneventfully. Peter's brother was there and his cousins and their children; it was busy and noisy. Peter had even managed to avoid the dreaded chat in the study with the Air Vice-Marshall. His father had never forgiven him for leaving the Air Force.

Jamie had been fine, fussed over by everyone. Then on the evening of Boxing Day he slipped through Emma's arms as she tried to take him up to bed, threw himself down on his back and began banging his head on the floor. It was horrific; everyone was stunned. Peter rushed forward and tried to pick him up, but he screamed and struggled like a wild animal and Peter had nearly dropped him. When he was finally able to take secure hold of him, Jamie stopped dead and went limp in his arms, his head hanging down sideways, eyes staring as though his neck had snapped.

As he grew older the tantrums became less frequent but more violent and on a couple of occasions he injured himself, drawing blood by gnawing on his knuckles and once cutting his head on the pavement whilst out shopping with Emma. Doctors had been consulted, various theories put forward and medications prescribed – mild sedatives mostly, rarely used and of limited use as the attacks came without warning and were usually short-lived. But they were baffled, the general consensus of medical opinion ruled out epilepsy, scans and encephalograms indicated no irregularities of the brain. Nor was the intermittent and infrequent pattern of the outbursts indicative of a readily definable behavioural disorder. Mostly they encouraged the Deacons not to worry and suggested he would probably grow out of it in time.

And it seemed that he was. Intervals between outbursts grew, months would elapse, but then he might have a spate of several over a few days. Once or twice he had lashed out at an unwary Sally, once only narrowly missing her eye with a toy car. But mostly his furies were directed at himself. And recently there had been a greater tendency to withdraw rather than externalise. It was worse in some ways.

'Go away.' The voice was tiny.

'What is it Jamie? Won't you tell me?' Peter stroked the head, bitter at the unfairness of it. 'What is it?' he murmured. What drives the anguish within you? How can a blue-eyed, frail-boned shrimp of just six years feel such terrible rage? Suddenly pity overcame him like a storm. He gasped, bunching a fist to his mouth, startled by the rush and power of the emotion. For a second he thought he might cry, but he stiffened, rigid and unbreathing until the spasm passed. He waited, exhaling slowly through his nose until certain that the crisis was fully over. Then he bent and kissed Jamie's head, before rising to leave the room. 'I must be overdoing it,' he said quietly, as he closed the door behind him.

'Hello Dad.'

'PJ. Emma told me. So sorry.' Peter sat in the Windsor chair swirling the golden brown around the bottom of the tumbler. He'd put it off. Subconsciously hoping to have the matter resolved before telling the old man. But Emma had spilled the beans. She wasn't to know.

'Bit of a blow but it's under control. I would have let you know sooner but, it's been pretty hectic.'

'Of course. I'd seen something in the paper anyway.' He knew, shit! He was just waiting for someone to call and tell him.

'What's the form?'

Here we go. 'Well, lots of irons in various fires. Two or three definite possibilities. I'm going to sit it out for a bit though, compile a shortlist when I've heard from everyone, then come to a decision.' He could hardly believe he was saying this.

'Write your own ticket as they say?'

'Hmm, something like that. How's mum?' He swallowed more whiskey.

'Terrific form. Wants to know when you're coming to visit. Now that you have more time on your hands that is.' There was a new note in the voice. An appeal?

'Well I don't really Dad, less if anything.'

'So you're too busy...'

'I didn't say that. Look Dad, we'd love to come, and we will. Soon.'

'She misses the children.' Why was he incapable of expressing his own feelings?

'I know. We will come up, in a couple of weeks or so.' There was silence on the line.

'Bit of a dead end really wasn't it?'

'I'm sorry?'

'That United Aerospace thing. Hasn't really got you anywhere.'

Peter threw his head back, took the receiver away from his ear and rubbed at his eyes with his free hand. Here it comes again. 'Dad, I can't agree. Yes, it was relatively high risk, but that's the defence procurement game, you know that as well as anybody. It was my judgement that the product base was sound, and if I may say so, I did a good job for them. It went wrong; these things happen. It's happening all over the industry.' He didn't mean to put it like that. This was not going well.

'Shall I have a word with Teddy Rawlings at the Ministry?'

Ministry of Defence, God! Coffin corner. Heaven forbid. 'Thanks Dad but I really don't think that's necessary.'

'Just a suggestion. You could have been well up the tree there by now.'

He finished it as quickly as he reasonably could. Then poured himself another drink and sat at his desk, sipping and watching as the light faded from the sky outside. The evenings were drawing in. He'd sensed a strong hint of autumn about the air as he walked back from the station this afternoon. He was exhausted, drained. What a day. And he hadn't told Emma yet.

He drew a bath for the children while she prepared dinner. As he was mixing in cold water, sleeves rolled, Jamie walked in. He was already naked, his body skinny and pale. And emaciated. His arms were like sticks, his skin practically translucent. Peter was shocked. He tried to remember the last time he had seen his son's naked body, or paid attention to his eating habits. Jamie went to the lavatory then carefully squeezed toothpaste and brushed his teeth. Peter was careful not to stare. Sally strolled in and began to undress: it was painfully slow, fumbling patiently with the buttons of her blouse. He bent to assist but she swung away. 'I can do it.' She did it, by herself. He had no idea.

They got in the bath together, Jamie washing himself in silence then quickly out, Sally lounging like a Botticelli cherub, first on her back, then her side, then her front. Wittering on and on to herself about somebody called Jambo and singing about a cat that came back. He got her out but she wanted to dry herself, huddling in a mound on the floor with the towel completely covering her, curled up just as she said, like a little mouse. Jamie left without uttering a word, his face expressionless.

Peter carried his daughter to her room, turned on the nightlight, was permitted to assist her into her nightgown and bed. They kissed and said goodnight. He looked in on Jamie next door. The light was already off. He went to the bed and kissed the pale forehead. 'Goodnight Jamie.' There was no reply.

'How's the Air Vice-Marshall?' Emma ladled bolognaise sauce onto his spaghetti. She'd got it from a bottle, mixed it with some mince, thrown in a chopped onion, a tin of tomatoes, garlic. He lowered his nose to the plate.

'Smells good.' He poured Chianti; they began eating. Not brilliant. 'He wants us to visit.'

'You mean he said your mother wants us to visit.'

'Precisely. You told him then. About UAS.'

'That's why he rang.' She put on a deep voice and spoke through stiff lips. 'I hear Peter's got a spot of bother.' It was a fair impersonation.

'Ah.'

'Don't say ah. Why didn't you tell him sooner?'

'The usual chestnut.'

'Pride, prejudice and the second begotten son. I do wish you two would sort it out.'

Later, she came from the bathroom, rubbing cream into her forehead, slipped off her pants, dropped the American football shirt over her head and slid into bed beside him. They lay on their backs, elbows touching, hands clasped on chests. Then she leaned out and flicked off the light. There was silence. He was dead tired, felt himself slipping away.

'Explain what?'

'Hmm?'

'Bishop, the bank. Remember? You said you'd explain later.'

He hauled himself back. It wasn't difficult. He took a deep breath, cleared his throat. 'He's prepared to help us out.'

'The way Dracula helps out with a cut finger no doubt.'

'Not necessarily, but—'

'Of course but.'

'We are going to have to come up with some sort of security. Just until I'm back in work. The moment I'm on a payroll we can reschedule the entire debt into loan and pay it off gradually.'

'Sounds good. One thing though.'

'What's that?'

'We're not staking the cottage. And that's final.'

CHAPTER

3

From the outside, the place looked like any post-war public service building. An unimaginatively conceived and hastily erected utilitarian box risen from the rubble of the Blitz. Square, ugly and functional, with tall frosted glass windows set high above the pavement, it could have been a school, or a library, or even a chapel. From the outside. He walked in.

The main part of the building consisted of a single large and open room, like a hall. It was lit by fluorescent tubes. Dozens of them, suspended in groups of four by chains from the top of the high ceiling, their diluted, milky glare casting a sickly pallor over the expressionless faces below.

Towards one end a counter divided the room. Behind it sat a row of department officers, screened off from each other in little hardboard booths, like bookings clerks at a railway station. Above their heads, an electric sign called their customers in by number. Mostly these sat patiently on rows of brown moulded plastic chairs arranged around the room. Others lounged along the walls, leaning against pamphlet dispensers and 'Back to Work' posters depicting brisk and cheerful men in clean dungarees and shining shoes carrying ladders on their shoulders.

A large sign advised Peter that new claimants were to take a ticket from the dispenser and wait. He hesitated at the threshold, tightly gripping the hand-tooled burgundy leather briefcase at his side. He was acutely aware of his appearance. He'd dressed casually but without due consideration: handmade shirt, with cufflinks for God's sake, cashmere wool V-neck sweater, light brown designer cords, soft red Italian moccasins. God he stuck out like a dog's balls. Might just as well have hung a notice around his neck, 'fallen yuppie'.

It was not too late. He could get out – cast about him uncertainly, damn, wrong building, quick check of the wristwatch, about turn and away to the street. He nearly went. A girl was leaning against the far wall, one foot up on the scuffed green paint behind. She caught his eye, nodding slowly. She was young, perhaps eighteen, hands thrust deep into the pockets of her heavy black leather motorcycling jacket, thick black woollen tights beneath an absurdly short plastic miniskirt, black again. Dark, dark red–blue lipstick, heavy black make-up around the eyes, which watched him beneath sharply angular eyebrows. Her expression was amused and scornful: this isn't for you mate, your sort don't have the bottle. Go on clear off out of it quick.

He walked over to the dispenser and took a ticket. There were no seats free so he stood by the wall near one corner. He looked at his ticket. Seventy-eight. The digital counter above the booths said forty-nine. He raised the briefcase to his chest self-consciously and began checking the contents.

'Got a light?' The girl had come over. She was tall, pretty beneath the war paint.

'I'm sorry. Don't smoke.' He smiled politely. She popped the Silk Cut back in the pack with a shrug and stood next to him against the wall, elbowing an elderly Indian aside to make room. Peter continued to sort through his briefcase, well aware that they were both now under scrutiny from their neighbours.

'Well, what happened to you then? You look like you just had the Porsche nicked.'

He kept rummaging. Where the hell was his P45? 'I lost my job.'

'Well I know that don't I?' she said slowly, as though he was deaf. 'Didn't pop in here to see yer mates didya?' The counter clicked. Fifty-two.

'No I suppose not.' He snapped the case shut, slotted it between his ankles and folded his arms.

'This your first time?'

He looked around. The air was thick with smoke and smelled like an abused telephone box. It was mostly men – all colours creeds and ages. African, Caribbean, Caucasian, Oriental, Indian, young and old. A powerful pot-pourri of exotic cultural strains and diverse ethnic bloodlines, yet linked by an invisible shortcoming like a common gene fault. Some talked, most just waited in silence. Impassive and resigned, slow moving or still like coralled livestock awaiting shipment, their individuality unnoticed and irrele-vant beneath the harsh glare of the strip lights.

'Yes, yours?'

A snort. 'Hardly.' She looked him up and down. 'What are you doing here anyhow? You don't need this.'

'With respect, how would you know?'

''Cos I've seen your sort before.'

'My sort?'

'Privileged. You may think you need help, but you don't. Not from the likes of this place. Your kind take care of themselves.' He began to get the impression it was a favoured line of rhetoric. Fifty-eight. 'It's all to do with class.'

The others around them were losing interest, perhaps they'd heard it before too. He wished she'd leave him alone, but she stood right next to him, sideways to the wall, very near, practically touching. Studying him. He could smell her, chewing gum, leather and cigarettes, and something else. She had black, close cropped hair. But there was lighter brown at the roots, and her eyes were blue.

'I'm sorry but I can't accept that. My situation is no different from yours. I'm out of a job and need support from the State.'

'Bollocks. Bet you've got a house, car probably, family with money. You won't starve. You're not on the street.'

'That's hardly the point.' He checked the counter anxiously. A couple of the cubicles were empty of customers, the ticket clerks sorting through card indexes or writing notes. It was desperately slow. Sixty-three.

'Yes it is. Look. If you had to raise some money, you know like life or death or something, really had to,' she jabbed him lightly on the shoulder for emphasis. 'How much could you lay your hands on?' She'd sprung this trap before all right. 'Fifty grand? A hundred?' More probably. He considered it. His parents. Emma's mother, Dan and Mitch, even Bishop if the chips were really down. She had a point. But under what circumstances? He couldn't imagine. Kidnap ransom on the children maybe? 'Get my drift?' Sixty-seven.

'Take these forms away with you and send them to the DSS as soon as possible. They will then assess your eligibility for income support in addition to the unemployment benefit.'

'How much is that, er, likely to be?' He sat in the cubicle across the counter from a middle-aged woman with frizzy grey hair and glasses.

'It's hard to say Mr Deacon. It depends upon a number of factors: whether your partner works, the number and ages of dependent children and so on.'

'But what, approximately, can I expect?'

She sighed, removed her glasses. These ones were the worst. Pitiful, they had no idea. 'Basic single man's unemployment benefit is thirty-seven a week. Assuming your partner is not declaring a separate income you can claim another twenty-three, bringing it up to around sixty, this may then be adjusted further depending, as I said, on other factors, but perhaps another twenty or so.' Eighty pounds a week. He needed over five times that.

'And what if, for the sake of argument, my wife has a small income from part-time work?'

She held his eyes. 'As I said, assuming your partner is not declaring a separate income, you may be eligible for support supplementary to the basic single person's benefit.' But he'd declare it all right. His sort always did. Lose out both ways.

He began collecting his papers, the cashflow analysis, expenses breakdown, bills. None of it looked at, none of it relevant. Tidying it all away into his briefcase along with her forms and pamphlets. She felt a sudden tinge of compassion. 'I'm sorry Mr Deacon.' She leaned forward across the counter, smiled kindly, suppressing an urge to take his hand. 'You see the system is not really appropriate to, well, to your kind, of situation.'

He smiled back weakly. 'So I have been told. Thank you.' He got up and left the cubicle.

'Good-morning. Mr Williamson please.'

'Yes sir. May I ask who is calling?'

'Peter Deacon.'

Momentary pause. 'May I ask what it is in connection with?'

'Yes, I am a surveillance avionics consultant calling with regard to a meeting Mr Williamson and I had at a symposium we attended together at the Paris airshow last year.'

'I see.' No she didn't but it was good enough.

'I'll just enquire whether Mr Williamson is free.'

'Many thanks.' He leaned back in the Windsor chair and crossed his legs. His feet were bare. He ran a hand over his chin, he'd forgotten to shave that morning. Or was it yesterday? A click.

'John Williamson.'

He swung forward quickly, grabbed the magazine cutting with the copy of his letter stapled to it. 'Mr Williamson. Thank you for your time. My name is Peter Deacon, I wrote to you a week or two back with regard to a position within your electroptics division.'

'What position would that be Mr Deacon?'

'Ah, no specific position. I have several years relevant management experience in the marketing of related equipment, and wrote to you on the offchance that there were some areas of common interest that might, er, warrant discussion.'

'Yes Mr Deacon I do recall your letter now. So sorry that I have been unable to reply. UAS wasn't it?'

'That's right.'

'Shocking business. It must have been quite a blow.'

It was, Peter agreed. Within a minute he had steered the conversation back to the central issue. But Williamson was sorry, he was unable to help at this time, market uncertainties, the entire defence sector in flux, cutbacks across the industry. He promised to keep Peter's details on file in case the situation changed. After they hung up he buzzed through to his secretary, told her to send Deacon a note and reminded her that all job enquiries should be routed through personnel.

Jotting a note on the bottom of his letter, Peter filed it

away and checked his list. He picked up the phone again, dialling one of the recruitment agencies.

'Hello Miriam, Peter. Any trade?'

'Ah Peter. Glad you called. How do you fancy some sun, sea and sand?'

'Don't tell me, deck chair man on Brighton beach.'

'Bit further south. Qatar actually.'

'Tell me more.' Sally walked in. She was holding one of Emma's lipsticks, there were vivid lines across her cheeks and forehead. 'Is it lunchtime Daddy?'

'Well it's via an associate of mine specialising in fixed term consultancies in the region. Variety of projects, this one is building an airport.'

He beckoned at Sally, but she made no move forward, standing in the doorway frowning down at the palm of her hand as she smeared circles on it with the lipstick. 'Sally!' he hissed. The crotch of her trousers was dark. Holding the phone at arm's length he made a grab for her, but she was out of range. 'Have you wet yourself?'

'Peter?'

'Sorry Miriam, babysitting. Er, airport construction? Yes, great. But I'm a sales manager, not an engineer.' Qatar. Fixed term. Twelve to eighteen months unaccompanied in the desert, then what? Back on the street.

'Lunchtime Daddy.'

'It's all project management Peter. This kind of opportunity doesn't come up often.'

'Bit risky though, wouldn't you say? As a career move I mean. A bit thin on security.'

'Daddy!'

He covered the mouthpiece. 'For God's sake Sally don't interrupt when I'm on the bloody telephone!' She dropped to her knees like a wounded animal.

'Up to you of course.'

Christ, two offended women. Sally lifted her hand from the carpet leaving a cherry smear on the beige. 'Jesus! Hold on a second Miriam. Sally come here!'

'Don't like you any more.'

'Hello, are you there Peter?'

'For Christ's sake give me the lipstick. Don't touch the bed!'

'Perhaps you'd better give me a call when you're less busy.'

'Just come over here with Daddy. For a moment. And you have wet yourself. Hello. Miriam? Hello?'

He cursed and checked his watch. It was lunchtime. He got up, holding Sally's hand, it felt wet and greasy. 'We'd better clean you up and then we'll go downstairs and have a sandwich.'

'And a drink.'

'You can count on it.' The telephone rang, he waited, Sally tugging at his hand. The answerphone intercepted the call, he listened as his message played, free hand hovering, ready to pick up.

'Er, yes Mr Deacon, my name is Garner of UK Car Leasing Group. Could you possibly call me as soon as possible with regard to non-payment of a standing order on your wife's Volkswagen. Thank you.'

Peter watched as the machine wound back and re-set. 'Hmm, no I don't think so.' He followed Sally down to the kitchen.

Emma got back late from the agency. She was working two days a week on a cover for a children's book and a brochure for a bank. She walked into the house at seven thirty and through to the kitchen. The children's tea things were all over the table. There were unwashed dishes in the sink, soiled clothes on the floor by the washing machine. She sighed and took off her coat, began clearing. Peter was upstairs bathing the children.

They were out of food and neither of them felt like doing a shop at the Indian store, so they ordered a Chinese takeaway for dinner. She drank lager, he Scotch.

'How was your day?' She studied him anxiously. It was six weeks since he had lost his job; it seemed much longer. It was amazing how quickly they had adjusted. He was much the same, plugging away in the spare room every day, talking on the phone for hours, writing letters. But there had been subtle changes. He rarely got up at six any more, or went running. He kept less regular hours, often working late into the night, or going to bed early only to get up again a couple of hours later. She would hear him through the wall, padding about, playing the CD or the radio, printing off on his word processor, murmuring to himself. Then he would creep back to bed again during the early hours and she would pretend he hadn't woken her. But he invariably did and it was becoming tiresome.

He was scruffier too. For pottering about the house he would pull on jeans and a sweatshirt, not bothering about shoes and socks, or underpants sometimes. And he showered irregularly, cleaned his teeth and shaved when he remembered, his entire routine upset by the erratic hours he kept.

It was becoming a strain on them both. He was certainly less tolerant, snapping at the children, lapsing into moody silences, drinking more. She had noticed him behaving strangely too. He didn't go out much any more during the day, but wandered off for hours at night. And he was oddly obsessive about their mail, running for the door when the postman came, scurrying upstairs to the spare room with their letters.

She was aware she could have been more supportive, but

55

it was a real bore not having Mrs Newton at all now. Or the nanny. The housework was endless: cleaning, washing, ironing, cooking. All that plus going out to work. She didn't feel supportive, she felt resentful.

'Got an offer today,' Peter said.

'Hey, well done darling.' Damn, too patronising. 'Well, don't keep us in suspense.'

'No good. Fixed-term contract in the Middle East.'

'Doing?'

'I don't know, some airport construction project. I was hopelessly unqualified.'

'Don't sell yourself short. Good money?'

He stopped eating, stared across the table at her. 'I don't know, Emma, I didn't consider it. It would mean leaving you here, trekking off to some God-forsaken, sun-baked hole in the desert, only to come back a year later with a tan and still no job.'

'Okay, okay. I just thought maybe as a short-term filler . . .'

'Do you want me to go?'

'Of course not Peter, I'm just trying to be practical.'

He drained his glass, confused and angry. He never considered she might seriously want him to accept the damn offer, well the enquiry. He felt tired. He always felt tired these days, yet as soon as he went to bed he was wide awake again.

Apart from a few audiences with headhunters, and despite best efforts, he'd only managed to secure two interviews in five weeks. But even those, strictly speaking, were more along the lines of informal chats. Both had gone well but neither company had suitable vacancies at the time. He was awaiting replies from a dozen or so other applications and continued to send out fresh ones at regular intervals, but the truth was, he had heard from most of his hottest prospects. UAS's demise was no mere coincidence, the industry was in recession, the outlook gloomy. Many businesses were laying off staff, and there was no immediate prospect of a trend reversal. Many of the people he was approaching were fearful for their own jobs.

Their finances were balanced precariously on a knife edge. He'd managed to hold John Bishop at bay with bullish talk of mortgage arrangements underway on the cottage in Suffolk. In turn Bishop allowed them to continue to cash cheques, but he had frozen all standing orders, including mortgage repayments on the house in Fulham – now over two months in arrears, as well as leasing and hire purchase agreements on Emma's car and some of the house's furnishings. Every day he received letters and telephone calls from creditors.

Emma knew little if any of it. She was aware of the lamentable state of their general financial situation of course, but not its frightening immediacy. Since she had refused to discuss the sale or mortgage of the cottage, he had been unable to tell her that their continued credit facility at the bank, albeit limited, was based upon that premise. Peter regretted ever having mentioned the cottage to Bishop, alarmed at how readily the banker had latched on to what had been intended as little more than a chance remark. But what other choices were there? They had to have an income line from somewhere. Anyway it was only a delaying tactic, as soon as he was offered a job the whole matter would become superfluous.

But the strain of the double deception was enormous. He had to intercept the postman to prevent her from seeing the threats and demands, and he disliked leaving her in the house during the day for fear of telephone calls. His blood ran cold at the prospect of an inadvertent conversation between Emma and John Bishop.

'How was work today?'

'Good. I had lunch with Charlie Gladstone.'

Gladstone, good God, where did he pop up from? He was an old boyfriend from years back, he and Emma had been graphics students at the University of East Anglia together. Back in the RAF Coltishall era.

'Good heavens, how was he?'

'Fine, he was in seeing Lawrence; he has his own consultancy now in East Anglia. Doing well.'

'Good for him, Got a family now?'

'Divorced. Two years ago. One child I think. He's going to come and see us next time he's up in town.'

'Great.'

After dinner he went for a walk. The night was cold and clear, a few stars visible through the glare of city lights. There was a chill wind, he turned his jacket collar up and set off briskly along the pavement, leaving the quiet residential streets for the neon signed shopfronts and bustling pubs and restaurants of Chelsea.

His nocturnal strolls had become a regular feature. He looked forward to them, to escaping from the house and putting mileage between what he began to think of as his real self and the other existence. Once out of the door and around the corner, he slipped the burden of responsibility effortlessly from his shoulders, cloaking himself instead in the warm fabric of anonymity, free to wander at will like a benign spirit, unfettered and invisible.

It was temporary relief, he knew, but harmless enough, and with positive therapeutic benefits. He was able to rationalise his predicament objectively, when he so chose. Bolster his flagging morale, soothe his frayed nerves and return, refreshed to the fray. In theory.

Sometimes he carried his anonymity into a pub for a brandy. Busy central London publicans thrived on the trade of strangers, asked no questions, serving with a nod and a passing word on the weather. Respectful, even protective of a man's right to be permitted to drink in peace. Inevitably these places were also haunted by other wraiths. Alone but discontent in their solitude, advancing on him with pints of light and bitter and a cheery: 'Haven't seen you around here before.' When politeness failed to dislodge them from his space, he learned to banish them with a look to freeze oceans.

But mostly he walked, sometimes north through Earl's Court and into Kensington, Notting Hill and beyond, or he headed south, tramping across a bridge – Putney or Wandsworth and into residential south London. Occasionally west, although careful to remain in charted seas; it was too easy to sail clean out of the safety of a city alive with character and vibrancy and drift into still and ominous waters, deserted, forbidding streets littered with wrecked cars, while unseen eyes watched from the shadows of brooding tower blocks.

He struck out eastwards, walked along the King's Road for a while, then turned right on a whim and cut through to the Embankment, strolling beside the river for a distance before forking left again to pass behind the Royal Hospital at Pimlico. In no time he was at Victoria, vaguely following a meandering course for Buckingham Palace, before turning west again for home. He went into the station and bought a drink and a roll at the railway tavern. The bar was quiet although the station was quite busy with travellers for the south and European arrivals off the boat train. He left by the main entrance tossing the half finished roll into a rubbish bin at the bus station as he passed.

'Got any spare change?' An invisible voice, from a doorway, deep in shadow. He nearly walked on, there were beggars everywhere these days, they were as familiar to the

London pedestrian as double decker buses. But there was something about the voice, thin, very young. He stopped, walked back a pace, peering into the shadow.

He was hunched into the corner, hugging knees drawn up to his chin and wrapped in an old overcoat several sizes too large. His head was bare, the toes of his trainers were badly scuffed, worn nearly through.

'Got any change?' he asked again more hopefully.

'How old are you?'

'Seventeen,' piped the unbroken voice. 'Spare us some change mate.'

Peter squatted in front of the doorway. The eyes watched him suspiciously. 'I don't believe you. How did you get here?'

'I come on the bus. With me brother.'

'Where is your brother now?'

'I dunno, gone off.'

'And how long have you been, out here, staying on the street?'

'Dunno, few days. Spare us some change.'

'Is there anywhere you can go?'

The voice cracked. ''E said he was coming back for me. Told me to stay here till he got back. But he never come. He never come.' He buried his face in his knees and broke off with a sob. Peter exhaled slowly, his breath misting in the cold. Debris from scrounging forays was strewn about the doorway, sweet wrappers, crisp packets and empty coke cans. He reached behind him and pulled some notes from his back pocket. There was enough for a taxi. He could take him back to Fulham by cab, get Em to fix him up with a decent meal and a bath, and a bed. Contact his parents, get him picked up. He reached into the shadow, patted the hunched shoulder, 'It's all right.'

The blow came out of the darkness like a bullet, catching

him hard between the eyes, right on the bridge of his nose. He reeled back on his heels, tried to rise but faltered and fell onto the pavement, stunned. His nose poured blood, his eyes filled with tears, he lay helpless, dazed and blinded, while something tugged at his arm. There was a sudden chill at his wrist as his watch went, and there was shouting, a child shouting, the shrill voice screeching like a cat, receding as he ran away. 'He abused me! That bastard tried to feel me up. Abuse, abuse, abuse!'

He lay motionless on the pavement, dizzy and disorientated. Around him the night city's pulse beat on without a break, he could hear the squeal of braking taxis as they slowed at the lights, the two-tone horn of a train pulling out of the station, the thump of rock music from a nearby bar, and people, everywhere his fellow human beings. Nobody helped him. Absurd. He groaned, choked, tasted blood and spat. Eventually he rolled over, and rose slowly and painfully up onto his knees, holding his head down as a wave of pain and nausea swept over him, the red stream running unchecked down his chin and neck, spattering crimson onto his jacket lapel and the white of his shirt. He looked down at himself, absurd, then slowly up and about him at the busy streets; there must have been a hundred people in the vicinity. Absolutely absurd.

His chest heaved suddenly in spasm and he choked, spitting again. Then his shoulders began to shake, gently at first, then uncontrollably. He snorted through the blood, wondering idly if he was about to blub like a schoolgirl. But he wasn't. These were sniggers gurgling in his throat, bubbling up through the pink mucus. Just as bad really, equally incapacitating, very embarrassing, completely, uncontrollably absurd. His head came up, struggling for air. In panic he fought the spasm, forcing cold oxygen deep into his chest then, replenished, a moment's respite, his body hesitated, teetered before he was nudged into the abyss once more. Head back, he surrendered, releasing a storm, a gale of strangled sweet bitter–sweet laughter which clattered into the night sky like startled pigeons. He was still there, kneeling, bloody and laughing, when the policeman arrived.

It took about three quarters of an hour to convince them at the station that he was not mad nor a prowling child molester but the victim of a mugging. At first they had been less than hospitable: 'Well sir it smells to me like you've been drinking; you say you've walked all the way from Fulham Broadway; you have no money; no identification and, well just look at the state of you.' Eventually common sense prevailed, but not until they had telephoned Emma who insisted on coming to collect him. They took a statement, gave him a cup of tea and some tissues for his nose and advised him to be more careful 'next time'.

Emma's eyes widened in shock as the desk sergeant showed her into the waiting room. 'My God, Peter, what the hell happened?' He took the blooded tissues from his face and grinned sheepishly. His jacket was filthy and stained, his trousers had picked up a tear in one knee and his shirt was covered in drying blood.

'Hello Em. Thanks for coming.'

Once out of the station and into the car her shock quickly gave way to anger. 'So humiliating, picked up on the street like a bloody tramp. What on earth did you think you were doing?'

He tried to explain, staring forlornly ahead through the windscreen, his head throbbing, the clotting blood blocking his nose. 'I had to stop, Emma (Ebba) – it was his voice. He couldn't have been more than twelve or thirteen.'

She glanced across at him and sighed. 'Peter,' she began softly. 'What is it? What's the matter? Please tell me.' He said nothing, keeping his gaze fixed ahead. 'I'm trying, I really am trying to understand what is happening, what it is you are going through. But you won't let me, won't let me help.'

'I know,' he said eventually, his voice a whisper. 'But you can't. It's not your fault, but you just can't.'

'Mr, er Greville Fulton please.'

'Yes sir, may I ask who is calling?'

'My name is Deacon.'

'Hold on please Mr Deacon.' Lengthy pause this time. Deacon? I don't know any Deacon do I? Hold on, there was a letter wasn't there, somewhere round here, did I throw it away, just a minute. Peter felt his bare wrist for the hundredth time. He missed the Rolex, its solid presence, reassuring reliability.

'Mr Deacon?'

'Yes.' Not put through, bad sign.

'Would this be in connection with your letter of application to Mr Fulton?'

'It would.'

'Ah yes. Mr Fulton has asked me to thank you for your interest but regrets he has no requirement for your services at this time.'

'I see. Is he there?'

'Yes he is, but he's rather tied up at the moment. In a meeting. Was there something else?'

'No. Yes, could you give him a message for me?'

'Of course.'

'Could you tell him that perhaps he might have had the common decency to write and say so himself.'

'I'm sorry?'

'You heard. Good-day.' He slammed the phone down, then sat staring sightlessly out of the window, surprised at himself, the depth of feeling. Quite out of character. The telephone rang. Not again. The machine picked it up on the third ring. It was Dan.

'This is Dan Mitchell calling for vigilante Pete, formerly Flight Lieutenant P.J. Deacon of Her Majesty's Royal Air Force, now starring as Charles Bronson in Deathwish twelve – the umpire strikes back. You there Peto?'

'Hello Dan.'

'Well hello sport, screening our phone calls these days are we?'

'Obscene callers, heavy breathers, advertising executives, all sorts of perverts you know.'

'Of course, wanted to get them on tape for playback later in the bedroom no doubt. What are you doing for lunch?'

Emma had called him first thing from the office. Told him of the events of the previous night, of her concern. 'You see if you can get through to him Dan, he won't open up to me.' She said he was alone all day, both children at school, no engagements.

'Nothing much, a little thin gruel perhaps, couple of paracetomol.'

They met in an Italian restaurant in West Brompton. It was a favourite haunt. Peter arrived first, the manager recognised him, sat him at a window table. He ordered Chianti and garlic bread. Dan arrived a few minutes later and made a big show of stopping in the middle of the floor and pointing at Peter.

'What have you done to your face?' he said loudly. Heads turned.

'Thanks a lot Mister Best Friend, may your gonads wither.'

'Any time, have you ordered?'

'The works, you're paying remember.' He fingered the bridge of his nose self consciously. It was red and tender, there were livid crescent shadows beneath his eyes.

'Big bastard was he?' said Dan innocently.

'Big knuckles for a twelve-year-old bastard anyway.'

Dan raised his voice again, turning his head to one side. 'Oh, you got mugged by a primary school kid then did you?'

They had antipasta then tagliatelle, he carbonara, Dan a seafood house speciality. They ordered a second bottle of Chianti. The place was filling up.

'Emma put you up to this of course.' Peter dabbed at his mouth with a napkin, and took a drink. He was two glasses ahead of Dan.

'She's very concerned Peto. We all are.'

'We? This smacks of conspiracy.'

'Don't be daft. What's going on?'

He hesitated. What could he tell him? And what could Dan do if he did tell him? A group of Japanese tourists was peering in at them from the street. Dan stared back, pulling faces and making little shooing motions with his hands.

'We don't have to talk about it you know. I'm not your blasted shrink, thank God.'

'Sorry Dan. It's okay, I'm just a bit up against it right now. Financially, you know.'

'Anything on the horizon, job-wise?'

Peter couldn't help resenting the question. 'Not yet,' he said wearily, as though tired of reciting the same lines. 'Some good, firm possibilities but nothing definite.' He drained his glass again. Dan refilled it.

'What about something temporary, stop-gap?'

'Oh she told you about that too did she?' He dropped his fork and sat back, face flushed, glassy-eyed. 'Anything else she happen to mention in passing while we're at it? Sex life not up to much these days Dan. And he's hitting the sauce a bit hard after dinner.'

'Easy Peto. It's me for God's sake.' He changed the subject but he'd blown it. Peter knew the lunch was a set up and remained sullen. But Emma was right, Peter was changed, suspicious and withdrawn. It was worrying, Dan had known him for fifteen years but he'd never seen him like this. Naturally some of it was probably attributable to delayed shock from the events of the previous night, but there was something else, a sort of aggressive defensiveness. Like paranoia.

'Do you know,' Peter said later, over coffee and Cognac, his voice distorted by blocked nostrils and too much alcohol, 'last night, when that little sod belted me, it was the first time, anyone had really, apart from boxing matches at school that is, the first time anyone had hit me. You know really hit me. First time in my life.'

Dan considered the notion. It was four o'clock and they had both drunk too much. He could forget going back to the office, but it was not a problem; in his business long lunches were the norm. And he felt he owed it to his friend. Even if he could offer him no comfort, he could at least stay and get drunk with him. The other tables had emptied long ago, most of the restaurant staff gone for the afternoon. The manager stayed on, cashing up the till. They were good customers, he'd give them another fifteen minutes. Outside the light was failing, it was grey and gloomy, a threat of rain in the November overcast. 'What about that time when the squadron was in Germany, you know, that bar in Dusseldorf?'

Peter shook his head blearily. 'Nooo. That was just a pub brawl, a bit of fun. Nothing like this. This was the real thing.'

'What did it feel like?'

'Well it hurt like bloody hell of course.' His eyes followed his finger as it gingerly touched his nose. 'Hurt like bloody hell. But! Do you know what?'

'What?'

'It felt great, actually. It felt bloody great.'

CHAPTER

4

'Hello Miriam? Peter.'

    'Peter.' No recognition.

    'Peter Deacon?'

'Oh, Peter of course. So sorry, it's been so busy. Hold on let me check your file.'

'Oh, Miriam—' But she'd flicked him onto hold. He waited while she rummaged.

'Here we are, now then, got nothing further for you at this time.'

'I was calling about the airport construction job you mentioned a while ago. In Qatar. Is it still open?'

'Qatar. Oh yes, no I'm afraid not and anyway you were right, they were looking for someone with a civil engineering background.'

Then why did you mention it to me you stupid bitch. 'I see. Well if anything comes up, anything at all, I'm widening the net.'

'Temporary assignments too? What about location?'

'Anything at all and I'd like to hear about it.' He hesitated. 'Does anything spring to mind?'

'Not immediately, but I'll ask around.' Uneasy pause. 'I

won't pretend it's going to be easy Peter. It's your qualifications, and experience.'

'What's wrong with them?'

'Nothing at all. They're excellent. In their field. It's just that it is a very specialised field.'

She promised to keep trying, they hung up. It was a problem he had already encountered since he began applying for jobs outside the aerospace industry. He had little experience of anything else. None at all really. He took the *Sunday Times* from the top of the bureau and turned to the management recruitment pages. There was no shortage of positions, well paid and interesting many of them. But invariably there was a 'preference will be given to applicants with relevant experience' clause.

Lately he had been sending letters of application which began:

'Dear Sir,
With reference to your advertisement for a marketing manager enclosed please find my curriculum vitae. Although at first glance it might appear that my experience and qualifications are not directly related to your company's business ...'

The replies, when they came, invariably cited the deficiency as grounds for not pursuing the application.

The telephone rang. He jumped. The answering machine took it. He had taken to leaving it on all day, telling friends and the recruitment agents that its constant interruptions had become a major distraction, but to hang on, say who they were and he'd pick it up if he was in.

'Peter. This is John Bishop. If you are there, could I please speak to you. Now. If not, please call me back urgently, before close of play today.' He waited on the line, as if he knew that Peter was there in the room, not daring to breathe, eyes staring transfixed at the slowly turning tape, listening to the gentle hiss of the open line, willing him to hang up. Two seconds, three, a click, the phone went dead and the machine stopped.

He breathed out slowly, shaking his head. This was it. He knew what Bishop wanted. He wanted the cheque, today. The cheque from the building society. The cheque that had been promised him a week ago. The cheque representing thirty thousand pounds worth of non-existent mortgage on Emma's cottage in Suffolk.

He leaned down and pulled a whiskey bottle from the bottom drawer of the bureau, poured some into an unwashed coffee mug on his desk, then a little more, half-filling it. He raised the mug, toasting the answering machine, then took a swallow. The neat spirit burned his throat, and tasted faintly of coffee dregs, but it warmed his stomach and eased his mind. It definitely helped him think. 'Cheers, John.'

He walked wearily over to the bed and lay down on top of the covers, his feet denting a pile of newspaper clippings and notes. It was over, there was nothing more he could do. In a way it was a relief, an enormous burden lifted from his back. Suddenly he laughed, out loud, slopping whiskey on his chest as he imagined the forthcoming conversation.

'John. Old thing. How are you? Fit and flourishing I trust?'

'Peter, thank God you've called. I'm in deep trouble with credit control. What about the damn mortgage?'

'Mortgage? What mortgage would that be then Johnny?'

'The mortgage on your cottage. You know in Sussex or wherever it is.'

'Oh that. Never was one. Sorry.'

'What?'

'No. Made the whole thing up. Good eh? Had you going for a bit.'

The laughter subsided. If only there had been more time. Perhaps he should have applied for a mortgage anyway, gone through the motions. Impossible, they would need Emma's signature on all the documentation: the property was in her name. He sat up. Wait a minute. Swinging his legs from the bed, he strode back to the bureau, tearing open drawers and rifling the contents. He found the estate agent's particulars on the cottage and some odd notes and letters, but not the deeds. He remembered they were lodged with Emma's family solicitor, the whole transaction had been handled by him in order to ensure that her father's will was properly discharged.

He sat at the desk holding the particulars and gnawing his thumbnail. Did he need the deeds? He didn't know – probably. And anyway there wasn't time. Bishop wanted something today. Pity, he might have been able to apply for the mortgage in her name, making sure she didn't see any of the correspondence of course. When the money came through he could pay off Bishop and still have plenty to live on, then pay it off monthly in the normal way. She need never know. Blasted building societies, it would take weeks.

His eyes fell on a letter he had received that morning from the building society holding the mortgage on the Fulham house. They were requesting urgent clarification of the situation regarding non-payment of their standing order. He had no idea what to say, make something up probably. Then it struck him. He picked up the letter. It was short, four lines. Maybe it could be done. He turned to his word processor, selected a fresh letter template and began typing.

Half an hour later he removed the single sheet of plain paper from his printer and held it up to the light with the letter from the building society beneath. It matched up perfectly. The date, the references, the name at the bottom, everything. Taking scissors, he trimmed around his page until when he lay it over the letter from the building society, the text underneath was completely obscured by his. A touch of glue and it was finished. He could never use it as an original of course, but the bank wouldn't expect him to send an original, he hoped.

He picked up the phone, then immediately replaced it, hand shaking. What on earth was he doing? He must be out of his mind. Pouring himself another stiff one he began pacing the room. He could call Bishop, tell him the truth, what could the man do? His imaginary conversation on the bed did not seem so funny now. Bishop would cut them off without a cent and without a second's hesitation. Then what? Begging and borrowing from friends and relatives? Two grand a month? Unthinkable.

It was all just a question of time. Just a little more time. He was bound to be back in work soon, bound to. He had that interview with Fielding Aero coming up, practically a sure-fire certainty. And if that one didn't drop into place, something else would, very soon. Then all this chicanery and deception could stop, it would suddenly become irrelevant. What? Regular income line again? Oh well, that changes everything of course! The credit squeeze instantly slackened, the debts rescheduled and life, normal ordered routine daily life could go on as before. That was all he wanted, all he had ever wanted. Just a little time. He drained his mug and sat down at the desk.

'John, Peter Deacon. Sorry I wasn't in earlier, just got back from an interview.'

'No problem. How did it go?'

'Hard to say, they'll let me know. Now John, I was going to call you, I've been on to the building society a couple of times during the last week, God they've been slow. But I've finally received a letter of confirmation from them that the mortgage on the cottage has been accepted and that transfer of funds will take place within fourteen days.' He bit his lip, there was a long silence at the other end.

'Fourteen days? Why so long?'

'God knows. I can't say I'm terribly impressed with them, but it all seems to be coming together now, finally. Would you like me to pop a copy of the letter into the post, or I can fax it to you from the print shop down the road if you need something today.'

Bishop sighed. 'I don't know Peter, I was really hoping for a cash transfer. Fourteen days, Jesus.' He came to a decision. 'Yes, okay, fax a copy of the confirmation today, if you would, and you might as well mail me another copy for good measure. I'm going to have to take this upstairs, but I expect they'll agree a further limited extension. Can't do anything about the standing orders though I'm afraid.'

He walked down to the print shop and ran off four copies of the letter on their photocopier, faxing one to Bishop at the same time. On the way home he tore up the original forgery and dropped the pieces into a rubbish bin. 'Piece of cake,' he murmured. 'Should have gone for thirty days.'

'Mr and Mrs Deacon? Would you like to come in now?' They followed her into the office, standard hospital fare, but she had made an effort, it was bright and cheery, the walls covered with children's pictures, many presumably by her patients. Jamie sat in the middle of the sofa, chewing a sweet and swinging his legs. They arranged themselves either side of him, smiling and cooing down at him self-consciously. 'Hello darling.' 'Everything all right Jamie?' The doctor sat at her desk, picked up her notes and smiled warmly.

'Well, we've had quite a chat haven't we Jamie?' He nodded, chewed on. 'First of all we took our clothes off and did some weighing and measuring.' Peter's expression remained fixed and impassive and attentive, but his mind wandered off track slightly. She was young, good looking, it was an intriguing notion. 'Jamie is slightly underweight for his height and age, but nothing we can't put right. He says he would like to be a bit bigger.' She spoke to them all, but constantly looked to him, smiling conspiratorially, he nodding back, and smiling too. 'And so he has promised to make a list, with Mummy, when he gets home, of all the things he likes to eat, and all the things you don't like too.' She screwed up her face and stuck out her tongue at him, he giggled. 'So that next time he comes we can see if he can't push those scales down a bit further. All right Mummy?'

There was more of the same, but little of any new substance. They were to participate in various activities, doing more things together as a family. She asked if anything came to mind. Emma said they could all go to the cottage next weekend for a treat; Jamie thought he might like that. Peter felt a shock like a belt of static electricity at the mention of the place but recovered quickly enough to mutter agreement.

Finally she stopped, looked at each in turn and said that she was very pleased with today's progress and perhaps that was enough for the moment. They began gathering themselves up.

'Mr Deacon, perhaps you and I might have a quick word together, in a second?' He looked at Emma, she was busy zipping Jamie into his anorak. She glanced up at him, made a tiny, frowning nod.

'Of course.' He sat down again, Emma hurried out of the room, Jamie in tow. The doctor watched the door until it closed. He felt a nudge of unease. What was going on here?

'I thought it might be helpful if we had quick word in private Mr Deacon.' Her tone had changed now that Jamie had gone. Businesslike and brisk, but still friendly; professionally amicable. 'Tell me, if I may ask, how would you describe your relationship with your son?'

He shifted on the sofa, crossed his legs, composing carefully. 'Well, until relatively recently, I would say he was opening up well.' He paused.

'Indeed, but with respect, that's not what I asked.'

'With respect, I hadn't finished.' His tone was icy.

'I'm so sorry, please go on.' Wow, what's all this then?

'I was going to add that I had begun to sense the foundations of a rapport developing between us. Although, I have to admit that we didn't spend as much time in each other's company as I would have liked owing to the nature and demands of my job.'

'I understand you had the misfortune to lose your job.'

Jesus Christ, Emma. He forced a wry smile. 'Ah, my wife has briefed you on recent events I see.'

'She mentioned it on the telephone when the appointment was made.'

'Of course she did.'

'Would you say that your change in circumstances coincided with a deterioration in your relationship with Jamie at all?'

'My relationship with Jamie?' He sat up on the sofa, jabbing a finger at his chest, eyes ablaze. 'What about his relationship with me? Or his relationship with his mother? Isn't this about all of us?' God, how typical! The woman had already made up her mind. Yes, had a chat with the boy's parents, the mother filled me in, the father's definitely the problem in that family . . .

'Of course it is. But whether you like it or not Mr Deacon, Jamie looks to you for emotional support and encouragement. Approval, approbation. It's absolutely normal in boys of his age.'

They eyed each other warily. She had to probe further. It was almost too text book: at the root of every troubled child was a screwed up parent. That may be, but she hadn't expected anything like this. The man was a pressure cooker. 'I'm sure you would agree that if a young boy's father is undergoing some, personal difficulties, of whatever nature, then the child is going to respond accordingly.'

'Yes, I can appreciate that. But I must point out that you appear to have overlooked the history of Jamie's "condition" Dr Pryce. It goes back almost to his infancy.'

'I hadn't overlooked that point. I was merely exploring the possibility that this latest recurrence may be connected with your change in circumstance.' He conceded the point grudgingly. She made one last attempt to draw him out. 'Is there anything at all about your own situation that you wish to discuss?'

His mind raced: I'd like to discuss why Chelsea have lost four games on the trot; why I get so tired but can never sleep; how on earth it can be that I cold-bloodedly perpetrated a serious fraud; why time contracts, shrinking in inverse proportion to my expanding need for it; how I can't talk to my father who is ashamed of me, nor my son who hates me, nor my wife who plots against me. I'd like to discuss why I can't do it with her any more but would like very much to do it with you, right now over your desk. I'd like to discuss how great the City streets feel at night, and the extraordinary cleansing purity of a punch from the dark. Global warming, the trashing of Antarctica, the obscene profligacy of the society we choose to live in. What magnificent stuff Scotch whiskey is; why it is that intelligent, rational human beings believe in God as a force for good; and I'd like to know, *what* it is that continues to drive me, compels me to restore a status quo founded on a premise for life that my heart keeps telling me is flawed.

'I thought we were here to discuss my son.'

*

The traffic on the drive back was heavy, the roads glistening wet in heavy rain. Emma sat, half turned in her seat, chatting to Jamie in the back, planning the forthcoming weekend in the cottage.

'Sally could miss school on Friday, we'll pick you up at lunchtime and we could get down in time for tea. How would that be?'

'Fine.' He was examining his new paintbox, selected during the obligatory post-examination visit to the hospital shop.

'Well that's opportune anyway,' said Peter, slowing for traffic lights.

'Hmm?'

'Sally. Got a letter this morning. She's got to leave.'

Emma glanced back at Jamie, he was engrossed. She turned forward. 'Why for God's sake?'

He enunciated the words slowly, an exaggerated stage whisper. 'Because we haven't paid the bill.'

'Peter. You said we were covered. For small expenses.'

'Em, we still owe them for last term.'

She stared ahead, the reflected rain on the windscreen pouring down her face. 'God I hate this.'

'Welcome to the real world.' He jerked the steering wheel suddenly, hit the throttle, forcing into a small gap in the next lane. The driver behind had to brake sharply, flashing his headlights and sounding his horn.

'Emma?' He looked across at her, she was tight lipped, stony. 'There really are some things we have to talk about.'

'If it's another of your economic dramas, no thanks. I saw the last one.'

'We have to face facts.'

'Wrong. You have to face them. I merely have to live with the consequences. You're the one who keeps saying he's going to sort it out remember?'

76

'I am sorting it out for God's—' Turning quickly she scowled at him, eyes flicking towards the back seat. He checked himself, glanced at Jamie in the rear-view mirror. His head was down, still looking at the paintbox.

'I am sorting it out,' he said quietly, through clenched teeth.

'Well, if you'll forgive me, you have a peculiar way of going about it.'

'I've got an interview tomorrow.'

She stared at him. In the back of the car Jamie gazed down at the decorated tin lid of the paintbox. The bright colours wavering, misted and blurred through the tears which he could hear tapping on the box as they fell.

He'd seen it in the *Telegraph* management recruitment pages. It was a marketing manager's position for a Heathrow-based business specialising in supplying technical services to the airline industry. The advertisement was rather small and irritatingly ambiguous about pay: 'An attractive remuneration package, salary commensurate with age and experience.' But he had applied anyway.

He took the car, misjudged the traffic on the M4 and arrived three quarters of an hour early. He drove past the entrance and on until he found a high street café. He sat, sipping frothy coffee and flicking sightlessly through a discarded copy of the *Sun*. He was nervous, working hard to suppress an urge to flee home. Sorry Em, vacancy already filled, complete waste of time. Standing in front of the bedroom mirror that morning, he had caught his own eye. A momentary glimpse of a frightened stranger in pin-stripe suit and shining brogues. He had felt nauseous at breakfast, panicky as Emma kissed him on the cheek at the door of the house.

The hands on the nicotine stained face of the café's

electric wall clock told him there was still plenty of time, but he mistrusted it. God how he missed that Rolex! He went back to the VW and double checked the facia clock, still twenty minutes to go. He sat in the driver's seat with the radio on, forcing himself to wait another five. Then, glancing round to check he was unobserved, he took a double pull from the half bottle of Bells in the glove compartment, grimacing as he chased it with a squirt of breath freshener, started the engine and drove back along the road.

'UAS, I see here. Unfortunate business.' Fielding held his unopened spectacles in front of his eyes while he peered at the application. He had his jacket off. The office, more a small conference room, was hot – he'd already apologised about the runaway central heating. Peter had declined the offer to remove his, said he felt fine thanks. Now there was a sheen of fine droplets covering his forehead and temples, and the neck of his pale blue button-down collar was damp and uncomfortable.

There were three of them at the table. Deacon sat at one end, his back to the door, Fielding at the other, painfully bright early winter sunlight pouring through large windows behind him, throwing him into partial silhouette. To his left sat a smartly dressed late middle-aged woman who smiled as she was introduced: 'Mrs Kavanagh, my Human Resources Manager,' said nothing during Fielding's discourse on the company, but wrote notes throughout his discussion with Peter.

'Yes it was. Something of a shock.'

'How long have you been out of work?'

'A little over two months.' A little under three actually.

'Have you, if you'll forgive me, have you applied for many positions in that time?'

'Yes, quite a few.'

'I see. The reason I ask is, what attracted you to this one?'

Nothing, I'm desperate, can't you see that? He tried to concentrate, looked up at the ceiling, pursed his lips, pausing for reflection. But his mind wandered, suddenly he was thinking of Dr Pryce; he'd handled that interview badly too. Come on man think! 'My background is er, in aviation. I would like to remain within the industry, your position would seem to offer both the potential for challenge and er, the opportunity to exploit my experience and qualifications.' What on earth are you talking about?

'In what way?' Fielding asked pleasantly.

'Well, er, Fielding Aero has a reputation for providing a quality range of aerospace support services, but mainly to the domestic market. It is my perception that your organisation possesses the basic infrastructure to expand that service into Europe. I'm thinking particularly of the supply of contract aeromechanical staff, and product support.' Now you're talking.

'And you believe you are the person to market this expansion?'

'Yes I do.' Mrs Kavanagh was writing furiously, Fielding was pensive, his chin on his hands, forefingers steepled at his lips. Deacon relaxed, in control again. After so long in the wilderness, he'd almost forgotten that he was a natural leader in his field, competent and capable, the wielder of great professional potency.

'Would it not be fair to say that it was a similar expansion, into what is generally perceived at the moment as being a contracting and unstable market, that was at the root of UAS's problems?'

Deacon sat forward on the edge of his seat, most of his weight on his legs which were taut and set like a sprinter's beneath the chair. Above, his left arm rested on the table top, fist clenching and unclenching. A droplet of sweat finally detached itself from the wetness of his hairline and trickled down his cheek in front of one ear. 'Yes, but UAS relied exclusively on the military market, your business base is oriented towards the civil sector.' A tiny warning flag fluttered somewhere deep within him. He ignored it, plunged on. 'Although in my view there are certainly niche markets within the defence sector, which I am intimately familiar with, and which I consider Fielding Aero could penetrate to great effect.' Come on Kavanagh, keep up.

'That might upset established suppliers to those markets, possibly damage them irrevocably. Does that bother you?'

Deacon shrugged. 'I've always believed in a competitive marketing policy.'

'Tell me Mr Deacon, just for our records, could you tell me the full names and dates of birth of your children?'

'Whaa . . .?' It was Kavanagh, speaking for the first time. A strong Irish lilt in her voice. She waited, pen poised, eyebrows raised. Polite and expectant. Her eyes boring like lasers into his.

'Oh, um, yes James Alexander, eighteenth March nineteen eighty-four.' Wasn't it? 'And Sally Anna, twenty-second – no twenty-fourth of June eighty-seven.' Damn, not right, one of them.

He drove out of Fielding's car-park, and along the road until he came to a housing estate. Turning at random he finally pulled up in a cul-de-sac outside a modern semi-detached house with a small, neatly maintained front garden and a sign saying 'Llamedos' on the gate. 'You're a long way from home, boyo,' he sighed, reaching for the glove compartment.

He was shattered, completely drained, it felt like he must have been in there for hours. He upended the half bottle to his lips, checking the facia clock. God, twenty minutes, incredible! Reaching down to his side he wound at the seatback until it was semi-reclined, wrenched his tie loose and collar button undone. He drank again and sank back, feeling the wet shirt pressing against his skin. Christ what an ordeal. Still it didn't go too badly. Fielding was impressed, certainly should have been. But the Kavanagh woman ...

He closed his eyes, tilting his head back on the neck rest, waiting as the alcohol began working its infallible magic. Soon it came, its golden caress drawing the tension from his neck, easing the runaway pounding in his chest, cooling the fever in his head. Five minutes. Just five minutes then head for home. His breathing became deeper. God he was tired. Just five minutes. He sank into the waiting black, chuckling. Llamedos. Not Welsh at all. 'Sod 'em all' spelled backwards. When he woke up it was dark.

'Daddy, my daddy! You've been to work today.' She hugged his knees for a couple of seconds then ran back into the playroom. Emma and Jamie were there watching television.

'What happened? I was getting anxious.'

'Sorry Em, the interviews were all backed up, mine was over an hour late. Any chance of a cup of tea?'

'I was late picking Jamie up from school, had to get a taxi.'

'Sorry. Hello Jamie, how was school today?'

'Okay.' His eyes remained fixed to the screen.

'Was it all right – about the taxi?' He munched slowly on a biscuit, leaning against the French window. The refectory table was laid for dinner. Five places. He'd forgotten. Had she told him?

She shrugged. 'You know Jamie, it's impossible to tell. But I was late getting there which obviously didn't please him. Really you should have called.'

'Sorry. It was difficult.'

'Tell me.'

'Fairly standard inquisition. About an hour.'

'God! Many inquisitors?'

'Two. The usual format, one good guy, one bad.'

'Bright lights and electrodes, eh ... What do you think?' Her tone was light.

'Hmm, very hard to say. Lot of competition, but the indications were good. Definite hints of selection for short-list. Umm, guess who's coming to dinner?'

'Peter! Dan and Mitch. I told you this morning.'

'Oh, yes. And ...'

'Charlie Gladstone. Remember?'

He arrived first. Peter opened the door. He barely recognised the man. He hadn't seen him in nearly ten years. He remembered a gangly, intensely serious young man with lank, rather greasy hair worn very long in the fashion of the day.

'Charlie, good heavens. How are you?' They shook hands. He was slightly taller than Peter and barely recognisable as the Charlie of old. He had filled out, was broader, broad shouldered, broad necked. He was a big man, the hair was shorter now, professionally coiffed. And there was the beard. Flecked with grey and designer short, its sides trimmed neatly like lawn edgings. Peter ushered him into the sitting room.

'Mineral water, please Peter. I must say you have a delightful house. What terrific lithos. Where did you get them?'

'Oh, Emma collects them. Horrific price, I'm sure she gets ripped off sometimes.'

'Worth about twice what I paid for them now those two. Hello Charlie.' She looked stunning, Peter had forgotten how she could. Emerald green silk blouse and knee-length matching skirt, the blouse shot through with delicately patterned thread, gold it looked like. Flesh coloured stockings glistening with lycra and little green leather ankle boots. It all looked expensive, and new, but she'd deny it as usual. New? Don't be ridiculous, I've had this for years.

'Well!' said Charlie. She walked to him, chin up, smiling. He took both her hands, held her at arm's length. 'Will you look at you.' He did, for several seconds, then kissed her on both cheeks.

Peter started from his reverie. 'There she is. Drink darling?' The doorbell went.

They drank aperitifs in the sitting room for an hour while dinner cooked. Dan and Charlie thought they must have met before but neither could remember the other. They talked shop; they were in related businesses. Emma came and went from the kitchen. Mitch sat next to Peter on the sofa. At first he hurried about with dishes of nuts and Bombay mix, refilling the glasses. Soon his attentiveness faltered.

'Hey Peto.' Mitch was nudging him. 'How you doing?'

'Hmm? Oh fine, fine.' He glanced around uncertainly, as though suddenly surprised to find himself in the room. With these people. They were looking at him curiously. What? Had he nodded off? Dan grinned at him and made a big show of shooting his jacket cuffs, then slowly raising his empty tumbler onto his head with both hands, like a circus performer. Peter recovered himself, leaped up: 'Give me that thing you ill-mannered sot, Charlie let me get you some more of that stuff. Are you sure I can't fix you something stronger? Glass of lemonade perhaps? Mitch how's yours?' He fled for the kitchen, filled their glasses, and his.

'Nearly ready,' said Emma from the oven door. 'Another ten minutes. Peter, are you all right?'

'Yes, I'm fine. Bit dizzy.' He was leaning over the table, rubbing his temples with both hands.

'Peter I really hope you're not going to get drunk tonight, and—'

'And what?'

'And spoil things that's all.'

'Is that things in general, or did you have any particular thing in mind?'

'Have you checked on the children?'

He went up slowly. He was tempted to stop at the first floor, turn straight into the spare room and fall flat out on the bed. But he could hear laughter, Dan's guffaw wafting up behind him, and he knew he had to go through with it. And as for Emma and Charlie bloody Gallstone. The guy must think Christmas had come early, she practically went down on him right there in the middle of the sitting room. The unsolicited image presented itself on cue, he walked it around the strewn flotsam of his jumbled thoughts, shocked and aroused, until it slipped from his grasp and was lost in the wreckage.

Sally's tubby pink body was uncovered, face down and asleep athwart the bed. She had rolled her pyjama bottoms up in tight coils above the knees, why did she always do that? Her feet were sticking out over the edge of the bed, her head hard up against the side wall. He manoeuvred the limp form back under the duvet and left quietly. Jamie's door was shut but a crack of light shone from beneath it. He was about to go in, but hesitated, tapping lightly instead.

'Jamie, may I come in? It's Dad.'

'Okay.'

He was sitting at the little desk rinsing a brush in a jam jar of water, the paintbox open beside him.

'Do you mind if I have a look?'

'Okay.' It was a big picture. Although very obviously the work of a child, something about the thoroughness, the way the sheet had been completely filled, and the attention to detail, suggested patience and planning.

'Hey. That is great.' He lowered himself to his knees beside the desk and studied the picture. It was an island in the ocean. The island was hill-shaped and rose steep and green from the deep blue of the sea. There were some trees or bushes dotted on it and a few animals, sheep perhaps, or cattle; it was hard to tell. At the top of the hill stood a small brown house with big windows and smoke coming out of the chimney. The sky was pale blue with an orange sun and small white clouds. 'That looks to me like a really nice place to go.'

'One day I'm going to live on an island.' Jamie slid from the chair and went to his bed. Peter picked up the painting and followed. He couldn't take his eyes off it.

'Oh yes. Wouldn't that be great? Your own private island.' Jamie got into bed, Peter leaned over and tucked the covers under his chin, stroked the mop of dark hair.

Jamie's eyes fluttered shut. 'Thirty million miles away, and no people, just animals,' he said sleepily; yet sternly, those were the rules.

'Uh huh.' The picture mesmerised him. He sank to the floor, leaning back wearily against the bed, brushing the green hill softly with his fingertips. Outside a strong, gusting wind spiralled street litter into the air and shook the window frames, its fitful hum drowning the sound of passing cars.

Peter's eyes closed, God he was tired. 'I'll think of you there Jamie,' he said softly. 'Relaxing in your house on your island thirty million miles away. I'd really like to visit from time to time. Would you let me?' His head sank back against the mattress. Jamie's breathing was deep and even. 'Perhaps you could paint me a ship to sail there in. A beautiful wooden sailing ship, with tall masts and snow white sails.' His voice was a murmur. 'Called Hope. A ship called Hope.'

He started. Emma's head was at the door.

'For God's sake Peter come on!' she hissed. 'You've been up here for ages. Everybody's waiting.'

*

They'd already started, garlic mushrooms. He sat down at the end of the table next to Mitch and Dan.

'All right?' asked Mitch.

'Sorry about that. Got waylaid by the first born.'

'How is he?' Dan turned to listen, he was godfather. Emma and Charlie were head to head at the other end, hushed tones.

'Been up and down lately, what with all the, uncertainties. But right at this moment, he seems to be handling it better than any of us. Apart from Sally.'

'That's good, and what about his dad?'

He put down his fork, refilled the Mitchells' glasses, passed the bottle to Dan. Break it up down there ... Dan turned away dutifully, filled the others' glasses, picked up on Emma's last remark. Peter drank, Mitch watched him, waiting patiently. She wanted an answer.

'What happened Mitch? In the sitting room before dinner.'

'You frightened me, that's what.'

'Sorry. Um, how?'

'Do you remember anything?'

'Come on Mitch.'

She spoke quietly, the other three arguing shop again.

'One second you were "mein gut host Peto" of old, the next, Rip van Winkle.'

'Nodded off?'

'To another planet. Peter you were sitting there, right next to me, talking, then you, kind of looked blank, stared into outer space for, I don't know, probably half a minute, seemed like hours. Totally out of it. Then you, just sighed. This awful loud, moaning sigh. Scared the shit out of me, the others too.'

'Emma?'

'In the kitchen. Have you seen a doctor?'

'Mitch, I'm fine.'

'Sure. Don't eat.' She nodded at the barely touched mushrooms. 'Don't sleep; wander about the city at all hours, slipping in and out of catatonia. How many of these little interludes have there been?'

'Mitch I'm just fagged out. Been a busy day. Got a job offer.'

They cleared away, made space in the middle of the table for a large pot of steaming casserole. Game: pheasant, partridge and pigeon breasts. All remnants from the freezer, but marinaded, stewed slowly until rich and tender. They helped themselves with a ladle. Peter uncorked Brouilly.

'But if you could, would you really go back to work full-time?' Charlie asked, heaping salad onto a side plate, then holding the wooden bowl for Emma.

'Like a shot. I was born to it, you know that.' She flashed a dazzling smile at him.

'Why don't you then?'

She tasted the casserole. It was good, something had been in the freezer too long, the pigeon breasts probably but no matter. 'Up until now there was no need, and not much point. Plus there were the children of course. But since going part-time at the agency again, it's been fantastic.'

'Would they take you back full-time?'

'Possibly, but they don't really have the work right now. And anyway there's the house, and the kids, you know the little woman stuff?'

'Well Peter's here at the moment, isn't he? Have you talked it over with him?'

She chewed thoughtfully. God if only. 'No. It wouldn't work. He's going flat out for jobs – thinks he might have got something today. It's very important to him that he gets right back on the horse as quickly as possible. Anyway I

87

couldn't make enough on my own to keep him in the manner—'

'You know there's a job for you at my place Emma. I'm always short of streetwise creativity and with your London agency experience, and talent . . .' He winked at her.

'What, commute to the sticks? Hardly Charlie.'

'Why not? Lots of people do it, counter-commute. No queues, no crush. Better still, sell up here and move out to the country.' His eyes widened, fingers dancing, voice deep and chanting like a children's conjurer. 'You know it makes sense.'

CHAPTER

5

The drive was a nightmare. It took well over three hours to reach the cottage. They had to drive west out of London on the M4, past Heathrow, join up with the M25 London orbital and creep round the north of the city, stopping and starting in solid motorway traffic until they were finally able to head east on the A12. Even then the roads were packed with Friday afternoon commuters leaving early to escape town for the weekend.

The children fretted and fidgeted in the back seat. Sally had a cold and whined incessantly. Jamie seemed bent on teasing and tormenting her until she screamed and hit him with a book. In the front seat the atmosphere was tense.

'This is utter insanity,' said Peter at one point, as they sat trapped in a motionless logjam somewhere near the South Mimms services.

'We're doing it for Jamie, remember?'

'Oh yes, terrific therapy. Let's spend a family weekend tearing each other's throats out on the motorway.'

'Make him stop touching me mummy!'

Emma sighed wearily, turning once more. 'What is it now?'

89

'He did touch me.'

'Jamie, don't touch your sister.'

'She touched me first!'

'Why not leave each other alone, sit quietly and read a book.'

They crept onward. At Chelmsford there was a long hold up for roadworks. Peter fell into a moody silence, Emma was trying to listen to the news on the radio. In the back, desultory, half-hearted bickering. It was dark outside, the traffic inched forward then slowed again, a river of brake lights stretching ahead and out of view. Motorcyclists weaved in and out of the queues.

'Will you two please sit quietly. I'm trying to hear the news.'

'She won't give my book back.' Jamie tore the book from Sally's grasp, she screamed in protest, ear-piercingly loud with an amplitude and clarity of tone unique to three-year-old lungs and larynx. Peter stiffened suddenly, gasped as though wakened from a deep sleep by a bucket of icy water. Turning, he reached into the back and seized a wrist from each child, wrenched them forward, face working, teeth bared.

'No more!' he bellowed like an enraged bear, his face white and wild in the headlights of the car behind. 'You have to stop, now!' He held them in a vice-like grip, flecks of spittle at the corners of his mouth, a deep animal snarl escaping between the bared teeth. They were shocked into terrified, silent immobility, as if a cobra had suddenly reared up in the front seat and was poised, fangs bared, ready to strike at the first movement. Seconds elapsed, then Sally whimpered, 'Mummy.' Emma responded, instinctively deflecting his attention.

'Peter,' she said softly, mouth dry. He didn't move. The car ahead pulled away, opening up a gap. She reached a hand across to his left shoulder, pulling him gently to her. 'Peter. It's all right darling.' He resisted for a second more then slumped, releasing the wrists with a gasp.

'It's okay,' he whispered. 'It's okay, I'm all right now.'

She stared at him a few moments longer, her eyes wide and anxious, then she opened her door and leapt out. The driver behind sounded his horn impatiently. She flicked two fingers at the headlights as she strode round the back of the Volkswagen to the driver's door. 'Budge over, I'll drive.' Peter shuffled across obediently. They drove on in silence.

After Chelmsford the traffic finally began to ease. They bypassed Ipswich then turned off the dual carriageway and began winding along B roads, passing through villages, some of them no more than a collection of farm buildings at a crossroads, some even less – the momentary flash of a sign in the headlights, then nothing until the next sign. Sally slept, trussed open-mouthed and snoring into her child-seat, Jamie and Peter stared ahead into the darkness beyond the headlight beams, leaning synchronously from side to side as Emma propelled the car swiftly along the last few miles of twisting lanes.

Then at last they passed a village sign saying Bedingham. They drove on for half a mile, rounded a sharp bend and descended to a confluence of roads around a small green. They could see lights from houses dotted around the green, a pub called the White Horse and an illuminated church tower hidden among trees off one of the lanes leading away from the green. They turned left at the pub and drove out of the village along a quiet lane until, after another quarter of a mile, they came to the cottage on the right, standing alone and set back from the lane. It stood out low and white in the headlights, squat and solid. Emma stopped the car. A low fence surrounded the tiny front garden, beside her the front gate and an overgrown path to the door.

91

'Hello old friend,' she murmured. Then she drove on past the house pulling onto a grass parking space at its side. 'Come on everyone, we'll unload through the kitchen door.'

The place smelled damp, and cold. There was a box of groceries on the kitchen table and a note from Mrs Morrison at the Post Office Stores.

Dear Mrs Deacon,
Thank you for your telephone message, here is the groceries minus the sossages which we won't have in till Saturday. Hope you are well and the little ones too.
Best regards,
Anne Morrison.
P.S. I left the upstairs windows open to air.

'That was thoughtful of her,' said Peter, dumping suitcases. He sniffed disdainfully. 'God what is that smell?' Upstairs the children were running from room to room.

'It's just a touch of damp. Come on, we'll get some coal in, light the stove and the fire in the sitting room. It'll be great.'

Peter set off with the suitcases, clumping up the narrow stairs and muttering about the cold. It was smaller than he remembered. Much smaller. And uninviting on a winter night. There were two floors, three rooms on each. Immediately inside the main entrance was a small hallway leading to a steep stairway, to the right a door opened into the living room which took up the right-hand half of the house. The door opposite led into the kitchen. At the far end of the kitchen through another door was a tiny, icy cold bathroom, formerly a food store or pantry and converted in the fifties. At the top of the stairs a small landing, their bedroom on the right over the living room, two smaller rooms opposite, one with bunks for the children, the other, spare and accessible only via a door off the children's room.

There was no outside light, and they had forgotten to

bring a torch. He groped his way around the back of the house by the light of the car's headlights and managed to fill a bucket with coal using remnants scraped from the bottom of a concrete bin. An ancient cast-iron solid fuel stove sat in one corner of the kitchen like a boulder, heavy, cold and lifeless. Peter eyed it suspiciously, peering into its cobwebbed recesses and fiddling with its vents and levers. Eventually, and after several failures, he was able to light a small fire inside it, but an hour later the ironwork was still barely warm to the touch. Emma used a small electric cooker next to the stove to heat up a macaroni cheese she had brought down from London.

The children were entranced, the frustrations of the drive down from London forgotten. They were eager to get to bed, bundled up in duvets on their bunks and talking excitedly of their plans to get up early in the morning to 'explore'. Peter and Emma settled them, then took a bottle of wine into the sitting room, pulling old and worn armchairs close to the fire which sputtered and spat feebly on the damp coal. Outside a strong wind was beginning to gust around the cottage.

'It's a bit Bob bloody Cratchet isn't it?' grinned Emma, turning the collar of her cardigan up.

'These places were not meant for habitation in the winter. It's a fact. Bumpkins migrate to the tropics in winter you know. Have you been up to the bedroom? I had to take the electric fire out and put it in with the kids. They'd freeze to death otherwise.'

'They're tough as nails those two, they love it.'

'Give it a couple of days.' He looked around the room and shivered. The damp, uneven walls, ancient floral paper faded and peeling. The single bulb hanging from the cracked and stained ceiling, the dusting of white mould on the brickwork surrounding the fireplace. 'I'll have to scout about for some proper firewood tomorrow, and some coal for that blasted stove.'

'You could take the children. Gather faggots in the woods like Wenceslas—' They sang, 'Gath'ring winter fu–el.'

He laughed. 'God, only four weeks to Christmas.' You could take the children. What did she mean? 'Why, are you off somewhere tomorrow?'

'Charlie's invited me over to see his company's premises. It's quite near here. I'll be back for lunch. Do you mind?'

His stomach lurched, he picked up his glass – a reflex action, drink while the smile withers. His mind raced: is this really why we are here? Three hours of insanity on the roads, a weekend huddled around a cold fire in a damp and draughty hovel miles from anywhere, then another three hours in the car back to London? He waded back, confused and panicky. The dinner party, perhaps they had arranged it all then. He'd seen them, mooning together down at the end of the table. No, impossible, it was arranged before then. At Dr Pryce's. She had suggested it hadn't she? For Jamie. Good therapy, get away together for the weekend, as a family. That was it. No! Not Dr Pryce, it was Emma. Emma had suggested it! She must have planned the entire thing in advance, the whole freezing bloody lost weekend, just to keep a tryst with that smug bastard Gallstone!

He drained his glass, hauled himself to his feet with a grunt. 'Well I think I'll go on up, busy day ahead on the steppes tomorrow.'

'Peter. Do you?'

'Hmm?'

'Do you mind? Me going off tomorrow morning?'

'Good God, no. Why on earth should I mind?'

During the night the wind blew up to a full gale. He lay awake listening as it rose like a sea. Soon it was roaring around the outside of the cottage, whistling through gaps in ill-fitting doors and warped window frames, hammering at the walls and vibrating the floor like a passing express train. When he was certain it could blow no stronger, it withdrew and regrouped before hurling itself forward again, shrieking with renewed fury.

Sally began crying. He turned on the bedside light and scurried across the cold landing to their room, fetched her back into their bed. She burrowed deep into the warmth between them and fell into a deep twitching sleep like a hibernating hamster, her icy feet brushing at his bare back. Outside somewhere, a shed door was banging. Sometimes it was lost in the howl and rumble of a gust. Then, just as he thought it had stopped, it would begin again, beating an irregular tattoo. 'Leave it,' Emma said drowsily. But he was unable. It banged on insistently. In any case sleep was impossible, like trying to sleep through an artillery barrage.

He got up again and pulled his trousers on over his pyjama bottoms, then carried his shoes and sweater down the creaking staircase to the hall. The shed was at the back of the garage, the other side of the car-park. He went through the kitchen and opened the back door, struggling to close it behind him as he stepped out into the uproar. Outside the noise was indescribable. It was as if the world was trying to tear itself apart. The sky was mostly clear, scattered grey cumulus clouds racing by in the half moonlight. He could see the darker outline of trees in violent motion against the skyline, tossing and thrashing like hysterical horses accompanied by occasional sickening, splintering reports, barely audible above the tumult as a branch tore free. The freezing wind hurtled across the fields like the storm thrashed waves of an invisible ocean, the gusts breaking over and around the house with a boom. It drove clean through Peter's thin clothing, leaving him gasping and shuddering. But its terrifying power thrilled him and he was seized by an urge to confront it head on, taste the full extent of its strength. He staggered past the car and out of the cover of the house into the lane, faltering sideways with a gasp as an undeflected gust struck him. Tottering forward, he turned to face it, leaning like a ski jumper. Slowly he spread his arms and legs, leaned further, flying in the darkness, the wind flogging his clothes and buffeting his body as though in free fall. He threw his head back and opened his mouth.

He remembered coming out of a bar once late at night, years ago as a teenager in the Air Force. A seaside town on the East Coast: Cromer, Yarmouth? There was a bad storm going on, he had stood there on the front, awed by the power, the terrifying force of the sea's anger. In seconds the flying spray had soaked him to the skin, but he had stayed, the wind snatching the drunken shouts from his lips, as twenty yards in front of him, the ocean, furious and frothing, hurled itself against the sea wall with a noise like thunder, the monstrous waves exploding high into the sky, hanging for a second like a torn curtain before dissolving in the wind.

Bending low against the icy gusts he fumbled his way back around the car and towards the darker shadow of the shed, finally banging the bolt of the door across with a half brick. He struggled back across to the kitchen door. As he neared it there was a clatter from above as a roof tile broke free. He felt it pass close by his head to smash on the bonnet of the car.

Back inside he poured himself a large Scotch and pulled a kitchen chair up next to the stove, huddling against the last of its meagre warmth. 'What the bloody hell are we doing here?' he muttered, through chattering teeth. The kitchen light flickered, went off, on again, then off for good. 'Terrific.' He held the bottle by its neck and tried pouring by feel, but he missed, spilling spirit onto his leg. 'Sod it.' Upending the bottle, he put it to his lips and drank deeply in the darkness.

During the morning, while Emma was away, he walked around the outside of the house taking stock of the gale damage. Apart from some missing roof tiles however, he was surprised to find little in evidence. But there was plenty wrong with the house. An idea lodged in his mind like a fallen sycamore seed. He found paper and a pencil and began moving from room to room peering into corners, studying walls and ceilings, scratching notes like an estate agent. By the time Emma arrived back at noon, he had two filled pages folded into the back pocket of his jeans.

She parked the Volkswagen adjacent to the house and breezed into the kitchen. Peter was sitting at the square scrubbed pine table warming his hands around a mug of coffee. Outside the children were playing red-cheeked in the overgrown back garden, the wind had dropped but it was still cold and blustery.

'Got the power back on I see. And the stove is hot, coffee brewed, outstanding work Deacon!' She leaned down and kissed him warmly on the lips. He watched her closely as she walked around the table, unwinding the scarf from her neck, slipping the coat from her shoulders, shaking her hands through her hair. What was he looking for? Evidence of infidelity?

'Eastern Electricity must presumably accept the credit for the first, the last two I managed by myself. How was Charlie?'

'Fine.' Fine? She completed her orbit of the table and arrived back beside him stepping across his legs and lowering herself onto his lap without warning. She slid her arms around his neck and kissed him hard on the lips, watching him, eyes wide. 'I'd like to do it, right now.' She squirmed lower down his legs and put a hand down on him, squeezing hard.

He slid a hand up inside the back of her sweater, stroked the wide smoothness under the bra strap. Why? he wondered dispassionately. She tugged at his zipper. 'I must make coffee more often,' he said, then: 'Hah!' as she slipped cold fingers inside.

She was kissing him again, flicking her tongue in his mouth, breathing hard, buttocks squirming against his legs. God she was hot. 'Let's do it Peto,' she gasped, 'Let's do it right now!' She pulled him free from his trousers, the back door crashed open.

'Look what I did find in the garden today anyway Daddy!'

They walked down the branch-strewn lane to the pub at lunchtime. The public bar was busy with long-haired young farm labourers who told them that kids weren't allowed in and to try the lounge. This too was crowded: old men playing dominoes; local landowners in tweed jackets; a young couple holding hands in the corner; and some passing trade, Londoners down for the weekend, out for a drive in the Mercedes.

They managed to find a table in one corner. Ducking beneath premature paper chains and sprigs of mistletoe, Peter went to the bar and ordered drinks and sandwiches, packets of crisps and nuts for the children. There was a middle-aged couple sitting at the bar chatting to the landlord. Dressed like escapees from the city, he wore brogues and what was once an expensive jacket, now patched with leather at the sleeves, she had on worn and faded tan cords but with a designer label. They turned and smiled, made room for him at the bar.

'You must be the Deacons, from Walnut Tree Cottage.'

Peter looked taken aback. Unperturbed she went on: 'Sorry, a village the size of Bedingham holds no secrets and anyway, my middle name is nosy.' She grinned and offered a hand. 'Alice nosy Greenaway. And this is my husband Jack shy-and-retiring Greenaway. We live up by the church. In the Old Rectory. Did you suffer much damage last night?'

'Lost a few roof tiles, one hit the car, some branches down in the garden. You?'

'Two silver birch, a dearly loved poplar and a chicken hutch.' She looked mournful for a moment but quickly recovered. 'What beautifully behaved children.' They looked over at the table. Emma sat with a child on either side – they were all quiet. Sally was watchful, her thumb in her mouth. Jamie was observing the dominoes game on the next table.

'It's their first time in a pub.' He thought about it, yes it was. 'Give them five minutes and they'll be all over the place.' He hesitated. 'You must come over, and meet them, and my wife.' Jack said they would love to but would allow them to eat their lunch in peace first.

'I've been thinking,' he said, after a long pull at a pint of bitter. He was perching on a low stool opposite Emma, resting an arm on a small round wooden table with wrought iron legs. The children ate crisps and drank bottles of coke through straws.

'Hmm, me too.'

'Yes I had noticed. What was all that about?'

'I don't know. I just suddenly felt like ... it. Is that so terrible?'

'Absolutely not.' The other business could wait. 'Perhaps the timing could have been better, but then that's kids. How does it go? "Spontaneity, dead at the heels of the first born."'

'Slain, I think. Anyway women can't just switch it on and off you know. It was driving through the countryside, coming back just now. The sky was clear and blue, you could see for miles; there was this wonderful smell, I had the roof open and it just felt marvellous. I felt marvellous.'

Nothing to do with a morning spent in the stimulating company of your old flame Gallstone then. Peter felt guilty but he couldn't help it. 'And how was Charlie?' She looked thoughtful, sipped her lager.

The old man sitting next to Jamie on the adjacent table turned and winked at the boy.

'You play dominoes young man?' Jamie shook his head, anxious but intrigued. ''Ere let me show you. First we have to mix 'em all up on the table like this.'

'I'd like to live here Peter.'

'Wha...?' A touch on his shoulder, he turned, startled, the Greenaways, Alice and Jack.

'We're off, just stopped to say hello.' He stood up awkwardly, introduced them to Emma.

'And you're Sally,' Alice bent and squeezed the coyly proffered hand. Sally giggled.

'Are you down for the weekend?' Emma enquired.

Jack answered. There was a softness in his voice, he spoke slowly, deliberately. 'No, we live here now. Almost four years.' He paused, saw the question forming in Emma's eyes. 'Alice is a writer.'

'And Jack is a painter,' said Alice. 'A damn good one.'

'You live here? How marvellous.' Emma was enthralled.

'We sold up our place in town when Alice landed her first publishing contract. I used to be on the Stock Exchange.'

'Director of a broking house actually ...' interrupted Alice. Peter groaned inwardly.

'Would you like to come to tea?' said Emma. He glanced at her, her face alight with excitement, eyes wide, expectant and hopeful.

'Um Em, we're not exactly equipped er—'

'Come to ours, please!' said Alice. 'Bring the children, they'll love it.'

During the afternoon they wrapped up in coats and scarfs and went for a walk. There was a stile in the lane opposite the cottage; they clambered over it and set off along the edge of a field. The last time they had walked there the field had been tall with ripe barley, the ground hard and crumbly underfoot. But now the field was bare, the soil dark and slippery. Peter had no wellington boots, his shoes became heavy and caked in mud.

They walked gently downhill, beside another field with a small wood to one side, the treetops bending and creaking in the breeze, some showing the vivid white wounds of freshly torn limbs, battle damage from the previous night's fury. Sally ran on ahead, her berry-red glossy plastic mac and hat standing out bright and gleaming in the failing light. A startled cock pheasant exploded out of the rough grass beside her and set off noisily across the field, Sally squealing in pursuit like a shiny red pig. She tripped and fell face down into the soil after a few yards, but picked herself up quickly, wiped the dirt from her nose and ran on. Jamie watched, arms folded, shook his head and plodded on.

At the bottom of the field they came to a stream with a narrow wooden footbridge. They crossed then stopped and turned to look back the way they had come. A neat patchwork of hedgrowed brown and green fields rose to the horizon. Away to their left the stream meandered along the bottom of an ancient riverbed, now a smooth, cultivated vale a mile wide, worked and worn by an aeon of weather and unbroken generations of farmers. It stretched away, wide and flat, save for a distant clutch of farmhouses, a church spire two parishes away and a solitary spreading oak in a field in the middle distance. It stood, colossal and alone, the tractor's ploughed furrows parting neatly around its broad base, its right of tenancy unquestioned after centuries on the skyline.

'Look there's our cottage.' Jamie pointed back at the tiny white rectangle standing out from the darker ground rising behind it. Peter hopped awkwardly, digging mud from his shoe with a stick.

'Come on, we'd better get back. It'll be getting dark soon.'

The Old Rectory was big and Georgian. They were greeted at the door by Alice who led them into a large sitting room with a huge fire blazing at one end. It was warm and welcoming. There were odd armchairs and over-stuffed sofas; no carpets but rugs everywhere, strewn on the oak floor apparently at random, some overlapping or with one corner curling up a wall. There were piles of newspapers and magazines on every available surface and an enormous glass-fronted bookcase spanning the length of one wall.

'This is Jasper,' said Alice, as an enormous shaggy-haired golden retriever hauled itself up from the rug nearest the fire and loped towards them, panting and wagging its tail. Jamie inched behind Emma. The dog stopped by Sally, easily dwarfing her. She looked unsure but stood her ground.

'They, er, we don't know much about dogs. We taught them not to trust strangers' dogs. Well you know, it's such a risk in London.' Emma looked at the animal uncertainly.

'Of course. Don't worry Sally, you can stroke him. His name is Jazzy.' The dog panted damply in the bemused child's face, blinking as she smacked at the top of his head with the flat of her hand.

'Do come and sit down by the fire. Jack will be in with the tea in a moment. Jamie I hear you're an artist too. Perhaps you'd like to see Jack's studio after tea.'

She prattled on pleasantly. Peter looked around the room,

the stacks of magazines, the profusion of house plants –
some of the larger ones stretching to the ceiling like
pantomime beanstalks. Behind him, at the far end of the
room, stood a grand piano, lid gaping, a stack of sheet music
on the floor under the stool. There was a modern hi-fi system
in the alcove on one side of the huge brick fireplace, also a
portable television and shelves of videocassettes. On the
other side a six-foot pile of neatly stacked logs for the fire.
The walls were covered in posters, framed photographs and
pictures of all sorts. Some were old and valuable – oil
landscapes mostly, others modern, probably Jack's. Watercolours of town scenes, a market place, a street café. France
perhaps, or Italy.

'Aviation? How interesting. Are you a flier Peter?' She sat
attentively on the edge of her armchair, smoking a cigarette.
She was in her mid-forties, the once dark hair now
completely grey, she was still an attractive, striking woman,
lean and erect.

'Not since leaving the Royal Air Force. I'm in marketing
management, defence related equipment to overseas customers mostly.' He trotted it out, she nodded, but she hadn't
taken it in, they never did. Jack came in, pushing a rattling
trolley, heavily laden with tea things. Space was cleared on
the crowded cane coffee table. The children knelt on the floor
next to it, watching closely as plates were circulated and
filled.

'Peter used to be in the Air Force, Jack,' said Alice. 'He's
a marketing manager now, exports aviation related defence
equipment.' She shot Peter a glance. Okay, so she was
listening.

'Really? Where were you stationed in the RAF?' The soft
voice, smiling eyes.

'Coltishall, in Norfolk.'

'I know it. Near Norwich. Who do you work for now?'

103

'I'm, er, just changing jobs at the moment. Considering an offer from a Heathrow-based technical support organisation.' He drank, swallowed an improperly chewed scone.

'Peter was made redundant when his last company went into receivership.' Thank you Emma. 'United Aerospace Systems, you might have read about it?' Alice shook her head, if she had she would have remembered.

'Name rings a bell,' said Jack. 'Unlisted Securities Market probably. How long ago?'

'August,' Peter said quietly. Alice studied him from the rim of her teacup. There was a moment's silence, broken only by the crack of pine logs on the fire and the clink of china.

'Jamie!' Alice looked down at him in mock horror. 'You've hardly eaten a thing. One more crumpet, and a piece of fruit cake or else Jack won't show you his studio.' Jamie grinned shyly. Jack looked confused, pulled a face and shrugged. They laughed. Sally laughed too, everyone else had.

After tea they walked around the house, Peter side by side with Jack, Alice and Emma falling some way behind. The children ran ahead, bursting from room to room. Peter tried to stop them, they were getting over excited. Jack said it was fine: 'Delightful to hear children about the place again.' Peter was tense, he wanted to go. Tea had been embarrassing, humiliating, he couldn't understand why Emma felt compelled to blurt out their woes to everyone. And that Alice made him uneasy, the way she watched him like a hawk, a shrewd lady, no doubt about it. He longed for a drink, wondered if they might be offered one, it was gone six. But he'd seen no sign of bottles or glasses so far on their tour. He struggled to make conversation.

'You were on the Stock Exchange?' he asked.

'That's right. Got out just in the nick.'

Peter thought back. 'The eighty-seven crash?'

Jack laughed. 'No my crash. About twelve months earlier.'

Alice switched off the studio lights and pulled the door closed. 'Have you told him yet, talked it over?' They walked slowly along the corridor after the men.

Emma sighed. 'Not yet. It really only happened this morning, although it's been on the cards for a few weeks.' It was extraordinary, she hardly knew the woman, yet she felt so comfortable with her, able to discuss anything – even her most intimate thoughts. God was it really only today she'd first met her? 'And Peter, well he's under a great deal of pressure at the moment and has been a bit, unpredictable.'

'I can imagine, poor boy. How is he sleeping?'

'Hardly at all.'

'Does he drink?' She touched Emma's arm suddenly. 'I'm so sorry, I have absolutely no right to pry like this. Please forgive me.' They fell quiet, she looked thoughtfully at the retreating back of her husband, then spoke very softly, 'It's just that, well, let's just say I do know a little bit about these things.'

Emma smiled. 'It's all right, it's a relief to talk about it quite frankly. Yes he does drink a fair amount, in the evenings I suppose. We both do sometimes. I never thought of it as a problem.'

'Hmm. And er, aggressive sometimes, forgetful, just plain odd from time to time?'

'Yes. Yes all those. I know he's been worried sick about the job lately, he's obsessed with getting another. And there are, obviously financial, and other pressures.' They walked on in silence, turned a corner onto a landing, arriving back at the top of the stairs. Down in the hall, Peter was buttoning the children into their coats. 'It looks like we're off. Thank you Alice, it's been wonderful.'

Alice squeezed her hand. 'Keep an eye on him Emma, don't let him bottle it up.'

After the cheerful centrally heated warmth of the Old Rectory, the cottage was cold and miserable. The children turned fractious, complained of the cold and demanded to know why there was no television. Nor did they accept Peter's explanation that it hadn't been invented in their village yet: 'Typical,' said Sally, throwing down a doll. 'Yes it has, there was one at Jack and Alice's,' said Jamie. Emma went to use the bathroom and reappeared shivering. 'I think they can skip baths tonight, it's a little chilly in there.'

Later, she came down the stairs and joined Peter at the kitchen table. He poured her a whiskey, freshening his own. There was a bottle of Beaujolais open on the back of the stove, he'd thrown on more coal and fiddled with the vents in an effort to coax it to life.

'Last of the winter fu–el in the bucket,' he said. 'Better save it for tomorrow.'

She nodded. 'We'll stay in here tonight.'

'Good idea. Anyway there's something alive and rather unpleasant growing up the wall in there – behind the sofa.'

'How do you know?'

'I did a bit of an inventory this morning.' He produced the notes from his back pocket.

'Ah, this must be the thinking you were going to tell me about.'

He sensed her suspicion, plunged on. 'I just thought, while I was checking the roof damage, I started to jot down a few notes, you know what needs doing, to fix the place up.'

She sipped her Scotch. 'Go on.'

'Well quite frankly Em, it's horrific. Apart from the roof tiles, there is a serious damp problem, upstairs and down.

And rot. The window-frames are all completely shot, some don't open and are just held together with paint. None of the walls are sound, the plaster just comes off in your hand, same with the ceilings. The guttering needs replacing, the wiring is prehistoric, and dangerous – you've seen the socket in the bathroom ...' She watched him; he was becoming agitated, his pieces of paper fluttering in his hands, his voice rising. 'The outhouses are falling down and there's a crack running up the eastern end wall.' He turned the pages, checking he hadn't forgotten anything; reached for his glass and waited for her to speak.

'Peter, we knew all this when we bought the place. That's *why* we bought the place, and at such a good price. The surveyor's report listed all that' – she gestured at his notes – 'and more. But the basic structure is sound, he was quite specific about it, and the rest can be tackled in our own time.'

He thought about it. 'Yes I know, but my point is, it's not really habitable in its present state.'

'It's not that bad, a bit basic perhaps.' She looked around the kitchen.

'Emma! Come on.'

'Peter, we're not selling it.' Her voice was icy cold, each word delivered separately, in a monotone like slow dictation. 'In fact quite possibly the reverse.'

'I haven't asked you to sell it have I?' he bellowed, jumping to his feet. The chair skittered backwards, clattered to the floor behind him. He glared down at her, saw alarm in her eyes. Suddenly he was overcome by dizziness, her face dissolved into a blur, his field of vision contracted, shrinking into the distance, as though looking down a tunnel. He dropped his hands straight-armed to the table and leaned heavily, forcing his chin down onto his chest and screwing his eyes shut.

'Peter?' He shook his head and held his breath, building the pressure to his head from his lungs, fighting the faint. There was pounding in his ears. An instant of memory came to him, glimpsed like the flash of a photograph. Sitting in the back seat of an F4 Phantom pulling nine G during close-in evasive manoeuvre practice. The G-suit gripping his legs like a vice to hold the blood in his upper body, he screaming like a wild animal as trained, fighting to stay conscious as his vision turned grey and oblivion beckoned.

The pounding began to recede, his sight to clear. He sat down again, took a deep breath, two. Steady, steady now. In through the nose out through the mouth. He poured a refill, the bottle clunking against the glass. He drank it in one, poured another.

'Peter.'

He held his hand up. 'It's okay. Just stood up too quickly that's all. I'm fine now.' He smiled. 'Really.'

They drank the Beaujolais with a chilli Emma had brought down from London. It wasn't properly heated through in the middle but they were tired and hungry. Emma put hot-water bottles in the bed, the electric heater was in with the children. They undressed quickly, left their socks on. Emma was wearing a full length heavy cotton long-sleeved night-gown with buttons right up to the chin. Her 'passion-killer' she called it. It worked. She snuggled up behind him in the darkness, her feet resting against a hot-water bottle. She ought to say it. She was tired but she ought to say it.

'Peto?'

'Emma, I wasn't going to suggest that we sell, that *you* sell the cottage.' His voice was deep, the words slightly slurred. 'I was just going to suggest that you at least consider taking out a small mortgage on it.'

'What for?'

'Firstly to allow us to spend some money fixing the place up. Just the essentials. And secondly—' He paused, fatally. She'd worked it out.

'To give some money to the bank.'

'That's right.' He waited. She didn't move, he could feel her breath on his neck. 'Will you? Consider it?'

'On condition that you consider this.'

God! Anything! She's gone for it. His heart was banging in his chest, he tried to keep his voice calm. 'Go on.'

'Charlie Gladstone has offered me a job, down here. A senior, full-time position on his design staff. I want you to consider moving here, to the cottage.'

His mind reeled. What? What for? What about Fulham? How would he get to work? The girl's lost her mind. I'll be starting at Heathrow shortly. The kids back in school. It was utterly absurd, she must be besotted. Charlie Bloody Gladstone.

'Well?'

'Yes. Okay, I'll consider it.'

CHAPTER

6

Identifiable by a corporate frank, the letter from Fielding Aero arrived on the Monday morning. He picked it up from the hall floor, turning it over and over in his hand before stuffing it in his back pocket, waiting until he returned to the house after dropping off Jamie. Emma was at the agency; he had Sally all day. He shoved her in the playroom in front of a Walt Disney video and doubled up the stairs to the spare room, closing the door behind him.

It was from Kavanagh and was infuriatingly short. It simply thanked him for attending interview, said that unfortunately and after careful consideration his application had been unsuccessful. It finished up by saying: 'I feel sure you will be successful elsewhere.'

He was dumbfounded. Why? There was no logical explanation. Fielding had liked him, they had got on well together, he had given intelligent, articulate answers to all the questions. What the hell had turned him off? Kavanagh. He picked up the phone.

'Human Resources.' He was put straight through. The soft Irish, no mistaking it.

'Mrs Kavanagh?'

'Speaking.'

'Deacon. I came for interview last week.'

'Oh yes, Mr Deacon, what can I do for you?'

'I received your letter. I was wondering if you might be able to explain it. More fully.'

There was a slight pause on the line. 'There's not much to explain really, we interviewed several candidates, they were all of the highest calibre. We selected the one that we believe best meets our requirements.'

We? 'I see. What, if I may ask, was it that decided you against me?'

'Nobody was against you Mr Deacon, we merely selected the applicant who in our opinion was most suited to the position. It's unfortunate that there have to be unsuccessful candidates but that's the way it works. It is our right to choose freely, you must allow us that.'

'Yes but there must have been something, or things that prevented me from being that successful applicant.'

'Just a moment.' She sounded impatient. 'Right I have the notes here. Oh yes, well since you ask, we both felt that you were eminently qualified but were too aggressive. Now if you don't mind I have a great deal to get on with.'

Aggressive? What on earth was she talking about? 'Mrs Kavanagh—' He spoke quietly into the phone, his lips touching the mouthpiece, struggling to remain calm, still the tremor in his voice. 'I really need this job. Yes it is possible that I came over a little forcefully at interview, but it was just my eagerness. You see I know I can do the job well, you'd never regret it. Mrs Kavanagh, I am asking you to reconsider my application. Please.'

It was becoming distasteful, she wanted to end this. Her tone became brisk. 'Mr Deacon, you have been formally notified that your application was unsuccessful, we have your details on file, now should anything suitable come up—'

111

'You smug Irish bitch!' He banged the phone down, dropped his head into his hands, grinding the heels of his palms into his eye sockets. It was unthinkable. The job was his, Fielding as good as said so. Kavanagh must have talked him out of it. Call him, talk to Fielding, he'll see sense. But it was no use. He began going through the files. It had to be this week. Now. There were about thirty companies sitting on his application. None of them had vacancies the last time he spoke to them. He began dialling.

By mid morning he had spoken to two thirds. Many were unable to remember his application but were able to confirm, after some delay, that they still had his details and would contact him as soon as something came up. At about eleven the doorbell rang. He stood by the window, out of sight to one side, watching through the gap between wall and curtains like a nosy neighbour. But unless they stood back from the doorway it was impossible to see who it was. He waited, they generally did, two paces back, looking up at the windows as if considering a ladder. But after two minutes there was still no sign and no second ring on the doorbell. The spare room door handle rattled, he jumped. Sally walked in, her face and hands brown and sticky, a chocolate biscuit in both hands.

'Sally what are you doing? You're supposed to be watching television.'

'I don't want to, his mummy did die, Bambi's did.' She looked around the room then, as an afterthought added: 'And there's people in the hall anyway Daddy.' She'd let somebody in. He dashed for the stairs.

There were two of them, a teenager with close cropped ginger hair and an earring, and an older man wearing an anorak and holding a clipboard.

'Mr, er, P.J. Deacon?' the older man enquired politely. The other stood back looking around the hall.

'Yes.'

He flipped sheets on the clipboard. 'Ah yes, black Golf GTI. Could you possibly just sign here, and here, we won't keep you a moment. Do you have any effects you want to take out of the car?'

'What is this all about?'

'The car, Mr Deacon, a Volkswagen?'

'I know my car is a Volkswagen.' His voice was icy. He remembered, last week sometime, a registered letter.

'We're here to return it, to the owner. You received the order last week.'

'I'm the owner!' Too loud. The ginger haired youth began paying attention, stood at the older man's shoulder, looking from one to the other, arms folded.

'Well that's not strictly true now, is it Mr Dorking? That vehicle is the property of the leasing company. You signed a lease agreement with them.' He recited his lines patiently, Ginger nodding where appropriate. Peter stared at the ceiling and sighed. 'You have broken that agreement, therefore the leasing company is entitled, by law' – he emphasised the word, Ginger nodding sagely – 'to take action to recover the property. It was all explained in the order.'

'Get out of my house.'

'Of course. I must advise you however that we will be removing the vehicle.'

He watched from the playroom window, Sally at his side. They went across to the car and found a key to fit the door from a bunch taken from their van. Next the older man made a complete inspection of the vehicle inside and out, marking notes on the clipboard, reaching out to finger the dented bonnet, crouching to examine a scuffed wheel hub. At the same time the youth produced a black dustbin liner and went right through the interior, removing everything

113

not originally delivered with the car. They could hear him calling out each item like a prison warder listing a condemned man's personal effects.

'One ballpoint pen, black, one woollen glove, child's, one London *A to* Z street atlas, with loose pages in the middle.' The older man wrote it all down. After twenty minutes they returned and rang the doorbell.

'Sally get it,' his daughter said.

He lunged, caught her by the shoulder, hoisted her to his chest. 'You must never, ever open the front door to strangers,' he hissed, a droplet of spittle hitting her cheek. The letters flap snapped open, the voice floating into the hall.

'We're leaving now Mr Dorking ... Do you want us to leave your effects on the step? Mr Dorking?' An envelope dropped to the floor, the flap snapped shut. Ginger got back in the van, the other got in the Golf. He started it up, made a note of the contents of the tank and the mileage on his sheet, manoeuvred it carefully out of the parking space and drove off, the van following.

'That man's got mummy's car.'

He went to the kitchen but they were out of whiskey. There was vodka, and tonic. He called Emma at the agency.

'You'll have to meet Jamie from school. Take a cab home from there. The car's gone.'

'What?'

'Gone, repossessed.'

'For God's sake.' The line went quiet, crackling with unspoken recriminations. 'It wasn't that much, we could have borrowed it. Mummy would have lent us enough for the bloody car.'

'It's a bit late for that now isn't it?'

'What on earth are we going to do? Without a car ...' The implications sprouted like weeds.

114

The rest of the day passed in a blur. At some point he emptied a tin of baked beans onto a plate and put it on the table in front of Sally. She ate some then tipped the rest onto her lap. The vodka was terrific, he never normally drank the stuff. It was a clean, hard hit, quite different from the smooth soothing balm of Scotch. He ran out of tonic but it didn't matter.

Emma arrived back with Jamie a little after four. There was a dustbin liner on the step, full of stuff from the car. She carried it in. She looked in on the playroom, it was empty, toys everywhere, the contents of the biscuit tin all over the floor, a spilled can of coke. She sniffed. There was something. Burning? She went back into the hall. 'Peter?' It was coming from the kitchen. Jamie called. 'Mum come quickly!' She ran.

'Sally was baking cake for tea anyway Mummy!' She was standing on a chair in front of the cooker holding a wooden spoon. Her face was a mask of tomato sauce and chocolate, the front of her dress plastered with, God knew what. The front ring of the stove was on, there was a saucepan on it, the underside glowing angrily. A steady plume of brown smoke rose from the saucepan to the ceiling where it spread out across the kitchen like an inverted mist layer. The smell was awful, acrid.

She moved down into the kitchen, swiftly, with her arms out so as not to startle her. 'Really darling? That's nice.' She reached her in a second, swung her up and back, away from the cooker, snapping the ring off with the other hand. 'Could you go into the playroom with Jamie for a minute sweet-heart? I'll be through in just a moment.' She was astonished how calm she was.

'But my cake mummy.'

Emma coughed and glanced into the saucepan, bits of blackened bread and something else. Sugar? She knelt.

'Darling we have said that you are not allowed to touch the cooker. It could hurt you very badly.'

The child sensed the mother's fright, the close proximity of crisis, and the tears rolled. 'But that's why I did, 'cos Daddy is asleep.'

He was on the spare room bed. She tried to rouse him but he was out of it, incoherent and burbling. She went back downstairs and cleared up the kitchen.

Much later he woke. The room was dark. His head was splitting, mind numb, he sat up, feeling nauseous and dizzy, staggered into the bathroom to urinate, dry retched into the sink. He focused groggily on the old Timex he was using in place of the Rolex. Shit, nearly ten! He splashed water onto his face, running wet hands through his hair, bent his mouth to the tap. He looked dreadful, bleary and puffy, red-eyed in the mirror. He struggled to remember. Kavanagh. He groaned. And the car. Watching the car go while Bambi played on the video, Sally in his arms. Sally! Baked beans for lunch, then what? God knows. He trudged through to the bedroom. She wasn't there, the place was in a mess, bed unmade, piles of washing, open suitcases from the weekend.

She was in the sitting room, working on something. She glanced up as he came in, then went on with her notes.

'Emma—' His voice was a croak.

'I don't want to hear it. There's some shepherd's pie in the oven; you should eat something.' Her tone was matter of fact, she didn't look up.

He wasn't hungry but he went to the kitchen and spooned some of the food onto a plate. The place had been tidied, a bit, but there was a peculiar smell. He poured a glass of water in the sink, drank it down, poured another. A saucepan stood on the draining board, full of water, a black lumpy crust on the bottom. He went back to the sitting room, squatted on the floor, picked cross-legged at the plate.

'You'd better tell me what happened,' she told him. There was no need to dramatise; it was a miracle Sally hadn't been hurt, the nick of time, he knew it. He felt sick again and put the plate aside, burying his face in his hands. 'Would it help if I said I was sorry and it will never happen again?'

'It might if only I could believe you meant it.'

'I mean it Emma, you have to believe me,' he pleaded. 'It was the car going, something just snapped. And—' He trailed off, looking away.

'And what?'

'The job. At Heathrow, I didn't get it.'

There was silence, then she jotted some final notes on her pad, dropped the books by the chair with a thud and stood up.

'I'm going down to Surrey tomorrow to visit my mother. On the train. I'm taking Sally with me, we'll drop Jamie at school on the way to Waterloo. You can pick him up. We'll be back about seven. Got it?' He nodded miserably from the floor. 'This can't go on Peter.' She walked out of the room, a moment later he heard her thumping upstairs. He sat for a while, then hauled himself to his feet, walked to the hall, took a raincoat off the hook and went out into the street.

Emma came down in her dressing gown at seven. He hadn't been to bed, at least not in their room. They were in the kitchen, all three of them, sitting at the table having breakfast. Boiled eggs and toast. He'd cleaned the place too. The floor had been washed, all the dirty crockery washed and put away. The work surfaces wiped down, the cooker spotless. The washing machine was on, churning away in the corner.

'Coffee.' He poured for her. He looked tired, pale but presentable. He was dressed, changed from last night; clean jeans and a white tennis shirt. And shoes. 'The saucepan's had it I'm afraid, tried Brillo but I couldn't shift it. Sorry.' She shrugged.

'We're going to Granny Fairbright's on the train today Mummy!'

Jamie was frowning. 'Why can't I go?' Peter cut more toast into strips and slid them onto Jamie's plate. 'Because you have to go to school today, sweetheart. But I'm going to be there to collect you, and if you like we'll come home on the underground. Then I want to sit down with you and write your list to send to Father Christmas okay?' Jamie considered the offer. It was a reasonable trade-off. 'Okay.'

'I want to go on the underground and see Father Christmas.'

Peter plucked Sally from the high chair. 'Come on you, we've got to get you dressed ready for Granny.' They disappeared upstairs.

After they'd gone he went right through the house. He began in the bedrooms, throwing piles of laundry onto the landing, changing the sheets, dusting and hoovering. Then he did the bathrooms, making sure there was fresh soap in the handbasins, scrubbing the bath, cleaning and disinfecting the lavatories, polishing the mirrors and tiles. He finished off with the vacuum cleaner again, reversing his way across the landing and step by step down the stairs.

Emptying another load into the washing machine he was stunned to discover it was noon. He sprinted upstairs again and into the spare room, began gathering and tidying his heaps of paper. He had to pause momentarily, drop onto the edge of the bed as a wave of dizziness swept over him. He forced his head down between his knees until it passed. Made a mental note to take more exercise. He made the bed and opened the window, swapping the rather foetid sweat and dirty sock smell of the room for the equally toxic but less offensive west London winter.

By two he was at the Unemployment Office, joining the shortest queue for regular signees, then hopping to the next, slightly longer one once he had checked out its composition. He knew how to spot the bad ones, recent signers usually, black, female, children fretting at their skirts; bearing sheaves of incorrectly filled forms and bemused I-don't-understand-any-of-this expressions. It wasn't racist, or sex-ist, he told himself, just a fact of life. Those sorts took hours, he'd learned that the hard way. Stubbornly standing two from the front of a queue that hadn't moved in twenty-five minutes while in the next line they went gliding smoothly by him as if on a conveyor.

He was out again in ten minutes, a record. Next back down the North End Road and into Tescos. He drove swiftly along the aisles, flicking packets and tins into the trolley as he rolled by, list clamped between his teeth ready if he needed it. Without bothering to stop and queue, he plucked a ticket from the dispenser at the delicatessen, rolled on to the bread counter, and picked up two wholemeal browns, the last Danish and a pack of pitta bread which he bullied the assistant into marking down as it was past its best-by date. Next he went on to the fish counter, then spun the heavily laden trolley back to the deli as his ticket number was coming up. At checkout he cruised down the long line of desks and parked his trolley at the back of one. It was a longer queue but there were more baskets than trolleys – fewer goods and cash payers probably. And the cashier was good – middle-aged Pakistani woman, had the bar code reader down pat, if it didn't work first pass, she didn't bother with it again just entered it manually, fingers dancing across the keypad.

He left the trolley and darted over to the drinks. He hesitated, gnawed his lip, choosing guiltily. He checked his watch, there was no time for this. He stuffed a bottle of Bells

119

under one arm crushing squash, beer and wine against his midriff before hobbling awkwardly back to check out. He paid by cheque, his face expressionless as he tore out the sheet, then he wheeled the cardboard boxes into the street. It took nearly ten minutes to get a cab, he had the driver stop at the house to dump the shopping then straight on to school. He arrived with five minutes to spare and waited on the cold pavement, stamping his feet and blowing into cupped hands amid a loose knot of murmuring mothers.

He was in the kitchen, going through one of Jamie's Roger Red-Hat reading books when he heard the front door. A moment later Sally came running in.

'Daddydaddydaddydaddy!' She clung to him, her face pink and cold on his neck. Emma followed.

'Hi, how's your mum?'

She looked tired; he helped her off with her coat, poured her a gin and tonic. She blew her nose, drank.

'What about you?'

'Later perhaps. I'll get the kids down.'

He made dinner for her, grilled pork chops with honey and mustard, sprouts, baked potato. Supermarket plonk.

'Thanks for doing the house. It looks marvellous.'

'No problem. How was your mother, you haven't said?' Nor have you said *what* you said.

'She's fine, keeping busy, sends her love.'

'Good, good. Did you, ah—'

'What?'

Come on don't be obtuse. 'Say anything. Fill her in on, things.'

'No. I was going to, but then I thought about it on the train down and it seemed so pointless. She's on her own. I don't want to worry her, you know what she's like.'

She's a widow with spare cash, that's what she's like!

Living quite comfortably off her husband's pension thank you and enough in the bank to see her through and no worries. How on earth could you go all that way and come back empty handed? Incredible! So, no help forthcoming from the in-law. Well done Emma.

'Quite. I think I'll have that drink now, I'm going to need it. Join me?'

'Why?'

'Because I prefer not drinking alone?'

'Why are you going to need it Peter?'

He got up and went over to the sideboard, cracked open the Bells and poured. 'I rang my father this afternoon, had a chat. I'm going up to see him tomorrow.' He took a swallow, it felt good, straight away. He was dead tired, he'd take a stiff one up to bed with him, try and get a decent night's sleep. Please God. 'It must be visit a parent week.'

'Crikey.' Emma was astounded. 'What are you going to see him about?'

He waved his glass. 'He knows a few old farts at the Ministry, might be able to swing something.'

'But you'd hate working at the M.o.D. You've always said so.'

I know that. 'It might not be such a bad move, until something better comes along. Anyway, beggars, remember ...' They sat at the table in silence. But something was bothering her. She licked her lips. Not the Charlie thing, please. Not now.

'Peter. How are we going to manage without a car?'

Give me a break for God's sake woman! He felt anger rising in his throat like bile, his face reddening, his fists bunch. His whole body trembled, he longed to cry out, to discharge his frustration like lightning, spewing fire from his fingertips just for the satisfaction of incinerating something, anything, with the heat of his fury. But he mustn't. Deep within him a warning bell sounded, its persistent clamour drilling through the molten rock of his ire. He mustn't, not after yesterday, he was on probation. Swallowing, gasping, he beat back the flames, dousing and smothering until there was nothing save dull, glowing embers amid the ashes.

Blinking with the effort, he levelled his voice, clipping the words off singly through gritted teeth. 'Emma. I am doing my best.'

During the night he dreamed. He was walking the streets of London. It was night but summer, it was warm and the city smelled differently. He was just wearing running shorts and a T-shirt. He was happy and comfortable. People smiled and nodded as he passed them, one or two said hello. He didn't know what his circumstances were but somehow he knew that he was content, unworried.

After a while, in a part of London he was only vaguely familiar with he walked into a pub. It was crowded with people wearing coats and scarfs, woolly hats. There were Christmas decorations. It was the White Horse at Bedingham. He wanted a drink, began to struggle towards the bar.

'Hello you!' It was Emma standing talking to Charlie Gladstone. They both laughed at him, he couldn't get to the bar and was having to duck round the back of people. There was Jamie. Sitting at a table with an old man playing dominoes. He was much older, late teens, relaxed and slender.

'Can you help me please?' he asked Jamie. 'I can't get to the bar.' Jamie smiled, clicking a domino onto the line. 'Grandpa's up there.' He kept going, he wanted to get out but he wanted to reach the bar more. He saw the Greenaways, they saw him and laughed. Then he caught sight of his father. He was sitting on a bar stool talking earnestly to a younger man whose back was to him. His father caught his eye and nudged the other man, they both turned to look at him. The younger man had long hair and a beard, he wore spectacles, but he looked familiar, he beckoned for him to join them at the bar. He tried, began struggling again, fighting to elbow his way past the crowd. He became desperate, felt fear and panic, he lost sight of them. The noise of the crowd was getting louder. There was shouting, and there was a voice, a little girl's voice rising above the crowd. It was Sally. She was screaming for him but he couldn't see her, couldn't get to her, couldn't move.

'Daddy! Daddy please help me, I'm burning. I'm burning Daddy help me. Daddy!'

'Peter. Peter! For God's sake, Peter!' He sat up, gasping and swallowing, the roar of the crowd fading in his head like a receding echo. He was soaked, drenched with sweat, and shaking. Emma had the bedside light on, was gripping his shoulder. 'Are you all right? You've been thrashing around like a madman.'

He swallowed again, his mouth dry, licked his lips. He could taste blood; he'd bitten his tongue. 'Yes,' he panted. 'Yes I'm all right. Just a bad dream. Sorry.'

'It's okay. You scared me that's all. Are you sure you're all right now?'

He threw back the covers on his side and swung his feet to the floor. They were still shaking and weak, as if they might not bear his weight. The bedside clock said it was two twenty. 'Yes, really. I'll just go downstairs for a bit. Have a cup of tea. Want some?'

She pulled the covers up around her shoulders and rolled over. 'No thanks. Do you want me to leave the light on?' She yawned.

'No. Go back to sleep.' She murmured a reply, he went downstairs and sat at the kitchen table drinking whiskey.

*

His parents lived in a village outside Bedford. In the car he could have driven door to door in an hour and a quarter, but by public transport it took double that. He caught a tube round to King's Cross changing onto the Circle Line at High Street Kensington. The first Circle Line train was packed with the last of the morning's rush hour commuters. As the doors slid open he was confronted by a mass of bodies in overcoats and scarves, eyeing him discouragingly. He could have got on, with a bit of a squeeze, but he hesitated, unwilling to join the throng. He could still hear it, the little voice, desperate and pleading: 'Daddy, help me!' He stood rooted to the platform, dry mouthed and panicky, then the doors slid shut again and the train rumbled off without him.

From King's Cross he took a main line train to Bedford then had to hire a cab for the twenty-five minute drive to his parents' house. As the taxi crunched through the pea shingle and pulled up outside the stone portico, he felt a familiar mixture of anticipation and foreboding. The faded oak front door opened before he could knock. They were both there to greet him.

His mother looked the same, pleased, almost relieved to see him. They embraced, she clung to him a second too long. He shook hands with his father, he had aged since they had last seen each other five, six months ago. Or last night. For the first time in his own life it occurred to him that his father was drawing towards the end of his.

'Good to see you PJ,' he said, throwing a mock punch at Peter's chest. 'You growing your hair or something?' He ran his fingers through it self-consciously. It was longer, but hardly long, just not regulation length any more.

They made the usual pre-luncheon tour of the garden. It was something his parents always did, if they had guests or family staying then they tagged along too, strolling along the neat paths, beside ranks of meticulously edged beds.

Stopping to admire a budding winter rose or point out an area of heather in need of attention. He knew the drill well, a stroll, a sherry, then lunch, probably something his mother knew he liked, or had liked as a child. Fish pie, or steak and kidney. Always a pudding, fruit crumble or a sponge, custard. Small talk first. Saving the serious chat for the private audience later.

They ate in the dining room. Just the three of them lodged together up one end of the long D-end table like the last beans in the bottom of the coffee jar. The room surrounded him with memories of his childhood, shrinelike in its constancy. Every nuance of its decor as familiar to him as the small hairs on his wrist. The tick and chime of the brass carriage clock over the unlit stone fireplace. The walnut sideboard with the silver candlesticks and cut-glass ship's decanter on it. Framed photographs of them as a family, twenty and thirty years ago – of Peter and his brother, as children; on holiday, in the first fifteen at Wellington. A large silver framed portrait photograph of him in Flight Lieutenant's uniform, his eyes darkly proud, serene beneath the peaked hat.

'Any news from David?' Peter asked. His brother lived in California – Professor of Marine Biology at San Diego University. He had always been destined for a life of academia. Scholarship to Cambridge from Wellington, post-graduate doctorate, then the invitations began arriving from institutions abroad. Kiel, Seattle and now San Diego. There was never any question of the RAF for David, the idea was laughable.

'Your mother had a letter about three weeks ago. Said he wouldn't be home for Christmas. Some time in the early spring probably.'

'He's got a steady girlfriend,' said his mother. 'Said infuriatingly little about her. Has he mentioned her to you?'

'No, I haven't heard from him in a while.' But then he hasn't heard from me either.

It was spotted dick. It lay on his plate like speckled leather. He forced it down, smiling as his jaws wrestled with the unyielding lumps. His mother was crestfallen when he declined a second helping. 'Such a shame and I made it just for you.'

He helped clear the table, but his father was impatient. 'Got a wee drop of the Macallan left from last Christmas, if you'd care to join me in the study.' This was it.

Peter sat in a high-backed leather chair in front and slightly to one side of the big knee-hole desk, his father rested his elbows on the blotter, pointed forefingers brushing the short white bristles of his moustache. Why did he keep the thing? It was practically invisible. On his desk, anchored to the same patch of mahogany for as long as Peter could remember sat two treasured mementoes, the same two artifacts that had fascinated Peter as a boy, seducing his imagination and painlessly predetermining the constitution of his adolescence. One was a framed photograph of eight men, teenagers, his father among them. They were grouped in front of the wingroot of a scuffed and filthy Spitfire fighter, its pale underside muddy and streaked with cordite. They had just landed after a sweep and were laughing and joking self-consciously in front of the camera. Many were still wearing Mae Wests and flying boots, holding cigarettes along with helmets and goggles. Peter had studied every detail a thousand times. He was fascinated by its uncontrived immediacy, the clothes, the aeroplane and the young faces. Only two survived the war, his father and one other.

The other item was a silver model of a Spitfire in flight. It was mounted on a stand, canted over at an angle that caught perfectly the grace and agility and power of the aeroplane. Its gleaming and stylised profile was at odds with the oil stained and battleworn example in the photograph, yet somehow enhanced the picture of gladiatorial warfare, stout-hearted mother's sons clambering aboard their machines in shirt and tie, duelling at dawn, returning in time for breakfast. These images together with his father's damp-eyed reminiscences of squadron life, overwhelmed his callow and impressionable soul at an early age, sealing his smooth passage into the Service.

'Your mother's worried about you.'

'There's no need.' Peter swirled the measured single of malt in the bottom of the glass. Now that the moment had come he was having difficulty with the words.

'Then why have you come?'

'Hmm?' The question caught him off guard. Bounced by the old aviator again.

'Well Peter, we don't see you for months, too busy even to call and tell us what's going on, then suddenly you're here. What are we to think?'

The Macallan went down, a single golden swallow. There'd be no more. 'Well Dad, I am in a pickle.'

'Still out of work?' Peter nodded. The old man tutted and looked out of the window, drumming his fingers on the desk. Sympathy? Or contempt.

'Money problems too eh?'

'Yes Dad.' It was like an interview with the headmaster. Important to let him make the running, exert full control. He was still looking out of the window. Never make eye contact.

'I have made provisions you know. One day this will all come to you and David. The grandchildren. There's not much else. I don't believe in it. Everything we have is bound up in this house. And the contents.'

What was he talking about, doesn't believe in what? 'Dad.' But his father held up a hand. Peter fell silent, this was a prepared speech.

'You and I may have had our differences over the years, Peter. But I want you to know that I always had your best interests at heart and tried to bring you up according to what I believed was right.' He paused, took a drink, his hand was trembling. He flicked a glance at Peter then resumed his window vigil before carrying on, less hesitantly.

'I don't believe in bailing a man out. I raised you to stand on your own two feet, deal with your own problems—' Peter groaned inwardly. He shouldn't have come, he should have written, it would have been far less painful for both of them. Just a short note: 'Dear Dad, help me find a job and lend us ten grand.' This was dreadful. '. . . But then again blood is thicker than water and although you have reached an age when you should be able to take care of yourself, and your family, I owe it to your mother not to turn down a request for help. For the sake of the grandchildren.'

'Dad, I haven't asked for your help.'

'Don't insult me by pretending that's not why you're here.' Now there was eye contact all right. He glared at Peter, daring him to deny it, a tinge of pink suffusing the grey hollow of the cheeks.

'Just as I thought.' He pulled the centre drawer of the desk open and drew out a chequebook, scribbled and tore, folding the paper in half before handing it across. 'You're a great disappointment to me you know.'

Peter hesitated, holding the stare. There was a pounding building in his ears like distant artillery, his chest felt constricted, the hairs prickled on the back of his neck. 'Keep it. I can't accept it. Not on your terms.' He got up from the leather chair and left the room.

'Cup of tea darling?' His mother turned as he entered the kitchen, her face falling as she saw his eyes.

'I'd better call a taxi Mum. It's time I went.'

'Peter sit down.' She pulled up a chair next to him at the

128

table. 'What happened in there? What did you say?'

He sighed. 'Very little. I began to tell him about, the situation, he launched off into a sort of final settling of accounts speech, then it all went wrong and I walked out. Mum I shouldn't have come. I'm sorry.'

'Tell me then Peter?'

'What?'

'The situation. Tell me.' She waited, the grey eyes wide, expectant. Sally had those eyes.

'Well, in a nutshell, I don't have a job yet and we are in some financial difficulty as a result. Oh and we don't have a car any more either.'

'Take mine, the Morris. It's in the garage, I never use it.'

'Mum—'

'Peter, your father is sick—' She sighed, put a hand on his. '—Well actually he's dying. It's a lump, in his chest. He won't have the therapy any more, not after last time, and the doctors say it's inoperable.'

His mind reeled. That's why. That's why the speech. 'Mum I'm so sorry. How, how long do they think?'

'Six months, maybe longer. He's not in any great discomfort, not at the moment. It's a blessing. Peter, he does love you. I know you find that difficult to believe; he's never been any good at expressing his feelings, to anyone.' She paused, smiled, squeezed his hand. 'But in his heart I know he loves you and he desperately wants to find a way to say so before, you know. But you'll have to help him. Will you, please try?'

He leant forward and kissed her gently on the forehead. 'Yes Mum, I will try.'

'Good.' She sniffed, conjuring a tiny hanky from her sleeve. She blew neatly. 'There's something else you should know. There's no money. Oh we get by on his pension and some small savings, but there's no real capital or anything.

This house is all there is. It costs us everything just to keep it from falling down. I keep going on at your father to sell it and move into something more practical, but, well you know.'

The dark green Morris Traveller stood in the cold garage under a thick layer of dust and bird droppings. Split potato sacking was draped across the bonnet. 'To keep it warm in the winter,' his mother explained. Peter walked around the car, eyeing it doubtfully.

'It still runs you know. Dad puts the battery back once a year and starts it up, goes like clockwork.'

'When did you last take it out on the road?'

She blew a cloud of condensation, hugging the dufflecoat closer around her. 'I don't know. I took it to Auntie Esme's, that time I went and stayed with her in Wales.'

'Mum, that was donkey's years ago.'

'Well I can't remember, we always use the Rover.'

'Where do you keep the battery?'

'It's in that cupboard.' They both turned, Peter's father was silhouetted against the gaping doorway, squat and bulky in his big anorak and cap, a torch pointing down at his feet. There was an awkward stand-off, nobody moved, nobody quite sure what to do.

His mother was looking from one to the other. 'John?'

He came into the garage, his face a pale mask beneath the fluorescent glare of the strip light. 'You'll need to check the distilled water, the caps are off. Here, I'll give you a hand.'

Ten minutes later he peered around the raised bonnet at Peter sitting in the driver's door, a smudge of grease on his cheek like warpaint.

'Ready?'

Peter held his fist up through the window, thumb down. 'Switches off.'

There was a hint, a faint glimmer in the eyes, then he

ducked behind the bonnet again. A moment later came the shout: 'Mixture!'

'Set!'

'Throttle!'

'Set!'

'Switches!'

'On!' He turned the key, the ignition light glowed red. He turned again, the engine cranked over, two seconds, three, then it burst into life in an explosion of blue smoke and dust. His mother clapped her hands to her ears, bouncing with delight, his father's face reappeared, triumphant over the closing bonnet. They grinned at each other. 'Contact!'

The Morris sat idling on the gravel, he arrived back at the driver's door, stooping to the window, wiping his hands on a rag. 'Lights all check out okay, but the rear offside is a bit dodgy. And you'll have to get it taxed. Check the tyre pressures as soon as you can and go easy on the brakes for a bit, until they settle down.'

'Dad. Thanks.' He reached his hand up through the window. They shook. His father produced an envelope from his pocket. 'Take it Peter, please. For your mother's sake.'

'All right Dad. Thank you. And take care of yourself.' He let the clutch out, and set off down the drive.

At about eleven the very next morning it finally happened. Peter was working in the spare room, Emma had taken the children to the shops in the Morris. She had been delighted with the car, walking round it, bending to examine the scuffed paintwork on the wheels, patting and cooing over the bodywork as though it were an old carthorse. 'Perfect,' she said repeatedly, despite obvious signs of wear. 'It's absolutely perfect.'

Peter had begun the working day by sorting through his day file but his attention had been diverted by an article in

Flight magazine about space propulsion and he had quickly become engrossed. He had even begun pencilling notes on a scrap of paper. Then the telephone rang. He paid little attention as the machine answered it, listening idly to his own barely recognisable and disembodied voice, the message crisp and confident, waiting until the caller was identified.

'Mr Deacon, my name is Fournier, I am chief executive of PGT Strategic Systems Limited. I understand from an associate at Racal that you have experience in the marketing of high capital value defence products.' The voice was accented, French perhaps, but cultured and fluent. And quick, too quick. Deacon stared at the machine. Who? Fournier? PGT. Racal? He frowned. Who the hell was Fournier? The voice went on: 'I have to leave for Switzerland later this afternoon. If you do return to your desk before, say two-thirty and would like to discuss possible areas of mutual interest perhaps—'

Deacon snatched the phone up. 'Mr Fournier? Peter Deacon here, I'm so sorry I have only just this minute got in.'

They spoke for a few minutes then hung up. Peter sat and gazed at the phone. He couldn't believe it, he must have imagined the whole thing, it was all so unreal, and so fast. His mind whirled, it was a dream, had to be. In a moment he'd wake from a desk top reverie, properly this time, rub the bleariness from his eyes, shrug ruefully at the extraordinary clarity of the fading vision and square his shoulders once more to cold reality.

But the tape! It was all on the tape. He rewound the machine and played it back, then again. Halfway through the second playthrough he found himself on his feet. 'Yes.' He muttered to himself as he began pacing the floor. The tape finished, he rewound it once more, pressed play. 'Yes.'

Louder this time, he began beating his clenched fists against his thighs as he paced. 'Yes, yes, YES!'

They had arranged to meet at 3 p.m. at Terminal 2 at Heathrow. Peter showered, shaved and dressed in a frenzy, choosing a double breasted charcoal grey wool suit from the selection of uniforms in his wardrobe. One of the handmade shirts from Hong Kong, pale blue with PJD stitched discreetly on the breast pocket, black brogues and a silk tie bought at absurd cost from Daks when he had been in Manhattan last January.

There was a period of panic when he realised he had insufficient cash to get to Heathrow and back – even on the tube. Emma had the car and anyway the cost of airport parking was prohibitive. He withdrew a slim calfskin wallet from his jacket pocket and flicked through his worthless credit cards, studying the fan dubiously like a poor poker hand. They were all stopped, probably, but unless the ticket seller at the underground checked . . . Hardly likely for a few quid. He'd have to chance it. He slipped the wallet back into his pocket, picked up his attaché case and overcoat and made for the door. As he opened it, Emma looked up from the bottom of the steps, arms laden with supermarket shopping bags. Her expression was stony, lips tight. He hesitated, desperate to get going. Then he dumped his case on the hall table and ran down the steps to help with the bags.

'Sodding children, I'd like to kill them.'

He looked up and down the road. 'Fine. I'll help. Er, where are they?'

'Playing hopscotch in the heavy traffic I hope.' She nodded towards the end of the street. 'I couldn't get a space so had to park in Willstead Road. I locked them in the car.' She looked him up and down as she spoke. 'You look nice, been somewhere special? Be an angel and go and fetch the

133

little darlings will you, I'll put the kettle on.' She started slowly up the steps.

'Em, look, can't stop, got to dash. Seeing a man about a job.'

She paused, turned on the steps, confused. 'What job?'

'A man called out of the blue, a while ago. Boss of some strategic systems outfit or something. Got my name through someone at Racal, he's leaving the country today, wants to see me at the airport. I don't know any more than that. But it's hot Em, I really think this could be it.' He couldn't stifle the smile from his lips.

She stared down at him, jaw working, frowning slightly as though momentarily distracted from some other, pressing matter. Just a second then the eyes crinkled and the face beamed. 'Well that's outstanding Deacon. Go to it.'

He crossed the fingers of both hands and shook them up at her from the bottom of the steps. 'Wish me luck?'

She dumped the shopping, came back down the steps, slipped both arms around his waist beneath the jacket and kissed him tenderly. 'Go get 'em airman.'

He stood back and came to attention, saluted. 'Lend us the bus fare missus.'

She smiled and shook her head, conjuring twenty pounds from her purse. She always seemed to have a supply of cash. He folded the notes into his wallet and set off towards the underground.

They met at the Swissair desk as arranged. Fournier greeted him warmly then led Peter to the terminal lounge bar. The barman rolled his eyes as Fournier ordered Perrier and Peter, after a second's indecision, a diet Coke. The bar was about half full, they sat at a table in one corner.

'It was very good of you to come out here at such short notice,' said Fournier pleasantly, the accent almost unnoticeable. He was tall, mid-forties Peter estimated, with attentive brown eyes and olive skin. His hair was dark and thin, swept back flat from a high forehead. He wore an expensive lightweight suit beneath a camel overcoat. 'Firstly, tell me a little about yourself and then perhaps I can explain something of my company's business and the vacancy.'

Peter cleared his throat and sat more upright at the table. He still found it hard to believe this was happening. The sights and sounds of the airport engulfed him, dizzying him with memories of countless arrivals and departures through innumerable and identical airports across the world. It was intoxicating and exciting even after only a few months away. The surroundings were as familiar to him as his own home, he'd travelled from this terminal many times over the years, sat at this bar, this table probably. Yet although he recognised it all, there was a feeling of unreality. It was different, like walking around your old house many years after someone else has moved in. A whole new perspective. Familiar yet strange.

They spoke for an hour. Peter handed over a copy of his résumé, Fournier studied it closely as Peter talked him through it, occasionally interrupting with questions about his family, education, hobbies and interests. Eventually Peter paused, he was hot and starting to feel light-headed. Fournier sipped Perrier and began to speak.

'Pan Global Trading is a recently established Geneva-based corporation specialising in the procurement and supply of defence related equipment to clients – mostly government agencies world-wide. In many respects the work involved is very similar to that which you carried out at UAS except for two major differences.' He paused, watching.

Peter's mind raced. 'Ahh, procurement and er—'

'Product base. Precisely,' said Fournier rescuing him with

a smile. 'Unlike UAS we are not restricted to the sale of our own manufactured goods, we seek to buy off-the-shelf products best suited to perceived requirements and then market them.'

Peter nodded. Fournier went on to explain that with deregulation and the opening up of the world's markets, the timing was propitious for organisations such as his; 'Centrally placed, well structured and professionally staffed, to establish themselves at the forefront of this unpredictable but challenging and ultimately rewarding marketplace.'

Peter was mesmerised. The voice flowed on, relaxed and mellifluous. 'But the ultimate success of the business is dependent upon accurately defining that market, anticipating trends, keeping abreast of current technological developments and so on. We need the very best management staff, people who are capable of using their own initiative, industry experienced, keen to develop and exploit their full potential.'

He rang home from a phone booth at the terminal.

'Hi Dad.' It was Jamie, the voice subdued. He felt a pang. God it had been rough on him lately. He spotted an array of toys at a nearby news-stand. He'd buy him something, and Sally.

Emma came on. 'You'd better have some good news mister,' she quipped like a Brooklyn moll, 'or else you might as well get your tail on the first plane out.'

'Emma.'

'Peto?'

'It's over.'

They went out to dinner. A French restaurant off the Fulham Road. Peter stayed in his suit, Emma changed into a skirt and blouse while he collected the babysitter. Then they took a taxi. On the way she dug her elbow into his ribs mischievously. 'But we haven't got any money for a taxi,' she said in a loud voice, the driver looked up at them in the rear view mirror.

'It's all right dearest,' Peter replied, enunciating the words slowly like an amateur dramatist, 'I got paid today.' The driver's attention wandered on.

He asked for a table near the window. 'I like to see people going by.' They ordered gin and tonics while waiters took their coats and fussed around with chairs and napkins, menus and winelists.

'Getting employed is one thing,' she said after they were settled. 'Getting paid on the same day is quite another. How the hell did you manage that one?'

Eyes closed, Peter drank, then exhaled slowly. He still couldn't believe it. It had all been so fast, so incredibly overwhelmingly fast. 'He said he appreciated the time and trouble I had gone to to meet him at the airport and insisted on compensating me for the inconvenience.' He paused. 'To the tune of a ton of compensation that is. In readies.'

'Good Lord. Mercy dashes to airport meetings, envelopes full of cash, all very John Le Carré.' She grinned at him. 'Let's have it then Smiley, from the top. You went by tube . . .'

They ordered, snails and salmon for Emma, eventually Peter asked for pâté and veal. He wasn't really hungry. He was exhausted, yet the tension in his chest refused to dissipate and his head buzzed. It reminded him of NATO exercises, the squadron held on twenty-four hours readiness for days on end. Scrambling to intercept bogeys at all hours, or screaming through the darkness, three hundred and fifty knots at treetop level to simulate an attack on a column of tanks or a bridge. Perpetually tired yet hyped up to the eyeballs on adrenalin. It generally took a week to recover.

He told her, blow by blow, as much as he could remember. Towards the end of the meeting Fournier had questioned

Peter about his earnings at UAS and his current expectations. Peter had blustered but indicated he would be happy to accept a similar package. Fournier had nodded then held out his hand. 'I am pleased to offer you the position of UK Marketing Manager. That doesn't necessarily mean marketing in the UK I'm afraid,' he said with a wry smile. 'It merely means UK based. I anticipate you will be travelling abroad a fair amount. Is that acceptable domestically?' Peter nodded, punchdrunk. Fournier went on. 'We are still in the process of finalising arrangements for our London office, at the moment I am working out of a suite in the Hilton, it's not satisfactory but we hope to complete on some office space in Chiswick very shortly.'

Peter paused to sip Pouilly-Fuissé. Emma let him talk, watching him closely. 'He wound it up with some more about duties and responsibilities and said he would be in touch very shortly.' He grinned at her, it was finally beginning to sink in.

'Incredible. How do you feel?'

He looked out of the window. There were few pedestrians about, it was late, and cold. On the other side of the road a bag lady in an old overcoat made her way slowly by, bent nearly double, head completely enveloped in coils of long woollen scarf. He'd imagined this moment. Not so much lately, but earlier on he'd fantasised about it a great deal. Triumph was a word he'd savoured then. Quiet triumph. And vindication. Of worth.

But it wasn't like that. Now that the time had come it wasn't like that at all. He was just glad that it was over. He raised his glass and smiled at her. 'Okay.'

The mood of restraint persisted. They talked quietly of readjustment and the practicalities of their impending change in circumstance. Although the short-term pressures were off, their lives would not be as before. Their indebtedness to the bank would skyrocket at first – Bishop would have to arrange extra finance to pay off everything; mortgage arrears, hire purchase agreements, the car leasing company. Of course, he'd have his pound of flesh. There would be years of burdensome monthly repayments to the bank before they finally crawled into the clear. But at least there would be order again. Control. He was back in control. It was a blessed relief.

'Sweet trolley?' he asked. Emma declined, she looked pensive. He shook his head at the waiter. 'Coffee? Cigar?'

She smiled, but without humour. 'Do you mind if we go home Peto? I'm absolutely whacked.'

In the taxi she snuggled next to him, resting her head on his shoulder, but she remained quiet. He stroked her hair. She'd been right through it too, put up with everything. It may not have been so obvious at the time, only now could he begin to appreciate her astonishing strength, the acceptance of deprivation, the readiness to make sacrifices, to step in and help. He kissed the top of her head. 'All right?' He felt her nod. 'Good.'

CHAPTER

7

He awoke with a start at around two. One moment he was deeply, blissfully asleep, the next his eyes popped wide open, blinking up at the pale shadow of the ceiling, his whole body awake and alert as though activated by switch. Something was wrong. Something about the job. It was too easy, too convenient. He hadn't seen it at the time, completely swept up in the torrent, bowled along by heady, fast flowing talk and his own breathless expectations. Or was he just panicking? After so long out in the cold he was just nervous, jumpy. Surely everything was all right, AOK, nominal, kosher.

Slipping out of bed he tiptoed through to the spare room. Fournier's card was on the desk, an address in Geneva. He sat for a minute tapping the card against his teeth. Then he turned and stared at his piles of trade magazines, clippings and files. About a year he had said, the company had been in existence for about a year. There would be mention of it, somewhere in those piles. He picked up an armful and two industry directories and began.

After about an hour he realised he was shivering, left the spare room for some clothes and moments later found himself vomiting in the bathroom. He stayed for a while, leaning heavily against the basin, studying the haggard and bloodshot eyes in the mirror. Then he fetched jeans and a sweatshirt from the bedroom and went back to the files.

There was nothing. No mention, anywhere. Not Pan Global Trading, nor PGT, PGT Strategic Systems, nothing. At about four he took a break from the magazines and directories and telephoned the number on the card. It rang, then there was a click followed by the piercing whistle of a telefax tone. He winced and put down the receiver. Next he tried international directory assistance for Switzerland and asked for any listings under PGT, Pan Global or Michel Fournier. There were none for the first two but six M. Fourniers listed in the Geneva area. He noted them all down for later then returned to the piles.

The door opened, it was Emma, tousle haired and frowning. 'What on earth are you doing?' she whispered. Then she saw his expression and came in.

He shook his head. 'I can't find him. Not a line, not a word anywhere. It's not necessarily significant, it is a new company but, there is something peculiar about it all.' His voice was calm but his stomach churned. He wondered if he was going to be sick again.

She sighed, sat down on the bed, hunched forward resting elbows on bare thighs below the football shirt. 'I knew it was too good to be true.'

'Well it's not dead yet Em, I could be worrying about nothing.'

'Of course. Have you phoned his number?'

'Fax machine. I'll just have to wait until office hours and call some contacts.' Racal. Fournier said he had got his name from someone at Racal.

'Right.' She ran her hands through her hair. 'Look, I know this sounds fatuous, but you mustn't worry. If this all goes to ratshit I mean. We'll work something out; we will manage.' She got up to leave. 'I'll make some coffee.'

'Okay, thanks.' Mustn't worry? What on earth was she talking about? His stomach had stopped churning, silenced by the steady settling of a heavy, cold leaden weight.

It was nearly noon before the bubble finally burst. Just twenty-four hours after it had first inflated. At nine he began by calling Racal. On file he had the business cards of three members of the sales team. Only one was in.

'Who? Fournier? Sorry Pete, never heard of him.'

'Somebody there has, gave him my name, must have been either Rhind or Williams.'

'Bill Rhind's in Santiago, Dave Williams will be in later, I'll ask him to call you back.'

While he waited he tried some of the Geneva Fourniers, eventually establishing contact with two and relatives of two more. His French wasn't fluent but it was evident enough that none were connected with his Michel Fournier.

Emma popped in from time to time to see 'how it was going'. He began to resent her hovering, he couldn't shake the impression that somehow she was almost hoping it would all fall through. Eventually at his prompting she agreed to take the children out to the park leaving him in peace with his growing despair. 'It was never going to be that easy Deacon,' he found himself growling through clenched teeth at one point.

Then David Williams called back from Racal. 'Not me Peter, must have been Bill, but I'm sure he meant no harm by it, you did say you were job hunting.'

'No, yes. So you know him then?'

'Fournier? Lord yes. He's been sniffing around for months. And elsewhere too, by all accounts, Thorn, Marconi, BAe.'

'What's it about? Is he for real?'

'Who knows. From what I gather he made very plausible and attractive overtures to some of the boys here, which so far haven't come to anything. They might one day of course, that's probably why Bill put him onto you. Could turn out to be a live one, he certainly wasn't short of cash. But you can never tell with his sort.'

'So what's his angle?'

'Search me. But he's very keen on news, you know, latest technological innovations, any R & D gossip, whispers on contracts.'

Peter felt a sudden chill. His mind raced back to the airport. Fournier had tested him, speaking knowledgeably about the Jaguar, close support, strategy, armament, but at the same time asking, pumping him for more. Peter had spoken freely, after all he was trying to impress the man. But had he strayed into sensitive areas? He rubbed at his forehead, God, this was turning into a nightmare.

He tried to keep his voice level. 'So you think he might be just your friendly neighbourhood intelligence gatherer then?'

Williams paused for a moment to consider. 'Hmm, no. Probably just your friendly neighbourhood bullshitter.'

When Emma returned he was out. She found a note on the kitchen table. 'Job a dud – sorry. Gone for a walk. P.'

'Look what is it with you two? I leave you here for two minutes and a fight breaks out. I don't care whose fault it was Sally, you are a big girl now and unless you can find a way to get on and play sensibly with your brother, then I can personally guarantee that there will be no Father Christmas. Got it?'

Sally looked shocked, lip quivering. The playroom was a mess again. Books and toys strewn all over the floor, just pulled from cupboards and shelves at random it appeared.

'No such thing as Father Christmas.' Jamie sat amid the debris, banging a piece of railway track against his shoe defiantly. He had been impossible since school broke up.

Peter thought quickly. God it was hard to maintain order using the threatened non-appearance of a fictional, over-weight old man in ridiculous clothes as a deterrent against unruly behaviour. 'Fine. Then I can just phone him up and tell him not to bother stopping by here as none of the children in this house believe in him; or the presents he would have been bringing.' He winced, the conjugation was amiss somewhere, he hoped they were following the general gist. God, his head ached. And his neck, shoulders. And his throat was sore; he'd been going down with something for days. They were unsure, silent. 'Right then you can start by clearing up this lot.' He jabbed a toe into a pile of puzzles. 'I'm going upstairs and I will be listening, so don't let me hear any more fighting.' He trudged out and back up to the spare room.

He was losing it. His forged fourteen-day breathing space with the bank was up. Bishop had phoned twice so far that week but Peter hadn't picked up either call. Another repossession notice had arrived, this one on the washing machine, dishwasher, television set and the dining-room furniture. Unless they heard from him 'in the very near future' they would be round with a removal van.

And the job situation had moved no further forward since the Fournier fiasco of the previous week. He picked up the file, thick with correspondence and dog eared from use. There were any number of possibles. There were well over twenty companies that had acknowledged his application and confirmed, in writing, that they would contact him as soon as they had a vacancy. He spoke to them all regularly, but was conscious that his persistence was becoming counter-productive. Most had told him not to keep calling –

they would let him know the moment there was any news.

It was the same with the headhunters. He'd spoken with one that morning. 'Martin. It really doesn't matter what it is, I'll take anything, anything at all to be going on with.'

But the Martins and Miriams did not deal in just 'anything', their positions were all top drawer. If they began sending unsuitable applicants for interview their clients would drop them like hot bricks. In any case, any hint of desperation was distasteful, common. They rarely returned his calls any more.

His father had given him a couple of names at the Ministry. Senior names to be fair but one was retired, the other shortly to be, and neither were directly involved in recruitment. His application had been accepted, but there were to be no short cuts, it would be routed through normal channels. In a month or so he could expect to be called for the first in a series of interviews, and then assuming he was successful in completing the long and idiosyncratic selection and screening process, he might, three or four months hence, be offered a medium grade desk post at DESO or procurement or even the foreign office, fagging for the chinless wonders and earning about half what he was on at UAS.

It was the money that was killing him. Money and time. Emma was working three days a week at the agency, but even full-time, her earnings barely covered the grocery bill. He drew the latest bank statement from the drawer, forced himself into a rough reconciliation. It was appalling, con-demnation by numbers. A lone entry in the receipts column marked the point in time when his father's cheque had vanished unnoticed into the void. Five hundred pounds. A measure of the gulf between them. And he still hadn't written.

The bills were piling up too. The latest quarterly batch

were already hitting the mat. He just threw them, unopened with most of the rest of the mail, into the back of the finance drawer.

There was a commotion downstairs, shouting. Then Sally's scream pierced his consciousness like a hot needle. That scream. Not pain, not anguish but protest. He willed it to stop, begged it to stop, hunched over the open front of the bureau, hands clamped over his ears, but it went on and on, long, long bursts then blessed relief as she paused to gulp air between red and tear stained cheeks, then again, loud and shrill.

Snarling like a dog, he leaped downstairs and across the hall in a series of adrenalin charged headlong bounds. But he misjudged the turning into the playroom and struck his elbow hard on the doorway. The pain made him giddy, disorientated, deflecting his attention like the barbed stab of a picador's lance. Instinctively Jamie shuffled backwards, sensing danger. Sally, misinterpreting the speed of his response to her summons, screeched on with renewed vigour. He bent and gripped the front of her dungarees with one hand, twisted and lifted, whisking her effortlessly into the air above him, then flexing until his upturned face was inches from hers. He yelled into it, enveloped it in a gale of heat and noise, a lungful for each word, ears popping as the scream rose to a bellow.

'Shut the fuck up!'

She stopped. Went limp like a kitten, the colour evaporating from her cheeks. He held her there dangling in space, it was close, still close, his arm shook, there was roaring in his ears, and something else.

'Dad. The doorbell.'

'Whaa?'

'Somebody's at the door.'

He hesitated, confused, then lowered her quickly to the

146

floor, she sobbed convulsively and crawled towards Jamie, first time he'd ever seen her turn to him for sanctuary. He flattened himself against the wall and slid towards the window. Nothing. Then a moment later he appeared on the step, taking the two paces back, staring at the upstairs windows. It was the postman, again? But a different one from usual. This was a special delivery, the red van double parked in the street, engine idling. He went forward again disappearing from view. A moment later the doorbell. Peter went to the hall.

It was a letter, recorded delivery. The postman checked his watch, made a note of the time and date and had him sign the form twice. He left the children and went through to the kitchen, dropped the letter on the table while he washed three aspirins down with the first drink of the day. He was more careful now, he regulated his alcohol intake, rationing himself so that he rarely became seriously drunk, or completely incapacitated, except perhaps late at night. During the day he started as late as possible, sometimes not until noon although he usually had a small one mid morning, his 'post opener' he called it. But it was under control, he remained coherent and together all day.

But the quantity surprised him, and the cost. He was up to about two thirds of a bottle a day, if Emma joined him for two or three in the evening it could be the whole bottle. He was buying the cheap supermarket brands and decanting them into a Bells bottle for the sake of continuity, she couldn't tell the difference. The empties he kept in a carrier bag under the spare room bed to take out and drop in lamp post litter bins when she was out. And when he remembered. The other day he had found himself staring at the shelves in the Indian store on the corner with the realisation that he hadn't enough money for the usual two bottles. The shop was empty, the manager watching a portable television by the till. Without thinking, almost without realising it, he slipped a half bottle of the good stuff into each coat pocket, carrying a one litre bottle of the cheap blend up to the counter. The proprietor took his money, muttered Merry Christmas, his eyes never leaving the screen.

Finally he opened the envelope. It was a court order. Couched in the complex idiom of the formal legal notification. It was some minutes before its full meaning became clear. He felt his mouth go dry, his heart pound as the realisation dawned. It was an eviction order. In effect. Oh there were caveats all right, let out clauses and escape options, but the long and the short of it was pay up or get out. Within twenty-eight days.

He took the bottle upstairs with him and sat at the desk reading and re-reading the letter. Frantically searching the lines in a forlorn effort to divine some other, less extreme message from the theretofors and whereases. He needed legal advice. Quickly. His own solicitor was out of the question, the man had resorted to a court action of his own to settle his account. There was Emma's family solicitor: Watkins? Wallace? Peter knew where to find the number. But could he rely on impartiality? Would they not feel obliged to offer advice only with her best interests in mind? You mean your wife is completely unaware of this situation? That does place us in an extremely difficult position Mr Deacon.

He rang the court. They could explain it. Eventually he was put through to a clerical assistant in processes or administration who located the details of his order.

'What exactly does it mean?'

'Well, er, it means that unless you can come to an agreement, a separate agreement that is, with the trustees of your mortgages, the court will authorise repossession of the property. Um, vacant repossession.'

'But they can't do that can they? Physically throw people onto the street?'

'Well, issuing an order is one thing, of course enforcing it is quite another. But legally they are entitled to sequestrate goods to the value of outstanding repayments, or if the agreement is deemed null and void as a result of breach of contract, as would appear in this case, they may simply take repossession of what in effect is already theirs. The property I mean.'

'Yes but the house is worth nearly double the value of the mortgage.'

'If you say so. But if I may say that's hardly the point, they are still entitled to recover their loss. And costs.'

'I could sell it.' Though that might take months.

'Not while it is the subject of a court order I'm afraid.'

He was speechless. It was incredible, unimaginable. 'So what the hell do I do?'

'I'm sorry, I am not able to offer legal advice.'

That night he said nothing to Emma about the order. He ate dinner in a moody silence then went out walking, stole a half bottle from a corner store in Battersea and drank the lot sitting on an embankment bench hunched up in his coat and coughing like a tramp. He got home after two and collapsed on the spare room bed.

In the morning he didn't appear at the breakfast table. Emma went upstairs and found him stretched out sweat-soaked on the spare room bed, mumbling and shuddering. She got him undressed and into bed, took his temperature and called the doctor. It was flu, he said, nasty bug going around at the moment. Keep him in bed and warm for a few days. Plenty of fluids. Peter dozed feverishly most of that day, she stayed at home with the children, looking in on him from time to time, helping him to the bathroom.

During the night he woke her twice, terrifying her with meaningless high-speed chatter and garbled shouting. The second time she ran in to him he sat bolt upright and grabbed her arm, squeezing it violently with both hands. He stared at her wild eyed and unrecognising, his dark hair dishevelled and wet, face flushed. 'I'm sorry I'm sorry I'm sorry I'm sorry.' He clung to her, she had to prise his fingers off her arm.

The next morning was much the same but late in the afternoon when she checked on him, the fever had broken. He lay quietly, blinking up at her in the doorway.

'Well hello there', she said. 'How are you feeling?'

'Thirsty,' he croaked, smiling weakly. Later in the evening he tottered downstairs in his dressing gown and sat with her in the sitting room, sipping vegetable soup in front of the fire.

'Mitch called. Sends her love.'

'How are they?'

'Fine. She says it's high time we came over for dinner.'

He nodded, staring into the flames as they flickered around the lumps of concrete coal. 'Remember Orlando? That was this time last year.' The four of them had flown to Florida for a week, stayed at the Sheraton, eaten at the best restaurants, danced at the most expensive clubs. During the day they hired cars and drove to the beaches, visited the sights; Disney World and EPCOT, an alligator farm, Kennedy Space Centre. Or they just lay by the pool smelling of coconut oil and drinking daiquiris. Sleek, shiny and content like basking sea-lions.

'Don't, I can't bear it.'

'Em.'

'Perhaps, when this is all sorted out and normal service is resumed, we can take off for a few days. Hit a beach somewhere.'

'Count on it.'

'Antigua maybe, or the Seychelles.'

'Kenya. You do beaches, I'll do game reserves.'

'Fine.' She closed her eyes and leaned back in the armchair, arms and legs outstretched, face raised in anticipation.

'Emma?'

'Not now. I'm on holiday.'

He slept well but woke early, he felt his mind was clear and alert. He crept out of bed and took a shower, made coffee and went to the spare room. Taking a clean sheet of paper he wrote 'Situation Report' and the date at the top. He then stared at it for ten minutes, his mind leaping off at tangents each time he tried to assemble his thoughts. Eventually he wrote 'Finance' near the top left-hand side of the page then: Bank Debts total circa 15k. Standing Orders, etc., 2.5k. Mortgage repayments approx 4k. Immediate requirement minimum 15k then 5k in short-term plus 1700 per month. He checked it through. It made sober reading. He added a postscript: N.B. Bishop expecting immediate 20k cottage mortgage.

The next heading was 'Job Sitrep'. He studied the file, grouping the prospects according to his completely arbitrary perception of each one's probability of success. He then regrouped and averaged the figures, tabulating them on the sheet in summary form. Total Possibles: 20. Firm Prospects: 8. Percentile probability of offers Long Term (6–12 mths): 100%, Medium Term (1–6 mths): 50%, Short Term (1 mth): 20%. He pondered this last statistic. He knew somehow that his logic was flawed. Also in reality his chances of finding employment over the Christmas period were slim in the extreme. He scratched out the twenty and wrote ten.

The final heading was 'Action'. But he could think of nothing. He doodled at the bottom of the page, a complex pattern of interlaced straight lines, then a filigree and intricately ornate question mark. Finally he crossed out 'Action' and wrote 'Options': 1) Confront E re: cottage mortgage, arrange re-finance package through bank. 2) Dan? He hated the prospect but Dan had offered to help, and an idea was forming. He wrote the 3) but could think of no more options. Next, he re-wrote 'Actions': 1) Chase head-hunters. 2) Arrange meet with Dan. 3) Depending on outcome of 2) tackle E.

Putting down the pencil he studied the sheet. He was about to take his coffee cup downstairs and lay the table for breakfast when the still absent third option caught his eye. He picked up the pencil and scribbled 'Westminster Bridge . . .' smiled and left the room.

He called Dan first thing. His office said he was out and very tied up all week putting together a pitch. They suggested he call tomorrow as he would probably be in. Emma went to work; it was her last day at the agency before Christmas, and her last on the current project. There was no news yet if they had any work for her in the new year. Peter stayed at home lounging around in front of the television with the children. At lunchtime he felt the urge for a drink and had a long Scotch and water. It made his head spin but felt good. During the afternoon he sipped at a couple more.

The next morning he left the house after breakfast telling Emma that he was going to light a few fires under the headhunters. Dan's offices were near Sloane Square, he decided to walk. It was a cold, crisp morning, still and blue. He cut past the Sands End gasworks to the King's Road and tramped East with increasing numbers of muffled morning shoppers. After only a quarter of a mile he began to feel dizzy and hot. The flu had taken more out of him than he had realised. He rested outside a newsagent's shop, panting and clammy, surprised yet intrigued at the sight of himself in the window. His hair was definitely longer and though it had been going on for months, there was suddenly a noticeable weight loss evident in his face. Yet he felt the leaner look suited him.

He took a bus up the King's Road to Sloane Square, arriving at Dan's offices by ten thirty.

'Yes Mr Mitchell is in but he is rather busy, may I say who is calling?' The receptionist sat him down in a corner amid a profusion of tropical greenery and framed photographs of the agency's more successful campaigns. On one wall was a huge poster of a girl in a swimsuit sitting at a table on a wide sandy beach. She was sipping a wine cooler, the bottle on the table in front of her, the sea lapping gently at her feet. Under the poster was a framed award won by the agency for the advertisement.

Dan was in a darkened room two floors up from Peter. There were five other people in there focusing intently on the screen of the overhead projector; the agency's creative director and two assistants, the media director and the budgets controller. They were into their third day of frenetic activity, long hours, irregular meals and late nights. At the beginning of the week, and with the usual lack of warning, one of the agency's biggest accounts had announced they were taking their business elsewhere. It happened all the time in the industry, clients constantly on the lookout for fresh talent and new ideas, a different agency prowling for business makes an attractive offer, seducing the customer with tantalising new marketing initiatives and bullish predictions.

As account manager, Dan was responsible for masterminding the counter-attack. When customers announce they are leaving an agency, it may be true or it may be a feint: 'Come up with something original and exciting or we go.' For the past three days they had been working on the project, tempers were becoming frayed. They were in conclave, the entire staff at the agency trod softly, worked quietly around them, sensitive to the tension, waiting for the smoke. Dan's secretary was under strict instructions. No disturbances, no exceptions. When Peter arrived the receptionist had telephoned the secretary, she'd relayed the message to Peter.

'That's okay, I'll wait.' He picked up a copy of Marketing Weekly, settling lower in the seat. 'He says he'll wait.' The receptionist murmured into the telephone.

Thirty minutes later Dan's secretary came down, the receptionist nodded towards a rather unkempt looking dark-haired man wearing sweatshirt and jeans beneath an old raincoat, badly worn trainers on his feet. 'Mr Deacon?' she said. 'I'm Paula, Dan's secretary.'

'Hello Paula, we have met, some time ago I think.'

She smiled, doubted it. 'Oh, yes, how are you? Dan is really tied up this morning, with clients. He has said that he almost certainly won't be free at all today.'

'Have you told him I'm here?'

'Unfortunately he is in a meeting as I say and has asked not to be disturbed.'

'Well perhaps you could slip a note in front of him or something. I'm quite sure he'll be happy to pop out and see me.'

Paula sighed. She had put a phone call through to him at eight thirty this morning, an urgent one. He'd practically jumped down her throat. She knew he would probably apologise later, but there was no way she was going to risk his wrath again. 'Could you possibly tell me what it is in connection with, and as soon as he becomes free, I could get him to call you.'

'It's a personal matter, we're old friends. If you just tell him I'm here, it won't take five minutes.'

'Well I can't disturb him right now, he was very specific about it.'

'Paula, I'm an old friend. I know he would want to be notified that I'm waiting out here.' She said she was sorry, but there was not much she could do. He asked her to try, she went back to the office. 'No chance,' she told the receptionist quietly over the phone. 'Let me know when he's gone.' A little later the receptionist phoned her back with the news that the dark-haired visitor had fallen asleep in the chair. 'Good grief,' she replied. 'What is he a vagrant or something?'

Peter woke with a start about three quarters of an hour later. He looked around, dazed and disoriented, completely at a loss as to his whereabouts. It was several seconds before he remembered, glancing sheepishly at the receptionist who pretended not to notice as he approached her desk.

'I'd like to speak to Patricia,' he said. 'Now if possible.'

She was baffled, turned the corners of her mouth down, shrugged. 'Patricia?'

He rubbed his forehead. 'Mr Mitchell's secretary?' She put him through.

'No, Mr Deacon. No luck yet. He's still tied up.'

'You haven't told him I'm here then.'

'He left strict instructions not to be disturbed. By anyone. I'm sorry.'

'Well I'm sorry too. Because now I'll just have to go and find him myself.'

The receptionist froze; this was getting creepy. Paula covered the mouthpiece. What the hell was she supposed to do? She could put him on hold, phone through to the post room, ask a couple of the lads to come up and escort him from the premises. They'd love that. She could even call the police, technically he was trespassing. Wasn't he? But what if he really was a long lost friend of Dan's, recently returned from years lost in the Amazon basin or something. Sorry Dan, he said he wanted to see you urgently, so I had him forcibly evicted. Nice going Paula. She swore under her breath, took her hand away from the mouthpiece.

'Would you wait there Mr Deacon, just for a few minutes, I'll see what I can do.' She gritted her teeth and dialled the conference room number. Dan came on.

'Peter? Here? What on earth does he want?'

'I'm so sorry Dan, but he said he was going to come and find you if we didn't—'

'It's okay, um, look take him up to my office, give him another coffee or something, I'll get there as soon as I can.' He put back the phone. The others were evidently unimpressed but agreed to break for ten minutes.

'Look, Peter, I'm sorry, I must have missed something here. It's been a hell of a week. Just run it all past me once again, please.'

Peter got up and began walking around the office. Dan was only half listening; he couldn't believe the change in Peter. He was thin and scruffy, pacing up and down like a nervous schoolboy, talking ten to the dozen, and utter nonsense by the sound of it, something about a short-term loan in advance of some imminent re-financing deal.

'Let me get this straight. You want me to lend you fifteen thousand pounds to get the bank manager off your back while a mortgage deal goes through on the place in Suffolk.'

'That's right. It should only be a couple of weeks. Then as soon as the cheque comes through from the building society, I repay you. Three, four weeks tops.'

'Well if the cheque's coming through in a couple of weeks, why bother?'

Peter stopped pacing, sniffed noisily, quickly wiping his sleeve across his face. 'Because ... the bank are expecting it sooner than that. Now actually.'

'Ah. I see.' He didn't really. What on earth was going on? He stifled an urge to look at his watch, he had to get back to the conference room. 'Emma?'

Peter shook his head. 'In the dark.'

'What, completely? I thought it was her cottage, Fairbright Folly you used to call it.'

'It is. Look Dan, are you going to help me out or not? You know this isn't easy for me.'

'Okay, okay. Right, first: I said I'd help, and if I can I will. But fifteen k is a lot of dosh to rake together at short notice. I'm running a national debt sized overdraft same as everyone else, I'm also running a darling wife who scatters cash like confetti. I can write you a cheque for about a grand right now, and probably make arrangements for the rest . . .' He flicked through his desk diary, muttering about Christmas and holidays. '. . . in a couple of weeks.'

Peter turned suddenly for the desk and brought his fist down with a crash. Dan sat back, startled. 'That's not good enough! I need it today, tomorrow at the latest!'

'Now just wait a minute.' Dan was on his feet now. 'You pitch up here without a word of warning, camp out in reception scaring the shit out of the girls like some sort of wandering pervert, and then have the gall to come storming in here demanding suitcases full of money!' They glared at each other across the desk.

'That's about it,' said Peter, eventually, with the ghost of a smile. 'Dan, I'm right in it. Up to my neck.' He drew a finger across his throat.

Dan's telephone warbled. 'I'm just coming.' He hung up. 'Peto, I'll get onto it but I'm not going to be able to raise anything significant before Christmas. It's the best I can do. But I really think you should at least be talking to Emma about it. She has a right to know.'

Peter stared at him over the desk, considering. Then he

157

straightened abruptly. 'Fine. Don't bother. Sorry to have troubled you.' He walked out.

He wandered back to Sloane Square in a daze and sat on a bench beneath the bare trees, in the middle near the silent fountain. Pigeons strutted about at his feet hopefully, or dozed, squatting, their necks withdrawn into the dishevelled plumage of their chests. The traffic arrived and circled and went, rumbling inexorably clockwise around him, passing like moments as steadily as sand through the neck of the glass.

He just needed more time. The situation was temporary, a change in his fortunes inevitable, as assured and certain as the passage of time itself. At some point ahead on the horizon was the instant when order would return out of the chaos. It was moving towards him, when it arrived he could resume his life as it was meant to be, a little older and wiser for the experience perhaps, but restored, refreshed.

He wanted a drink but had barely enough money on him for a single short in the pub. He hauled himself up wearily from the bench and began walking slowly back down the King's Road. After a while he came to an off licence. He walked in, moving slowly along the shelves, watching the cashier. He reached the spirits and studied them. Too long.

'Can I help you?' The cashier was peering over the top of a six foot pile of beer cases.

'Umm, no thanks.' He crawled back down the shelves, past the fortified wines and soft drinks and out of the shop.

'How did it go today?'

'What?' His mind went back to the agency, Dan's office, then he remembered. 'Oh well it's pretty hopeless, the whole world grinds to a halt at Christmas. They all say I might as well twiddle my thumbs until the second week in January.'

Emma opened the oven door and withdrew a pie dish. The

pastry on top looked cooked but flat and solid. 'Not sure about this, not so much puff as puffed out. God knows how long that pastry's been in the freezer.' There was no Scotch, keeping his back to her he poured them both another gin and tonic. It was the last of the gin, he drained the bottle into his glass, half-filling it. 'It'll be fine. Anything happen here?'

She closed the oven door and took the glass from him. 'Nothing much. The kids were ghastly, I took them out for a walk after lunch to try and cool them down, but as soon as we got back they were at each others' throats again. So I told them I was going to telephone Santa and tell him not to bother with the Deacon kids this year. Guess what?'

'What?'

'They said I was wasting my time, Dad's already rung him.' It was a joke but her voice had an edge to it and she wasn't smiling. 'Guess what else?'

'Hmm?'

'John Bishop phoned.'

Oh God. His hand lifted the glass from the table. A reflex reaction, a knee jerk. He gulped. 'Oh yes? Dear John. Let me see, invitation to lunch was it?'

'Last supper more like.'

Come on Emma let's get it over with. 'So, well?'

She tilted her head, looked at the ceiling, lips pursed. 'Hmm, no you first I think.'

He took a deep breath, exhaled through puffed cheeks. He thought of his options and actions sheet. It might as well be now. 'The mortgage thing.' He kept his head down, glanced up at her leaning against a work surface, arms folded.

'Indeed.'

'Emma, we have to do it.'

'Not strictly true. If anyone has to do it, it's me.'

'All right. You have to do it.'

'Why?'

159

Another sigh, he couldn't look at her. 'Because I told Bishop that we've already done it.'

She looked baffled. 'You told him that I had agreed to take out a mortgage on the cottage?'

'Yes.' Tiny sparks of rebellion were flickering within him. He felt a sudden recklessness. He sat up at the table, tilted the chair back, faced her. 'No. I told him, in effect I led him to believe, that we both owned the cottage and had already applied for and been granted a mortgage on it. It was a way, in my view the only way, to secure an extended line of credit from him.'

'And he believed you?'

'Yes. Although after a while I had to, er fabricate confirmation from the building society.'

That got through to her. She pushed forward, straightened. Put her glass down on the work top. 'You did what?'

'I faked a letter from the building society, faxed it to him.'

'I don't believe I'm hearing this.' She was shaking her head, stunned.

'So you see we have to, sorry, you have to apply for a mortgage now. Immediately. I have the forms ready filled out upstairs. Otherwise I will probably go to prison. Obtaining money by deception or something.'

There was a long silence, he watched her defiantly. Something was popping in the oven. Go on, say it. Her voice was a whisper. 'What in God's name did you think you were doing?'

'What was I doing?' He got to his feet, stabbing his finger into the air towards her. Mind racing, stuttering and stumbling in his haste over the words, his desperate hurry to spit them out. 'I'll tell you what I was doing. I was trying to deal with an impossible situation the best way I knew how! A situation that you were more than partly responsible for yet refused to have anything to do with. I was trying to

160

protect you, and the children from all of this for as long as possible, in the hope that in the end, everything would be sorted without you ever having to get caught up in it!'

'But I had a right to get caught up in it, didn't you consider that?'

Now he was furious. 'Don't you give me that you lying bitch! Every time I tried to bring up the subject you switched off. Just didn't want to fucking know!' He spat the words at her contemptuously, only partly aware that he had moved across the kitchen, was right in front of her, his finger inches from her throat.

The tears were welling up in her eyes, but she was fighting them, she didn't want his pity. 'You tried to mortgage my cottage. My cottage, my Daddy's cottage ...' The tears sprang, she choked, sobbed.

He felt a pang, glimpsed the little girl, in the photograph, at her mother's house, the little girl, seven or eight, sitting on her father's knee. Just a pang, but the fire engulfed it before he could draw back. He growled at her, lips drawn and quivering. 'Don't try and lay your guilt over your dead father at my feet. This has got nothing—'

She slapped him hard on the right cheek. He took the blow with the same bemused surprise as the punch from the child at Victoria, but this time he reacted, immediately and spontaneously. His left hand came up like lightning and whipped across her jaw with phenomenal speed, barely a half second after she had struck him. He saw it as though in slow motion, he couldn't stop, it was a conditioned reflex. She'd rung the bell, he'd salivated. As the clenched fist soared upwards towards her face he sensed its huge destructive power, as if every cell in his body, every fibre of his being was concentrating, focusing energy onto the hand. At the last moment, the split instant before it struck her, something deeply embedded inside caused his fingers to unclench.

Clutching a hand to her lower cheek, she gasped and took a step sideways. She stood, half crouched in the middle of the floor, looking up at him in surprise, disbelief. Then she sank to her knees, a tiny siren wail began, as though from a distance, the note rising and growing louder until it cracked and she broke into uncontrollable, shaking sobs.

'I'm sorry. God, Emma I'm sorry.' He knelt at her side, his arm around the shoulders. She tried to shrug him off but he encircled her with his arms, crushed her to his chest, holding the shaking head against him as she wept. Soon she grew quiet, but he held onto her a while longer, rocking together on the floor. Then she said she had to get a handkerchief and slipped from him.

A few minutes later they reconvened in the sitting room. He assumed she had gone upstairs for good, but she reappeared in the kitchen, blowing her nose and moving her mouth about, exercising the jaw. Her voice was calm, she even managed a wry smile when she saw his face. There was a perfectly formed hand outline glowing red on his cheek. 'Let's go and sit down, have we got anything left to drink?'

'You're incredible, you know that?' He found a bottle of German wine someone had brought to a dinner party as a gift. It wasn't chilled and it was too sweet but they drank gratefully.

'Emma I'm sorry I hit you.'

She held up a hand. 'So am I. But we have to decide, now, what we are going to do. Remember you agreed to consider my proposal, if I considered yours?'

So this was it. Bent and battle damaged though she may be, she was not about to leave the field and risk losing everything. This was her moment of triumph, when she snatched victory from the bruised jaw of defeat. The fact that they had come to blows was merely a distraction. He sighed, 'Yes.'

'Well irrespective of the fact that you seem to have already gone ahead with your plans, I think the time has come to consider my suggestion as a serious option.' Another prepared speech. She blew her nose again. 'Therefore I think that if by the end of the year your situation is, unchanged, we should move down to the cottage. I can provide enough for us to survive on, we'll get the children into local schools and you can continue to hunt for jobs using the cottage as a base.'

'But that's only a couple of weeks. My situation is not going to change before the new year.'

She shrugged. 'That's as may be, but we can't go on like this. I can't.'

They drank in silence for a while. He looked around the room. 'And what about this place?'

'I don't know. I don't really care. Put it on the market, sell the bloody place, clear all our debts and still leave a nice lump to start again, get something else, smaller. A flat or something.'

'You've thought it all out haven't you?' She didn't answer. 'What if I say no?'

'Peter, you're not listening. I'm going. With the children. You can come too, or not, that's up to you. This has gone on too long and cannot go on any longer. It's not your fault, God knows you've tried, but we have to be practical.'

Practical. Abandon any hope of restoring the situation to normal. Flee a comfortable house in the heart of the business capital of Europe and for what? For an unheated, uninsulated, improperly plumbed, damp, draughty hovel set in darkest Outer Beyond. In the middle of winter. It was insanity. 'What if I do get a job, *when* I get a job, here in town. What happens then?'

'I don't know. We'll deal with that when it happens. Maybe we'll all move back. Maybe you could commute – lots of people do you know. But that's then, this is now.'

He was appalled. He looked appalled, his dark eyebrows set in a deep frown, eyes staring sightlessly at the floor, fingers plucking a piece of loose rubber on his shoe. His lips compressed so that his mouth shrank to a thin, straight line with the ends turned down. Head hanging, shoulders slumped.

'Peter. It won't be so bad.' Her voice was softer. 'You'll see. Tomorrow we'll start phoning. We'll talk to Bishop and sort out the mortgage thing, we'll contact some estate agents, maybe get someone over to give a valuation on this place. Try and get hold of some builders around Bedingham, give them your famous list of defects.'

Don't patronise me. 'Hold on. End of the year you said if I remember correctly. Let's not get ahead of ourselves.'

'Okay. End of the year. So it's agreed then.' She was finding it hard not to smile, there was still a small livid purple patch on her right jaw but she seemed oblivious.

'It would appear I don't have much choice.'

She grinned, clearly delighted, she practically clapped her hands. She got up from the chair, came over and kissed his cheek, tenderly. Then she headed for the door.

'One thing.'

She stopped. 'Hmm?'

'What did Bishop want?'

'Oh. Nothing. Wouldn't say, just wanted to speak to you.'

CHAPTER

8

B ut it wasn't the New Year. It was the next day. They
were both up early. Sitting at the kitchen table
drinking coffee even before Sally padded in, slippers
on the wrong feet, sleepy eyed and yawning.

'Is it Christmas today?'

'Not today sweetheart, soon. Come and have some
breakfast.'

Jamie arrived, they sat and breakfasted together. Emma
cooked scrambled eggs for all of them. Jamie stared at his in
amazement.

'What's this for anyway?' asked Sally.

'Scrambled eggs is for teatime.'

'I just thought we should all have a proper cooked
breakfast this morning. For a change.'

Afterwards they adjourned to the spare room. The children wanted to come too, sat bouncing on the bed, sensing
something unusual. Peter was bemused and perplexed. This
was his room, he was used to having it to himself, their
presence made him uneasy.

'Can I see it?'

He hesitated, then dug deep into a bureau drawer,

produced a clear plastic document folder containing letters and forms from the building society. He withdrew a single photocopied sheet, handed it to her nervously.

She cast a professional eye over the forgery. 'It's very good,' she said eventually, holding it up to the window. 'Different typeface from their usual house style of course but the bank would never know that. Very handy piece of cutting and pasting. You should have a go at bank notes next.' In the light from the window he could see a faint discolouration on one side of her jaw, a barely perceptible yellowing, unnoticeable unless you were looking for it. But a bruise nevertheless.

'Ha, Ha,' he said, faking a humourless grin.

'Ha! Ha!' said Sally.

'Where's the original?' His fingers made delicate paper tearing movements. 'Good.' She nibbled her thumbnail thoughtfully. Jamie was leafing through a back copy of *Flight* magazine. Sally was trying to crawl under the bed. 'Right. How about this. I'll call him, or you, and tell him that we've decided to cancel the mortgage application, we'll think of some excuse – the building society were messing us about, or we've had a better quote, anything.'

'Emma, he'll go ballistic. He'll shut us down, we'll have no way of cashing cheques, that' – he gestured at the page – 'was the only thing keeping us going.'

'I don't think he'll do anything. We could tell him we're having a complete re-think, considering selling this house instead. He won't cut us off, he can't. Anyway what's more important is it gets you off this hook.' She fluttered the sheet. There was the sound of clinking bottles from under the bed. Only Sally's ankles and feet protruded. Emma studied him, elected not to comment. 'Come out from there Sally, it's time to get dressed.'

Peter sat in the Windsor chair in a daze. Everything was

happening so quickly. 'It won't work,' he muttered over and over. But a little while later he found himself on the telephone to John Bishop. He said his lines and waited. There was a long pause.

'I see. Well I can't pretend I'm not disappointed Peter. I'll have to, er, review the matter and get back to you.' He rang off. Emma looked at him expectantly.

'Well? What's he going to do?'

'Nothing. He's going to review the matter and get back to us.'

'Precisely. All sizzle and no sausage. Banks need people like us, it's how they make so much money. He'll come back with a new loan package you'll see – probably ask you out to lunch.' She screwed up the fake letter and threw it into a corner. 'Now what about this place, I've been thinking, we could let it, make a bomb, you know a series of short lets, to respectable families. Or sell it? What do you think?'

It went on like that for most of the morning. She was unstoppable, blazing away like a bushfire in a drought. He'd never seen anything like it. It was as though she had suddenly discovered some fantastic and hitherto dormant talent, tap dancing or trick cycling or something. She couldn't stop, had to keep doing it, proving to herself – and him – that it was no mere transitory fluke. Mostly he was quiet. Part of him was amazed, dazed at the speed at which she grasped the situation and seemed able to deal with it, dismissing each problem with a contemptuous wave and moving on to the next.

Part of him grew sullen and despondent. He was losing it, losing control, the reins slipping inexorably from his fingers. The smell of failure hung in the air, invisibly polluting the atmosphere like the stench of the mouse that had died undetected in the kitchen. Lingering long after it had eventually been found and disposed of.

Still another part of him was growing increasingly irritated by her gross oversimplifications, her unspoken condemnation of his handling of matters. But he kept counsel, he knew that it wasn't all as straightforward, as cut and dried as she thought. Sooner or later, as she burrowed deeper and deeper into the mess, she would strike bedrock.

'You can't sell this house, or let it,' he said at one point. 'There's a court order on it.' She blustered and flustered something about coming to an agreement with the building society, an interim out of court settlement. But as the full scale of their situation was becoming evident her pace began to slow.

The telephone rang, she answered it then handed it to him. 'Bishop.' There was a tiny crack in the façade, a chink of vulnerability in the armour. The doorbell rang before he could speak, he covered the mouthpiece: 'For Christ's sake don't let the children answer it!'

'What?' She was bewildered, momentarily.

'Go!' She ran for the stairs.

'Yes John, yes Peter here.'

'Peter, I'm sorry about this, it's out of my hands now. I'd really hoped there was another way, believe me, but, since your call this morning, it's gone too far now.' He was rambling, almost incoherent. His voice very subdued and muffled, as if he was holding the receiver somewhere down on his chest.

'John, what are you talking about? I can hardly hear you.' A dreadful, cold foreboding was forming in the pit of his stomach.

'We're petitioning, Peter. The bank is. Petitioning the court for bankruptcy. It's for your own protection.' He went on, began explaining, recovered his senses, quickly becoming lucid again now that it was over, the news delivered. He talked, Peter asked questions, only half listening. His mind

168

wandered through the window, up into the grey sky. He missed flying, he never thought he would, but there was still no sensation like it. You did it every day, it was a job, taken for granted. But even so, taking off in a fast jet, holding it low and level with full reheat while the mach needle crept round the dial, then haul back, the G-forces driving you down into the seat as the aircraft rotated, rocketing skywards, punching straight up through the overcast to burst into the dazzling blue like a gleaming bullet, higher and higher in a perfect vertical until the sky grew dark, the speed decayed and the controls became sloppy. Then slowly push over until the nose was vertical again and plummet like an arrow towards the distant white carpet ten miles below.

'Yes, yes, John I understand. I'll talk to you later, there's er, someone, something going on downstairs.' He could hear Emma's raised voice. He hung up, went to the landing. There was a man there, standing in the hall at the bottom of the stairs, he wore a short blue coat, like a shopkeeper. He was holding the television in his arms, awkwardly, Emma was remonstrating, he arguing with her in a 'I'm-only-doing-my-job' voice. Sally and Jamie watched to one side; Sally was crying. It was as if he had arrived late at his seat at the theatre, the upper circle. Standing in the gods watching the second half of the opening scene. Quickly piecing together the plot. They stopped arguing and turned their faces up the stairs. It fell to him to adjudicate. Audience participation. He felt a familiar welling inside him. He began descending the stairs.

'Put it back and get out of my house.' The line was familiar somehow, but then not, someone else was speaking it.

'Listen mate. Don't give me a hard time. I'm just the driver. I do as I'm told. They send you the advice note; I just come and collect. It's all legal and above board.'

He reached the bottom of the stairs, joined the other players, placed himself in front of the man in the blue coat, fixed him with a cold stare. Spoke quietly, slowly, enunciating clearly, so the words would be heard at the back.

'I don't give a damn. Put it back. Get out of my house.'

The driver hesitated. He was quite within his rights. He knew the law. If they let you through the door you were entitled to walk out with the goods. He'd done it before, loads of times. But he usually tried to arrange things, time his visit for when the man of the house was out and there was just kids and women standing about wringing their hands and propping the door open for him. But this was different, she was a feisty bitch no doubt about it, and as for him, something definitely odd there. Dangerous eyes. Could get ugly. Rule one: never get into unpleasantness with the punters. Not with your arms full anyway.

'Right then, please yourself.' He lobbed the television towards Peter, who fumbled, nearly dropped it, recovered. Taking full advantage of the new scenario he turned sideways, cocking his head close to Peter's. 'But you're wasting your time mate, we'll come back tomorrow, bring the law with us. What'll your kids think about that eh?' He stuck his finger under Peter's nose, it was dirty and nicotine-stained. Peter didn't blink, just stared back dull-eyed. 'Your sort make me sick,' he hissed. Peter smelt the staleness of the breath, felt a droplet of spittle hit his nose. The man sneered at him for a moment, took one last look around at Emma and the children, then swaggered across the hall. He threw open the front door so that it crashed against the wall and walked out onto the steps.

That was his mistake. The door, leaving it open. Peter felt something snap in his head, like a switch, and there was a lightning flash, then he was moving towards the light, the blinding, painfully bright light flooding into the dim hallway through the open door. He broke into a heavy lumbering run, turning sideways as the light grew closer. Faster and faster as he neared it, he could feel its coolness. Then he was there, suddenly. He stopped dead, bathed in its glow, twisted and heaved upwards and outwards, like an olympic hammer thrower, releasing the load with the same explosive grunt.

The driver turned on the pavement at the sound. His eyes widened in shock as the television sailed through the air towards him. He was too late to escape, too slow. Instinctively his arms went up in front of him, he uttered a small, childlike shout of alarm: 'Ah!' and ducked sideways.

The television exploded onto the pavement at his feet, chipping the paving stone and scattering glass in all directions, it bounced onto its side, and rolled on into the gutter, fetching up hard against the side of the driver's van.

The man looked open-mouthed up the steps at Peter, still half crouching, one arm crooked above his head. 'You mad fucker.' His voice was quiet, shaking. 'You could have killed me ...'

Peter said nothing, just stood in the doorway staring emptily down at the shattered carcass of the television. The noon light throwing his back into relief and casting a long shadow across the hall floor.

'We'll have to go now, today.' They were in the kitchen, Peter sitting at the table, both hands around a full whiskey glass, Emma pacing the floor. She'd had to pull him in from the door. He was just standing there in a complete daze. She feared the driver might come up and hit him. But the man had scurried back to his van, thrown the remains of the television into the back, muttering curses and threatening to 'go and call the law right now!'

As soon as she got him inside he began shaking,

shuddering like a winter bather, hugging himself while his teeth chattered and his body shook, Emma and the children watching anxiously. At first he couldn't speak then gradually the spasms eased. 'Em. I could really do with a drink.' It wasn't an observation it was a plea.

'Me first.' She'd run up to the corner shop and bought a bottle; he'd run to the lavatory and thrown up.

'Hmm?' He took another pull from the glass, the shaking had almost stopped.

'We'll have to go right away. What exactly did Bishop say?'

Bishop. The telephone call. But that was so long ago. He groaned, trying to recall. 'Er, it was a lot of legalese, but he said it was like being in receivership, a sort of protection.' He remembered that bit. 'We are protected from all our creditors, um by the court who appoints the bank to administer the receivership, er bankruptcy.'

'What was the bit about goods and effects?'

'They can freeze any assets and seize any goods, er and effects for liquidation and distribution on behalf of creditors.'

'Including property.'

'Yes, he did say something about property.'

'Did he mention the cottage, specifically?'

'Yes, um no. He mentioned property specifically, and he does know about the cottage of course.'

Emma stopped pacing. Jamie came into the kitchen, Sally was already there, kneeling on a chair over the table with a colouring book. He went and stood next to Emma, watching Peter warily. 'Mum.' His voice was very quiet, confidential. She ruffled his hair thoughtfully. He went on. 'First, we didn't have Daddy's car any more, then we didn't have your car. Then the man came to take away the television away . . .' He was counting on one finger.

'And I did stop going to school anyway.' Sally broke in.

'And I've been thinking that all these happened because Daddy hasn't got a job.'

She stroked his head. 'Don't you see, they can't seize this place, it's already under court jurisdiction. They'll go after the cottage, particularly if it's empty.'

'So why doesn't he just get another job?'

'What?'

'Let them have all this.' She gestured around the kitchen. 'There's a lot of effects here and ultimately the courts will have to come to an agreement over this property, it's still worth far more than we owe. Don't you see, we have to go, right away! I'm not going to let them take the cottage. They can't, not if we're living in it.'

'Are we going to live in the cottage?'

Yesyesyes!' Sally climbed down from the table and began pulling his hand. He couldn't think. It was all happening too quickly. Suddenly the prospect of escaping from all this mess did not seem so unattractive and, though he felt sure her logic was flawed, something in what she said made sense.

'We'll just take what we can fit in the Morris, the essentials, just load it up and go.' She waggled her fingers through the air.

'And what do we live on?'

She hesitated; he wasn't going to like this much. 'I have a thousand pounds. My mother gave it to me, when I went down to see her, remember?' She watched as he digested, his lips pursed, nodding thoughtfully. Of course she had, the sly old goat, she'd never allow her baby to come back empty handbagged. 'I've been saving it, for an emergency.'

'Well maybe one will come up.'

She came over, sat on the chair beside him, rested a hand on his. Sally added hers to the pile. Emma held out her free arm for Jamie, he walked over slowly, stood next to her. It

173

was a conspiracy. 'Peter, it's a chance for a fresh start, a clear breathing space. We can get clean away from all this mess, leave it for them to sort out while we regroup, plan our next move. But we have to do it now. Right away, before it's too late.'

The afternoon passed in a blur of suitcases, phone calls, errands to the corner shop and confused shouts to each other from different parts of the house. It soon became clear that shutting down the London house, properly; stripping the beds, removing all personal effects and clothing, packing away china, cutlery, books, dust sheets on the furniture and so on, was completely out of the question. There simply wasn't time. And there was only limited space available in the back of the Morris. In the end they decided on one suitcase each for essential winter clothes and as many cardboard boxes of other belongings and provisions as could be squashed around them in the car. They would have to come back at some point and close the place up properly. Gradually a pile of baggage accumulated in the hall.

Dan called. Peter was in the spare room, sorting through his job applications file.

'Dan. Look, sorry about yesterday, out of order you know.'

'Don't be daft, I was a prat. Now listen, the gravy train is rolling. Been on to the Gruppenfuhrer at the bank, had a little discussion about Christmas and goodwill and the photos I've got of him and the chief cashier, and guess what? He graciously agreed to leave a suitcase full of used tenners in the gents at the King's Arms, bless him—'

'Dan, Dan whoa there. Thank you, but I can't.'

'Why the hell not? They're unmarked.'

'It's too … Well, we're leaving.'

'Leaving what? Where? You mean fleeing the country or something?'

Emma's head appeared around the door, she had a scarf tied round it, refugee style. 'Dan!' he mouthed at her. 'Tell him we'll be in touch soon,' she hissed, and disappeared.

'Sort of. Fleeing to the country as a matter of fact.'

'Good God. Not the folly! But why, what the hell is going on?'

He didn't have time to explain, he promised to contact them both as soon as possible.

At teatime they gathered in the kitchen and had mugs of tinned soup. The children were excited and impatient. The heating was off, the house cooling. There was an urgent sense of departure, of rushed leave taking, they sensed it, fretting to be off. There were boxes everywhere, carrier bags full of clothes next to bin liners of rubbish. Cupboard doors and drawers thrown open and left, their contents hurriedly rifled then abandoned. The whole house looked as if it had been rapidly and inexpertly burgled.

Once the volume of baggage in the hall had grown to at least twice the available capacity of the Morris, Emma had taken to roving furtively from room to room like a dog with a cache of bones, grimly searching for improbable places to conceal her gains. And muttering to herself as she went about her work, secreting pictures under mattresses, candlesticks under towels in the airing cupboard, her worthless but prized costume jewellery at the back of a drawer full of underwear. 'They're not having this. The bastards won't find these.'

As he fetched and carried, Peter found himself constantly side-tracked, setting off upstairs intent on retrieving his business cards folder, reaching the landing only to divert to the bathroom to reset the water thermostat. After a while he stuffed a notepad and pencil into his pocket, jotting reminders to himself as he went. He kept thinking of a scene from a movie, American Civil War, or Second World War, he wasn't sure. James Caan as a battle-fatigued and blood-stained Confederate, or was it a grizzled and grimy GI? Crashing through the front door of the homestead. 'They're coming. Take only what you can carry in the wagon and get the hell out!'

This was insanity! He yelped, cursing furiously as the slipped screwdriver skittered away across the kitchen floor. He knelt in front of the boiler, sucking hard on the injured finger, then withdrew it to examine the cut the screwdriver had gouged in it. The white-edged gash quickly disappeared beneath a seeping spring of crimson which dribbled round the finger and dropped to the floor. He sucked it again, tasting the warm saltiness, found a tissue and went back to the hall. They were all there, sorting through the pile.

'Emma this is insanity. Why don't we take our time and go tomorr—'

The doorbell stopped him. They froze, staring at each other, Emma opened her hands, a silent questioning shrug. He put his bloodied finger to his lips. The children looked from one to the other. 'Daddy?' It was Sally, she was holding the plastic fishing net on a stick he had bought her for the beach last summer. He took one step, swept her up onto his chest, Emma reached down and took Jamie's hand. The doorbell went again. They froze again. Grandmother's footsteps. Their eyes locked together, hers alarmed and questioning, his angry. Shaking his head he tiptoed over to her. 'Get back,' he whispered.

They pressed back against the wall, in a line. Jamie between them, Sally in his arms, he muttering soft gibberish in her ear. The doorbell rang again, then the letter flap snapped open. He couldn't see it, kept his head back against the wall, pressed hers hard down onto his neck. The hall light was on, so was the playroom light. The pile of baggage was in the middle of the floor. The letter flap stayed open, he heard a man's voice, talking to someone else. The doorbell went once more, long and hard, Sally clapped her hands over her ears. Just take only what you can carry and get the hell out! He closed his eyes, willing it to stop, begging it to stop. He felt the heat rising again. If that bastard didn't stop soon, didn't get off that doorbell, right now . . .!

It stopped, the silence shocking. They waited, scarcely breathing. There was a long pause, finally the letter flap snapped shut, they heard footfalls descending the steps. He made them wait, another minute, then crept through to the playroom, crouching at the sill, watching the empty, streetlit road until he was certain they had gone. The Morris stood waiting outside, its chrome hubcaps gleaming against the dark paint of the wheels. He came back into the hall and began gathering up suitcases.

'Right, let's go.'

It was still nearly an hour before they were finally ready. There was far too much luggage to fit in the car, they had to thin out again, discarding all but the absolute essentials. Peter lashed two suitcases to the roof using the mattress from Sally's old cot for cushioning. Emma agreed to sit in the back, with Sally on her knee, that left half the bench seat free for boxes and bags. Jamie went on the front seat, the floor well full around him so that his feet stuck out straight ahead, propped on a box of kitchen utensils. Peter packed and re-packed the boot space until it was stuffed to the roof, jamming last minute items into every available crevice until finally he had to lean on the back doors to prevent everything cascading out again. With a last shove he twisted the handle, locking the doors shut with the key. They were set.

He leaned down to the window. It was cold; a light drizzle drifted past the yellow glare of the streetlights.

'I'll just go in, switch off and lock up.' She nodded. 'Don't be long.'

He walked through the house checking windows, switching off lights, closing doors. He paused only once. In the spare room, looking at the bureau, running his hand around the curved rim of the chair, his chair. He wished he could take it with him, thought back to that first week when he'd carried it upstairs to his 'office'. How he'd sat in it, blithely masterminding his strategy, enjoying an objective analysis of the hiatus. Supremely confident, mindnumbingly naive.

And he'd sat in it when the serious struggle began. When what had started out as a brief, intellectual exercise in logistics planning grew into full-blown conflict and a long drawn-out campaign to restore order from a chaos not of his making. A hard, bitter, dirty, foot-slogging war of nerves that ground him down, tiring him to exhaustion, eroding his will, chipping away at his capacity for reason. And something else. It was changing him, the way he felt and reacted. Subtly altering the landscape of his personality.

He shivered; the house had grown cold. Nor was the war over. He felt a bone chilling weariness at the prospect. No, not over. Just moving. He switched off the spare room light, closing the door softly behind him.

They watched him through the misted windows of the car. He double locked the front door, took two paces back, looking around at the upstairs windows, then turned abruptly on his heel and walked briskly down the steps. We're doing the right thing, he told himself.

'Everybody set?' There was a chorus from around the car. He twisted in the seat to check on Emma, jammed into the corner by a barricade of baggage. Sally on her knee, sucking her thumb, waggling the other fingers in greeting.

Emma smiled, reached out to touch his arm. 'We're doing the right thing.'

'Look, there's the moon!' Jamie pointed. The drizzle had stopped, the thin cloud dissolving into ragged patchwork. The moon gleamed like new platinum, gibbous and glowing.

'It's an omen,' joked Emma from the back.

He snorted. 'Star in the East?'

'What's an omen?' Jamie asked. Peter turned the key in the ignition, nothing happened.

'Oh good grief.'

'What Daddy?'

'I don't believe it.'

'Typical.'

The car was badly overloaded, a deadweight. He and Emma shunted it back and forth at the kerbside, manoeuvering it into the road. Jamie got out and helped, Sally stayed inside, under protest. Eventually they had it lined up.

'Ready?' Peter was sweating already, could feel his heart pounding.

'No! What do I do?'

'You mean you've never done this before?'

'Not in this life.' She leaned anxiously out of the driver's window.

'Clutch in, select second gear, when I yell, let the clutch out and go. Got it?'

'Right.' She sounded uncertain.

By the end of the third attempt the car had reached the end of the road. So had Peter. He staggered round to the front and collapsed over the bonnet, coughing and retching. His ears roared and lights like distant fireworks burst and faded before his eyes.

'Are you all right?'

He rolled onto his back. Along the street, curtains were twitching, he could see the outlines of several spectators silhouetted in their windows. So much for a quiet getaway.

179

Nobody offered to help. 'God I'm in bad shape,' he gasped. 'I can't understand it, the bloody thing doesn't even fire.' They would have to unload it all, return to the house for the night. He groaned at the prospect, swallowed, hauled himself upright, crouched at her window.

'Does this mean we can't go to the cottage?' said Jamie, puffing manfully at his side. Peter was staring at the dashboard, slowly he reached in past Emma, felt for the key, turned it one click.

'No it doesn't,' he said calmly. 'Would you ask your mother to step out of the car for a moment Jamie?' He went round to the front and leaned his hands on the bonnet to push it back up the road. 'Daddy has to kill her now.'

CHAPTER

9

They finally arrived at the cottage just before ten. The drive had been uneventful, but slow. There was little traffic about and by and large their progress was unimpeded, but the Morris, down on its springs and seriously overladen, steadfastly refused to go more than fifty miles an hour on the level and considerably less than that whenever it was presented with an incline.

The last few miles of narrow country lanes and short hills had nearly finished it. The car grew hot and cranky, bottoming on its springs on the uneven roads and protesting noisily through gear changes. Peter had to work hard to keep it moving at all. Hunched forward over the big steering wheel, he coaxed it along gently at thirty miles an hour or less, rarely out of second gear, dabbing cautiously at the hot and fading brakes. At his side Jamie murmured encouragement: 'Come on car, nearly there now, keep going, that's it.'

At last he pulled onto the grass beside the cottage and switched off. They sat in silence, listening to the ticking of the engine as it cooled, the whisper of the breeze through the trees. Emma touched him on the back. 'Well done darling.'

The house was like an ice box, much colder inside than out. After weeks of non-habitation the cold had soaked right through the walls, permeating deep into the foundations. They stood shivering in the kitchen, wreathed in clouds of condensation, the table piled high with boxes, luggage dropped at random around their feet. Emma checked on the bedrooms. 'Bracing,' she said on her return, rubbing her hands briskly on her shoulders.

They still had no coal or firewood so were unable to light the stove or the fire in the front room. The children wanted to sleep in the bunks in their bedroom but Peter was genuinely concerned about the cold and damp. 'Believe me Em the temperature up there is only just above freezing.' So they ended up in the double bed in the main bedroom. All four of them, with socks and jumpers worn over their pyjamas, hot water bottles in the bed and both electric fires going on the floor.

The adults slept badly in the overcrowded bed, Peter dozed at intervals, rising as soon as he could detect the first faint lightness through the curtains. He creaked down the stairs to the bathroom where he stood, shivering as he urinated a steaming jet, scratching lace fingers of frost from the glass of the window with his fingernail. In the kitchen he began boiling water on the electric cooker, darting outside to retrieve another box from the car. He stopped, startled by the stillness, turned and looked out across the fields, past the wood, on down towards the distant stream where they had walked. The entire landscape frosted ghostly white in the half-light, the air solid and unmoving, the silence complete save only for his own breathing and the soft crunch of his footfall on the crystalised grass.

He made tea for them all, weak and sweet for the children, carrying the mugs up to them, sitting on the edge of the bed while they sipped and smiled sleepily.

182

Emma sat up straighter, pulling a cardigan round her shoulders. 'I've been thinking.' He held up his hand like a traffic policeman, put his mug on the floor and withdrew the notepad and pencil from his pocket with a flourish. 'List man!' she sang.

They spent that first day unpacking and running errands. At the Post Office stores Mrs Morrison gave Peter the name of the local coal merchant and sold him two bags to be going on with. When he enquired about firewood she gave him a curious look and said: 'Most folk have their own.' He persisted, she told him to leave it with her. She would arrange for one of the farm labourers to deliver a trailer load for twenty pounds. He thanked her and ticked it off.

Emma produced a long list of groceries to be collected later in the day. On the matter of telephones, Mrs Morrison said that incoming messages for them 'of an urgent nature' could be rung through to her at the Post Office, and they could buy cards from her to use in the payphone outside.

'Will you be staying right through to the New Year, Mrs Deacon, or just over Christmas?' she asked, with the characteristic native soft rising modulation of voice.

Emma glanced at Peter; he was studying Mrs Morrison's unusual range of wines and spirits. Jamie was browsing through a basket of second-hand children's annuals and Sally was standing hopefully at the sweet counter. There was another local couple in there. They were elderly, bundled up against the cold in old-fashioned winter coats, and woollen gloves. He had a cloth cap, she wore a piece of heavy mauve millinery dating from the sixties. Emma had twice offered to let them be served ahead, but they had declined politely, content to wait their turn wandering around the little shop frowning myopically at can labels held out at arm's length.

'No, we'll be staying down for quite a while now, it's er a

183

semi-permanent arrangement.'

'Oh. I see. Semi-permanent, that's nice.' She looked away, busying herself behind the counter.

Peter came over. 'Would you happen to know the name of a good local builder? Also a plumber and possibly an electrician. There are a few things need fixing up at the cottage.'

'Well now, let me have a think.' The momentary embarrassment swiftly passed. 'I tell you what, you leave it with me. I'll look into it.'

'Thank you,' said Peter, scribbling again. 'Though I don't suppose there'll be much chance of getting anyone out until after the holidays.'

'Hmm.' Mrs Morrison tilted her head, scratching absently at her eyebrow with a little finger.

'Also,' Emma lowered her voice, leaning over the counter, this was delicate. 'If you happen to know anyone who could help out, you know, around the house, and things, perhaps one or two mornings a week . . .'

'You leave it with me—' Peter murmured to himself.

Mrs Morrison straightened with a conspiratorial nod. 'You leave it with me. I'll see what I can do.'

'Amazing!' said Peter in the pub afterwards. 'Perhaps if I drop her a copy of my CV she could fix me up with an interview at Lockheed.'

'Don't knock it,' said Emma, sipping ginger wine. 'We may have struck the motherlode with that one.'

During the afternoon Emma and the children unpacked clothes into chests of drawers and wardrobes, Peter cleaned out and lit the kitchen stove and the fires in the front room and their bedroom. At one point Emma came into the sitting room holding a framed picture, he was crouched over the fireplace blowing onto damp kindling.

'What's that?' It was one taken from the dining-room wall

at Fulham, a large, warm watercolour of fishing boats at anchor in the clear cobalt blue waters of a Cycladean harbour. An island bay ringed by white, sunbleached cottages, burnt umber hills rising steeply behind to a shimmering skyline.

'Very seasonal.'

'I thought we could stick it on the wall over the fireplace. Pretend we're on Paros.'

'You've been at those mushrooms growing on the bathroom wall.'

She patted his arm and disappeared upstairs. He fetched his toolbox from the car, but when he tried banging a picture hook into the chimney breast, a large piece of plaster fell off revealing bare brickwork behind. At the same time there was an ominous rumble from further up the chimney and a moment later a bucketful of sooty rubble crashed onto the fireplace, extinguishing the newly raised flames and scattering smutty embers onto the floor.

'What the hell was that?' Emma's voice floated down through the ceiling.

'Er, looks like a little piece of upstairs just came downstairs.' He sighed, swept the wreckage into a pile with his foot and went in search of a shovel.

The 'outbuildings' referred to in the original advertisement for the cottage, consisted of a well-proportioned but structurally untrustworthy wooden garage with dry rot and a leaking corrugated tin roof. It was located adjacent to the house on the other side of the parking area. In the back garden to the rear of the cottage was a small free-standing brick and timber greenhouse in reasonable repair, apart from a few cracked panes.

Leaning up against the back of the garage and running its full width, was the shed. Peter had never looked in it except for a cursory, disparaging glance the first time Emma had shown him round the property. He flicked the catch of the wooden door and went in.

The smell immediately reminded him of home, in Bedfordshire. Standing in the potting shed as a small boy, watching while the gardener tinkered with a lawnmower on the bench. It was a smell of old men, soil and hand-rolled cigarettes, of old fashioned oil cans and shelves of brown cardboard boxes and rusting tins of weedkiller or bonemeal, rooting compound, rat poison. It was a comfortable smell and apart from the cold, the shed had a dry, comfortable feel. And oddly familiar. Stepping in had been like shrugging on a favourite old jacket. It was dry too, in better condition than the garage. He thought it must be a more recent addition, erected with care and attention to detail by someone wishing to spend many hours there.

He stepped inside, trying the heavy black bakelite switch by the door. A single bulb lit up, suspended from the ceiling. The shed was long and narrow, its width restricted by a sturdy workbench running down one side. There were small, square windows set into the length of the long side wall above the bench. At the far end, its tubular flue disappearing up through the low timber roof, a small cast-iron pot-bellied stove stood, squat and black. In front of it an old armchair with a split and faded cover, tufts of horsehair sprouting through a hole in one arm like weeds. It was the strangest sensation. He wanted to light up the little stove and make himself comfortable in the old easy chair, relax, browse through a seed catalogue or something. He would do it, he vowed, this was his.

The shelves and toolracks were empty, but in one corner a collection of old gardening implements leaned up against the wall. He found a spade and after a last look round, switched off the light and went back to the house.

*

'Mitch?'

'Peter! Hello, are you all right? What's going on? Is Emma there?'

'Hello, I guess so, don't ask me ... No she's back at the cottage with the kids.' He hopped from foot to foot in the cold booth, tapping his little stack of green phonecards against the glass. 'Look I'm in a phone box, Mitch, just wanted to let you know we're here, and all right, and beg a favour.'

'Anything.' He didn't sound all right, as though he was carrying the phone box on his back, along with the rest of the world's woes.

'We're going to be down here for a while. If we mail you a set of keys, could you look in on Fulham, keep an eye on the place for us?' I've failed Mitch; I've really cocked up. Don't ask me how it happened but it has. One minute fat and happy, the next, running away like a trespassing schoolboy, hiding in the hills like fugitives.

'Of course. Dan's here, wants a quick word. Peto, take care eh?' Dan came on the line: 'Earth calling Walton mountain, come in please over.'

'Hi Dan.' The voice flat, deflated.

'Do you want to tell me what's going on?'

He sighed. 'The bank's filed a bankruptcy petition; there's an eviction and repossession order out on Fulham; I don't have a job, Emma does, we just thought it would be better to lie low down here for a bit until the heat dies down.'

'We?'

'Well, you know, I had my chance, now we get to do it her way. She sees it as a clean break, turn our backs on the other mess.' You don't have to say it Dan, I know that won't make it disappear. 'Look I'll have to ring off now, got to break it to the Air Vice-Marshall.'

'Ouch. Good luck with that one. Stay in touch, if there's

anything we can do, just fire off a carrier pigeon or something.' They rung off.

'Hello Mum.'

'Hello darling, where are you?'

'We're at the cottage.' He took a deep breath. 'How's Dad?'

'He's resting, had a bad night. Anything the matter?'

He hesitated, the meter on the phone counting down the seconds. 'No, no. We've come down here, for a bit. For Christmas. Get away from it all.'

'That's nice. How's the car?' Talk to me Peter.

'Going like a Trojan. I'll have to go now Mum, time's up. Give you another call, in a few days.'

He walked back down the lane to the cottage, relieved Emma who went to phone her mother. She was nearly an hour.

'Mum's fine. I saw Jack and Alice going into the White Horse, had a quick one with them. They've invited us all over for lunch on Christmas Day.'

'Ah.'

'Ah nothing. We haven't exactly got anything else planned have we? And they're all on their own rattling around in that great big house. It'll be fun. They really want us to come, they told me.'

And what did you tell them? He held up his hands. 'Fine, fine we'll go.'

She turned her back on him to stir the casserole. It had taken all day, but the stove was actually hot, radiating warmth, the kitchen almost comfortable. 'I also spoke to Charlie. Everything's fine. I start on Tuesday.'

'Right-oh.'

They had bought a handsomely marked-up bottle of Rioja from Mrs Morrison. 'She probably can't afford town prices, doesn't have the turnover.' It had spots of mould on the label and tasted musty, he suspected it had been stored out at the back of her shop, through frost and heatwave, for far too long – years probably.

They drank it anyway, sitting in the kitchen mopping the casserole off their plates with wedges of farmhouse bread. Emma was excited, ebullient, her cheeks glowing pink from the stove and the Rioja, her eyes wide and sparkling. She talked quickly, bubbling and chattering like a stream in flood, bowling him along with animated talk of an imminent upswing in their fortunes and the manifold and varied joys of bucolic life.

He watched her rejoicing in her fulfilment, his spirits sinking as hers soared. Forced for the first time to acknowledge the unpalatable realisation that she had been dissatisfied with her former existence, perhaps even despising her life as socialite and hobbyist, hostess and homemaker. Wife and mother. The realisation that while she browsed through shops, or sat in exotic restaurants with her friends, applauded the prima ballerina from the dress circle, or just daydreamed at the warm hands of the masseuse, she yearned for something else. Craving, contriving even, despite the complete suite of material trappings, limitless credit and unrestricted freedom from responsibility, to assume the role of provider and decision maker. Despite? Or because of . . .

'Em. The other business, London. It isn't just going to go away. It has to be faced, dealt with. There'll be letters, court appearances, God knows what.'

'I know that. Mummy's going to get Mr Wallace onto it. He'll take care of all the unpleasantness.'

Wallace, the Fairbright family solicitor. Terrific. 'So Mummy's in the know now is she?' The sneer was unintentional.

Her cheerfulness became impatience. 'Look, you said it has to be dealt with, he's dealing with it. You . . . we need legal representation – you're not exactly talking to your man these days, so what's the problem?' She sat back, hands in the air, cheerfulness resumed. He shook his head, finished the Rioja. She didn't see, it was his problem, not hers, not her mother's and certainly not that weasel-faced vulture Wallace.

She put her hand on his, squeezed. 'Peto, we're safe here, they can't touch us. Don't you see? I feel in control here, and protected, like a fortress. I feel ... impregnable.' She squeezed again, pumped. She felt horny. He looked at her, she was smiling mischievously, eyebrows hopping. 'Not completely impregnable. Fancy your chances airman?' What was it about this place? Weeks, months of tacit mutual indifference and sporadic activity, then a few hours in the country later and suddenly it's clear all decks for action.

She went up ahead while he tidied away the plates. He was ready, God knows it had been long enough, but there was a nag, an uneasiness. He suspected that this concupiscence was just another symptom of her burgeoning independence, her quest for domination, and his emasculation. But he was also suddenly conscious of his own powerful lust, recently so erratic and transitory. He poured himself a large Scotch and drank it slowly, standing by the stove, savouring the warm spirit, flexing his desire. 'Ten to one she gets on top,' he mused.

He never found out.

'What's up?'

'Not much apparently.'

'Well I can see that.' She stroked him encouragingly, sliding her cool flanks against his side, passion killer ready on the floor beside her. He tried to concentrate but felt panic and mild irritation at her coarse ministrations. She was amused, intrigued. 'This is a first.'

He struggled, screwing up his eyes to summon porno-
graphic imagery: a couple doing a floor show in a bar in
Hamburg; a video someone had lent him at work; the
masturbating woman he had stumbled upon as a twelve-
year-old walking on the beach in Devon; Dr Pryce gasping
over the desk in her office. But they were no more than static
depictions, like a series of almost tastefully and cleverly
contrived tableaux, posed by bored professionals. And each
designed to trigger a distraction, an association guaranteed
to sap his ardour. The contemptuousness of the bar perfor-
mers; the laughable production quality of the video; the
woman's sneer; Dr Pryce's reproof.

'Would you like me to, you know?'

God she must be eager. Suddenly he despised her conde-
scension and her wantoness, his rising anger completing the
final attenuation. 'Sorry Em, I guess the special's off
tonight.'

The hand stopped. She paused, her breath warm and
moist on his neck. Then she licked her lips and withdrew.
'No problem.' She reached for the nightie. 'I could have
picked a better time.'

'What do you mean?'

'Well you have been under a certain amount of pressure
lately. Putting it mildly.' She kissed him on the cheek. 'Don't
worry.'

He lay still until her breathing steadied then slipped
downstairs. The kitchen was warm, he pulled a chair next
to the stove, propped another under his feet, drank purposefully.

The next morning at breakfast, Sally made her customary
enquiry and was surprised to learn that although, no it
wasn't Christmas today, it was however Christmas Eve. But
the children's cheer at the news quickly turned to
complaints that there was no Christmas tree and, more

191

importantly, no evidence of presents beneath it. 'I'd better go into Ipswich,' he said quietly across the table. 'But we'll be pushed to find a tree this late.' After breakfast he made a list and stood around awkwardly in his jacket. 'Er, could you let me have some cash?' She produced a roll of notes from her handbag.

'Don't forget something for the Greenaways.'

Ipswich was dreadful. It was a Saturday and the place was packed with last-minute shoppers. There was nowhere to park and the one way system was incomprehensible. Eventually he found space in a car-park some distance from the shopping centre. After nearly an hour spent jostling with impatient and parcel-laden crowds he was about ready to give up. He was dizzy and dazed, stupified by sleeplessness and an excess of alcohol. His ears ringing with the exasperated shouts of the throng, seasonal department store music and the thump and crash of a Salvation Army marching band as it forged a passage back and forth through the multitude of shell-shocked pedestrians.

At one point, head reeling in an atmosphere saturated with atomised perfumes, he found himself staring earnestly into the bloodshot eyes of a heavily made-up sales assistant at the cosmetics counter in Debenhams. He had been queueing endlessly but now that she was ready to serve him, eyebrows raised, upper lip sweaty with pasty foundation, he quite forgot what he wanted. After five seconds of his inaudible stammering, she passed him over for the credit card toting woman behind. He ducked away from the counter and fled for the street.

He found a pub off the main square behind the town hall. It was surprisingly quiet, he bought a large brandy and re-grouped, running an audit of his pitiful list of acquisitions. So far he had managed one blouse and the usual annual supply of Marks and Spencer underwear for Emma.

He ordered a second double and went through the list, revising its contents to better suit a short assault on as few shops as possible. The barman gave him directions for a garden centre on the way out of town where he might be able to pick up a late tree, he jotted them down and thanked him, tossed back the drink and headed back into the fray.

He became aware that he was sitting. It was cold, he was sitting on the pavement, there was noise all about him, confusion, music and shouting. He felt giddy and nauseous and there was a throbbing pain behind his right ear, a trickle of wetness. It was Victoria station, a half scale fist of tightly balled white knuckles had exploded out of the darkness and into his face rocking him back sprawling onto the pavement. But it was light and this wasn't Victoria. A woman's voice, authoritative and persistent in his ear, a burst of radio static, an unintelligible exchange on the UHF. 'Tango Foxtrot check gear down cleared number one to land touch and go.' He shook his head, blinking in the sudden daylight. It was a policewoman, crouched next to him, her face inches from his, a hand under his arm. 'Sir? Sir. Are you all right?'

It was twenty minutes before she let him go, and only then if he promised to get the bump over his ear looked at as soon as possible. She sat him in the back of a parked panda next to a muttering shoplifter, and squatted by the open door, feeding him sips of cold water and quizzing him on his personal details. It was several minutes before he regained his senses, but there remained a disconcerting gap – an interval of about twenty minutes from the time he left the pub to the moment he came to in the street – about which he could recall nothing.

She eyed him doubtfully, unwilling to believe that this good-looking, dark-haired man with exhausted but fiercely compelling eyes was just another fall-down-in-the-street

Christmas drunkard, yet apparently accepting his explanation that he must simply have tripped and knocked himself senseless on the ground. He almost believed it himself except for an uneasy suspicion that the fall and the unconsciousness were in reverse order.

But he kept the suspicion to himself, instead choosing to endure the reproachful looks and cautionary admonishments about excessive alcohol so early in the day. At last he convinced her that he was really quite all right, and no he wasn't driving. 'The parking is impossible.' He was going home on the bus. She loaded him up with armfuls of shopping, little of which he could recall buying, and sent him on his way.

Once sure he was unobserved, he doubled back and made his way wearily to the car-park, stopping several times en route to rest and redistribute the packages about him. Once back at the car he threw the lot into the back and collapsed gratefully into the driver's seat. On the way out of town he remembered the Christmas tree and spent twenty minutes trying to find the garden centre. He got there to find they had sold out but they knew of another place he might pick one up.

It was half past one before he finally arrived home. Wearily he switched off the engine, allowing his head to sink forward onto the steering wheel. This was absurd, he was wrecked, completely shattered. He snorted, his forehead pressed against the rim of the wheel. 'How did you get on darling?' 'Fine, fine, you know, the usual Christmas mayhem – had an attack of amnesia, fell down, woke up in the gutter. Still, got the shopping done all right ...'

'Daddy my daddy! Come quickly to see our Christmas tree that I did some decorating today!' She pulled open the door of the car and began tugging his hand.

He kept his forehead against the wheel. 'Sally,' he said

quietly. 'The Christmas tree is here, tied to the roof of the car, see?'

She looked. 'That's not our Christmas tree silly. That's because ours is inside, with baubles [boar-bells]. Hurry Daddy it's inside, come on, quickly!'

It was in the corner of the sitting room, baubles, lights, tinsel, everything. There were paper chains looped across the beams and along the walls, twists of crêpe paper around the windows, sprigs of holly, even a bunch of mistletoe. A compilation of carols played on the portable compact-disc player.

'Hi how did you get on?' She was standing on a chair, fixing a little plastic fairy to the top of the tree. Sally looked up at her intently, mouth agape. Jamie was lying on the floor fiddling with the graphic equaliser on the hi-fi, *In Dulci Jubilo* emanating first muffled then tinny.

'A tree,' he said quietly.

Emma stepped off the chair. 'Jack and Alice dropped it off, and a huge box full of decorations. Wasn't that thoughtful? They really are very kind.'

'We have a tree. It's on the roof of the car.' His face was expressionless, his voice icy calm.

Emma was confused. 'You, but you said, oh, well never mind, we've got this one now, we can always have two, put the other one in the kitchen, or the children's room.'

Sally was confused as well. 'Two Christmas trees? But that's silly.'

'You don't understand. I have been all over this God-forsaken county to find a tree, our tree. And I found it, now it's outside tied to the roof of the car.'

She was hesitant, he had the same glazed look she'd last seen in Fulham, when the man had come to repossess the television. And there was a bruise, a cut of some sort over his ear. 'Peter, it's really not worth getting steamed up about. What happened to your head?'

He turned and left the room. A moment later she heard the kitchen door slam. She expected to see him walking around the front of the house on his way to the pub or something. Instead, a minute or two later he reappeared at the doorway, embracing the tree awkwardly in front of him. His face was flushed and he was breathing heavily. 'This is our tree. The only tree we shall have in this house.'

They all looked at him. Emma grew exasperated. 'Peter for heaven's sake, this is ridicul—'

'This is our tree!' He strode across the room, tore the other from the bucket and flung it aside, scattering tinsel and broken baubles across the floor. Sally screamed and put her hands to her ears; Jamie cowered against the wall.

Emma put her hands on her hips and glared at him. 'You really are an arsehole these days you know,' she shouted above Sally's sobs.

Jamie was still on the floor, his back against the wall. He could make it stop, he liked Peter's tree better. 'Dad.'

'Get out!' he roared against the thunder in his ears. Get out before I kill someone. Please, quickly, just go.

'But Dad.'

'GET OUT!'

During the afternoon a youth arrived on a tractor pulling a trailer-load of firewood. Peter finished reinstating the Greenaway's tree in its bucket, cleared up the mess on the sitting-room floor then set to, stacking the logs against the wall by the kitchen door. He stood the tree he'd bought in a corner of the shed. A little later they were all in the kitchen, the children eating at the table, Peter standing next to the stove sipping tea.

'Sorry,' he said. 'Everyone. About the tree thing. It was silly.' It was mainly for their sake, the apology – the children.

He waited for her to reciprocate, some condescending acknowledgment of a just grievance.

'Too right it was silly.' No chance, she was still fuming. 'I tell you buster, you'd better just begin dealing with this or—'

'Or what Em?'

There was a discreet tap on the door. Outside it was practically dark. Peter reached for the handle. Not the Greenaways, please not now.

It was the old couple from the shop, the ones they had kept waiting. There was a girl with them, sixteen or seventeen. They stood on the step. The woman was in her Sunday overcoat and hat, hands clasping her handbag in front of her. 'Mrs Clements,' she said, by way of explanation.

'Hello there.' He looked uncertainly from one to the other. The girl looked past him into the kitchen.

'This is my husband Arthur, and my granddaughter Mandy.' Emma appeared behind him, smiled politely, shook hands. 'You wanted someone to carry out some repairs on the house? And a domestic?' The penny dropped. They were ushered in. Extra mugs found, tea poured. Mandy sat at the table next to Sally. 'Daddy did smash up our tree but now it's mended again,' she confided.

'Arthur is retired now, used to run his own building business, didn't you Arthur?'

'How marvellous,' said Peter. 'Perhaps you'd better take a look at our chimney while you're here.'

'What for?' Arthur said, sinking dentures cautiously into a slice of Christmas cake. His wife nudged him. He looked at her, manoeuvering cake to the side of his mouth. 'But the wiff's bugg—, er shot. It was shot ten years ago when I last looked. It won't have got any better will it?'

'Go on!' she mouthed at him furiously. He sighed, put

down his plate, wiped his hands on the back of his coat and limped after Peter. 'Mandy here is training to do secretarial at the Poly but she can help out with a bit of "doing" for you two mornings a week, Tuesday and Thursday, two pounds an hour. And she can babysit if you and Mr Deaking want to go out of an evening, in't that right then girl?'

Peter showed Arthur the rubble in the fireplace. He sniffed and poked at it with the toe of his shoe. 'As I said boy, it's the wiff – shot to buggery.'

'Wiff?'

Mr Clements hawked noisily, spat into the rubble and explained, mostly with his hands, about the single course of bricks running up the inside of the chimney breast, dividing it into two flues.

'So it's not structural then – the chimney isn't going to fall down?'

'Noo boy, nothing like that.'

'And we can use the fireplace in the meantime?'

'Shouldn't be a problem.'

'Good, so, er, no great panic to repair it.'

The old man sucked in noisily through his teeth, lips pursed, head shaking. 'Well boy, you do as you please of course but my advice is get it fixed and quick. You don't want another lot come crashing down here one night while you're upstairs abed with the missus eh?' He winked mischievously.

Peter nodded back. 'I'll bet you're a man who wouldn't say no to a drop of Scotch on Christmas Eve.'

'Thought you'd never ask boy.'

He was walking along a deserted beach. It was long and wide, stretching straight ahead to a single point far ahead on the distant horizon. It was a beach of deep soft sand like light-brown sugar, nearly white against the pale and deep blues of sky and sea. To his left the sand rose gently and smoothly to a ridge. A long way beyond the ridge, the terrain climbed lush and green in a rolling sweep of distant foothills. To his right the waves rolled ashore slowly and hypnotically.

He had been walking for a long while, his steps falling to the steady rhythm of the sea, his toes sinking into the warm sand in time with the bursting waves beside him. He was wearing shorts, and a straw sun hat. Nothing else, his feet were bare and his back and shoulders. He could feel the heat of the sun on them and the backs of his legs. He was relaxed and at ease, he felt no discomfort save a pleasant fatigue from the effort of walking across the soft sand.

On he travelled, his eyes shaded from the sun's reflected glare by the frayed brim of his straw hat. He was unaware of the purpose of his walking yet felt a sense of familiarity and belonging, as though he lived near the beach, perhaps in the fertile lower reaches of the far hills.

After a while he could see a group of dark dots peppering the sand in the distance ahead. Drawing closer, the dots grew into a small gathering of people close to the water's edge, there were ten or twelve of them, dressed formally in dark suits or dresses, arranged in a semicircle around a single figure clad in a long white robe standing shin deep in the water. Soon he could hear voices above the gentle rumble of surf, the lone voice of the white-robed figure, deep and stentorian, followed at intervals by the respectful, murmured response of the others. The tongue was unfamiliar but the solemn tone and pattern of the voices told him he was intruding upon ceremony. Conscious suddenly of the impropriety of his dress, he stopped and joined the back of the group, stooping ludicrously close behind the bent back of an old woman, so near that he could see individual threads on her black wool coat, aroused by a distantly familiar damp muskiness of her grey hair beneath the smoke-coloured veil covering her head.

He began to recognise faces among the gathering. His mother in dark overcoat and hat, black gloved hands clutching a patent leather handbag to her midriff. Dan, an arm around his wife's shoulder, their expressions mute, pensive. Mitch glanced at him, her eyes showing disapprobation at his appearance, but no recognition. Mr and Mrs Clements were there, dressed exactly as they had been in Mrs Morrison's shop. Their granddaughter was with them, she wore a short, emerald green dress and a wide brimmed hat. She caught his stare, suppressed a smile, winking at him quickly before averting her eyes again.

The tall white clad figure was holding a child's bucket in the crook of his arm. After several more exchanges with the congregation he paused, then lifted his face to the sky. He was young, tall and very thin with dark hair and eyes. Something about his eyes was familiar, and he wore about him a vulnerability, a protectiveness as though bruised from past injury. After a long silence broken only by the soporific lapping of the surf, he lowered his face and looked at them all. Peter felt the eyes upon him even though his were averted and he was still cowering behind the old woman. Then the figure made the sign of the cross to the congregation with the edge of his hand, turned to face the sea and began taking handfuls of sand from the bucket, scattering them on the surface of the water like seed.

The back of the old woman in front began to move away; he followed it, crouching awkwardly. He saw his arm reach out, the skin deeply tanned, the short hairs baked blond and dusted with sand grains. He touched the old woman's shoulder, she turned and glowered at him, the lips compressed, brown eyes frowning.

'You might have had the common decency to stay away

today,' said Emma, her voice like ice.

The arcs of sand fell on the smooth water like fine rain. Beyond the breakers the sea stretched smoothly to the horizon, unbroken in all directions save for the distant outline of a single sailing ship. He watched as it stood away from the shore, its hull gleaming in the sunlight as it rose and dipped in the swell, tall masts heeling as snow-white sails appeared, snapped taut and full in the breeze, driving it steadily out to sea.

'We are glad you could come. Christmas just isn't the same without children.' Alice took them by the hand and led them into the house.

'It's so kind of you Alice,' said Emma. 'And thank you again for the tree and all the decorations. It was terribly thoughtful, wasn't it Peter?'

'Absolutely. Impossible to imagine what we would have done without it.' He pecked Alice on the cheek, shook Jack's hand and followed them into the sitting room.

'Daddy smashed our tree up,' said Sally to Alice, 'but then he mended it again.' Jamie freed his hand from Alice's and scowled at Sally.

'Don't say that stupid!' he hissed.

'Now then, I want you two to have a look at our tree over here by the piano. I've got a feeling there might be one or two parcels under it.'

They sat down in front of the fire, the children at the far end of the room unwrapping furiously. 'They're thoroughly over-excited I'm afraid,' said Emma.

'Early start to the festivities this morning?' Alice smiled at Peter.

He rolled his eyes at her. 'About five, I think.' He'd been awake anyway, dozing restlessly after the dream. Before he knew it Sally came running in clutching a handful of sweets

201

in one hand, brandishing the still bulging stocking in the other. 'Daddy, Mummy – he came, he came!' Emma groaned and rolled over, he turned on the light and sat up with Sally, watching sleepily as she rifled the contents of the stocking he'd filled seemingly minutes earlier. Jamie appeared around six. Peter went down, made tea and brought it up to the bedroom.

Emma wanted to go to church. There was a brief discussion at the breakfast table.

'Why for heaven's sake?' he repeated. 'Why go and sit on a hard bench in a draughty old building paying cash to some feudal institution and homage to a God you don't believe in?'

'For the sake of tradition, and the children.'

'But what are the children to think the other three hundred and sixty-four days of the year? It's the ultimate hypocrisy.'

'I believe in God,' said Jamie quietly.

'So do I, he made baby Jesus and Father Christmas.' Emma raised her palms and tilted her head to one side. Discussion over.

The church was small, the pews full. They found one near the back and slid onto the pine, Peter against the wall. Emma next to the aisle, the children between them. It was a family communion service, Emma knelt and stood and sat where appropriate, singing lustily and chanting responses confidently like a well-rehearsed actor. Peter sat mostly, leaning against the wall which deposited white powder on the shoulder of his jacket. Sally fidgeted, swinging her legs and talking during the sermon. Eventually she clambered onto his knee and watched the proceedings dispassionately, sucking her thumb noisily and winding his tie round her fingers. Jamie watched Emma, following her actions and copying her murmured responses.

Towards the end, the vicar, a smiling young man with sandy hair and a powerful singing voice, invited all the children to the altar step to look at the crib. Sally leapt off Peter's knee like a cat and set off for the front at the trot. Jamie looked momentarily panicked but followed with the others. Emma glanced at Peter, they shrugged, craning their necks and swaying sideways to see past rows of similarly bemused parents.

'Now, do you all know "Away in a Manger"?' The vicar began arranging the twenty or so children in a line on the step facing the congregation. Sally quickly broke ranks, choosing instead to remain on one side next to the crib. She hunched over it, her head practically inside the open-fronted model stable, peering minutely at the clay figures, sniffing suspiciously at the tiny baby doll on its straw bed. The organist struck up the opening bars of the carol; the vicar moved to the centre. Jamie was in the middle of the line next to a little girl with a hearing aid and a fat boy in a Dennis the Menace jumper. He looked pale and anxious but determined. Peter found himself rising slowly to his feet to see. At the other end of the pew, Emma leaned far out into the aisle.

The children were to sing the first verse alone. They began slowly, hesitantly, grinning self-consciously at their families. The vicar joined in quietly, then a small voice was heard rising above the others. It was Jamie. He knew all the words, and the tune, his voice was thin and reedy but carried pure and clear over the heads of the assembly. The vicar standing right behind him rested a hand on his shoulder. Gradually the other children joined in, then their singing was swallowed by the congregation with the remaining verses.

As the last chords died away, the vicar closed his eyes and reached forward over Jamie's head to deliver the final blessing. Peter swallowed, staring spellbound as his son tilted his head up, his dark eyes watching as the hand slid slowly through the air above him, oblivious to his own as it followed through with the sign of the cross as though suspended by an invisible thread.

Eventually Alice offered them a drink. Peter had quietly tossed off a large one when they had returned from church and another just before leaving the cottage, comforting himself with the prospect of an afternoon anaesthetised from everyone by whiskey, fine wines, port and brandy. But since arriving at the Old Rectory there had been no sign of alcohol at all and he was beginning to suffer the cold and unwelcome effects of withdrawal. He sat straightbacked in an armchair, listening inattentively as Emma's animated prattle drowned out a recording of carols from King's College, Cambridge playing quietly on the hi-fi. He tried to catch her eye on a couple of occasions but eventually gave up, staring instead dejectedly into the flames of the fire.

'—A glass of wine? Yes that would be lovely thank you.' He started, Emma had finally got through.

Alice smiled at him. 'And I should think you're ready for one too. We're not great drinkers here I'm afraid. Perhaps you would accompany me to the kitchen and give me a hand with glasses.' She held his gaze, the warning clear. He followed her into the kitchen, watched as she bent to the Aga, prodded the turkey, put on the vegetables. 'There's a bottle of white wine in the fridge, please help yourself. Corkscrew in the drawer next to it, somewhere.' She turned back to the cooker. 'So how are you Peter?'

The inquisition again. He rummaged through the drawer, eventually found a corkscrew. 'Oh, fine, thank you. Well enough I suppose. You know.' Why was he babbling?

She straightened, turned and faced him again, leaning back against the rail of the Aga. She was dressed in black trousers, a cream silk blouse and a little dark blue quilted silk bolero, her hair was back, she looked gorgeous, barely forty. 'Yes I think I do.'

He stopped in mid screw, exhaled slowly. No you don't you smug bitch. 'You don't know anything about me. Nothing at all.'

She cocked an eyebrow at him. 'Is that right? Well let me see now, you drink, a lot; you sleep very poorly if at all; you suffer uncontrollable mood swings, hysterical laughter, then towering rages or dark depressions. What else? You are fearful of the future, feel you are losing control over your own life; you are bitter and resentful of Emma for trying to cope. Am I close?'

His mind whirled, had he spoken? Surely not. Jack. 'Jack?'

She nodded. 'You see I've seen it all before Peter. Jack had his breakdown three years ago.'

He scoffed. 'Who said anything about a breakdown?'

She shrugged.

'Alice.' He was still holding the bottle. 'Why are you telling me this?'

'You have to break out of it Peter. You have to!' She spoke passionately, through gritted teeth, clenched fists banging against her thighs. 'It's a dreadful, vicious spiral. And it gets worse, much much worse than you could ever imagine.'

'Really?' he was entranced, vaguely amused by the strength of her emotion.

'Yes really.' She stared at him then sighed. 'You don't believe me do you? Well have it your way then.' Her voice grew calm. She began counting on her fingers 'You find it hard to concentrate, you have no patience, you hear strange noises, you dream, sometimes you are awake when you dream – that's called hallucinating Peter.' He held her gaze, the fixed smile slipping from his face. He felt his head go cold. 'You behave irrationally, are forgetful, confused. Pretty soon you start to have little blackouts, losses of memory, and that's when it gets dangerous.'

'Dangerous?'

'Of course, you're not in command of your faculties. You are capable of becoming a danger to yourself, and others, usually those in closest contact to you.'

'You mean I might hurt somebody, I hardly think—' He stopped, she had pulled the front of her blouse out and was tugging the waistband of her trousers down with her thumbs. For a moment he thought she was going to undress, he saw the pale, smooth flatness of skin below her navel, the black elasticated top of her underwear, a trace of fine hair. Then he saw the scar. It had faded but was clearly visible. About an inch long, pink and raised with tiny stitch marks on either side.

'I've never shown this, nor spoken of it to anyone except the doctors, and Jack. It was a kitchen knife, not deep but deep enough. He remembers absolutely nothing about it Peter, nothing at all.'

CHAPTER
10

'**H**ello Miriam? Peter Deacon.' He stamped his feet, hugging his chest with his free hand. His breath misted the plastic of the handset.

'Hello, Peter. How are you? Still at the country residence I take it?'

'Fine. Look I'll be basing myself down here for a while longer. Only snag is we still have a problem with the phone so I'll have to keep calling you to check in, say once a week. Stay on the case; I'm still in the game, and if you need me urgently you can leave a message on the following number – it's the local post office, okay?'

'Of course. Nothing moving at all at the moment I'm afraid but we are still working on it.' From her tone he doubted it.

He hung up and went back into the shop to thaw out and buy more phone cards. Sally was sitting on the counter eating a biscuit and looking at a comic.

'You'll be glad to be getting your own telephone connected I should think,' said Mrs Morrison, glancing curiously at his skiing boots.

'Three weeks they promised.' He stood in front of her gas

207

heater rubbing his hands briskly. He was wearing tracksuit trousers over his jeans, two sweaters, his overcoat, scarf and woollen ski hat. But the skin of his cheeks visible above the two weeks growth of beard was pale with cold.

'Right then, here we go. Is she being a nuisance?'

'No Daddy!' Mrs Morrison patted her head. Sally smiled up at her angelically, helping herself to another biscuit. He left the comparative warmth of the shop and crunched out onto the green. Everything was frozen. The grass of the green, the roofs of houses around it, the bare limbs of deciduous trees, and the foliage of the evergreens thickly coated on all surfaces as though sprayed with adhesive and dipped in icing sugar. Even the slash of normally jet-black tarmac bisecting the green was dusted white with powdered ice, motorists creeping through the village in slow motion, their cars trailing clouds of freezing exhaust vapour.

Dialling again, he wondered about the Morris and whether it had made it to the comparative safety of the salted main roads. He'd offered to drive Emma to work but she'd scoffed at the suggestion. He considered phoning her at the office to check, decided against it: 'Hello dear just calling to make sure you were there . . .'

'Mr Wallace please.'

'Hello, Peter isn't it? We have met I believe.'

Pleasantries over, they discussed formalities. Or Wallace discussed, Peter listened, pulling his hat down over one ear and shifting his weight from foot to foot. The man spoke confidently and without deference, his tone brisk and impersonal.

'You'll have to let me have copies of all correspondence between you and your bank, details of all financial agreements, hire purchase, mortgage arrangements, bank statements and so on. Also a complete summary of all and any assets, likely inherited benefits, covenants, trusts etcetera.

Also pertinent background financial information relating to your parents, grandparents and other next of kin.'

Peter stopped shuffling and broke in. 'But why?'

'I'm sorry. Why, did you say?'

'Yes, why do you need personal financial information about my parents?'

'Peter, the plaintiff may seek to prove that you had, or still have for that matter, the resources to settle your debts. At least in part.'

'Well I don't.'

'That's hardly the point. For all they know, you might have transferred assets to your family to avoid sequestration. Believe me there are innumerable precedents, people hiding paintings or furniture or simply cash with their relatives.'

'Well I haven't done it and I don't want my parents brought into this, is that absolutely clear?'

'I'm afraid it is not that simple, my instructions—'

'Yes I've been wondering when we'd be getting round to those.'

From behind her counter, Mrs Morrison could see him through the window of the shop. One minute he was stooped forward in the little glass cubicle as though examining those extraordinary spaceman's boots of his, the next he jerked his head back suddenly, spinning round to face the other way and chopping his gloved hand through the air like an imaginary axe. She could make out the agitated tone of his voice when he raised it too, although she couldn't actually hear what he was saying. But then she didn't need to and anyway it was none of her business. She patted the little girl on the head and went on sorting the mail.

The phone rang twice then his father picked it up.

'Hello Dad, Peter.'

'P.J. How are things in the frozen wastes?'

'Not so bad. Well a bit of a mess actually. There are a couple of matters I have to brief you on ...' He closed his eyes and drew a deep breath.

'Hold on, your mother's here, she wants to speak to you.'

'Dad ... Dad? Damn!' His mother came on the line.

'Hi Mum. Why does he always do that?'

He walked back down the lane to the cottage with Sally. They held hands and took small steps on the icy road. Back in the cottage he put the kettle on the stove and went to check on Mr Clements. He was in their bedroom. In fact he was sitting on the end of their bed hand-rolling a cigarette.

'All right boy?' he said casually. Peter stopped in the doorway and gaped. The room looked as if it had been bombed. There was a two-and-a-half-foot wide gash in the chimney breast from fireplace to ceiling. The old man had torn the plaster off the wall then chiselled or levered out the brickwork with an iron bar, tossing the bricks into a heap on the floor. Those that broke and smaller pieces of rubble he threw onto a separate pile, both heaps had grown, amalgamated and spread right across the floor.

Every flat surface was coated with brick dust and soot. As he walked slowly into the room, Peter's boots left huge, sharply edged imprints in the thick smut like an astronaut's footprints in the lunar crust. Dense, acrid particles hung in the air like smog, the smell reminded him of a London Underground station.

He began to speak, coughed. 'Um, so how's it going?'

The old man flicked cigarette ash onto the rubble pile and sucked air through his teeth as though filtering it. Bright sunlight streamed into the room behind him, highlighting the brick dust settling on his shoulders and trapped in his wispy hair, throwing his shadow, solid and spectral, into the room. 'Well not so bad now the wiff's out, some dozy bugger never tied it in see, when they built the place, so I 'ad to strip

210

out the whole course before the bloody lot come crashing down and so now we're about ready to get right in there and 'ave a bloody good sort out.'

'I see.' He had absolutely no idea what he was on about. 'Can I help?'

'Dunno boy, can you?'

Peter humped fresh bricks up to the bedroom from Mr Clements' van. He also carried up a square of hardboard from the garage and watched in horror as the old man mixed up mortar on it in the middle of the bedroom floor. Then with the two of them balanced precariously on a plank supported by two easels they began rebuilding the inside of the chimney. Peter kept him supplied with fresh mortar and bricks, watching entranced as Clements cut them precisely to fit with sharp taps of his trowel, then with deft flicks of it, lobbed dollops of mortar into impossibly inaccessible crevices. At one point Sally appeared and clambered over the rubble to peer suspiciously up into the gaping maw of the chimney. 'What have you two done to my mummy's bedroom?' Peter checked the time and took her down to the kitchen for lunch. Clements declined sustenance, he'd eaten his sandwiches at half past nine, sitting in his van with a thermos flask and newspaper.

By mid afternoon the new wiff was in place and the chimney bricked up. There was still a large amount of rubble on the floor.

'What about that lot?' said Peter, wiping grime off his forehead with his sleeve.

Clements spat onto the pile, 'Well the missus won't be wanting it in her bedroom. I daresay it had better go outside for subsequent disposal.' Peter groaned at the prospect, but Clements was giving him a curious look, winking and nodding towards the bed. Peter thought he was about to make another of his lecherous jokes, but it wasn't the bed, it was the window. While Clements applied fresh plaster to the chimney breast, Peter pushed the bed aside and began depositing rubble out of the window.

Soon Emma arrived home, he called down to her, heard her on the stairs, Sally leading. 'You're not going to like this one little bit my mummy.'

'Well Arthur that is wonderful!' cried Emma. She stood in the middle of the bedroom beaming at the old man, Sally looking around suspiciously for the now absent mountains of rubble. The chimney breast had been completely bricked up again and freshly plastered.

Clements lit the ever present roll-up. 'Soon as the plaster's gone off you can paint it again. Don't light the fire until the cement's had a chance to harden – say three or four days. You'll have to find other ways to keep the chill off till then.' He cackled. Sally was looking under the bed. 'There's still a bit of dusting – get young Mandy to go over the place for you tomorrow.'

'It's marvellous. How can we ever thank you?'

He stood almost to attention, hands at his sides, head inclined towards Emma. 'Prompt settlement of my account would be greatly appreciated. I'll drop you a note in the morning.'

'Of course.'

He stood easy again. 'In the meantime I wouldn't say no to a drop of the hard stuff – just to ward off the chill you know.'

Sally emerged from under the bed. 'But Daddy where's all the mess gone to?'

Peter and Clements exchanged glances. 'We took it outside darling, left it in a pile by the front gate.'

He lit the stove in the shed then left it to warm up while he cooked sausages for the children and fixed a drink for Emma.

She thanked him with a kiss, sitting at the table flicking through a design magazine while he waited on the children.

By the time he had cleared up, the shed was warm and comfortable, he threw a couple more logs into the stove, sat down in the armchair and opened his briefcase.

In the two weeks since Christmas he had continued to follow up his old job applications as well as applying for new ones. He kept his applications file up to date, meticulously dating and annotating each contact, weeding out those that appeared dead, writing follow up letters, maintaining contacts.

He had made one trip to London, setting off by himself in the Morris early one Saturday morning to collect their mail and pick up another load of clothes and belongings. He had arrived in Fulham mid morning and spent ten ludicrous minutes driving around and past the house peering about for signs that the place was being watched. Eventually he parked and ran up the steps to the front door.

It was almost a surprise to find the house exactly as they had left it. He stood in the cold hall surveying the mess: half-filled cardboard boxes, dustbin liners and the discarded bags he'd pulled out of the overloaded Morris just before leaving. His mind went back to those last frantic minutes, the shouting and running up and down stairs with arms laden, the frozen terror of the ringing on the doorbell. The television man.

There was a large crop of post heaped up against the door, he picked it up, sorting carefully through the envelopes. Those that displayed recognisable company logos or franks, or postmarks that he could positively cross-reference to his applications file, he tore open. There was one from an airline saying the marketing director was abroad and would respond upon his return, the rest were merely acknowledgments of his follow up letters. Apart from Christmas cards and junk mail, the remaining post: demands, formal notifications, solicitors' letters – he was not sure but he could guess – he left unopened in a heap on the hall table.

He shivered, gave in to a strong urge to finish and leave as quickly as possible. Doubling up the stairs he went straight to the spare room, sniffing at the faint mustiness. He tried the telephone but it had been cut off. The message light on the answering machine was flashing, he hesitated then pulled the plug on it, dropping the machine into a box along with the telephone. He packed up the word processor and carried it down to the hall on the Windsor chair.

Checking off each item as he went, he moved quickly from room to room. Some office clothes for Emma, school things for Jamie, Sally's Hickory Dickory Dock nightlight. He had some difficulty disconnecting the washing machine and dragging it out onto the street. But once there he begged assistance from a passing youth and together they man-handled it onto the Greenaway's borrowed roofrack.

Within forty-five minutes he had loaded up the Morris and was ready to go. Closing the front door, he paused then unlocked it again, snatched up the unopened and junk mail from the hall table, slammed the door and pushed the fat bundle back through the letter flap. He backed slowly down the steps, mentally checking that there was no other evidence of his visit, yet unsure why, if at all, it was necessary to cover his tracks. By mid afternoon he was unloading at the cottage.

He flicked open the door of the stove with his foot and poked at the burning wood with a stick. The word processor now sat on the bench along with his reference books and files, London telephone directories and ordered piles of trade journals. The legs of the Windsor chair were chocked on bricks so that he could sit at the long bench to work at his papers.

214

He'd begun to keep a diary, or at least a notebook of dated observations and impressions. He felt absurdly self-conscious about it, keeping its existence completely secret and denying himself all but the most rudimentary freedom of expression. In the privacy of the shed he jotted surreptitious and abbreviated notations, their style and content more like entries in a businessman's appointments diary than the ruminations of a troubled spirit. It had been Alice's idea, that and going on the wagon. The one would be good therapy and keep his mind off the other, at least so she said. He badly missed the drink, its absence made him jittery and denied him even more sleep than before, but he'd glibly promised her he'd try. 'It's really not a problem Alice, I can stop any time.' And something about the urgency of her plea had shocked him. He often sat in the armchair in the shed or lay awake at night recalling her powerful and passionate entreaty, and the starkly, shockingly erotic images: the desperate tugging at her clothing, the worm-like scar on the milky skin of her bared abdomen.

Much to their surprise, a place for Jamie had been found at the local primary school without difficulty, despite the short notice. The school was much smaller than he was used to, had fewer facilities, 'but there's no computer!' and he didn't know any of the staff or children. The first few days had been tricky, with increasing signs of a renewed outbreak of the old conflict. On the third day Jamie sat sullenly in the back of the car throughout the two mile drive and refused to move when Peter opened the door for him.

Just as an ugly scene seemed unavoidable, his smiling form teacher appeared at the car door as if by magic. 'Come on Jamie,' she said briskly, taking his hand. 'We've got to finish that picture you were doing yesterday. Did you know that most of the boys and girls of your age round here come to school on the bus? I expect if you promise to be very grown up about it, you might be allowed to do the same. Shall we ask Daddy?'

His streetwise city-bred mind was appalled at the notion, even Emma had doubts. But it turned out to be absurdly simple and Jamie responded well to the small measure of extra responsibility and freedom. In the mornings after breakfast, Peter walked with him down the lane to the Post Office where at eight thirty the bus picked him up, returning to deposit him at the same spot seven hours later.

Emma had started work at Charlie Gladstone's. Most mornings she took the car, which left Peter without transportation, but until their financial situation improved it was an inconvenience he could put up with. She made a token effort not to appear too pleased with herself at the end of each day, but her delight in work was unsuppressable.

'Oh Peto,' she exclaimed one evening as they were hurriedly bathing the children, 'the staff are a hoot and there are some fascinating accounts. I thought I was going to be working alongside a load of hayseeds designing fertiliser bags, but it's not like that at all.'

He lifted Sally out of the warm water into the cold, bundled her up in a large towel and propelled her, shuffling like a geisha, into the kitchen to dry off by the stove. Jamie sank down into the water so that only his head was exposed to the cold. Emma, still wearing her coat, sat on the lavatory holding a gin and tonic. The smell of it was a major distraction, the clink of ice on glass mesmeric. 'Well that's good, a little bit of Mayfair-by-the Moor. So what are you working on?'

The complete lack of sexual contact between them was worrisome. He had designed a coded lettering system to encrypt any activity in his diary, but as yet there had been no occasion to use it. A warlock's brew of dark and powerful desires fermented in his subconscious, but although they surfaced frequently, their appearances were promiscuous and short-lived, a few seconds at most. He had decided not to worry about it, Emma appeared disinterested, or at least unconcerned – returning to full-time work exhausted her, most evenings she went to bed early and dropped quickly into deep sleep. Peter had begun rising early again, even on weekends, so opportunities for congress were minimised. Most of all he feared a repeat of the previous ludicrousness.

'Two book jackets.' She pulled a face. 'I know, but!' She held up a finger. 'We're also pitching for a big corporate commission, whole new company image for a high street retailer: shopfronts, logos, stationery, letterheads, point of sale, the lot.'

'Fantastic.' He pulled the plug on Jamie who grimaced and slid out of the water like a thin white seal, accepted the proffered towel and scampered into the warmth of the kitchen.

Peter jotted in the diary, referencing the morning's telephone contacts and noting that he and Arthur Clements had made a good start on the demolition of the cottage '... Should have it all down in a couple of weeks ...' Then he shut the notebook and closed his eyes, leaning his head back against the frayed cover of the armchair. Is this it? he wondered. Househusband, or homemaker as the Americans tactfully put it. Thirty-five years old, over-privileged product of an elite education, trained by the Government and at considerable expense to the taxpayer to operate the world's most sophisticated combat machinery moving at the speed of a rifle bullet, ten years spent developing a powerful business potential of global proportions and unfettered by barriers cultural, political or lingual. At the very peak of his intellectual acuity and how does the man pass his day? He makes tea for his kids and lives in a shed.

*

The next day he rose at first light, struggled blearily into trainers and tracksuit and stepped into the cold. Turning right into the lane he checked the time on his wristwatch and set off at a slow jog. It was overcast and damp, the surface of the lane shining greasily in the half-light. On walks he had discovered a circuit of tracks and paths that took him in a wide circle ending up at the stile across the lane from the cottage. He estimated it was about four miles. The lane led to a farmyard where it petered out and became a muddy track. From there he skirted fields of low winter corn, passed some derelict farm cottages and followed a narrow twisting path through a dank wood.

By the time he reached the wood, and despite the gentle pace, his breath became laboured. Soon he found himself gasping, open mouthed like a beached fish as he choked the moist air into tortured lungs. He stopped, lowering his head and propping his hands on his knees, coughing and swallowing, as bright flashes and swirls of colour danced before his eyes. His head reeled and there was a familiar thunder in his ears. A hot, sharp pain pierced his ribs and his legs shook like rubber, wobbling warningly. He sat down heavily on a fallen tree trunk until the turmoil eased.

'Fastest middle-distance runner in the squadron,' he panted. Three feet away a rabbit emerged from a thicket, studied him for a moment then hopped away along the path into the wood. He hauled himself to his feet and jogged heavily after it. 'You're going to have to get in shape boy.'

In all it was nearly three quarters of an hour before he arrived back, flopped over the stile and staggered across the lane to the cottage. Sweating and mud spattered, he half sat, half lay on the step outside the kitchen door, eventually peeling off his tracksuit and lurching inside to bathe. Jamie was at the kitchen table building with Lego. 'Hi Dad,' he said absently, 'been running again I see.'

Fifteen minutes later he had bathed and laid for breakfast. He called up to Emma who clattered downstairs, muttering and cursing about being late. Her skirt was misaligned, blouse undone to the waist.

'I can see your boobies Mummy!'

'No you can't Sal, I'm wearing a bra.'

'Don't let Clements see you like that, give the poor old boy heart failure.'

'God he's a lecherous sod, did you see the way he was gaping at me yesterday? He must be in his eighties for God's sake.'

'Don't knock it, must be something uplifting in the air down here.' He winced but she said nothing.

It was Sally's first day at a nearby pre-school. She fretted and fussed over her wardrobe and what toys to take with her; it was the nearest Peter had ever seen to her showing nervousness. They all piled into the Morris, and shouted encouragement to it as he cranked the starter. It had become crotchety recently, reluctant to start and rough running. Within seconds the badly depleted battery gave up trying to turn over the engine.

'Jamie, starting handle, go!' Jamie leapt out and ran round to the back of the car to retrieve the starting handle. Hissing curses through clenched teeth Emma hitched up her skirt and threw her right leg over to the driver's side, sliding halfway across so that her foot reached the throttle. Peter paced about out front, licking his lips and spitting on his hands, eyeing the car as if he was about to wrestle with it, try and lift it off the ground. Jamie inserted the handle into the slot.

'Can I have a go this time Dad? You did say.'

'Jamie, it's a real bast ... very difficult. And it might kick and hurt you.'

'But you said ...'

219

'I know, and I will give you a proper lesson, but not today, we're late.' Jamie's head sank. 'Anyway, I need you to stand next to the window and make sure Mummy does it right.' Jamie went, slowly. 'Ready?' he called.

'Ready!'

'Switches off?'

'Turn the switches off Mum!'

'I know I know. Yes, switches off!'

'Gears in neutral?'

'What? Oh yes, yes. Come on for God's sake.'

'Right then, here we go.' He took hold of the handle with both hands and swung, slowly at first then faster. 'Now!' She turned on the ignition, the engine sprang to life. She kept her foot on the throttle until he was back aboard.

'You did say you'd take a look at the blasted car about a week ago,' she said testily.

'I know. I'll try and get to it today.'

Jamie jumped out at the Post Office, then they drove on to drop Sally.

'Don't be long,' hissed Emma as he took Sally's hand at the car door. 'I'm bloody late.'

'Don't say bloody, Mummy!' He spoke briefly to the head teacher of the kindergarten then bent to peck Sally on the nose. She walked boldly into the room of noisily playing children without looking back.

'How was she?' Emma applied make-up as he drove.

'Sally? Oh, unconcerned as usual. Busy place too.'

'Nothing phases that girl; it's incredible.'

'I'm not altogether sure that it's an entirely healthy outlook,' he mused, turning the Morris onto the main road. 'It's an indictment on the times, but little girls should grow up to be mistrustful of strangers.' Emma grunted, peering into a compact mirror as she rolled pale gloss between her lips.

He dropped her outside the converted schoolhouse that headquartered Charlie Gladstone's company, then drove straight back towards Bedingham. About a mile outside the village he turned off the road and bounced along a rutted track into dense and pungently smelling pine forest until he came to a clearing. Surrounding the clearing were tall piles of neatly stacked pine logs, roughly cut to four-foot lengths. He opened the back doors of the Morris and loaded in as many as he could safely fit before tying the doors half shut again with rope.

It was the landlord of the White Horse who had told him, crooking his finger and leaning confidentially across the bar when Peter had enquired about cheaper sources of firewood. It turned out that the forestry commission had just left the timber: 'More or less for folk to help themselves to,' the landlord murmured, his eyes swivelling around the bar. 'They got more of the stuff lying around than they know what to do with since the great gales.' The farm labourers took it by the trailer load, chopped it into smaller pieces and sold it to the unsuspecting.

He drove on to the village, picked up a box of groceries from Mrs Morrison, checked for messages and returned to the cottage.

Mandy was there, sitting at the table drinking tea. 'Morning Mr Deacon. Cuppa?' She fluttered heavily mascaraed eyes at him, grinned mischievously and helped herself to another digestive.

'Morning Mandy.' She was a competent cleaner, but only when under supervision. 'No thanks. I think we'll go straight upstairs to the bedroom.' He smacked his palm to his forehead and rolled his eyes but she went ahead and milked the line anyway.

'Ooh, Mr Deacon, you are wicked.'

Not me Mandy Clements, he mused, you and your wicked

grandfather. They started in the main bedroom, Peter pulled the furniture out from the walls, she began dusting, polishing and vacuuming, swinging her hips and bending over provocatively any time she thought he might be watching. He stripped the bed completely and carried the bedding downstairs. He had plumbed the washing machine in at the kitchen and rigged up a rope and pulley drying line that ran from the window out to a post in the back garden.

'What the hell's that for?' Emma had joked. 'Signalling the fleet?'

'My grandmother had one,' he replied proudly. 'Simplest piece of ingenuity since the invention of the wheel.'

'And so quick,' she quipped, in a soap powder advertisement voice. Outside steady rain ran down the window. 'Only three weeks to dry one pair of socks.'

Chopping onions, carrots and floured stewing steak into a pot he added water, seasoning, a pinch of dried herbs and a stock cube, placing it on the simmering plate on the stove. Next he emptied ash from both stoves, re-laid and lit the one in the shed and re-stocked the wood and coal supply for the kitchen stove.

Next he backed the Morris up to the garage to unload the timber. Gingerly pulling one of the garage doors open, he jumped back as it dropped off the door post and crashed to the ground at his feet. He ignored it, stacking the logs along the side walls of the garage to dry out. He sawed up two or three for the kitchen stove and after a quick inspection of the garage door, took an axe to it.

The clattering down the shaft of the screwdriver was clear enough. He slid it along the outside of the rocker cover and bent over the Morris's roughly idling engine, pressing the plastic handle into his ear again. The last one sounded better. But the tappets on the middle two rockers were badly out of adjustment and probably at the root of the rough running problem. He sighed and gazed down at the grumbling engine which, as if to reinforce the point, wheezed asthmatically, misfired, shuddered and stopped.

Mandy appeared close by his side. 'Brought you a nice cuppa.' He thanked her and took it. Resting her hand on his shoulder, she leaned over and peered into the engine bay. 'I don't know how you men get to understand any of this mechanics stuff; it's quite beyond me.' She faked a shiver, wrinkled her nose distastefully and minced back to the kitchen door. 'I'll be off home in a minute then,' she called.

He didn't have a set of feeler gauges, nor a workshop manual on the car, but by using strips of aluminium cut from a Coke can, folded and beaten flat with a hammer, he made a feeler to fit the good tappets and adjusted the others to its thickness. The improvement to the engine running was immediate. Encouraged by his success he cleaned and replaced the spark plugs and reset the mixture adjustment nut on the carburettor.

He was thirsty. Licking his lips he checked his watch. There was still time for a quick orange juice at the pub before closing time. God how he longed for a beer. He was tempted, as a reward for good behaviour and high productivity. As if on cue Alice's silver Range Rover appeared in the lane and drew up on the grass by the cottage. His heart skipped a beat.

'Hi handsome! What's that all over your face?'

He looked down at his filthy hands. 'Oil probably – the joys of motoring y'know.'

'Oh that's all right then, for one awful moment I thought you might be growing a beard.'

The Range Rover's engine was still running. 'Are you coming in, for tea or something?' Subtle. Come up and see my etchings.

'No I can't stop. I'm on my way to Ipswich to do a shop.'
She leaned over the back and retrieved a small paper parcel.
'I brought you this.'

'Ah, medication time I sense.' He took the parcel. It was
a book, loosely wrapped in a paper bag. *The Oxford Book of
English Verse*, rather dog-eared and much thumbed.

'Special prescription. I'd like it back, some time.'

'What's the dosage doctor?'

'Dip in at least once a day, more often if symptoms
persist.'

'At random?'

'Completely. And take notes. Now have you been a good
boy and no slippages?'

He clicked his heels together and bowed.

'Good,' she said sternly. 'Well I must be getting on with
my rounds.'

'Do you have many lame ducks on your list?'

She engaged gear and began to move off. 'That's quite
enough of that young man. But since you ask, none at all.'
She grinned, executed a neat three point turn and drove
back up the lane. He looked down at the book. He'd
forgotten to thank her.

He made himself coffee and a sandwich and took them out
to the shed. He sat up on the Windsor chair, took out his
private notebook and made a date entry in the margin.
Firstly he updated his list of actions. It was hardly recognisable in comparison to his lists of old. Those had consisted
of company addresses, contact names and numbers, job
descriptions, financial projections. This looked more like a
page from a DIY enthusiast's handbook, or a list of chores
for the handyman. He snorted. It was a list of chores for the
handyman.

He munched the sandwich and ticked 'car' off the list.
Then he jotted down that Alice had visited and noted that

she'd leant him her OEV. He picked up the book and opened it at random as instructed. 'Thomas Lodge,' he wrote dutifully, then added the title 'Rosaline'. He read for a while before pencilling a note. 'Would get on well with Arthur Clements. N.B. Check dictionary for "pap".'

He met Jamie off the bus then drove to collect Sally. The room was crowded with excited toddlers and their parents – mostly mothers. He put on his doting parent face and waded in to seek out Sally. She was dangling upside down like a pink cheeked bat from the crossbar of an indoor climbing frame. 'Daddy, my daddy! I'm a little orang-utan [raner-tan]!'

'Yes sweetheart, indeed you are but we have to go now. Come and put your coat on.' The noise was incredible.

'Mr Deacon? Mr Deacon. Ah, there you are.' It was the proprietress, smiling wanly, the strain of seven hours closely closeted with fourteen three-year-olds showed in the startled, faintly dazed look in her eyes. 'These are Sally's paintings. We've all had a lovely time haven't we everyone?' She handed him the sticky wet sheets and wandered back into the mêlée.

'Come on Sally! We have to go now.' He was virtually shouting himself. And there was somebody else, a woman over the other side of the room.

'Justin? Justin! Oh my God, Justin!' There was panic, adult panic, somebody screamed. Everyone was shouting. The head teacher was calling for calm. He craned his neck to see. Over the other side of the room some mothers were bending over a child's form on the floor. For a moment he was tempted to take advantage of the diversion and slip out. Then the woman screamed again.

'He's dead! Oh my God, he's dead. Justin!'

Without realising it he crossed the room, elbowed his way past two stunned mothers and knelt by the child. The face was blue, the eyes wide and bulging. 'What happened?' He looked up at the mother but she had her hands over her ears, was shaking her head, speechless.

'He swallowed summat,' somebody said. 'He was playing with a ball, had it in his mouth. I saw 'im.'

The mother wailed, 'He's dead, Oh my God, he's dead.' Peter reached two fingers deep into the throat. He touched hard roundness but it was wedged tight. He looked around desperately as he groped, precious seconds, the room suddenly quiet. Sally was still swinging on the climbing frame. Upside down. Something clicked. He grabbed the inert heels, swung the boy into the air with one hand like a newborn, he was heavy though, nearly dropped him. He gripped tighter, raised his arm up and out as high as he could, and slapped the boy on the back with the flat of his hand. Nothing happened.

Peter grunted, grimacing from the effort and strain of the weight on his arm. Deep growls escaped his clenched teeth in time with the repeated slaps. 'Don't take him, don't take him, DON'T take him.' But nothing was happening: his arm shook; his face was bright red; the veins on his neck standing out like knotted blue ropes. 'Don't take him – take me don't take him come ON dammit!'

In desperation he reached back for one last blow, balled his free hand into a fist and struck hard with its base, high, right between the shoulder blades. There was a noise like pneumatic brakes on a truck, the ball shot out of the child's mouth and bounced across the floor to rebound off the far wall. Peter sank to the floor gasping, cradling the boy in his arms and bending his ear to his mouth. He was breathing: fast, panting breaths, shallow at first but then gradually becoming easier, slower and deeper as the oxygen spread.

*

'How was your day?' Emma leaned forward in the car beside him and shook her fingers vigorously through her hair. 'God, mine was exhausting.'

He reached over and patted her back. 'You poor old breadwinner you. Mine was quite good actually, as you can see the car now runs like a Swiss watch, oh and we can put it away at night, the garage doors are no longer a problem.'

'You managed to fix the garage doors?'

'Sort of. And we've got enough kindling to see us through the winter.'

CHAPTER
11

He dropped the bag of carrots into the top of the groceries box and pulled it towards him across the counter.

'Mind the bottom as you lift now.' Mrs Morrison watched as he picked up the box and turned for the door. 'Oh Peter, I nearly forgot! Somebody telephoned for you. Hold on, I wrote it down somewhere, just a moment, here! Yes Stock, that was it; a Ms Stock, sounded like a London accent.'

'Stock?' He stood in the middle of the shop wondering. Stock, who the hell? God, Miriam! 'Stock yes, okay thanks Mrs Morrison.'

'About a job is it do you think? One of your head-shrinkers? Well good luck then—' But he was already in the phone booth.

He took the train from Ipswich to Liverpool Street. It would be far less hassle than driving and, as Emma had rightly pointed out, a useful exercise to time and cost the journey. He sat in the carriage next to the buffet drinking British Rail coffee and nervously rechecking the contents of his briefcase. He had the uniform on. A white shirt, practically new, the navy blue double-breasted suit made for him in twenty-four hours by the little man in Kowloon, Royal Air Force Association tie and freshly polished black brogues. It felt very strange, but he looked good, even with the beard and the hair.

'You look fine, darling, absolutely.' She had examined him closely in the kitchen that morning before leaving for work, straightened his tie, brushed faint traces of brickdust from the shoulders of his jacket.

'What about the beard?' He had debated whether to shave it off, but after a trim and a tidy up it looked quite presentable.

Emma checked her watch and drained her coffee quickly. 'It's fine Peter, stop worrying, you look terrific, *très élégant, absolument.*' She held her finger and thumb up in a circle. 'Come on Jamie we'll be late. Sal you behave yourself at Jack and Alice's, darling.' She leaned up against him, slid her hand around his back under the jacket, kissed him lightly on the lips: 'Good luck.'

Peter stood in front of the bathroom mirror waiting for Alice, tucked his shirt into his trousers again. They were too loose – he must have lost weight, combed his hair back. It was quite long, very long by his standards but there just hadn't been time to go to Ipswich for a haircut and anyway with it washed and combed back it looked okay, 'smart and stylish' Emma had said. But God was he nervous, he longed for a drink, just a small one to steady his nerves and settle the churning in his stomach.

The Range Rover drew up. 'My, my! Will you look at you then.' Alice smiled broadly; he must look presentable.

'Smart enough?'

'Oh yes, yes. The perfect balance between City formal and Hollywood chic, like a big time movie producer going to a business lunch, or—'

'A marketing executive?' She was building him up, he

knew, pumping up his ego like one of the children's battered and less than airtight inflatable bath toys.

She laughed. 'Yes! Even a marketing executive.'

'It's very kind of you to drive me to the station, and take on Sally at such short notice. I could easily have called a minicab.'

'Nonsense.'

Allowing for the traffic it was thirty-five minutes to the station followed by a fifteen minute wait for a slightly delayed train, then about an hour and a quarter to Liverpool Street. The interview was at Hammersmith; he took the tube, changing onto the Piccadilly line at Gloucester Road. In all the journey took just under three hours door to door.

But he still had a little time to kill. Borne on the tide of pedestrian traffic, he drifted past the squat smoked glass and steel office block without a pause until, a quarter of a mile further on, he reached a newsagent's shop. He walked in and began blindly browsing the magazine rack. The journey, the sudden bustle and noise, the speed of movement dazed him. In just a few weeks he'd forgotten, fallen badly out of step with the pace and rhythm of the City. It was as clear a case of culture shock as if he had just stepped off an aeroplane in Rangoon, or Rio or Reykjavic.

And he was nervous. There was an emptiness in his stomach and a light headedness. His mouth was dry, his mind in turmoil.

'Can I help you?'

He started, checked the Timex, pity about the Rolex, damn that kid. It was time to go. 'No thanks.'

It was a tough interview, but not as traumatic as the Fielding Kavanagh nightmare. There were two of them again, the sales and marketing director and the managing director, both sympathetic yet industry-wise and hard-working men. Dedicated to their company and the struggle to survive and succeed in the treacherous and quick-shifting sands of their chosen field. The company originally manufactured in-flight video entertainment systems for airliners but had recently begun developing external camera systems for integration into aircraft flight data recording systems. It was a new concept, with high development and start-up costs, but potentially lucrative, and topical – there had been several instances of both civil and military pilots making ill-informed judgements about the health of their aircraft simply because they were unable to see the problem with their own eyes. Sparks from a faulty turbine, damage to an undercarriage leg, a stuck missile.

They gave him coffee, invited him to join them in shirtsleeves (this time he accepted), apologised in advance for their haste: 'We've four to see and a production meeting at two.' Then launched straight in. They tested him on his knowledge of the whole industry and current technological trends, they questioned him about his work at UAS but dismissed its demise as an occupational hazard. 'Happens all the time – someone screwed up.'

Their speed was difficult to follow at first and they kept jumping track like a badly scratched record.

'I see you've travelled a lot. Worked much with the Chinese?'

'What was your assessment of the Kegworth findings?'

'How many sidewinder live firings did you make in the Jaguar?'

'Know much about our competitors?'

'Is your wife employed?'

He worked hard, scored points, lost them again, blunder and triumph. He completely forgot the details of a recent civil airliner crash in Kansas which bore direct relevance to their business, yet a minute later was able to recall the Arabic names of three senior Saudi Air Ministry attaches, a market they were eager to penetrate.

Suddenly it was over. The room fell silent, they conferred with each other, stood up and shook his hand.

'The position is a new one. We have an immediate requirement. We'll let you know within the next few days.' He thanked them and fled to the street.

He stopped by at the house in Fulham to check the mail. It was over three weeks since his last visit. The power had been cut off, and with the curtains drawn the place was gloomy and depressing. It was like visiting a closed museum, cold and lifeless, the main exhibits removed to storage. A sense of hurried departure continued to pervade the atmosphere but it was less tangibly associated with his family, as if someone else had lived there.

Wandering aimlessly from room to room he completed a slow tour of the house before returning to the hall to sort through the post. He discarded all the junk mail and old bills into a dustbin liner. It was no longer his concern; all creditors had been contacted by Wallace and advised to liaise directly through his office pending the bankruptcy hearing. There was an assortment of other letters; he glanced at the envelopes then tossed them into his briefcase.

There was a three quarter hour wait at the station for the next Ipswich train. He found a table at the railway tavern, bought a piece of rubbery quiche and a glass of orange juice and sat down to read the paper. But he couldn't concentrate – his mind drifted. He wanted the job, badly. It wouldn't be easy: the remuneration package was a considerably reduced version of the deal he had enjoyed at UAS; the company smaller; the position less prestigious. But that was not the point. It was a lifeline of a vacancy, a toehold on the crowded and precipitous slope back to normality. If he made it the next step would be easier, and the one after that. And if he failed? Something inside him – a dull, heavy cold weight – kept telling him this was his last chance. If he failed now, he would never get back. The pressures of the last six months, the disappointments and the strain had all taken their toll, denting his self-confidence, distorting his perspective and dulling the once keen edge of his professional competence. This was his last chance: he had to succeed, *had* to.

A card caught his eye among the scattering of letters in his briefcase. He picked it up. It was an appointment reminder from Dr Pryce. Checking the date he saw they had missed Jamie's last appointment. He hesitated, tapping the card against the table top. She'd drilled into him all right, on that last occasion, but he had probably deserved it. And that curious watchful, knowing look she gave him. A bit like Alice. He checked the time, still twenty minutes before his train was due to leave. There was a pay phone just below him on the main concourse.

'Ah yes Mr Deacon, I have it now, two thirty on the sixth wasn't it?'

'Yes, sorry about that. We moved out of town for a while, completely forgot.'

'No matter, would you like to fix another appointment?'

He hesitated. Was this such a good idea? Why was he doing this? 'Um, perhaps we could let you know, once we have a firmer idea of our movements.'

'Of course. How is Jamie?'

He told her. Still a little edgy, still quiet and introverted in the main, preferring his own company to anyone else's; still thin but eating better and settling in at the local primary school.

'Excellent, seems the move out of London is proving beneficial. He obviously enjoys the lifestyle.'

Obviously? He hadn't really considered it. The day to day

change in Jamie was barely perceptible. But now that he thought about it, it was a change, and an improvement. 'I'm sorry?' She was talking again.

'I said and how are you? How have you been?'

'Oh, er fit enough thank you. Still in the market for a job, but hanging on, you know.' Yes, grimly and to what? The last of your self-respect. Why are you having this conversation Deacon? Are you going to tell the good doctor about the continuing insomnia, and the impotency? How you eke out an existence as part-time domestic help and handyman, manfully standing by to watch your own emasculation?

'Are you hoping to find work in the country?'

'No, not especially. Naturally it depends on the work opportunities that come up but I, we, anticipate the country arrangement as temporary.'

'Well I wish you every success of course but have you considered the effect of another move on Jamie? Particularly one back to London?'

Time to end this. 'Yes Dr Pryce, we are considering all the effects, on all of us. If you'll excuse me, I have a train to catch. Sorry again about the appointment, as soon as we can we'll contact you to fix up another.'

'Fine. And er, Mr Deacon, please call me in the meantime, if anything comes up that you wish to discuss. About Jamie that is, or anything ...'

On the train home he had a couple of Scotches in the buffet.

'Now I want to hear it all, from the beginning.' They were sitting in the front room, flames danced brightly in the wrought-iron grate, new curtains hung at the windows, fresh paint on the recently re-plastered walls. Warm light diffused from brass wall-lights shaped like Edwardian gas lamps, softly illuminating a collection of local watercolours and framed prints. The floor was covered in fitted hessian the colour of autumn straw, an Aretha Franklin CD played in the corner.

He had taken a cab from the station, arrived home about six thirty. Emma wanted to prepare something special for supper so he bathed the children and sat on the wicker chair in their room reading Roald Dahl. Down in the kitchen he uncorked a bottle of Beaujolais placing it on a corner of the stove to chambré.

'Hello, what happened to the wagon?' said Emma smiling. She took the proffered gin and tonic.

'Jumped off it for the evening.' He sipped a whiskey and soda, slight guilt pang. He found himself glancing at the door, in case.

'Well you've earned it. Anyway it's dreary as hell drinking alone. Let's go next door and swap news.'

She had news too? He followed her across the hall. 'Well there's not much to tell.'

'Don't give me that Deacon. How was the journey?'

'About three hours.'

'Ouch. What about the offices – decor?'

She grilled him good naturedly. He told her all he could remember about the place, the people, their business. He remained deliberately, superstitiously non-committal about his performance at interview, preferring despite her persistence: 'Come on you must have some idea!' to leave it at five-to-one for all runners.

But something was not quite right. Maybe it was the whiskey: it was working its old familiar alchemy, a warm golden glow suffusing his body, relaxing his muscles and banishing the tension from his neck and shoulders. But the lay off had weakened his resistance to liquor, it rushed to his head and made him dizzy, yet at the same time apparently imbuing him with a heightened sense of perception. There was something false about her attentiveness, the detailed questioning, fascination with minutiae. She seemed tense beneath the nodding, smiling façade.

He realised it with a jolt. It was the main issue she was avoiding. They both were. Stamping about the place like Sumo wrestlers, parading and posturing, bowing and bending, anything to delay direct confrontation of the core issue. For an instant his heart softened, he wanted to reach out and fold her in his arms. But the unyielding strength of those bright smiling eyes deterred him. He got up to freshen their glasses. It was going to be a long evening. 'And what about your news?'

'Remember the big commercial job I was working on? The retail chain.'

'The corporate facelift thing yes.'

'We got the job, the whole account.'

'Well done Em, that's outstanding, really. That was mostly your design work too.' But there's more to come.

She basked for a moment, laughed. 'True, true enough, it must be said. But don't let the others hear you say that!' She laughed, sipped her drink.

'And ...'

'And Charlie wants me to head up the project.' She stopped smiling, watched him closely. 'It represents a ten per cent increase in the gross turnover of the company. He'll have to take on extra draught staff, more equipment; the whole building will have to be reorganised to fit everyone in.'

'Of course, but you'll manage – it's a fantastic coup.' He got up from the chair, went over and kissed her warmly. 'Congratulations – you deserve it. Really.' Was he overdoing it? His head swam. 'Any extra dosh in it?'

'Definitely. Maybe a car too once things get underway.'

'Oh to be an eight-wheeled family again!'

He sustained the party atmosphere throughout dinner, fresh mussels followed by fillet steak. ('Crikey surf and turf – we must be celebrating!') They toasted each other until the Beaujolais was gone, talked of the past and alluded to the future, or tastefully selected versions of it. They planned a list of improvements to the cottage: a proper damp course, central heating, an extension with an upstairs bathroom. 'New garage doors!' They promised themselves a holiday in the sun, new clothes, bicycles for the children. It was easy, she was euphoric and he could fake it with practised and well lubricated ease.

After dinner they took the whiskey bottle back into the sitting room and cuddled up on the two seat sofa by the fire.

'I'd like to make love,' she murmured wistfully. He stroked her hair, holding his breath. 'But we can't. Sorry.'

'Ah.'

'Peto.' She turned to face him, concern in her eyes. He smiled; here it comes. 'I know this hasn't been easy for you: UAS, the money, the house, moving here, everything. But I want you to know that I do appreciate all your support, and the sacrifices you've made.'

He kissed her on the forehead, caressed the soft warmth of her back under the blouse. 'Thank you.' Suddenly he felt a deep sense of foreboding, an icy chill down his spine, the hairs prickling at his neck. A fragment of Donne came to him, glimpsed probably somewhere in Alice's book, something about his grave being broken up: '... Some second guest to entertain ...'

'Will you accept it? The Hammersmith job. If you are offered it?'

Yes Emma, I have to. Can't you see that? He sighed. 'I don't know.'

She went up. He cleared, then went over to the shed. It was cold, but he'd laid the stove the previous evening. He needed time, time to work it out. He lit the stove, went back inside for an extra sweater, made coffee and carried it over with the rest of the Scotch.

Having noted the day's movements in the diary he then went on to summarise the dilemma. It didn't take long. He wanted the job. It wasn't really practicable to commute to Hammersmith on a daily basis. Six hours a day! I'd have to get up before I went to bed. Perhaps for a few weeks, *in extremis*, but no more. That left one alternative. Two. Return to London to live. Or turn down the job if offered.

He considered each in turn. Sitting in the tatty armchair next to the little stove, listening to it ticking as it warmed up. Outside it was clear and moonless, a light breeze sighed through the trees in the back garden. A long way off, somewhere down towards the farmyard, he could hear animal noises: a curious almost human yowl, something between a cat and a baby. Without thinking he jotted 'fox' in the margin of the diary.

All of them return to London? Impossible. He couldn't even bring himself to mention the possibility to Emma this evening. There was something defiant, an unbreakable resolution about her triumph. She'd made it, her feet were firmly locked under the table, the heels deeply dug in, but he sensed she wanted the issue confronted, now that she was ready: 'Come on buster let's have it out.' But he could present no cogent, logical basis for his argument. Where would they live? The house was probably going to be sold from under their feet. Of course, there should be enough cash to buy something smaller later. But it could be months, a year even before that mess was sorted out. He sloshed whiskey into his coffee mug. Then there were the children.

He'd tacked up some pictures on the wall of the shed. A poster of a Jaguar cockpit, as familiar to him as the dashboard of the Morris, even after ten years out of the saddle. His office photograph of Emma and the children, a couple of Jamie's paintings from school. There was also a thank you picture from the kindergarten boy Justin, next to one of Sally's indecipherable potato cutting messes, smudged with spilt paint and smeared green hand prints added for reasons known only to her. 'Daddy!' she had scolded, 'It's a monster.' Sally was not a worry, she accepted change readily and without question. Relished it. If he told her they were going to live on the moon she'd have her case packed in minutes and be waiting impatiently by the car yelling for everyone to hurry up.

But Jamie. The Pryce woman had a point, he had as great a say in this as anyone, greater perhaps, he was more vulnerable. But it was always difficult to gauge his true feelings. He shared his sister's independence of spirit, but not her ready expression of feeling. And none of her confidence. Peter sighed, scored heavy lines in a box around Jamie's name. He had to acknowledge there was a powerful argument for leaving him undisturbed. He could see battle lines drawing up. Emma and Jamie on one flank, he and Sally, his unreliable and capricious ally, on the other.

He could commute weekly. Rent a single-bedroomed flat in town. Leave Suffolk on Monday mornings, return home on Friday evenings. Spend the week on his own in bedsit-land, and a weekend visitor to his own home, a stranger to his wife, an 'uncle' to the children. Hardly. And the cost would be astronomical.

The cold woke him up. The stove had gone out, through the windows he could see it was getting light, the sky a pale smoky blue tinged with pink. He straightened slowly, sharp stabs of pain lancing into the side of his neck, his throat was dry, mouth sticky. A familiar dull ache throbbed in his head, his feet were numb with cold. He picked the notebook up from the floor where it had fallen by his feet.

The empty whiskey bottle lay by its side.

The house was quiet, the kitchen warm. He went to the bathroom then crept upstairs avoiding the worst of the creaking steps. The bedroom was cooler, but the second-hand night storage heater kept off the worst of the chill. Pre-dawn light diffused through the curtained windows, drowning the soft electric glow of the Hickory Dickory Dock nightlight. 'Hi Dad.' A whisper from the bottom bunk.

Peter put his finger to his lips, lowering himself to the floor by the bed with a soft grunt. The wide eyes watched him curiously, above Sally stirred, muttering then snored on. Outside the dawn chorus was tuning up. 'Hi Jamie.' He stroked the head, ran a finger lightly down the nose, across the soft valley of lips, on down to the angular hardness of the chin.

'What is it?'

Leaning into the enclosed shadow of the bunk, the whisper was soft, almost silent. 'Jamie, do you like it here?'

The breath smelled, sort of sweet and stale like rotten apples, but Jamie didn't mind, the dreamlike presence was comforting, protecting. The hovering face was indistinct, the dark hair and beard melting into the gloom. Like matt black camouflage paint on a night fighter. But he could see the eyes, there was sadness, and worry. He thought hard, this was important, there was a right answer, and a wrong one. 'Yes.' The eyes blinked.

'What if we were to go back and live in London, and you went back to your old school?'

It doesn't matter Dad. I just want you to be happy again. Was it the wrong answer? Perhaps he didn't believe him. He must have thought he had just said yes to please him. 'Dad I really do like it here.' The eyes hung above him, motionless like a kestrel.

'Okay.' He stroked the head again then got up and left.

*

Voices. Outside the door. 'How long has he been out here?'
'Three days, on and off.' Women's voices. He licked his lips,
slowly lifted his cheek from the bench. A sheet of paper was
stuck to it, pasted to his face by his own saliva; he could see
it reflected in the window. 'Drink?' 'Yes, I don't know,
probably, and pills, he got something from the doctor. They
were supposed to help him sleep.' 'Jesus.' What the hell were
they on about, twittering away outside the door like a couple
of fishwives? He knew the voices too, just couldn't quite . . .
'Does he come in at all?' 'Yes. He comes in, mooches about,
picks at his food, cracks jokes one minute then says nothing
for hours, goes to the bathroom then wanders out here
again. Alice, do you think I should call the doctor or
something? Was Jack like this at all . . .?'

'Let me have a word with him, on my own.'

There was knocking at the door. Oh God, now what? He
levered himself straighter in the chair, it wobbled on its
bricks, must have shifted. 'Er no thanks,' he called, his voice
gravelly. 'I don't think so, not today.'

'Peter, can I come in?' It was that other woman, the one
with the scar. Alice.

'No!' His head jerked back, ouch! He threw his hands up
to his temples, the chair rocked again on the bricks, teetered,
crashed to the floor.

'Peter!' The door flew open, she rushed in on a sudden
blast of light. He lay there groaning, feet tangled in the legs
of the chair, one arm crooked over his eyes against the
blinding glare. The groan became a snort. He giggled. 'Oops-
a-daisy.'

'I suppose you think this is funny.'

She was cross with him. Standing up there straight and
tall in the doorway, a perfect silhouette framed against the
harsh light. Haughtily glaring down at him like that, legs

241

apart, hands on hips like— He began to speak but a spasm overcame him, driving the breath from his chest, the tears starting from his eyes. He tried again 'Wonder—' but the next wave of laughter swept over him before he could speak. He kicked feebly at the chair to free his legs, gasping to control his voice, thrusting a clenched fist into the air he finally sang it out: 'Wonderwoman!'

'Have you any idea how pathetic you look?'

He hauled himself to his feet, covered in dust; he flicked a bit off his chest. 'Yes thank you.'

'Do you seriously think that this is going to solve anything?'

'Yes I seriously think!' He glared at her, she didn't bat an eyelid. 'I seriously think all right. I seriously think that you don't know everything.' He was pointing, stabbing the air in front of her nose, his face a sneer. 'In fact you don't know anything at all. You think this is all about money, and bills and solicitors. Well you are wrong, Miss Smartarse, totally out of the ballpark. That's what I seriously think.' She said nothing, just shook her head slowly, contempt in her eyes and worse, pity. 'And what's more I seriously think that these guys' – he snatched up her poetry book from the bench – 'Don't know damnation. Just a bunch of day-dreaming bloody self-deluding loonies!'

She held his gaze. He began to wither, feel ridiculous. Her voice was quiet and cold. 'You want damnation, try Coleridge. Lunacy? John Clare.' She nodded once, turned and walked out into the light.

He went for a walk. The usual round, turn right out of the driveway, down to the farm and round the fields. He'd given up jogging – it wasn't working, just made him sick and dizzy. But walking was pleasant. It gave him time to think, and notice things. There was a hint of spring about: snowdrops, crocuses, clumps of daffodils poking up through the rough grass in the back garden, clearly visible through the shed windows. There was more daylight, he could feel the sun's meagre heat soaking through his clothes, warming the flesh of his back. The crops, their growth suspended up until now, were suddenly coming alive again too. One day he watched for hours as a farm labourer drove up and down top dressing the stunted winter corn. In no time the scruffy and frostbitten leaves appeared to shake free from hibernation and begin pushing fresh shoots clear of the ground.

In the woods the trees were still bare, silently awaiting the shot of the starting pistol, a critical temperature threshold, a day length, a soil-borne enzyme, agents signalling the end of the cold wait, the start of new and vigorous growth. He sat on the fallen bough and watched for the usual rabbits and squirrels to appear. He'd heard in the pub that there were badgers in these woods, he meant to hide out one night to watch them. And the deer allegedly wandering nearby in the hundreds of acres of serried pines planted decades ago by the Forestry Commission.

He crossed the stream by the wooden footbridge, stopping for a while to watch the muddy water swirl slowly beneath his feet. It amazed him. By looking out across the flat bottom of the vale he could see the course of the glacier that had gouged it out of the bedrock aeons ago. A mile or more wide, mighty and relentless, but now reduced to little more than an itinerant brook. Looking around he could see the cottage in the distance, a thin smudge of smoke above the chimney. He set off but when he reached the stile decided to wander up the lane to the green. Groceries, that was it, pick up the groceries.

'Hello Peter,' smiled Mrs Morrison. 'It's all here ready for you.' She slid the box towards him.

He frowned, studying the contents. 'Ah, I think we'd

243

better just stock up on the old firewater while I'm here. Could you stick a couple of bottles of the usual poison on the slate for us, better still make it three, thanks. Have you been out yet today Anne? Grand day.' He slotted the bottles among the groceries and picked up the box. 'You can see for miles.' He winked at her and turned for the door.

'Well aren't you going to open it? It's been sitting there all day.' Emma forked tinned steak and kidney pie from her plate, tapping the envelope with her finger. 'Jamie, I'd like you to eat a little more of this please. And you Sal, right now or no ice cream.'

'It's yuk!'

'No it isn't, it's very good for you.'

'S'gustin!'

He snapped forward in his chair. 'How dare you speak to your mother like that!' She froze, eyes wide, face inches from his. 'Now you listen to me young lady, you have a simple choice.' His teeth were clenched, voice a growl. 'Either you eat it all, by yourself and right now or else you get a smack and go straight to bed and no ice cream. Now which is it?'

'Peter it's not . . .'

'Yes it is! It is important. You have to choose Sally, right now. There is nothing else.' Her lip quivered, she stared down at her plate the tears splashing onto the gravy. Slowly she took up her spoon, raised it to her mouth. 'Good.' He looked at Emma, eyebrows raised. 'Choice. Important lesson.' Sally sobbed, coughed, gagged on the spoon.

'For God's sake.' Emma got up and took the plate from her, put it in the sink.

Peter sighed. 'Important lesson wasted.' He got up and cleared away the rest. Nobody liked the pie anyway; Emma's was the only clean plate. The envelope remained on the table, white and pregnant, the postmark London W6, printed on the back flap was the company logo.

Emma bathed the children and put them to bed, he tended the fires, emptied the ashes from both stoves, restocked the buckets and baskets with coal and wood, swept up after him. A little later they met in the kitchen. 'Are you going over to the shed this evening?' She began spreading papers out on the table. He made a maybe grunt, poured his first official whiskey of the evening, she declined with a wave, already engrossed; 'No thanks, I've got to work. Next week is going to be murder. I shall probably be pretty late most nights.' She glanced up at him. 'Is that okay? I mean, I'll have to keep the car all week.'

He shrugged. 'Fine, not a problem.'

She looked at him a moment longer, her eyes perplexed.

He tilted his head. 'Was there something else?'

She exhaled through pursed lips. 'Are you going to open it?'

'Hmm.' He picked it up as if noticing it for the first time, turned it over in his hand. 'I don't know. Is there any point?'

'There's always a point. Curiosity if nothing else.'

'Perhaps. But then it's not going to change anything, whatever it says. Is it?' He emphasised the question, he wanted her to come right out and state her position.

'Don't try your bully boy tactics on me; they don't work remember?'

'All right let's just cut to the chase. If I get this job, are you going to drop everything, pack up and come back to town with me?'

'And live precisely where?'

He shook his head, took a large swallow from the glass. It was important to remain calm. 'Ignore that for a moment. Ignore everything! Just answer the question. Hypothetically if you like.'

'I can't do that. My answer would depend entirely on the circumstances.'

'Please?'

'Don't be so ridiculous! Look, if you are asking whether I'm prepared to camp out with the children beneath the arches of Hammersmith flyover then strangely enough my answer is no. Present me with a proposal, a sensible plan. One that makes sense, covers all the angles. As soon as you do, I will consider it.'

There was silence. She continued sorting through her papers. He drained his glass, rinsed it and put it on the draining board. 'Fair enough,' he said briskly. 'I'll pop over the other side. I won't disturb you if I'm late coming back.'

'Fine.' She didn't look up.

But he didn't feel like staying in the shed. He felt the old urge to take solace in the streets. He retrieved one of the bottles hidden in the shed, dropped it into his coat pocket and slipped out, treading softly in the lane until out of earshot. He walked through the village and out along the road towards Jamie's school. But it wasn't the same as London. There was no pavement for a start. He had to walk along the unlit road and scramble up onto the steep grass verge every time a car came along. And there were no people to look at or follow. No busy restaurant windows to gaze through, no hustle and bustle. No life.

At the first opportunity he turned off the road, following a wide service track that led into the pine forest. The track doubled as a fire break, soon turning out of sight of the road. As he walked on it grew quieter, the crunch of his footfall on the cinder track loud above the gentle breeze moaning softly through the trees. He came to an intersection of tracks, took a turn at random, then another, soon he was deep in the forest, wandering aimlessly between tall, brooding ranks of silent conifers.

After a while he paused, the sudden quiet thick and oppressive, took the bottle from his pocket and drank, tilting his chin to the narrow strip of star-specked sky visible above the forest roof. Around him the trees waited and watched, dense, black and impenetrable until finally their motionless reproof drove him on.

Much later he found himself outside the Old Rectory, staring up at ivy covered walls, shivering as he hesitated on the threshold. He watched curiously as his arm reached out for the bell. After a long time, a light came on above the door, he heard a man's voice: 'Who is it?'

He cleared his throat, working his jaw. 'Peter here.' He said gruffly.

There was a long pause. 'You'd better wait there.'

She came to the door, tying a silk dressing gown, peering at him half in, half out of shadow on the step. 'Peter? What on earth are you doing here?'

'I came—' He cleared his throat again, his mouth wasn't working properly. 'I came to apologise. About earlier, you know?'

'If you are referring to your performance in the shed, that was two days ago.'

'Yes. Exactly. Whenever.' What was he doing here? It had all been so clear to him earlier. He needed her support again, and her advice, badly. But he had let her down, behaved ridiculously (wonderwoman, Jesus!) He must apologise. 'Anyway, the thing is, I behaved like an arsehole. I want you to know that and—' His hand swung in the air like a puppet's. 'I'm very sorry about that because, you really are a wonderful woman, actually and even though I may not have said it, I really do appreciate your, help.' He tried to smile but it came out lopsided. Why didn't she say something instead of just standing there, shaking her head. 'And! I may not have said this either for that matter, but I never said thank you for the book which was bloody rude, so I'd like to say thank you now. And—'

247

'Don't you think you've said enough.' There was a hint, a glimmer of a smile in the eyes. 'Go home Peter Deacon. Do you think you can manage that?'

He nodded, more of an unsteady bow. 'Not a problem. Alice, sorry again, and thank you. Again.' He turned and strode down the drive. She watched him go. Just as she was closing the door he spun around, walking backwards. 'And—' he called loudly. 'You were right about Coleridge. I'd forgotten about that poor old sailor. Damned to buggery and back poor bastard.'

CHAPTER

12

'Right then, we're off. Into the car everyone and hurry up about it. Now, Danielle's mother is going to collect Sally from school then drop her back here after tea so you don't have to worry about that. That just leaves Jamie to be met at the green at three fifteen and— Peter, are you listening?'

He waved her towards the door. 'For God's sake Emma, I've got it! Go, or he'll miss the bus.'

'Right then,' she said again, patting her coat pockets for car keys.

'On the hook, by the door.' He picked up his coffee mug.

'Oh yes. Okay. See you, don't wait up, it could be late.' She hesitated at the open door. 'Right, bye then.' He nodded, wiggling his fingers from behind the mug. A minute later he heard the car start and drive off towards the green.

He sat at the table relishing the sudden quiet. He was bone weary, had sat up half the night scrawling notes in his diary then crashed out on the spare room bed only to find his head filled to bursting like a simmering stew. Eventually he had taken a couple of those pills, but before he knew it it was time to get up. There were things he ought to do today. They were low on chopped firewood, the water supply to the washing machine needed attention, there was a mass of laundry to catch up on, a ton of junk in the garage to be sorted and cleared; the list was endless.

But the urge to sleep was overpowering; he could feel his eyelids drooping as he sat in the peaceful warmth of the kitchen. Perhaps he could just go upstairs and lie down for half an hour. But his head was already sinking, sliding slowly down until it rested on his arm. All right, just a few minutes or so . . .

The door opened. It was Mandy Clements. 'Hello Peter what you doing, having a quick snooze?' She took off her anorak, hung it behind the door, slid the kettle onto the hot plate and flicked on the transistor radio by the window. Pop music filled the kitchen. 'Poor thing, just look at the state of you. What you need is a nice hot cup of tea.'

He sat up, blinking blearily. His left eye refused to focus properly, he ground the heel of his palm into it, shaking his head until it cleared. She was wearing a thin white wool sweater, the usual ridiculously short denim mini skirt and tatty little black suede ankle boots. Her legs were bare, her breasts unrestrained beneath the sweater. She paraded about the kitchen as though on a catwalk, every move, every posture planned to best display her so recently acquired voluptuousness.

It must be an extraordinary, intoxicating, yet humbling phenomenon for a young girl, he mused, as she stretched up for the teapot, bent for the mugs. One minute a child, graceless and gawky perhaps, puerile, completely unremarkable. Then in the space of only months, transformed into something that half the membership of her entire species is suddenly salaciously, competitively desirous of. It was a terrifying responsibility for one so young. How did they cope? He wondered if she was still a virgin.

'Mandy—'

'You're out of sugar again; we'll have to use brown.' She looked at him, his face pale and drawn, the long hair dishevelled, the beard unkempt. She wrinkled her nose; he did smell a bit. Not bad, not like real BO or anything but a kind of earthy man smell. And thin, with sunken cheeks and those eyes, red rimmed and hooded, but watchful. She knew he liked to watch her. 'You're too thin you know. Doesn't she feed you or what? How about if I cook you some breakfast, a proper fry up? Then I could run you a nice hot bath.' She winked saucily. 'Scrub your back.' She could take care of him all right. He was lovely.

He pushed back the chair with a screech and got to his feet. 'Mandy Clements, you are a delight and a siren. Some day you and that magnificent body of yours will make some wholly undeserving slob very, very happy. I'll be in the office, if anyone rings—' He nodded towards the new wall phone.

'I know, you're out unless it's a major emergency.' He bowed and backed out of the door.

About an hour later there was a discreet tap on the door. He scowled, deeply engrossed sorting through the exercise books and piles of loose papers in an effort to transcribe some of his notes onto the word processor. 'Not now, kids. Daddy's got a lot of work to get through. I'll be over later.'

'Peter, it's the vicar.'

'What? Oh, Mandy what did you say?' Vicar? What was she on about?

She took it as a clearance to enter. Her head appeared, eyes ricocheting around the little shed. Paper everywhere, pictures and notices covering the walls, hanging from clips nailed to the roof, more of it pinned to the carved up cardboard boxes taped over the windows. Heaps of the stuff all over the floor. 'Phew it's a bit dingy in here. Why do you

251

keep the windows blocked up like that?' There was just a single bare bulb hanging from the ceiling, the glow from his computer screen casting a ghostly green shadow across his face.

He shook his head irritably. 'It's, um part of a limited sensory deprivation chronology study I'm looking into and it's important to exclude all external visual cues Mandy so, er what was it you wanted again?'

'The vicar. He's in the kitchen, wants to know if it's "convenient".' She laboured the word, rolling her eyes.

'No it isn't. Tell him to go away. No! Wait a minute.' He began searching through the papers on the bench, muttering curses. 'Tell him I'll be over in a minute.'

'I'm so sorry to drop in unannounced like this. Please say if it is inconvenient.' The vicar tried not to stare as Peter pumped his hand warmly.

'Not at all Vicar, not at all.' He'd seen him a couple of times since Christmas, in the pub, Mrs Morrison's. Not in church. He was young, about his own age, so much the better.

Mandy made yet more tea, hovered like an attentive waitress. The vicar explained that he had heard that Peter was 'based mainly at home for the moment', and thought he would take the opportunity to stop by and introduce himself. They talked a little of the village, the vicar's association with the area, the dimensions of the parish. Then Peter suddenly produced a wirebound shorthand notebook, flicking through the sheets with a moist finger like a bank teller.

'Vicar—'

'Alan, please.'

'—Alan, do you mind if we cut the er, cut through to the core issue here. You see, I'm a total unbeliever essentially, yet I'm very interested in your profession, and how you entered it, and the way you see your role in the community.

Not so much in the pastoral sense but as our, well spiritual welfare officer. I have some questions here, would you mind?'

The vicar looked slightly taken aback, glanced at Mandy busying herself at the sink. 'Well of course not, anything to er—'

'Fantastic! Firstly the big one, and I know it's an old chestnut, but I'd be grateful for your indulgence.' He was speaking very quickly, a pale wet tide mark forming at the corners of his mouth. 'You see the whole of your profession – and I'm really speaking multidenominationally here, is peopled by intelligent, well-educated, often very well-qualified, and in the main rational human beings presumably from a diverse range of backgrounds. Of course, there are also idiots and charlatans same as any other profession. But generally I believe you are considered a bright enough bunch.'

The vicar smiled. He'd heard rumours but hadn't suspected anything like this.

'So how, and this is my question, how can it be, when our species' history has been one of logically reasoned and scientifically proven self discovery, that you, as a body, profess faith in something that becomes daily more improbable?'

'You mean how can I believe in God when there would appear to be a scientific explanation for everything?'

'Precisely. Granted we don't have all the answers yet; we've barely scratched the surface, but as we grow we learn. What was incomprehensible and readily attributed to God in say, the middle ages, such as a plague or something, can now be given a universally acceptable explanation. Similarly things that are a mystery to us now will, over the centuries, find definition.'

The vicar drank his tea; he would have preferred a vodka

and tonic, but he was rarely offered it. Sweet sherry if he was lucky. 'I suppose the short answer, for me anyway, trite though it sounds, would be the one about the more we discover the less we comprehend. Remember the two goldfish swimming around in their bowl?' Peter shook his head, scrawling furiously. 'One says to the other: "Do you believe in God?" The other replies: "Of course! Who do you think changes the water?" Well who's to say that's incorrect? To them we are a higher being, completely unimaginable—'

'But nevertheless fulfilling all the requirements of a God, yes, interesting; may I come back to that point in a moment. Second question: how can you profess faith in a God of love that has had more conflict, pain and suffering perpetrated in its name than any other single cause in history, and which is also demonstrably non-interventional?'

It went on like that for three quarters of an hour and would have continued for longer had not the vicar, punch-drunk and awash with tea, pleaded another engagement and escaped to the fresh air. As he pedalled back up the lane to the village he felt as if he had just emerged from a tough university viva.

Most of it had been awkwardly couched but fairly standard agnostica. But there had been one or two personal questions: how did he sustain his own faith (prayer, self-discipline and one day at a time); how did he feel about a church attendance that averaged around one per cent of the parish population (frustrated); and an odd one about the sanctity of life: 'Do you support the Roman Catholic doctrine prohibiting the taking of one's own life under any circumstances?' Despite Peter's persistence he had declined to state a firm position, insisting his work with the terminally ill made objectivity impossible.

Before he left he tried to draw Peter into more general

discussion but learned little except that he was very busy and the family were fine. They shook hands again, Peter thanked him for a 'most stimulating chat', then disappeared back into the garden shed.

He'd barely sat down and begun the laborious task of deciphering and rewriting the scrawl in the notepad when there was yet another tap on the door. He threw down the pencil and bellowed, 'For God's sake leave me alone and go away!' There was a long pause, just sufficient to pick up the pencil, find his place and begin again. Then there was another tap, softer. He ignored it, cursing under his breath. Whoever it was went away.

A little later he heard a car pull up outside, engine idling, doors slamming shut – it wasn't the Morris. Then an unfamiliar woman's voice with a local accent, calling his name. He cursed again and went to the door.

It was dark outside, and drizzling. He stood outside the shed, looking up and around and behind him at the sky and the dim outline of the cottage, the grass damp beneath his feet. As if for the first time. There were shadows moving over by the kitchen door. 'Hello?' The woman again. 'Mr Deacon is that you?' She came towards him, walked through the light from her car's headlights, beams of softly falling rain. She was holding Sally's hand.

'Daddy, my Daddy!' She ran to him, hugged his knees.

'I hope she's not too late; they were having such a wonderful time.'

'No. No that's fine, hello sweetheart.' Jamie. Where's Jamie? Christ!

He tore across to the house, flung open the door and ran into the darkness, cursing as he collided with the table. 'Jamie!' The sitting room was dark too, he sprinted up the narrow stairs and swung left at the top into their bedroom. 'Jamie!'

255

He was sitting at his desk. He was surrounded with books and toys, some damaged, strewn around the floor at random like so much discarded flotsam. He was looking through a book on classic American cars that Peter had given him for his last birthday. There were pieces of torn pages on the floor around him. Without looking up his hand slowly closed around the next page of the book until it split from its binding, then he crumpled it into a ball and dropped it.

'Jamie, what are you doing?' There was no reply. The next page went. 'Why are you doing that – it's your best book?' Jamie ignored him, tore another page out, screwed it up, dropped it to the floor. 'I am sorry I wasn't there to meet you off the bus. I forgot. The time. That was unforgivable Jamie, please stop it now!'

He looked up, his face shaking and flushed as he struggled to tear out a handful of pages. The eyes were round and hot, lips pressed and locked. Half a dozen pages came away with a sickening splitting sound.

'Stop it now!' He lunged for the book but Jamie ducked away.

'No!' he screamed. 'I hate you!' He tore handfuls and threw them into the air around him. 'I hate you, I hate you, I hate you!'

Peter stepped away. 'Don't Jamie, please don't hate me. I'm sorry, really I am.'

'It's not just that!' The tears started, and the sobs. The book defeated him, he slumped to his knees, flung it aside. Peter moved towards him but he shuffled away backwards through the litter.

'But why?'

His scream was a tortured, shrill damnation. 'Because you hate me!'

'Hi, Been out?'

'Hmm?'

'I called around six but couldn't get a reply.'

He took the receiver away from his ear for a second, reached out to the table for his glass. 'No, we were here, probably upstairs and couldn't hear. Where are you, still at the office?'

'No we're at an Indian restaurant in town. We decided to take a break, then work on later.'

Oh yes? 'Ah, right. Many of you there?'

'Just the three of us on the project. And Charlie of course. He's paying!'

'I should bloody well hope so. Have a chapatti for me while you're at it. What time will you be home?' What time was it now. He had no idea.

'I'm not sure. It depends how we get on. Actually I might stay up here. Last night was awful, I was practically asleep at the wheel then had to be up again at six. Would you mind? We'd be able to really crack on, probably break the back of it by the end of tomorrow.'

'No that's fine, makes sense. Where will you stay, Debbie's?'

'Yes or Charlie's, he's got masses of room.'

'Which?' His heart missed, he felt the back of his neck go cold.

'I don't know! We're all going back there from here to carry on working, possibly all night for all I know. If not then I might go back to Debbie's or I might stay at Charlie's or I might come home. I'll make a decision then.'

'Are you sleeping with him?'

'Oh for God's sake!' She hung up. He stood by the phone, hefting the receiver in his hand. It was a reasonable enough question. She was a healthy young woman with normal physical needs. Their life together had always been sexually active, yet through no direct fault of her own she was now

257

denied that which she had enjoyed and grown accustomed to. And Charlie was an old boyfriend, they'd probably slept together long before he'd even met Emma.

He topped up his glass. The ridiculous thing was he didn't really mind. Oh he disliked the idea of Emma and Charlie actually doing it. Heaving and grunting about between the sheets like a couple of barely post-pubescent teenagers. Happily reliving bedroom encounters of yore. But the continual self-reproachment over his failure to fulfil carnal obligations had become burdensome. Part of him longed to be shot of the responsibility if only an acceptable means could be found to resolve the moral dilemma.

No it wasn't so much the possibility of Emma's infidelity that irked, although the concept both fascinated and appalled him. What really made his blood boil was her refusal, yet again, to give him a straight answer to a direct question. He paced around the kitchen brooding angrily. He found Charlie's number in the telephone address book and called a couple of times but reached his answering machine on both occasions. He considered leaving a message then decided against the idea. It was a fair question; he'd have it out with her tomorrow. Face to face.

He slept in their bed. Or rather lay fretting in a restless waking sleep, tormented by fantastic and lurid imagery that alternately shocked and tantalised him. At some point during the night he jerked upright and blundered through to the children's bedroom to rescue a wailing Sally from her sleep demons – of the eight legged and hairy backed variety. 'Spiders can't hurt you sweetheart,' he murmured groggily, stroking her golden hair by the glow of the nightlight. 'Only people hurt people, and generally then only the ones they really care about.'

'Alice, hello. What? Oh yes fine, fine, thank you. Look could

I possibly beg a favour? It's Sally. I've got to er go out, for a bit this morning and I wondered if you would mind . . . huh? Yes that would be great. Thanks. What? Oh, er just visiting a relative. Right. Bye.'

He made them hot chocolate, real Scots porridge and toasted muffins for breakfast. The three of them sat together in the kitchen. Sally, talkative and cocksure, when he asked her about her nightmare, she just gave him a funny look and denied everything. Jamie remained silent and reproachful. He no longer spoke to Peter except in monosyllabic responses to direct questions: 'Would you like another muffin Jamie? Have you got PE today?' Nor would he be tricked or cajoled into meaningful dialogue. When Peter tried to interest him in a new photograph of Saturn in the newspaper, he just said: 'I saw that yesterday,' and excused himself from the table.

But there had been a noticeable change from the troubled Jamie of old. He was no longer so helpless. He remained isolated and withdrawn, but there was a spark of defiance, a hint of inner strength. Although it was apparent he loathed his father, his hatred was not incapacitating him. It was a small crumb of comfort.

He dressed them warmly against the cold and together they strolled up to the green. Jamie walked on ahead; he could do this by himself. Next term, when the light was better and the ice gone, they might ratify the arrangement. He would be seven soon. He could ride a bike now. They might consider allowing him to take it up the lane, leaving it behind the Post Office to come home on in the afternoons. Next term.

Alice came to the door. 'Hello Sally, you're coming to spend the day with us I hear. Jack will be pleased. And Jazzy, they're in the kitchen.' She bustled off along the big hall.

'Bye Sal,' said Peter with a shrug. 'Thanks Alice, this is

259

very kind, um not sure what time I'll be back.'

'Whenever. Unwell?'

He shook his head. 'I'm sorry?'

'The relative. Mercy visit is it?'

'Something like that.' He thanked her again and headed back down towards the Green. On his way he passed the church, the vicar emerged wearing bicycle clips and carrying a bundle of leaflets, he dropped them in the basket and pedalled across the churchyard towards him. 'Good-morning,' he said cheerfully. 'Looks like a fine day ahead.' All things bright and beautiful. 'By the way, I haven't said how much I enjoyed our little discussion the other day, made a welcome change from the usual flower show committee meetings and youth club outings I can tell you. Mind you, if I'd known I was in for quite such a grilling I would have boned up.'

Peter smiled politely. What was the man on about? 'Yes, right.' He waved as the vicar pedalled on with a happy goodbye and a Latin *bon mot* that he didn't catch. How can anyone, he wondered, particularly someone in the vicar's line of work, be so irrepressibly optimistic? Probably been at the communion wine.

It was a laborious process. A straightforward journey that took twenty-five minutes by car stretched to three times that by bus and foot. Eventually an Ipswich bus arrived which took him about halfway. He waited for another that would take him to the Old Schoolhouse but after a while he gave up and began walking.

The vicar was right, it was a fine day, warm and refreshing once he had walked for a bit. He followed the main road then turned off to try a backroads short cut. The lane wound through a wood then broke clear into the open. Descending a short steep hill, he rounded a bend and found himself entering a village he'd never seen before. Smaller than Bedingham, just a confluence of minor roads, a scattering of houses, pub and a craft shop. He wandered in and looked around at the wares. Shelves of locally thrown pottery, hand-knitted sweaters, home-made marmalade. He picked up a card mounted sketch of two children sitting by a stream in summer. Dragonflies hovered over the water, cattle grazed in the meadow behind them, beyond lay fields of ripe corn. It could have been anywhere, any children, but to him it was Jamie and Sally down at the stream below Walnut Tree cottage. There was a reassuring warmth about the picture, a sense of timeless and dreamy tranquillity.

He took it over to the deserted cash desk and rang the bell. A man appeared wearing jeans and a clay covered sweat-shirt. 'Delightful isn't it?' He took the money and slipped the picture into a bag.

'Oh yes, perfect. Local artist?'

'Chap from a village near here. Does some really splendid work.' The man was in his forties, and spoke with a London accent between puffs on a small pipe. There was clay drying on his hands, under his fingernails, a streak of it through his hair.

'Do you, er, if you don't mind me asking, do you make much of a go at it? All this I mean?' He gestured at the shop, absent-mindedly patting the pocket of his coat for a note-book. But he'd forgotten it.

'Barely.' The man smiled. 'But it sure beats the hell out of flogging commodities.' Christ, another rat-race refugee.

'Don't you miss it, at all? The pace, the cut and thrust, the thinking on your feet?'

Now the man was laughing. What the hell was in that pipe? 'Nope. Not a bit.' He stopped, looked thoughtful. 'I thought I might, and it was a while before I got it completely out of my system, but well you learn to adapt.' He shrugged, puffed again.

261

'Incredible.' He took the picture, tucked it carefully into his coat and set off once more into the sunshine. Just beyond the outskirts of the village, the road began climbing again. After a little way he came upon an old man sitting on a bench by a weatherworn milestone. Peter frowned, staring at the bench, his head swivelling on his shoulders as he walked slowly by. There was no visible reason why there should be a bench there, nor any reason that he could think of why the old man should be sitting on it. He stopped, went back to the bench, and with a nod to the old man who replied with the usual, 'All right?' he sat down next to him on the bench.

The man was in his Sunday suit. It looked thirty or more years old in cut and was worn beyond repair but he still appeared incongruously formal. He sat quite straight on the bench, leaning both hands on a walking stick. He wore no coat but had a woollen waistcoat and a cloth cap. There was a clutch of campaign medals pinned to his breast, the ribbons faded and frayed, the medals tarnished.

They sat in silence. Cars came and went; the old man turned when they approached, watched them pass then stared after them when they had disappeared. They didn't speak, but occasionally and without explanation the man would tip a meaningful nod towards Peter after a car had passed. Soon, Peter began nodding in agreement.

He stayed for a while; he had no idea how long. Ten minutes, three hours? Eventually he rose to his feet, brushed off the back of his coat and turned, thrusting out a hand to the old man. 'Peter Deacon.' They shook, the old man's hand bony and spotted. 'Fascinating.'

It seemed to take much longer than planned to reach the Old Schoolhouse. The back roads' short-cut turned out to be the long way round, finally leading him to the place from the opposite direction from normal. He nearly missed it, plodding steadily along the road engrossed in thought. Then he looked up and saw the Morris. It was parked outside the building with several other cars in what used to be the playground. He lifted the latch on the gate and walked up to the front door.

The receptionist's desk was empty. He hovered uncertainly then looked through a glass panelled door on his right and saw Emma. She was standing at the far end of a large room, leaning over a table with her back to him, discussing something with two people he didn't recognise. He went through the door. It was a bright, spacious open-plan office, probably the school's assembly area once, no ceiling but solid timber A-frames supporting a high steeply angled roof. Bright spot lights supplemented the original school lights which still hung from the cross beams, their dark green metal lamp shades like dustbin lids.

About fifteen people, mostly young, were working at tables or drawing boards. Some looked up and exchanged glances as the rather scruffy, bearded man with long dark hair and pale skin ambled into the room in worn running shoes and a dirty old overcoat, and began studying the ceiling. Bemused, a couple even followed his gaze to discover what he was looking at. Mostly he was ignored. Pop music played from a radio somewhere; outside in reception the telephone was ringing. Emma still hadn't seen him, he went over, came up behind her, leaning around the side of one of the people she was talking to. It was the girl, Debbie he presumed, she turned suddenly and saw him, started, letting out a little cry and clapping a hand to her mouth.

'Peter? What on earth? How did you get here?' Emma was astounded, she glanced around the room nervously, it had grown quiet.

'Surprise!' He threw up his hands. 'I came on the bus, and walked a bit. It was fine, really very interesting.'

'But what are you doing here?' Her eyes widened in alarm. 'Where's Sally?'

'I've come over for a chat and Sally's at the Greenaways.'

She still didn't get it. 'Chat? Peter, I'm working. Couldn't it have waited until I got home?'

'Mmm, I didn't think so. You see I felt that it was important. Still do.'

'What is?' She was hissing at him, quiet but ferocious. She held her head rigid, but still her eyes kept darting around the room to see who was watching.

He noticed. 'You're ashamed.' He stepped back in surprise and considered the notion, as though sampling a bold new wine for the first time. 'Good God, I embarrass you. I do, don't I?' He looked around the room, his voice louder.

'Peter,' she pleaded, 'Please go home and whatever it is we'll talk about it later.'

'Hey! Everyone! Peter Deacon. I'm this lovely girl's husband, how do you do!' Hands raised, he turned this way and that before them, smiling and nodding like a newly elected politician. Emma buried her face in her hands. He went on, his voice conspiratorial but clear, like a theatrical aside. 'Last night, I asked her if she was sleeping with the boss. She refused to give me an answer then, so I'm here to get one now!'

'Peter, for God's sake.' A face appeared at the glass door at the far end of the room. It was Charlie, he came in and walked over to them. He eyed Peter cautiously, then he recognised him. 'Good Lord. Peter, how are you? Look at all this hair!' He tried not to look shocked, at the same time glancing at Emma for clarification. Her eyes were pleading, her cheeks pinched and flushed.

'And here he is!' He shook Charlie's hand energetically, clapping an arm around his shoulders. 'Actually Charles, I do want to say that there is absolutely nothing personal about this. In fact your role, if any, is completely irrelevant.'

Charlie smiled uneasily, glancing from Peter to Emma and back. 'I'm not sure I follow you old man. I tell you what, why don't we all go next door into my office, have a coffee and we can sort it out there.'

'Here's fine.' The voice had changed suddenly, clipped and icy. He was looking at Emma, his eyes dull and dark like bottomless wells. 'I can wait. All day if necessary.' Nobody moved; the room was silent, somebody tactlessly turned the radio volume down, the better to hear. 'Are you sleeping with him?'

She spoke slowly and quietly, biting each word off through gritted teeth. 'I am not discussing it here.'

'I say, I don't think that's the sort of question a gentleman—'

'You keep out of this Gallstone!' The eyes were wild, the danger palpable.

But this was Charlie's patch, his people. Like it or not he had to act. He snapped his fingers towards two youths working at a table by the window, at the same time he reached forward, gripping Peter by the elbow: 'Brian, Kevin I think we'll escort Mr Deacon—'

Peter's fist hit him just below the left eye. It was not as hard as he intended, the angle was bad for a proper swing. But it was enough. Charlie reeled back clutching his hand to his eye, stumbled on a chair and crashed to the floor. There were gasps, somebody, one of the girls let out a strangled scream. Emma pushed past Peter and knelt by Charlie who groaned, rocking slowly from side to side on his back. Everyone else gaped. After a moment the two youths looked at each other and began moving reluctantly towards Peter. His shoulders slumped, he sighed: 'Shit.' Then began threading his way back towards the door. 'It's okay guys. I was on my way out.'

*

He wandered aimlessly until he came across a pub. He ordered up doubles and set to with a vengeance. When he emerged two hours later it was dark and he was drunk. There were houses and streetlights visible a mile or so along the road, the other way darkness, he struck out towards the lights, hungry for humanity and the comforting solidity of an illuminated pavement. Blearily calculating he was somewhere on the residential outskirts of Ipswich, he walked on until he reached a busy main road, then took signs for the town centre.

It was Friday night, the place busy with people out for the evening. He passed a cinema complex with a long queue waiting patiently outside and stopped to listen to a busker playing jigs on a violin. 'This guy is good!' he told them, tapping his foot and bobbing in time to the fiddler. He picked up the busker's hat and began walking down the line demanding contributions. 'Come on madam, the bloke is busting his arse out there. Thank you mate, very generous. Thank you sir, thank you madam. Oh look, ten pence from the man in the camel coat, sure you can spare it? Right which one of you put in the apple core . . .?'

The manager of the complex appeared from nowhere in a dinner suit. 'You'll have to clear off, soliciting is not allowed.'

'Steady on maestro, what's the difficulty?'

'He can play and people can make contributions if they want, but you're not allowed to solicit. Now clear off before I call the law.'

Further on he heard music coming from the door of a wine bar. He went in and hoisted himself onto a stool, noisily disgorging handfuls of loose change and crumpled notes onto the bar. He took the little picture he'd bought earlier out of its paper bag. One corner of the mounting was bent. Squinting at the wine list scratched on a blackboard, he waved the barman over. 'I would like to order a bottle of your finest champagne.'

The barman looked at him dubiously, leaning over to peer at the clothes. 'Planning a little celebration are we?'

'Hmm? Oh yes, perhaps. Actually, it's more like celebrating a little plan.' He laughed, banged his hand onto the bar then stopped, frowning at his dwindling pile of cash. 'The thing is, I can't.' Mystified, the barman shook his head, and looked along the bar, other customers were waiting. 'Buy a bottle of your finest Champagne that is. In any case I rather doubt that it's up to much. No offence mind.'

'None taken. Drink or door buster.'

'Bang open a bottle of Jacob's Creek quick.'

A young woman was sitting alone at a table. Something about her looked vaguely familiar. Her hair was dyed black and fluffy. Her face heavily made up with thick dark eyeshadow and purple lipstick. She wore a lacy black top, thigh length red PVC skirt, black tights and a short mock-fur jacket. He helped himself to a spare glass, picked up the bottle and shimmied towards her table in time with the music. 'Excuse me, my name is Peter.' He fumbled to disentangle a hand from the bottle and glasses, bowed as, after a bemused pause, she extended hers. 'I was wondering if you would care to join me in a glass of wine?'

She drew heavily on her cigarette, chewing on a piece of gum, looked him over. 'Okay.' She shrugged.

'Marvellous!' He sat down and filled the glasses. 'There you go, now you have a little try of that. Did you know that this stuff comes from down under? Incredible isn't it? Trampled by the feet of aboriginals . . .' He went on for half an hour without pausing, except to drink from his glass. In no time the bottle was empty and he had to signal the barman for another.

But she was growing impatient. The man may well talk

with a posh accent but it was non stop drivel, clearly pissed out of his mind. And he looked a bit dodgy, those eyes ... Eventually she leaned forward and interrupted him in mid flow. 'Look mate, if you're not here to do the business I will thank you to bugger off and leave the table free for those who are.'

'Business?' He looked around, confused and befuddled. The bar was filling up. 'Sorry, I—'

She rolled her eyes. 'Manual relief round the back for a fiver, oral'll cost you fifteen, straight sex thirty, in your car or I got a place five minutes away, strictly condoms, nothing kinky and no kissing.'

He sat back, threw his head up and laughed. 'Good Lord, you're a whore!' Heads turned, she caught the barman's eye, he nodded. 'That is fantastic. Really.' He started rifling through his pockets for something to write with. 'Look I'd like to ask you just a few questions, won't take a minute. God a whore, fantastic ...!'

The barman threw him out with the remains of the second bottle that he'd already paid for. He stuffed it in a pocket and staggered off into the night.

He woke up to feel rain falling softly on his face. It was still dark but the sky showed a hint of grey. He lay on his back and listened to the pre-dawn hush, a zephyr of wind rustled leaves on nearby trees, away in the distance an owl called. Something tiny was moving about in the undergrowth inches from his ear. He was cold and damp but comfortable enough. He had no idea how he had arrived in the ditch, nor where the ditch was; his recollections were a jumbled confusion of snatched moments, glimpsed faces and uncon- nected events. He tried to sit up but the effort made his head spin so he lay a while longer.

Eventually he struggled dizzily to his feet. The ditch was

beside a lane. He looked both ways, then set off wearily in the direction of the brighter horizon. He finally got a lift from a truck driver on his way to collect a load of poultry from a farm two villages from Bedingham. The man eyed Peter suspiciously at first but then took pity and drove out of his way, dropping him on the green outside Mrs Morrison's Post Office Stores. Peter thanked him, climbed down from the truck and walked off down the lane.

As he neared the cottage he saw his father's car parked outside.

CHAPTER
13

He froze. Stopped dead in the lane outside the cottage. Although he was exhausted, filthy and cold, desperate to go in, he couldn't. Not at the moment, he wasn't ready. Backing across the lane, he began moving towards the stile and the safety of the fields beyond. But he was too slow.

'Daddy! Grandma look it's Daddy!' Sally appeared at the side of the cottage, pointing and beckoning. A moment later his mother appeared. He groaned, walked back across the lane towards them. As he grew nearer Sally fell quiet, sliding into cover behind his mother's tweed skirt. 'Daddy? You're all dirty.'

He stopped in front of his mother, her eyes searching his, wounded and anxious like a hurt doe.

'What are you doing here?' he said quietly.

'We thought we'd just pop down for the day, and see how you all were.' There was no anger, nor disapproval. Just incomprehension, and the other thing, worse.

'Don't do that mum,' he said quietly, holding his hands up in front of his chest. 'Anything, anything at all, but not pity.'

'You'd better come inside.'

He followed her into the kitchen. They were all there, arranged in an awkward group, like amateur actors. Three generations of Deacons, Peter waited close by the back door with his mother who chose to remain next to him. Sally ran over and stood in front of Emma who was leaning against the sink, arms folded, face expressionless. At the table the young boy stood next to the old man. Jamie had been showing his grandfather some of his schoolwork, they both stared at Peter with the same shocked hopelessness. His father, drawn and frail, looked slowly from the top of Peter's dirty and unkempt hair, down past the red-rimmed eyes, the grimy cheeks, beard, and on down the length of the filthy and mud spattered overcoat to the sodden trainers. Peter ran a hand through his hair self-consciously, a couple of sprigs of moss fell out, falling like autumn leaves to the floor. His father sighed. Suddenly Peter snorted. This was absurd, there was nothing anyone could say, the play had departed the script, the wrong players were on stage together at the wrong time, and nobody knew how to break the impasse. Except Emma.

'You'd better go upstairs and change out of those things. I'll run you a bath.' Her voice quiet and matter of fact.

'Right.' Good old Em, pillar of strength. He remembered suddenly the last time he had seen her. Yesterday was it – at the office? Poor old Charlie. They passed each other on opposite sides of the table, she moving purposefully for the bathroom. 'Well it's good to see you,' he said, to the room in general. A moment later they heard him clump slowly upstairs. After ten minutes Emma went up to fetch him for the bath. He was spread-eagled on the spare room bed. Face down, shoes still on, the overcoat, the damp jeans. He was snoring softly. She closed the door and went downstairs.

They went for a stroll down the lane to the farm and back.

Walking slowly, pausing frequently, ostensibly to admire the view over the fields and across the vale, but mainly to allow his father to catch his breath. It had been his idea, his wife had fretted: 'Don't be ridiculous John; it's cold and damp out there. You'll tire yourself out, catch something.'

'My death of cold perhaps?' He'd gone anyway. Peter, clean, rested and refreshed followed obediently. He'd slept until early afternoon, would probably have gone on, but Emma had woken him eventually. 'They are leaving soon, you'd better come down and see them.'

They moved slowly down the lane, side by side but not touching. The pace was very slow, almost a dawdle. Apart from a vague, lingering muzziness, Peter's head felt clear and alert. He waited patiently for his father to open discussions in the usual manner.

'Your mother is very anxious about you. We hadn't heard anything for so long. You know what she's like.' They stopped where the lane bent, his father wheezing and coughing. He banged his stick on the ground, nodding defiantly as Peter bent to him: 'All right?' Gradually the spasm passed.

'Did you know that you can see the churches of seven separate parishes from here? On a clear day of course, and only in winter.' His eyes swiftly travelled the valley, but it was dull and misty, he found only four.

'It is a delightful spot.' He inclined his head towards Peter, but he couldn't look at him. 'So what happens now?'

'I've been giving it a great deal of thought. You know Dad, Emma's really doing very well here. I never realised it but she is much happier now. She thrives on it – full-time work, the demands, the responsibilities. She has regained her independence, her identity and I had never properly understood how important that was to her. Never really considered that she was entitled to these things.' He thought

272

back to yesterday and his performance at Charlie's office, wondered guiltily whether she still had a job.

'And what of your responsibilities?'

'Ah. Indeed.' He wished he had his notes with him; it was all clearly set out. They resumed walking. 'Well Dad, until recently I never seriously considered them. I worked, everything revolved around that. My responsibility, if you can call it that, my function more like, was simple, one dimensional. Just keep that old gravy train rolling.'

'What's wrong with that? Millions of people do just that all their lives.'

'Nothing Dad! But this is not about right and wrong.' He walked ahead, backwards so as to face his father, gesturing with his hands for emphasis. But the old man kept his head down as though studying the lane for hidden pitfalls. 'But when it suddenly stops, and stays stopped, things change, become different.' He was growing exasperated, this was hopeless. 'Try and imagine what it would have been like if, if the Government had suddenly scrapped the Royal Air Force. Shut it down overnight. Right at the very moment that you were poised to launch yourself up the ladder to the very top. Flight Lieutenant remember? Your whole life mapped out, Flight Command, Squadron, Group and on.'

'Well?' The voice was gruff, the head still down and shaking – make your point. Peter could see he was trying to understand, but he might as well have asked him to imagine they were walking on Mars.

'Well, if that was your whole life, all you'd ever thought about, been trained for, lived for, I expect there would probably follow a period of introspection, don't you? Re-evaluation?'

'You have to just pick up the pieces and get on with it. Responsibilities remember?' He shook his stick angrily.

'Exactly. But I would argue that the real responsibilities,

no, obligations is a better word, only become clear when everything else is stripped away. A single young man under normal circumstances has none at all, except to himself. But he is generally driven by instinct to establish a means to reproduce his genes. When he gets married he is obligated to his wife. But if she works, has a career, an income, her independence, then these obligations are intangible, almost entirely moral. He can go on just as before.' He paused, was he getting through? Impossible to say, he ploughed on. 'Until the children come. Then suddenly there are clear obligations. The parents' role in life, and, in my view their only genuine responsibility, is suddenly crystal clear. They must, as parents, do everything within their power to ensure their succession.'

His father stopped; he was breathing heavily again. His voice hoarse. 'This may be terribly old-fashioned, but I was brought up to believe that this was achieved by men providing for the women who raise the young. It's quite natural you know, happens right across the animal king-dom. Ask your brother.'

Ah David. He was bound to crop up sooner or later. 'I'm not disputing that. All I am saying, and I think we are in agreement, is that our primary and sole responsibility as parents is to provide the best environment in which to raise and prepare our offspring so that in due course they can go out into the world, compete and survive.'

'And this –' He flashed the walking stick about him like a fencer, stabbing ferociously at the Suffolk countryside, and at Peter, '– is it? A dingy little hovel in the back of beyond and a father who stays out all night God knows where, and comes back stinking of drink and covered in filth like a bloody tramp?' He doubled over, coughing violently.

Peter went to his side, put an arm across the shaking back, supporting him until the convulsions subsided. Gradually his father straightened, dabbing at his mouth with a handkerchief. Peter began leading him back towards the cottage. 'Believe it or not,' he said softly, 'I think it might be. At least in part.'

They left after tea. His mother led him into the sitting room to say goodbye. 'I'm sorry, we should have given you some warning, but he was absolutely determined.'

'It was good of you. The children were thrilled.'

'Yes they do look well. Jamie is really growing up.' She was searching his eyes again. 'What is it darling? What's happening? Is it you and Emma?'

He smiled. 'Me probably, Emma's fine, they all are. Really mum you mustn't worry.' He took her hand, squeezed. 'How is he coping?'

'Well he hates the debilitation, you know every day a little bit weaker. He just wants to get it over with I think.'

'Is he um, prepared?' He'd desperately wanted to ask his father himself. So many questions, it was crucial to everything. His mother scoffed; 'Good God, dying doesn't bother him, either of us really, we saw enough of that in the War.' She sighed. 'No, it's not the end of his life that frightens him, it's the continuation of it.'

They walked back to the kitchen and out to the car.

That weekend he moved into the shed. He felt there was much to do and he was anxious to get on. He began avoiding the house, whenever he went inside the atmosphere quickly became tense. Emma refused to speak to him at all, and Jamie. Even Sally was wary. Nobody disturbed him in the shed; it was warm and peaceful. He had everything he needed, when he was tired he slept in the old armchair by the stove. He rarely felt thirsty or hungry but kept a plastic container of tap water and a supply of biscuits and fruit in a box under the bench. The only time he ventured outside was to stock up on fuel for the stove and relieve himself in the overgrown pasture land around the far side of the garage.

He became engrossed in his linear time experiment. In the introduction to his notes he proposed: 'The body's natural rhythm is not circadian nor cyclical, in fact not a rhythm at all, but a stream of irregularly occurring events like random peaks on an endless oscilloscope trace. However, as a convenience, we have conditioned ourselves in accordance with the regime imposed by the earth's rotation ...' He went on: 'By removing all external cues – principally daylight – the fundamental composition of time becomes subjective, and indeed plastic, so that with practice it is possible to reduce the passage rate of perceived apparent time, almost to a standstill, or indeed speed it up, so that hours of work can be easily accommodated within the space of just a few minutes, or a moment's reflection expanded to fill a day.'

Eliminating all light from the shed was a problem. He finally succeeding by taping cardboard over the windows and sealing the cracks around the door with rags and newspapers. Then he had to devise a lightproof means of allowing air into the shed. At some point he crammed cotton wool into his ears in an effort to exclude the tell-tale sounds of birdsong and passing tractors.

He worked on other projects: meticulously drawing up preliminary plans for a new aircraft recovery system for ships at sea; studying books on the history and geography of the area surrounding Bedingham; devising a national marketing strategy for the goods he had seen at the craft market. Or transcribing poetry from Alice's book onto disk. Often he worked on two or more ideas at once, inevitably notes became muddled and confused; lines of Milton unaccountably appearing next to a sketch of a jet fighter's undercarriage; the words 'Event Horizon' in a heavily scored box in the middle of a map of Suffolk.

At some point he awoke in the armchair to see chinks of light around the doorframe. Somebody must have been in, he concluded irritably. Then on Tuesday morning Emma walked into the shed. He was sitting at the bench, staring into the screen of his word processor when the door opened suddenly, scattering his bits of rag and newspaper sealing and flooding the room with light. He gasped, throwing his arm up against the sudden glare. She left the door wide open and stepped back into the sunshine.

'Can you come out here for a moment please?'

He staggered into the light, eyes screwed up and blinking. The air was intoxicating, cool and fresh with a powerful scent of turned soil and new growth. On the other side of the lane, the crop fields beyond seemed flushed, viridescent, the sky cerulean, scattered cumulus clouds painfully, brilliantly white. 'Wow!' he gasped again. 'That is stunning.' He tore his eyes from the vista to look at Emma but she was checking the contents of her purse. She was in work clothes, jeans and a sweater but court shoes and pearls, her face carefully made up, her bronze hair clean and shining. 'You look very nice.' He meant it.

'Right, we're off. Mandy will be here in a while. I'd like her to do upstairs; can you make sure she does the spare room properly and if she has time ask her if she would mind having a go at the oven.' She snapped the purse shut, slipped it in the pocket of her jacket and began pulling on a pair of brightly coloured wool gloves. She looked at him dispassionately, her face set, voice matter of fact. He blinked at her, his eyes still smarting and watery from the sudden glare.

'I've just come off the telephone. I've had a word with the doctor. He's going to look in on you later this morning. I think it would probably be a good idea if you were to have a chat – please try and be as polite and helpful as you can.'

She finished stretching her fingers into the gloves, slid her hands back into the pockets in search of car keys. 'I will collect Sally from Danielle's, Alice is going to meet Jamie off the bus and take him back to the Old Rectory for tea. I will take Sally there and help Alice put them to bed.'

'Bed?'

'She is having them for the night.'

'Ah.' He bent down to see through the car windscreen, they were both in there, watching. He waved but could not see if either waved back. He doubted it somehow. 'What for?'

'So that you and I can spend an uninterrupted evening by ourselves. We have some matters we need to discuss.' She produced the keys and turned for the car.

The idea of the doctor intrigued him, wrinkling his nose he went back into the shed to retrieve a notebook. The air in there was warm and stale, but familiar. It was like returning to a dream after a brief spell of wakefulness, or was it like waking up after a short, explosively bright dream? In an instant he was engrossed but then he remembered the doctor, found a pencil stub and went over to the house.

In the kitchen, the smell reminded him that he hadn't eaten. He went upstairs to the bedroom and began searching through cupboards and chests of drawers for clean clothes, standing by the bed tearing off the ones he had on and throwing them into the corner. Again a smell arrested him. Emma's smell, shampoo and Rive Gauche, he sat down on the bed, leaned over the pillows, sniffing at her night gown like a curious dog. She had looked fabulous this morning, appealing and sexy. He sensed a momentary stirring, a fleeting pang of lust like the delicate touch of tiny needles at his loins. Then it was gone. He gathered the clean clothes up into a bundle and hurried down to the bathroom.

Mandy was in the kitchen. She froze, gaping open

mouthed at his nakedness, a jar of instant coffee in one hand, teaspoon in the other.

'Oh Mandy, hello. Coffee, yes please. And I don't suppose there is any chance you could do one of those breakfast cook up things. I'm absolutely ravenous.' He went through to the bathroom and shut the door.

The warm water was soothing and soporific, she had to bang on the door to rouse him. 'Your breakfast is ready. Peter? Are you there?' He appeared in the kitchen a couple of minutes later, his long hair slicked back wet across his head, his eyes red and his face pale, but clean, and clothed. He began eating. 'This is fantastic, Mandy, thank you.'

'You're welcome.' She was still recovering, her voice unusually hesitant. 'What's a girl to think?' she'd asked herself. 'Bare-arsed and bold as you please right across the kitchen like that.' She'd wondered if she ought to just get her coat and go straight home, but he seemed so innocent about it, as if he had no idea he wasn't wearing anything. Sometimes he could be so scatty. And sometimes he was just plain peculiar. She concluded that that was why she fancied him. In the end she had stayed and cooked his breakfast.

'Do you make a regular thing of it then?' she asked.

'Hmm?' He was thinking about the impending arrival of the doctor.

'Waltzing about the place in front of strangers in the altogether like that?'

He munched on a sausage, looked up at her, properly noticing her for the first time that morning. The little denim skirt again, and the ankle boots, and a plain white T-shirt. She'd tarted her face up too, lipstick and eyeshadow. He patted the chair next to him, she lowered herself slowly. He detected chemist's shop body scent over the smell of fried bacon. 'How old are you again?'

'Seventeen in April.' She kept her chin up, tried to sound

confident, but his sudden proximity, the way his eyes drilled into her like that, it was unnerving.

'Have you ever been to bed with a man before?' He put his fork down, sipped coffee.

''Course,' she lied nervously. 'I've had boyfriends since I was fifteen.'

He nodded. 'What would you do if I said I wanted to go to bed with you right now?'

She swallowed. He'd stopped eating, just stared. 'I don't know.' Her voice had grown small, and trembling like a cornered mouse. 'All right.'

A wince passed across his face like a fleeting shadow. He shook his head, the eyes boring deep, invading her once more. 'So, if I said I want you to' – he looked around the room then back to her eyes – 'to take off all your clothes right now, and dance about for me up here on this table, then lie on it so that I could fuck you, you would do it?'

Her eyes began to fill with tears, her lips to quiver. Why was he like this? He sounded angry, his voice hard. What had she done to make him cross with her? She was confused, and frightened. 'Yes.'

He sighed. 'But why?'

The reply was tearful, a whisper: 'Because I love you.'

'NO!' He leaped to his feet upsetting coffee over the table and knocking his chair to the floor. She gasped and shrank back. 'No, no, no! You don't love me, you like me and I intimidate you. It is not enough, not nearly enough!' He paced furiously around the floor, muttering and cursing to himself, suddenly he swung back to her, leaning low across the table on his palms until his face was inches from hers, his eyes darting about her as though in frantic search. 'Do it. Do it if it makes you happy. Do it for a laugh if you like. Do it if it turns you on. But do it only because you choose to, because *you* want to. Otherwise never do it and especially never do it just because some half-baked lowlife like me asks you to. Got that? Never!'

She was crying hard, shoulders slumped, head hanging, rivulets of mascara-stained water running down her nose to drop and splash onto the pine. He continued pacing, angrily back and forth like a Gestapo interrogator, watching her, crushed by his vehemence like a carelessly trodden crocus. 'Important lesson,' he kept muttering furiously to himself, then: 'This is really going to have to stop.' He came around the table and knelt beside her on the flagstones. 'Come here.' She turned to him and buried her face in his chest, sobbing and choking. He held onto her, rocking forwards and backwards and stroking her hair, murmuring meaninglessly.

He heard her voice, lower down, choked and muffled against his chest. 'I do though, I do. I really do love you.'

He groaned. 'Oh Christ.'

The doctor studied him professionally as they exchanged pleasantries, the way doctors do. He was in late middle age, experienced and mature, seasoned by a lifetime in General Practice, firstly in inner cities, then for the last twenty years in country practices. Though he was not in any way a conceited man, he wore about him the air of one for whom life holds no surprises. He had seen it all, the entire spectrum of human suffering; from morning sickness to senile dementia; from a child's finger cut on a penknife to a man's arm ripped from the shoulder by a corn thresher; from Aids to xenophobia.

He was also a thorough man. Although a colleague at the practice had written a prescription for sleeping tablets for Peter, there were only minimal notes. As far as the doctor was concerned, this was a new patient.

Nor did he begin by asking: 'What seems to be the problem?' The receptionist at the practice had just said that

the man's wife had telephoned to say that she was concerned about the state of her husband's mind and could
someone pop over and see him. Minds were tricky, so little
was understood. But every mind had a body and over the
years he had repeatedly found that problems with one were
frequently linked to trouble with the other. In any case he
always made a physical examination of a new patient.

'Wherever's most comfortable Mr Deacon.' They stayed in
the warmth of the kitchen. He sent a morose cleaning girl
with blotchy cheeks out of the room with a joke about her
not wanting to witness the 'horrific spectacle of her partially
clad employer'. She left without smiling. Peter perched on
the kitchen table, the doctor carrying out the examination
in the usual way, starting at the top and continuing down.
As he worked the man talked, a lot.

'Tell me doctor, would you mind if I asked you a few
questions? Without wishing to compromise your professional discretion of course, but I am extremely interested to
know your views on abortion for instance.'

The doctor tugged at Peter's earlobe, peering into the
eyepiece of the otoscope. 'I beg your pardon?'

'Abortion. Is it defensible? Under any circumstances,
apart from when the life of the mother is directly at risk?'

'I don't perform abortions Mr Deacon,' he said, with a hint
of irony. 'It's a surgical procedure, carried out in hospitals.'
He fingered the glands under Peter's neck, ticked off an
entry on the file.

'Yes, but you refer women to hospitals for abortions, that
makes you responsible, therefore you must have a view.'

The doctor stopped and looked at Peter. 'There are strict
guidelines for referrals for terminations. Laws, clearly defining the criteria from which judgements are made. My view
on the matter is not of relevance any more than the man in
the streets.'

'But don't you find that paradox difficult to deal with? I mean your view, your personal moral standpoint is bound to colour your judgement. Subconsciously at the very least.'

He managed to stem the tide briefly by asking Peter to breathe deeply during the chest examination but he resumed his theme immediately after, panting on about confidentiality pacts: 'What if someone agreed to be tested for cancer but said they did not wish to be informed of the result under any circumstances, or what if somebody tested positive for HIV but refused to tell their partner?' He grew excitable, gesticulating wildly, arguing each point ferociously, but also articulately and for the most part logically.

The doctor pencilled notes on the bottom of the examination form. Physically he could detect no signs of illness or abnormality. But Peter was underweight, undernourished and out of condition, in fact close to exhaustion. He reminded him of a sailor he had once examined after the man had been adrift in an open boat for five days. When asked to perform a few step-ups onto a chair, Peter's pulse had become fast, thin and irregular. He'd heard better lungs on a lifelong smoker and the blood pressure was way up. At one point after the exercising, Peter had completely lost the thread of his conversation and gone very pale, reaching out a hand to the table to steady himself.

Nothing that exercise, a regular diet and a few days uninterrupted rest shouldn't sort out. There was no question that he was in poor shape for his age. But why? He studied him, only half listening as Peter fired off another salvo of questions, something about compulsory organ donor cards.

'Are you a drinker Mr Deacon?' That stopped him.

Peter was thrown by the question. Good old Em. Drinker? Not lately, not since that night in Ipswich. When was that? Ages ago. He shook his head.

283

'Drugs?' You never knew with these London types.

Peter laughed. 'No. I did try LSD once though, extraordinary stuff, it's true what they say you know – it really does expand the mind, unlocking little compartments normally kept tight shut. But listen doctor I've been doing some research of my own lately, I'd like to tell you . . .' And he was off again, pacing around the floor in vest and underpants, rattling on about some linear time experiment he had been conducting.

'Doctor do you support the views of some so-called alternative practitioners regarding claims that clinically diagnosed illnesses such as cancer can in certain cases be treated and cured from within? Solely by the power of the mind?'

The doctor began returning instruments to his bag. 'Well it's an interesting concept, sadly there is not enough qualitative research being carried out on the subject. Certainly it is my experience that a positive outlook speeds the healing process in injuries and some illnesses, in the same way that a negative outlook can genuinely make people ill. But that is a far cry from the sort of miraculous recoveries you speak of.'

'Fascinating!' He drew breath to change tack but the doctor jumped in ahead.

'Tell me, Mr Deacon, are you regularly employed at this time?'

Peter laughed again. 'Yes I certainly am Doctor, never been busier. But if you mean do I have a conventional "job"' – he wiggled the fingers of both hands for quotation marks – 'then I would have to say that I do not, although it is my opinion that this, er situation is unlikely to continue for much longer. One way or another.'

'One way or another?' He needed specialist counselling, he had to admit it. He could detect no physical explanation for the patient's physical condition. That meant it was in the head and he was damned if he knew what was in Peter Deacon's head. He wasn't sure he wanted to know. He'd fix up an appointment for him at the hospital, let them sort it out. As he rose to leave, Peter grabbed his arm.

'Doctor! One last question, before you leave. Please!' There was alarm in the eyes. Panic. The doctor hesitated, sat down again. He was rewarded with a wan smile. 'Thank you.' Peter fell silent, pinching the bridge of his nose, eyes screwed shut. He felt exhausted suddenly, longed to lie down. The doctor waited, glanced discreetly at his watch.

'I'm sorry to keep presenting you with these hoary old moral dilemmas, but I would be genuinely interested in your views on this one.' The voice was calm, a hint of humour flickered across the face. 'Supposing you had a patient, say an old man, a widower perhaps who lived on his own. His family were long gone, he had no dependents in the world. Nobody in the entire world depending upon him, for anything. And suppose he was sick, suffering great pain and unlikely to recover. Yet you were entirely satisfied that he was capable of rational thought. One day you visit him and he tells you that he has concluded that it is time to end his life because the burden of sustaining it was intolerable and pointless. You have it within your power to provide the means for him to carry out his wishes privately, painlessly and with dignity. He asks you to provide these means. A) Do you accept his decision and B) Do you provide the means?'

The doctor sighed heavily, lowered his bag to the floor. 'Mr Deacon,' he began wearily, 'the American constitution provides a means whereby a citizen can refuse to answer a question, even under oath in court, if he believes his answer may implicate him.'

Peter nodded. 'The fifth amendment, I understand that but—'

The doctor held up a hand, he didn't have time for this. 'Nobody, no professional person in their right mind is going to answer a hypothetical question in a manner that appears to condone a breach of the law. What you are talking about here is professionally assisted voluntary euthanasia and whether we like it or not it is illegal. However,' their eyes locked, 'in my view it is the General Practitioner's primary responsibility to relieve suffering in the community, and that in doing so he should keep the well-being of the patient uppermost and always exercise care, consideration and discretion. It is also my view that he should be free to carry out his responsibilities unimpeded by insensitive and out-dated legislation. Now if you'll excuse me I do have several more visits.'

He wandered up to the Post Office and bought pasta and ham and cream for dinner, he'd make a Carbonara – it was an old favourite of Emma's. Picking up two bottles of Chianti, he hesitated at the whiskey display, Mrs Morrison watching discreetly over the top of her spectacles. But he decided against it, picked up a half of gin for Emma's evening heart starter and a miniature bottle of Sambuca to go with the coffee.

He bought a box of chocolates for Mandy but by the time he arrived back at the cottage she had gone home so he hid them in the shed. It was lunchtime but he wasn't hungry, he plodded heavily up the stairs, collapsed onto the spare room bed and fell into deep dreamless sleep.

The telephone roused him, early in the evening. He sat up suddenly in the gathering darkness, shivered and ran downstairs. It was Mitch.

'Hi there,' she said in awful Texan. 'How's things out there in Indian country?'

'Mitch.' The sound of her voice overwhelmed him. He

leaned his forehead against the wall with a thud. 'It's really, bloody good to hear from you.'

'You too Peto, what you been up to?' God he sounded low. She'd heard Emma's side the previous evening. It was unbelievable, living in a shed, sleeping in ditches. Punching out Charles Gladstone for heaven's sake – although she quite liked the sound of that one. Emma had hinted at a visit from Dan, or just a chat on the phone, assuming she could get Peter out of the shed and into the kitchen. But Dan had refused: 'I'm not getting into all that "Come along now old chap" nonsense again, not after the last fiasco. If he wants to speak to me, I'm confident he'll get in touch.'

But Emma's tone had bothered Mitch – hard, and resolute. 'We've got to have it out Mitch; this can't go on,' she had said.

Peter sighed. 'Well, this and that, I expect you've already heard via the bush telegraph.'

'I wanted to hear it from you.' She waited, listening to the soft rhythm of his breathing at the other end as if he was lying next to her, asleep. 'Peter?'

'Hmm. It's ah, all a bit of a mess really. I don't understand it, one minute I seem to be on top of the situation, the next I get distracted by something else, it's just a bloody mess.'

'How's Em? The kids?'

'Oh they'll be all right, much better off really. Your godson is really finding his feet; it's a good school – you'd be amazed at the progress. Sal, well she's a tower, running everything as usual, of course.'

Mitch laughed encouragingly. What did he mean: 'Much better off?'

Peter heard the Morris pull up outside. 'Mitch I'll have to go, got to get the dinner on.' He hesitated. 'One thing though, could I, if it became necessary, could I pop up and bum a patch of floor space off you for a few days, you know

287

while things sort themselves out?'

'Of course. Any time, you know that.'

'Thanks. You're a brick Mitch, always were. Goodbye.'

Mrs Morrison's ham was not right for the Carbonara and he overcooked the spaghetti, but it was edible and Emma was polite about it. Both of them were on edge. It was like a first date but less enjoyable, fraught with anticipation and unease. Peter was attentive and solicitous, he took her coat, poured her a gin and tonic and busied himself in the kitchen while she freshened up in the bedroom. By the time she returned the table was laid with a cloth and candles, supper was cooked and the wine open. He refilled her glass, she followed him into the sitting room, the freshly lit fire blazed in the grate, The Eagles (another favourite of hers) played softly on the CD; there were early daffodils on the mantelpiece and little dishes of nuts and olives on the coffee table.

'Peter, what is all this? You're not making things any easier you know.'

'Yes I do. I just thought, perhaps we could suspend hostilities until after dinner.' He grinned lopsidedly.

'If you like, but it won't make any difference.' And it didn't. She was determined not to be wrong footed, maintaining a wary distance throughout dinner. Although Peter worked hard to create an atmosphere of temporary normality and establish a neutral dialogue, it seemed that there were no non-contentious topics available for discussion and conversation remained stilted and desultory. Emma, fearful of attempts at pre-emptive mollification, was circumspect and monosyllabic throughout.

After dinner she accepted coffee but declined Sambuca; the party was over. He stood about uneasily: 'Well, um where shall we ...' They went through to the sitting room. She turned off the CD, sat down in an armchair by the fire.

He threw on a couple of logs, poked the embers to life and sank into the opposite chair. He said nothing, her ball. She drew a deep breath.

'I think it is fair to say that we have a problem, do you agree?'

'I think it would be fairer to say that I have a problem.'

She nodded. 'What did the doctor say?'

'He says he wants me to see a specialist.' He plucked at a thread on the arm of the chair.

Again the nod. She crossed her legs, steepled her fingers beneath her chin. 'What do you think?'

God, twenty questions. I just want to get it over with. Like Dad. He tried to concentrate but his thoughts crowded him. 'I think a great deal about matters that I believe to be of enormous importance.'

'Such as?'

He shook his head.

'Peter, don't shut me out! I'm trying to understand.' She checked herself, exhaled slowly, determined to remain calm.

'Don't lie to me Emma. This little chat is not about trying to understand anything. It's too late for that.'

She glared at him but did not argue the point. There was quiet save for the crackling of the fire; she stared into it pensively, flicking her front tooth with a thumbnail. Eventually she faced him again, spoke softly.

'Perhaps you're right. But I have tried, really tried to understand what it is that you want.'

'Ah, I can help you with that one.' He leaned forward. 'For a long time I just wanted everything to be the same as it was. Nothing more. My mistakes were essentially twofold.' He spoke quickly, well-rehearsed lines; it was all in the diary. 'Firstly I deluded myself into believing that this objective was readily achievable and secondly, I became tunnel visioned, completely oblivious to the signals around me.'

'What do you mean?'

Come on Emma, this is where you came in. 'I believed, wrongly as it happens, that the course I was bent on was the correct one.'

'I see.' She thought about it. 'But what about all this, this weirdness? And bloody behaviour?'

'What about my self-respect?' He felt the heat rising. 'Christ Emma you never gave me a single inch! Right down the line, everything exactly your own way. While I was trying to put up bridges, you were all beavering away building dams to divert the damn river.'

She shook her head. 'Who?'

'All of you!' His knees were jumping up and down. Exasperated, he got to his feet and began pacing, his mind in turmoil. It had all been so clear before. Why couldn't he make her see?

She uncrossed her legs and sat up straight, knees together, eyes focused straight ahead at the floor. 'Look. We're missing the point. The simple fact is, your, behaviour is very worrying. You may see nothing unusual about it, but in my view, and others' – fractional hesitation – 'it is at best unsettling, particularly for the children, and at worst potentially dangerous.'

This was not Emma speaking; her mother perhaps, or Wallace or that blasted Greenaway woman. 'Do you really believe that?'

'You hit Charlie!'

'He was out of line. I deserved an answer, still do!'

Now she was on her feet. 'You're out of your fucking mind. You come wandering in off the road like some filthy backstreet wino and subject me to a disgusting public humiliation for which I will never, ever forgive you. And then, when Charlie asks you to leave you hit him!'

'I just wanted to know if he was laying you!'

'Why, because you can't?'

He was upon her in an instant. There was the familiar thunder, a roaring, popping sound in his ears. He swiped at her wildly, caught her a glancing blow behind the ear; she stepped back clutching a hand to her neck, missed her footing and fell awkwardly onto the hessian. He dropped onto her heavily, driving the wind from her as he straddled her chest, pinning her arms back onto the floor above her head. 'So this is what it's all about.' His voice was a snarl, the face twisted and purple, the veins out on his neck, dark and bulging.

Dazed and winded she tried to struggle. 'No, Peter, no!' She began to slither back from under him but he slapped her hard across the cheek, kicked her flailing legs flat and began tearing at the button of her jeans. 'No, Peter please stop.'

'It's what you want isn't it!' He was screaming, his face contorted as he yanked at her zipper. In one lightning movement he jumped to his feet, turned and wrenched her jeans to the calf then completely off. She rolled onto her stomach and scrambled up onto her knees, but he was on her before she had gone a foot.

He could do it, he could feel the strength in his loins like hot steel. There was a deafening, pounding drumming in his head, like standing under a waterfall. The eyes were blurred, bright sparks of incandescent white light jumped and floated before him. His chest was bursting but he had the strength: boundless, terrifying like a vast machine. He flicked her onto her back again, effortlessly levering the legs apart with his knee. Fumbling at his own clothing he felt the steel jump free into the cool, then plucking aside the final flimsy barrier he roared and plunged in suddenly like a doomed bull, pumping viciously, head back, teeth bared, crazed and gasping.

CHAPTER
14

He woke up on the floor. The lights were still on but it had grown cold, the fire shrivelled to feebly glowing embers. He was alone. Slowly he raised himself to a sitting position, leaning back against one of the armchairs. He touched his face, the cheek was sore and pitted where it had pressed against the hessian, there was a dull ache in his head, the taste of blood in his mouth. And lead in his heart.

Alice, standing in her kitchen with the scar on her belly: 'You are capable of becoming a danger to yourself, and others, usually those closest to you.' He had scoffed of course. 'I hardly think ...' But she had been right again – right all along; he should have listened.

But now it was over and the crisis past, like a short but violent squall. There was a sense of calm and cleansing. He felt relieved, unburdened, buoyed up by a wonderful clarity of purpose, for the first time in, how long? He'd made a mess of it to be sure, although he believed that his predicament was not entirely of his own making, he was surely in part a victim of circumstance, an unlucky throw of the dice or draw of a card. Or perhaps every move, every folly was part of a meticulously woven web, the great grand design, and his fate, this outcome was as assured as the setting of the sun. From the moment he first struggled into the light as an infant, bawling and slippery. Or sooner.

It didn't matter, the moment for conjecture was past, it was time for action. Time. Suddenly it was important, he fingered his naked wrist, where the hell was that bloody Timex. Hauling himself to his feet he went into the kitchen, lights still on, plates and dishes on the table. The kitchen clock said a little after two, he searched through drawers and cupboards, quietly, like a burglar. Finally he found the watch in the bathroom cabinet, set and wound it, shook it to life, strapped it firmly to his body like a bomb. The clock was running.

He made coffee and cleared up the mess downstairs. In the sitting room he came across Emma's jeans, inside out in a heap against the wall, he also found one of the pearl earrings he'd given as an anniversary present years previously. He carefully folded the jeans and left them at the bottom of the stairs with the earring. When he had finished tidying up he slipped out of the back door into the cool darkness and across to the shed.

He was back at six, took a bath, dressed, made tea and carried it up to the bedroom. He placed the teacup carefully on the table next to his wife's head. She was awake, the eyes watchful as he moved about the room. Drawing the curtains back, he paused to look at the pale morning mist drifting across the fields. Down the lane he could hear the lowing of the dairy herd as they were led into the milking shed at the farm. He retreated to the far end of the bedroom, stood with his back to the wardrobe, formally like a servant awaiting her dressing instructions. Then he cleared his throat.

'I'm sure you'll agree it would be best if I go.'

She rose slowly to a sitting position, reached for the

teacup. 'Yes.' The voice was a whisper.

'And I think today would be best for everyone. I'll get some things together.'

'Right. Take the Morris; there is a car I can use at work.'

'Fine, thank you. How will you manage, with the children and everything?'

'I'll use a child minder for Sally on the days she's not at school and alter my working hours to be back in time for Jamie. There's a lot of work I can bring home. Also the Greenaways have offered to help out and there is a working mother's group at the Primary School, rosters for school runs and things.'

She'd got it all sorted out. Ages ago probably, a *fait accompli*. He nodded. 'Good. I'll aim to go this evening then. I have a few arrangements to make and I would like to see the children before I go, if that's all right.'

She shrugged. 'Of course.' She looked at him, the sheets held modestly to her chest. 'I'd like to get up now.' He left the room.

They collected the children from the Greenaways. They were excited; they'd slept in separate rooms 'but with a door in between, Mummy, so Jamie could come and see me if he got frightened'. Alice had spoilt them with cakes for tea and best of all, a Walt Disney video. They drove Jamie to school, the four of them together in the Morris, Sally talking non-stop, Jamie interjecting occasionally when she paused to draw breath. Emma, half turned in the seat, nodding and smiling at them, asking questions. He, silent behind the big wheel, changing down to coax the old car up a hill, half listening as the banter washed over him like a warm breeze.

'Jack an' Alice have got a little house right at the seaside, a beach house, Mummy, they said I can borrow it, can we go please, please, Daddy, can we go to the seaside?'

He flicked a glance across at Emma. 'Of course darling.'

'Today?'

'Not today Sal.' It was Emma. 'Soon.'

They dropped the children, then drove on in silence to the Old Schoolhouse. Pulling up in the road outside he could see figures moving about through the windows of the big office. 'I won't come in.' Not a flicker, she pulled her bags from the back seat and walked into the playground.

There was much to do. He stopped at the Post Office and bought stationery: brown wrapping paper, a selection of envelopes, adhesive tape. He also bought a quarter bottle of Bells. Mrs Morrison's face remained inscrutable. 'We've been cutting down lately,' he said, by way of explanation. Back at the cottage he went straight into the shed and booted up the word processor. Checking his watch he pinned the list he'd made during the night to the window frame. The shed was dim and stuffy. Before starting he tore down the cardboard from the windows and banged them open. The stove was out but he was comfortable enough with his jacket on. There was the promise of warmth in the strengthening sun; he inhaled deeply, the air clean and pure like spring water.

Letters first, beginning with the easy ones. Short notes of instruction: poor long suffering Bishop at the bank, Wallace the solicitor, his insurance broker. He rattled them off, printing out top copies and back-ups for the files. Mid morning he broke from the keyboard and began sorting through the scattered piles of notebooks and papers heaped around the shed. Most he stuffed into a dustbin liner, the rest he arranged into fresh piles along the bench. He updated the finance and job files, stacking them neatly at one end together with his general correspondence file and reference books.

The 'projects' notes he sorted into categories, binding each into a bundle according to subject. Where appropriate

295

he added explanatory magazine and newspaper clippings, or in the case of products, manufacturer's information, taking care to include the computer disk relevant to each project. Carefully he wrapped and sealed the slim packages using brown paper and tape, clearly labelling each with the subject title and date. Then he placed all the packs into a cardboard box and slid it down to the end of the bench, placing it neatly next to the other files.

Taking a second box he began collecting together items to take with him. The diary notebooks, the office photograph of Emma and the children, the letters and the little bottle of Scotch. While sorting through the last of the rubbish he came across the interview reply letter from the Hammersmith aviation company. He held it delicately, turning the sealed envelope slowly over and over in his hand. Through the open window he could see a pair of blackbirds darting about in the overgrown back garden, skipping nervously from branch to fence post, post to ground and back to branch again as, oblivious to his prying, they manoeuvred skittishly in preparation for union. There was the warm smell of damp grass as it dried in the sun, the distant rumble of military jet traffic drowned by birdsong. With a smile he dropped the envelope into a half-filled dustbin liner.

The telephone was ringing in the cottage but he ignored it. Seating himself once more in front of the bench he picked up his fountain pen and began on the personal letters. He started with his parents, apologising in advance for embarrassment or distress additional to that already caused, explaining briefly that the decision was entirely his, and had been carefully and impassively considered. '. . . In my view a rational course of action which, without doubt, will prove to be the best solution for everyone in the long run . . .'

Next and in a similar vein, Dan and Mitch. Harder, they were closer. Easier, he could lower the façade of formality:

... And don't try giving me any of that introspective hindsight crap, I know this is right and that's all that counts ...' He joked with them briefly about past times together and reminded them of their obligations to their godchildren; 'This is going to cost you a packet Mitchells.' He signed the letter: 'With all my love P.' Then underneath wrote: 'Flt Lt. P J Deacon. RAF (Retd.)'

Then Alice: 'Why? You know why – you taught me and I am forever indebted. Mind you, I don't want you waltzing around claiming any credit; this is all my own work thank you very much. Oh yes and you can forget any of that legal mumbo-jumbo about "the disturbed balance of his mind". Lunacy, you said, try John Clare, you said. The one he wrote in the asylum? I never read a saner eighteen lines in my life.' He hesitated, staring down at the page before finishing: 'Thank you Alice, you are a very remarkable woman. Oh and thanks for the book, it was a lifesaver! Love Peter.'

He sealed the letter, tossed it with the others into the box he was taking with him, then drew a fresh sheet of notepaper with a sigh. Emma. Before he could begin he heard a car slowing in the lane outside, then saw the bonnet of the Range Rover as it nosed into the driveway. He jumped off the chair, glancing quickly around the shed for clues, panic rising. There were none except his take-away box. He dropped it under the bench, threw a blanket over it, checked around once more. A tap on the door; Alice walked in. He smiled sheepishly.

'Hello stranger.' She stared around the shed in amazement. 'My word, we are having a clean out in here. About time too if I may say so. I was wondering if you'd care to join me at the pub for a bit of lunch?'

Lunch? God the time! He checked his watch, gone one. 'Alice I'd love to but I'm right up to my neck in it, as you can see, and I'd like to get it all tidied up. Rain check?' Her face fell; he guessed she was after the lowdown on last night. Perhaps Emma had already told her. Perhaps she wanted to hear it from him. Either way it didn't matter.

There was a pause while she continued to look around the shed. 'What's going on Peter?' The voice was softer but the eyes no longer wandered, focusing cool and immovable on his. The old familiar scrutiny.

He met the gaze for a while, exhaled wearily. 'I suppose you might as well know. I'm going.'

'Where?' She was staggered.

He shrugged. 'Back to London, some friends.'

'Giving up you mean.'

He held up his hands. 'Now don't start Alice, please. It has to be like this. Emma and I are both in agreement.'

'I see.' The voice was cold, the expression tinged with contempt, eyes still locked. 'So you think that just walking away from it all will solve all your problems?'

'It's not like that. I have to go. Remember at Christmas you told me that I would become a danger to others? I was too arrogant to believe it at the time, but you were right.' He sighed, glanced out of the window, up at advancing ranks of mares' tails, high thin lines of cirrus, ice crystals invading the sky to the west, a warm front approaching. 'You've been right all along. Well, it's happened, hopefully no lasting physical injury, no scar but bad enough and exactly the same as Jack and the knife.' He nodded at her stomach.

'But Jack didn't run out! It was then that he began, really began to deal with it. It was a turning point.'

'And why?'

'Because despite everything I still needed him!' She stopped, the trap sprung.

He smiled. '*Quod erat demonstrandum?*' Her shoulders sagged. He went to her, linked a hand through her arm, leading her gently out into the veiled sunshine. 'Do not feel bad about this,' he said firmly. 'Any of it. I have brought it upon myself and the plain fact is that they don't need me, in fact they are demonstrably better off without me.'

'But the children.' She was pleading.

He laughed. 'Alice, dear girl. Jamie doesn't speak to me. At all. Yet despite that, since moving down here, a decision incidentally that I was totally opposed to, he has really found his feet. He is stronger, fitter, happier. Emma must take all the credit. Sally? Well she takes everything in her stride; she is a strong, independent soul, like her mother.'

'You're wrong, I know it. Wrong about the children, wrong about Emma. They do need you, it's just perhaps they don't realise it.' She was floundering. 'You've just got to give it time.'

No. There was no more time. He had steered her to the door of her car, now he held it open for her, kissed her cheek. 'Thanks for everything.' She stepped up into the car, suddenly he remembered the book. 'Hold on, just a second.' He ran back to the shed, re-appearing a moment later clutching it. 'I promised to return it.'

'Keep it.'

He handed it to her through the open door. 'No. Thanks, really but I don't need it any more.' He didn't want other people's possessions cluttering the picture. No opportunity for self-recrimination.

After she left he went for a short walk down to the stream before returning to tackle Emma's letter. He stood on the footbridge and dropped pebbles into the gurgling water. The sun was gone, the next layer of lower, thicker cloud creeping like a blanket across the sky. There would be rain before nightfall. No problem. He began the slow walk back up to the cottage. He felt no fear, but there were regrets. He would have liked to have seen the countryside around the cottage in summer. Properly, now that he knew it, not like last summer's disdainful cursory glance but close up in all its glorious detail. He snorted, he'd like to have lived in the cottage in summer. Be able to pad around in shorts with the doors and windows wide open to the balmy air, sit outside and listen to the calm of the evening, walk down to the stream at dusk, with Emma and the children.

He would have liked to have seen how they turned out, as people, ten, twenty years down the line. Not like him he hoped. More like the grandparents, Emma's father, perhaps. And his mother. Warm, gentle people, caring and considerate. He wondered how, if at all, they would remember him. Sally, doubtful at three, perhaps a couple of hazy recollections. Jamie?

My darling Em,

This may have come as a surprise to you, but not, hopefully as too much of a shock. Please don't think too badly of me for lumbering you with this on top of everything else, but it really had to be now. I'm confident that you'll cope with your usual efficiency and in time come to see this as a logical course of action. It may not seem like it now but the intention was selfless.

I am deeply sorry about last night, it was inexcusable. My greatest hope is that the memory of it will fade quickly. Perhaps one day you may even be able to disassociate it (along with other recent events) from your recollections of the amiable if rather feckless individual you married all those years ago. If you so choose.

You are not in any way responsible for this; do not allow yourself to entertain the idea for a second. The decision to go was mine alone, taken only after careful and sober (yes!) reflection. Just think of this as a firmer commitment to that decision, a sort of emigration. Use it as an opportunity for a completely clean break, and a fresh start. You are young, and extraordinarily beautiful. My best advice is to put all this behind you as quickly as possible and enjoy your freedom. You deserve it.

I go in the knowledge that the lives of our children are in safe and loving hands. If it comes to their asking one day, and you decide to tell them, please say it was done with their best interests in mind and out of my deepest love for them both.

Thank you for the best years of my life.

All my love.

Peter

He re-read the final draft, then folded it quickly, sealing it into an envelope and adding it to the others in the box. He checked his watch again; they'd be home soon, yet there was still much to do.

He carried the box into the garage, placed it in the boot of the Morris then began sorting through his tool box. He cut two eight foot lengths of garden hose with a Stanley knife, offered them up, then threw them into the back of the car together with the knife, a large multifunction motoring torch and a roll of two-inch duct tape. He covered them all with a blanket and went into the house.

Suddenly he couldn't think what else to do. He was ready, just say goodbye and go. He felt sure he had overlooked something obvious but couldn't think what it was. While he waited he emptied the ashes from the kitchen stove and refilled it, topping up the coal bucket and log basket. He laid and lit a fresh fire in the sitting room.

As he bent to sweep twigs of kindling from the hearth the telephone rang. His head jerked up at the sound, he straightened up on the floor. He didn't want to speak to anyone. But what if it was Emma? The plan had changed; she couldn't get away. Or what if it was a problem with one of the children, fallen over at school, taken ill. Chewing at the moustache hairs at the corner of his mouth he went back to the kitchen towards the shrill ringing. After a moment's indecision he picked it up and listened, said nothing.

'Hello? Hello Mrs Deacon?' Woman's voice, vaguely familiar, he couldn't quite ... 'Hello, it's Stephanie Pryce here. Mrs Deacon?'

Pryce! God, what did she want? 'Dr Pryce hello, Peter Deacon here. Sorry about that, new phone, had a few problems with it—'

'Oh Mr Deacon, yes hello. Forgive me for calling, but I've got a note in my diary that we would speak some time this month about an appointment?' She paused. Peter said nothing momentarily confused. 'Now I'd be quite happy to see him here, or I can make arrangements for him to see someone in your area if you like, or not if you feel it unnecessary, but it has been some months now and I really should put something on the file, or close it.'

'Ah yes doctor, sorry, I remember now.' Jamie. Liverpool Street. The day of the interview. 'To be honest both my wife and I had more or less dispensed with the idea of therapy for Jamie at the moment. He's so much better, improving daily, hopefully there won't be any further need—' He stopped. There might be a need. In the next few weeks. 'On the other hand, who knows. Anyway I'll have a word with my wife, she can get in touch if she wants.'

'Your wife?'

Christ. 'Yes, or I will.' Oh what the hell. 'Well, no I probably won't, I'm er, we're separating.'

'I'm so sorry.'

'Yes, we've given it a great deal of thought and really it's in the best interests of the children, Jamie in particular.'

'Well of course you know best, although if you'll forgive

me, children rarely benefit from the break up of a family. Is this, arrangement something of a trial separation?'

'I don't think so.'

'But you will be seeing Jamie, and your little girl again.'

There was a silence, then he spoke again, his voice muted. 'I don't think so.'

'Oh that is a pity. Mr Deacon, I do urge you to consider the implications of such a decision very carefully.'

'I have considered, very carefully Doctor, but my mind is made up, the decision is irrevocable. It's too late to stop now.' The clock is ticking.

Too late? Irrevocable? 'Surely not, Mr Deacon, there's always room for discussion, perhaps you and your wife—'

'Doctor, I'm afraid you don't understand the full nature of the situation here. My presence is destructive, bad for everyone, possibly harmful, and therefore you must believe me when I say that removing myself is genuinely best for everyone.'

Something about his tone, his choice of words ... 'It sounds as if you blame yourself for all your family's difficulties – that hardly seems fair, or probable if I may say so.'

Fair? What has fair got to do with anything? 'No I don't actually. I don't blame anyone. You see Doctor, in my view, there are simply good people and there are bad people. Everything we are, every facet of our being is predetermined. At conception we are issued with our twenty-three pairs of chromosomes and as well as determining how tall we are, and the colour of our eyes, the size of our nose, those packets also ultimately decide whether we are good people or bad people.' He began to speak more quickly, became more animated as he warmed to his theme. 'Whether by nature we are generous or selfish, bad tempered or patient, violent or docile.'

'Yes but the whole meaning of higher intelligence is that it allows us to recognise our flaws and suppress them, concentrate on developing the more socially desirable elements of our personality. It's what separates us from the animals.'

'Yes, yes, I know that! Of course someone who recognises that he is jealous can train himself to suppress his jealousies and become a better person. Similarly someone who is naturally easy going may slide into sloth and become a worse person. Somebody who recognises he is seriously bad, naturally jealous, argumentative, lecherous, avaricious and so on, may take himself off, become a Trappist monk and do nothing but good all his life. But he still remains a naturally bad person. The point is, we are dealt this bridge hand and it may be good on balance, or bad. But nothing, nothing at all can change it, you can't just chuck it back and ask for another.'

'No, if it is bad, you learn to deal with it, like your Trappist monk.'

'Precisely and what if you find that you are unable to deal with it . . .'

The line went silent again. She felt a shiver run down her back. There was something wrong here. 'It's a very interesting theory, hardly original I must say, but you've obviously given it a great deal of thought.'

'Oh yes.'

'There are some fascinating philosophical counter-proposals you know. I'd like to put them to you, I think you'd find them interesting. Perhaps you might like to discuss them sometime soon.' She could beat his logic she knew, it was flawed, but not now on the phone, she needed time, to check, bone up, dig out some of her old philosophy papers.

'Yes I would.' He would, genuinely but it wouldn't change

anything, too late, the clock ...

Emma and the children arrived back late, they had stopped
to collect the children's night things from the Old Rectory
and do some shopping at the Post Office. Emma was driving
a two-year-old Ford Escort.

'It looks in good order,' he said, after a quick inspection.
It had begun raining. 'Run okay?'

'Yes fine.' She hesitated. 'Are you, all set?' She wanted
him gone, he could see. Perhaps in her own mind he already
had. So be it. 'What about laundry?'

God! He hadn't packed. Not even a toothbrush. 'Just going
up to finish off now.'

'There are a couple of shirts in the bathroom, I'll bring
them up.'

He tore upstairs, threw a suitcase onto the bed, began
grabbing handfuls of clothes from drawers, tearing shirts off
hangers, a few personal effects; another family photograph,
all four of them this time, taken at a theme park somewhere,
eighteen months previously. His quartz alarm clock, New
York Dodgers baseball cap. He picked up his leather cufflinks
box, saw the dull gleam of his wedding ring. He hadn't worn
it in years. He'd like to, when ... It would be appropriate, a
gesture. But not now, that would be tacky. He closed the box
and dropped it into the front of the suitcase. Straightening
from the bed he turned for more. She was standing in the
doorway holding the shirts in one hand, his sponge bag with
the other, shaking her head.

'Leave it. I'll do it for you.'

'Oh, er, thanks. Never was any good at packing. I'll, go
downstairs and speak to the kids.'

They were in the kitchen drinking juice and eating crisps.
Neither spoke when he entered. Jamie didn't even look up.
Peter was nervous, like a summons to the headmaster,

305

worse. And he was unprepared. One at a time would be best. 'Hi guys,' he said. Sally smiled up at him, stuffed more crisps into her mouth. 'Look, er, Daddy has something important to say to you both. But it's very important and I'd like to talk to you on your own for a few minutes.' They exchanged glances.

'Daddy I didn't do it. Jamie . . .'

He held up his hand. 'It's okay. It's nothing like that, nothing bad.' God they were nervous of him. 'Please, you mustn't be afraid. I just want to have a quick chat with you, by yourselves in the sitting room, okay? Now who wants to go first?' Immediately Jamie slid off the chair and made for the door.

He shook his head at the invitation to sit on Peter's knee. Peter pulled the two armchairs closer together then they sat, opposite each other in front of the fire, as he and Emma had last night. The eyes were round and watchful, the expression wary. But there was something else, he thought, a spark of determination in the lift of his chin, strength in the straightness of his back. 'Mummy and I have had a long chat Jamie,' he began hesitantly. This was going to be harder, much harder than he thought. 'And we've decided that it would be best for everyone, if I went away.' A blink, nothing more. 'I think you and I both know that you can get along much better without my, without me. And so can mummy, and Sally. So for this reason, mainly, I'm going to leave here, tonight.'

The eyes fell for a moment, considering. 'Are you going to come back?'

He blew out, forced a wry smile. Don't weaken, not now. 'I er, I don't know. I don't think so. I would have liked, very much, to come back and visit you, perhaps when you were much older, to see how you were getting on, but it isn't going to be possible.' His voice cracked, Oh God don't lose it, don't. 'But you can be sure that I will be thinking of you, all the time. For as long as I live.' He got up quickly and began tending the fire, clearing his throat gruffly, fighting the tears. 'Now I want you to be very grown up Jamie, as grown up as you can. You are going to be the man of the house now, and must help Mummy, take care of her, and be nice to your sister. Now I want you to promise me that you will try your best to do that.'

'I promise.' A whisper.

He didn't look, couldn't. He fixed his gaze ahead, at the blurred yellow flickering, feeling the warmth on his face, and the hot running wet. He swallowed, drew a deep faltering breath, one last hurdle. 'Before I go, I would just like to say that I am sorry, for everything and that, though you may find this difficult to understand, I do love you, very much. Perhaps one day, a long time from now, all this will make better sense and who knows, you may even be able to, feel a bit happy when you think of me.' Enough! He moved quickly, gripped the head between both hands, bent and kissed the forehead, held him for a second, two. 'Now I'd like you to run and tell Sally to come in.' He squirmed off the chair; Peter patted the backside as it went for the door.

Sally came in. Or rather her head appeared. The face was solemn. 'Daddy, it wasn't me. I didn't [didernt] do it.'

He beckoned to her from the chair, the storm passing. 'Yes I know Sal, just come and sit on my knee for a while.' He heard Jamie's feet running upstairs. She meandered over coyly, clambered aboard. They sat in silence for a while, listening to the fire and the fall of rain outside, after a minute she leaned back against his chest and slipped her thumb in her mouth. He stroked her hair, luxuriating in the smell of her. Gradually, softly, he spoke. It was a much abbreviated version of his talk to Jamie. And much easier. She nodded when he asked if she understood, although he knew she was too young to fully grasp it all. But he was satisfied she had the gist of it.

They sat peacefully until he heard Emma on the stairs, then they kissed and she hugged him round the neck. 'It's time for me to go now sweetheart.' 'Okay, my Daddy.' She jumped down, he followed her into the kitchen. Emma put the suitcase on the table.

'Don't bother coming out, the wet . . .'

She nodded. 'Where will you be?'

'I spoke to Mitch, made arrangements.'

Again the nod. That was it, nothing else. It was time. 'Right then, take very good care of yourself, and these two, I wish you every happiness.' They kissed, just a peck on the cheek, incongruous and awkward, but natural somehow, like leaving for the office.

'You'll ring or something, at some point. Let us know.'

'Hmm? Oh yes.' He picked the case up from the table and opened the door. 'Right. Goodbye and er, well I'm sorry. For everything.' He stepped out into the rain, pulling the door closed behind him.

Peter threw the case onto the back seat and drove up the lane towards the Green. Halfway along he stopped and peered back through the rain-spattered windows at the lights of the cottage. It was over, finished, complete. Now all that remained was the release, the mercy.

He drove around the Green and out of the village on the school road. He went cautiously, the rain was heavy, the little windscreen wipers jerking back and forth ineffectually through the curtain of water. Once clear of the village he drove on until he could discern the dark presence of the pine forest. He slowed right down, peering to his right until he saw the entrance to the access track, turning off the road to enter the forest.

The track was slippery with mud, the back end of the

Morris skidded from side to side; he had to work hard to keep the car moving. Twice the narrow wheels sank into mud, spinning uselessly. On each occasion he throttled right back, delicately slipping the clutch until the tyres began to grip and the car inched forward onto firmer ground.

He began turning into cross tracks, anxious to drive as deep as possible into the forest. But at the third turn the car slid to the edge of the track and a rear wheel sank to the axle in deep mud. He nursed the pedals for a while, trying to coax it out, but it was useless, with every attempt the car sank deeper. Cursing he ran round to the back and retrieved the torch, shining it onto the black ooze around the mired wheel. It was hopeless. Even if he had a shovel he doubted it could be dug out; he'd need a tow. Screwing his face up against the rain he shone the torch about him. It would have to do, not as far into the trees as he would have liked but completely out of sight of the road.

Leaning in through the back doors of the car he retrieved the lengths of hose and by the pale glow of the small fluorescent tube on the torch, he bound them tightly together with tape, side by side. Next he cut slits in the joined hose ends, then ducking out into the rain again, he forced them several inches into the car's exhaust pipe.

Sealing the union with more tape, he then led the two pieces of hose forward and into the car through the two rear sliding windows, one each side, carefully closing the windows until the hosepipes were gripped but not crushed. Then he climbed into the back of the car to seal the remaining gaps from the inside with tape. Ducking back out into the rain once more, he retrieved his take-away box and the torch from the back, and closed the rear doors, tugging on the handle to make sure they were securely shut. He dropped the box onto the front passenger's seat, jumped in behind the wheel and slammed the door. He was set.

He was also soaked, and shivering from cold. Propping the torch against the dashboard he dried his face and hands as best he could with the blanket, then unscrewing the cap of the little bottle of Scotch he gulped greedily. He tilted his head back and breathed deeply as the familiar healing fire spread from his throat, down and across his chest and into his stomach. He took another swig then replaced the cap, rummaging through the box for his diary. He also found the office photograph of the family and fixed it to the rear-view mirror with tape.

Flicking through the pages he found the last entry, drew a line and entered the date beneath. His hands were shaking. Outside the rain drummed on the roof. He checked his watch then wrote: '1920 hrs and I guess that's everything. I'll be on my way. I leave you with a few lines of verse written by a chap who truly understood. They all thought he was batty. I'm not so sure. Don't think too badly of me for this.'

He reached forward and turned the key, holding it until the engine clattered to life, the volume of noise surprised him, much louder inside the car now. He revved the throttle, feeling the pressure build on his eardrums, then he let it settle to a steady, burbling idle.

> I am, yet what I am who cares, or knows?
> My friends forsake me like a memory lost.
> I am the self-consumer of my woes;
> They rise and vanish, an oblivious host,
> Shadows of life, whose very soul is lost.
> And yet I am – I live – though I am tossed
> Into the nothingness of scorn and noise,
> Into the living sea of waking dream,
> Where there is neither sense of life, nor joys,
> Just the huge shipwreck of my self-esteem
> and all that's dear . . .

He coughed, his eyes watering. There was a grey–blue halo around the fluorescent tube of the torch and a dull pounding at the back of his head and at the sides of his neck. He shook his head, struggled to concentrate and focus on the paper. His writing was sliding off the page, he must just, finish it:

> ... Even those I love the best are strange
> – nay they are stranger than the rest.
> I long for scenes where man has never trod,
> For scenes where woman never smiled or wept,
> There to abide with my creator, God.
> And sleep, as I in childhood sweetly slept,
> Full of high thoughts, unborn. So let me lie
> The grass below; above, the vaulted sky.

The pen slipped from his fingers; the book dropped onto the floor; his head sank back ... There was a tightness in his chest; his head still pounded but there was something else building up – a deep whooshing, whistling roar. But no pain, just a light headedness. Then a violent choking spasm gripped him suddenly, doubling him over in the seat. It passed and he sat back again, felt himself falling, easy, easy, his vision darkening at the edges. Like in the Air Force, the hypoxia training chamber, just keep reciting Peter Piper while they drain away all the air until ... His head lolled back, his eyes flickered then fell on the picture, the two children, smiling at him behind the camera, Emma cool and serene. Like she was on the day he married her. The ring. The ring! He wanted it on. It had to be on! He tried to move but his body was like rubber, his arms and legs limp and tingling.

He struggled to turn in the seat, the pounding starting again in his ears like thunder. He reached back, half sitting, half lying in the seat. His right hand found the case, fumbled for the catches. But his fingers were numb and cold, paralysed. He beat at the catches feebly. Suddenly the lid rose an inch – it was free! The box, the little leather box he'd bought in Morocco. Desperately he fought, back towards the suitcase, but it was too late; it was as though the case, his hands, were miles away, at the end of a long tunnel, and receding, slipping further and further from him. Then somehow a hand was inside the lid of the case, it closed on paper, a large sheet of paper, pulled it out. It was a picture, a child's painting, fuzzy and indistinct in the fog. His cheek slid down the side of the seat as he slipped towards oblivion. A ship. It was a painting of a ship. A beautiful wooden sailing ship with tall masts and snow white sails. A ship which bore its name proudly in large letters on its prow. A ship called Hope. Beneath, at the bottom of the page three words, hastily scrawled, barely legible: 'Dont leve me.'

CHAPTER
15

Well he'd popped it in the top of the case just before Emma closed it of course. He told me later that he'd painted it some time previously and had 'sort of been thinking' of giving it to me as a present one day but not until I was being nicer. Can't argue with that.

I woke up forty-eight hours later in Heath Road hospital Ipswich with a hangover to beat them all. If I think about it very hard, which is not something I care to do much, there are vague, fleeting recollections, unconnected glimpses of the intervening period: whirling blue lights racing round the wall of the forest in the thin, pre-dawn mist. The bleep and hiss of two-way radio transmissions, the smell of damp pine trees and cigarettes, but then nothing, for a long time nothing mercifully, but a silent black void.

When I awoke it was evening, the lights in the room subdued, outside I could hear traffic down in the street, in the corridor footsteps and voices, passing trolleys, farther off a television set. The smell, the decor, the sounds told me it was a hospital. Beyond that I knew nothing, not even who I was or how I came to be there. Nor did I care to know; I'd find out soon enough. My bandaged head ached damnably, there was a blinding pain behind both eyes, excruciating, piercing like red-hot needles if I moved them. There was a dull, throbbing ache in my chest and my legs and arms felt numb and heavy like lead. Apart from that, and a killer thirst, I appeared to be in reasonable order.

I must have drifted off again, within a very few minutes a nurse looked in – they don't like to leave you unattended too long in case you wake up and decide to dive straight out of the window – saw that I had awoken and came bustling to the bed. 'Ah there you are,' she said cheerfully. She summoned another nurse with the buzzer over my head, told her to fetch Dr Sissons, chatted to me while she waited. 'And how are you feeling?' I opened my mouth and made a sort of gasping croak. 'Good, good.' She fussed around, straightening covers and fluffing pillows. 'Drink,' I croaked. In the end she got the message and lifted my head while I sucked on a plastic straw. There was a burst of explosions in my head as I moved and the pain behind the eyeballs made me want to throw up and pass out, but it was worth it, the touch of tepid liquid on my tongue and throat was heavenly.

Dr Sissons appeared and ran some checks, pursing his lips at my pathetic efforts to wiggle my fingers and toes, humming tunelessly while he shone lights into my mouth, and my eyes (ouch!) and ears, listened to my chest, prodded and poked. 'Well now, how many fingers can you see?' He waved three, easy. 'Can you tell me your name?' Not so easy. 'Do you know where you are?' Yes, thank you. 'And how you came to be here?' Not exactly.

Most of it came back to me during the night. It passed in a blurred jumble of vivid, fitful recollections and waking dreams. I'd doze for a few minutes then jerk awake suddenly, sweating and blinking in the dim light. Gradually the pieces came together. At one point I found myself overcome by an intense grieving shame, and lay there humbled and mortified, the tears flowing freely like forgotten taps. Later I awoke again, shaking with terror, as in my dreams I fled headlong through the pine forest, gripped by the horror of unseen pursuit. But by dawn I knew there had been a change, sensed a difference, like the sudden alteration of wind and temperature in a storm system at the instant of frontal passage. The bad weather wasn't over, not by a long way, but gradually the wind would back and slacken, the rain ease. And despite the discomfort of my predicament, the confusion of unanswered questions, the unknown path ahead, there was a feeling of receding crisis and a conviction that whatever the future held, it could be faced.

Early in the morning they brought me a cup of sweet tea jacking me up into a near sitting position to drink. The cup shook alarmingly in my hand, the fingers still numb and tingly – something to do with the carbon monoxide they said – but I drank gratefully. A little while later Emma appeared at the door, her face full of trepidation, clearly as nervous about the reunion as I was. I couldn't help it, I cried like a baby; her eyes went watery too. We smiled sheepishly at each other, sniffing and blowing for a minute or two, then she leant over and kissed me gently on the cheek.

'I'm so sorry,' I said, meaning it. 'For everything.'

'I know,' she said ruefully, frowning over the top of her handkerchief. 'I read the letter.'

Between them the women had worked it out, during that evening. Of course as Emma recounted it, blessed with the wisdom of hindsight, anyone would think I had left a trail as wide as the Grand Canyon. But to their credit they had pieced it together. Not that it would have made any difference if it hadn't been for Jamie's picture.

Emma said that she had been suspicious about the

suitcase, that apparently I was ready to walk out and leave for ever yet without so much as a change of underwear. As she spoke, I found, with an odd sense of bemused relief that it was as if she was talking about someone else, some cranky and dimwitted relative like a dotty old maiden aunt. She even slipped up herself once, said something like '. . . And he left all his shoes in the wardrobe . . .' I half listened. It was the sound of her voice as she sat on the chair next to the bed that I found heartening. It was the best medicine, soft and soothing like music. I longed to reach out and take her hand, but I hadn't the right.

Stephanie Pryce had telephoned the cottage about two hours after I'd gone. It was her input that really set the machinery in motion, well she was the professional. Apparently I'd dropped what she later referred to as 'some strong intent indicators' during our earlier conversation. Although off duty and due to meet her husband at the theatre, she had raced home from the hospital, and fished out a load of philosophy textbooks from her study. Her plan was to ring me back and divert my train of thought with weighty chunks of Socrates and Keynes or something, marvellous stuff some of it – she ordered me to read it subsequently, although to be honest I'm no longer that interested. But I still think the good/bad bridge hand concept had merit.

Anyway, Stephanie rang the cottage, but by then I was long gone, busy fugging up the Morris in the woods somewhere. She spoke to Emma and hinted in her 'don't-panic-but . . .' doctorly way, that all may not be quite as it appeared. Emma immediately rang Mitch who confirmed that I had only made the vaguest mention of a visit and that she wasn't expecting me that evening, in fact she and Dan were about to go out. The moment they hung up, Alice arrived in the Range Rover to see Emma. When she heard about Stephanie and Mitch she threw in her two bob's worth: 'I know he's up to something,' she said, apparently, 'nobody voluntarily hands back their only copy of *The Oxford Book of English Verse.*'

The police were called and appeared in a shot, took down the necessary information and set off in pursuit. 'He won't have gone far missus,' one of them had told Emma cheerfully. 'If he's going to do it, why go all the way to London?' They weren't that sure though, apparently they sent a patrol car round to the house in Fulham.

God it must have been ghastly for her. They left her in the company (she said it felt more like 'custody') of a well meaning but overweight woman Police Constable with BO, who spent the entire time boiling pots of tea and hovering around like the angel of doom. Alice took the children back to the Old Rectory, returning to the cottage once they were settled.

At about five in the morning an observant young patrolman cruising the area in a Ford Sierra picked out ridiculously narrow cross-ply tyre tracks leading off the road and through the soft ground to one of the Forestry Commission service tracks. He followed them into the forest. Later, as he sat by the bed taking a statement, he expressed cheerful amazement that the old car had made it so far through the mud – he'd very nearly put the Sierra in a ditch. 'So much for limited slip bloody differentials . . .'

He found the Morris in minutes, the engine still faithfully burbling away in idle hours after I'd driven it there. I was face down in the mud half in, half out of the car, unconscious and leaking blood into the quagmire from a handsome gash on the forehead. They worked out subsequently that I had probably struck it on the edge of the door as I fell out. The patrolman called for back-up and fairly soon afterwards they were hoisting me into an ambulance. He said that for the most part I remained out of it, but came to

at one point and 'turned fairly abusive' when an ambu-
lanceman tried to prise the sodden and mud-stained remnants of Jamie's picture from my fingers.

It was ruined incidentally, but I keep what's left of it
hidden away in a safe place; don't ask me why – one day I
may feel the need to look at it. Jamie produced another one
in no time; it seems children have no misgivings about
running off several copies of an admired work of art,
particularly if it is commissioned. Well he said he'd be
needing a bike – how else was he to get around on his island
paradise? I had the new painting signed by the artist,
mounted and framed. It hangs on the spare room wall next
to the window above my desk. This time the whole family
are aboard, four heads poking above the deck as the ship
ploughs steadily through the ocean towards the little green
hump of land away on the horizon.

They let me out after eight days. There was some lung
damage, further complicated by an unrelated infection
which knocked me down for another fortnight and left me
with a hacking cough for weeks. They muttered about my
liver and possible long-term damage there from the gas. A
succession of therapists, councillors, bone rattlers and
headshrinkers lectured endlessly on the mechanics of nervous breakdown and the error of my ways. Painstakingly
leading me through analysis of my motives and inter-
rogating me on the so-called logic of my reasoning. Raised
a few eyebrows there I can tell you.

They meant well, but it was all unnecessary – they were
preaching to the converted. But for the timely discovery of
Jamie's picture I would not be here; I have no doubt of that.
Of course, they were all very excited about that: 'And what
is the significance, Mr Deacon, of the symbolism represented
in your son's painting, and how did it relate to your own
personal situation then and now?' Four hundred words

please, by tea-time or else. But it was very straightforward as far as I was concerned, six words would suffice. Tangible proof that he needed me. That's all.

As the moment for release from hospital approached, the ticklish question of my place of residence arose. I told Emma I wanted to go and stay at my parents' house. It was true, I felt a strong urge to return to the home of my youth, to descend to base camp, regroup. We talked in hospital, at great length, but mainly about the past and present with only occasional oblique references to any possible future scenarios. There was a tacit understanding, truce but not reconciliation, it was far too soon. I was determined that she should enjoy a period of respite, a chance to gather her thoughts and feelings without me around cluttering up the place. At first she wouldn't hear of it but in the end she capitulated, and one sunny morning late in March an orderly wheeled me down to the hospital lobby with a blanket over my knees like an octogenarian on an outing, Emma picked me up in her company car and we made the two hour trip to Bedfordshire.

I stayed nearly two months. At first my mother was run off her feet what with both me and my father on our backs in bed. But as his health slid steadily downhill, mine gradually improved, and after a week or so I was up and about. I still had the damned cough, occasional dizziness and incomplete sensation in the tips of my fingers and toes. The headshrinkers' tests had flagged up a retardation of thought reaction time and some difficulty concentrating. 'Nothing new about that,' said my father. 'Just look at any of your old school reports.' But they were optimistic that eventually the effects would wear off and normal service be resumed.

I spent a lot of time at my father's bedside. When he was able he told me about my grandparents, his childhood in the

319

Dales, his induction into the Air Force. I knew so little about him and his background. It was a revelation. We talked of aeroplanes and flying. He quizzed me about the Jaguar; I asked him what the Spitfire was really like. 'A bit bloody slippery at first . . .' We discovered that the only aircraft type we'd both flown was the Chipmunk.

Gradually he grew weaker. At first he had been able to assist us when we manoeuvred him to the bathroom or his favourite chair by the fire in the sitting room, but soon we had to lift him in and out of a wheelchair. He bore the indignities of his decline with characteristic stoicism, but I could tell he was just going through the motions. We never spoke of my situation, nor our last meeting in Suffolk; these were matters over which we knew we would find little common ground, and were better avoided. Once, he did come close:

'I've got a feeling it'll all turn out all right for you PJ,' he said, one afternoon. 'Probably not in any way I can envision but your mother has a sixth sense about these things and I trust her judgement.' It was good enough, and when I put my hand on his, he smiled and left his there. For nearly a whole minute.

Under my mother's relentless regime of three full meals a day and hot puddings with everything, I soon began regaining weight. As spring matured and the evenings drew out, I started to exercise, gently at first, just strolls around the local area, then when the cough finally abated, running, a mile or so along the roads and lanes, then further afield as my strength returned. It became a kind of occupational therapy, focusing my mind on forgotten priorities like health and stamina, the pace and rhythm of mind and body, the concerted cooperation of heart, lungs, and limbs. Soon, to her horror I began rejecting the cooked breakfasts, apple crumbles and treacle puddings, eventually persuading her that two light meals and one modest but substantial one a day was plenty.

And drink was right out of course. Still is. Got well and truly brainwashed into submission on that score by the medics and headshrinks at hospital, not to mention cruising AA representatives. But I'm careful not to get complacent about it – after all, once an alcoholic always an alcoholic as they keep telling me. But to be honest I don't miss it, and I haven't been tempted.

Not even during the bankruptcy court hearing. Although court is perhaps too grand a word for it. It all took place in the beak's private office and was conducted civilly, almost cordially. Wallace was there, of course, and Bishop representing the bank. He pumped my hand, when we met in the car-park, seemed genuinely pleased to see me, asked after the family, said we should have lunch! Also present was a chap from the building society. Since the house in Fulham was the only asset, and they owned a good deal of it, most of the discussions centred around its disposal and the subsequent allocation of proceeds.

I was more than happy to follow my counsel's instructions and say nothing unless spoken to. There was the little matter of the fraudulent telefax to the bank to worry about and at one point things became tense when Bishop and the man from the society exchanged documentation relating to existing mortgages. But no mention was made of an application for a mortgage on the cottage. It turns out that the telefax was of limited significance, a facsimile transmission is not acceptable as proof of an agreement between parties nor is it admissible in court. In any case the letter merely purported that my application had been accepted, so Bishop had been unwise to use it as security. He probably hoped, as did the defendant sitting two seats away from him, that the paper never saw the light of day again. For all I know he shredded the damn thing.

Matters proceeded to conclusion in an orderly fashion. The building society man said that they were happy for the house to be sold; he even had a couple of possible leads on buyers. The most conservative estimates as to its market value meant that in theory nobody would end up out of pocket. The building society would recoup the full value of the advance, plus outstanding payments arrears, plus interest. That left more than enough to pay off all the bank debts and the other creditors, Wallace's fees, credit cards, everything. It was even possible there might be a few hundred in it for the Deacons at the end of the day. The beak explained that until the house was sold and all these debts discharged, I was still insolvent and subject to the jurisdiction of the court, but as soon as every last penny was paid, then I was off the hook. I don't know who was more relieved but I let John Bishop buy me a lemonade in the pub afterwards.

I called Emma with the news that evening. We spoke once or twice a week, sometimes I called, sometimes she did. Our telephone conversations were amicable, less stilted. We talked and listened to each other's trivia. It was just banter, polite, not intimate but pleasant. I grew to look forward to those phone calls greatly. I missed her badly, and the children. More than I would ever have imagined. We'd agreed to tell them that I was in Bedfordshire for a while because Grandpa Deacon was poorly. She said that apparently they talked of me: Sally had asked after that smelly old scarecrow that used to hang around in the shed, and Jamie was preparing a portfolio of work to show when I next came down to see them. I deliberately refrained from talking specific dates; I wanted Emma to call that shot.

My father died one evening in May. Although expected, it took us by surprise. He was propped up in bed dozing peacefully, my mother was sitting by the window darning and listening to her portable radio. I had just got back from a run and poked my head around the door to let her know. He opened his eyes: 'Oh you're home. Okay PJ,' he said, and died. My mother and I looked at each other, she took off her spectacles, went to his side and kissed him. I came in and the two of us sat there holding hands on the bed until it began to grow dark.

He didn't want any fuss at all – left explicit instructions of course. David flew over from San Diego the next day and the three of us saw him to the crematorium. Emma had a long conversation with my mother: she wanted to drive up but my mother said no, it was far too much trouble what with the children and everything. Afterwards I talked to Emma:

'Why don't you come down for the weekend, when the dust is settled,' she said. 'Bring your mother, and David, it'll do her the world of good to see the children.'

'Are you sure?'

'Yes. I'd like to see you.'

We left on the Friday afternoon. I drove them down in Dad's Rover; we arrived in time for tea. The last few miles were nerve-racking; I could barely stay on the road. I was frightened and excited, desperate to see my family yet terrified of their reaction. As we coasted down the hill into the village, the memories crowded back like ghosts. But it was different, the Green really was green now, the grass dark and lush, trees heavy with foliage. Around the village gardens were ablaze with colour, poppies grew along the hedgerows, there were hanging baskets outside Mrs Morrison's Post Office.

I crept down the lane and turned into the drive behind Emma's car.

'There's old Morris,' said my mother. It was sitting in the garage, something heavy turned over in my stomach. The kitchen door opened.

'Granny, Granny, my Granny!' Sally stormed out and into my mother's arms. I shrugged at David, then Emma was there. She came out to meet us; her hair had grown. 'You've cut your hair,' she said. We embraced, clung for just a second but it was more than enough, more than I'd ever hoped for. 'Jamie's upstairs,' she said quietly.

He was at his desk in the bedroom. He looked serious, shuffling sheets of paper around anxiously. 'I wasn't ready yet.' He sounded cross and flustered.

'I'm so sorry, would you like me to—'

'No. I was just getting my work ready. To show you. You've shaved off your beard.' I'd kept the moustache though, as a souvenir.

I knelt beside the desk and we went through his school-work, then he showed me some of his recent paintings. Finally he produced a black ring-binder and handed it to me. It was the American car book, or the twenty or so pages that had escaped the worst of the damage. He'd repaired them with tape and clipped them into the folder.

'Hey that's great, we've still got the Studebaker.'

'Yes and the Lincoln Continental, well most of it.'

'Jamie.' I looked at him, the eyes were still anxious but perhaps not fearful. Never again the fear please God. 'I really am very, very pleased to see you.'

The next day, mid morning, the Mitchells rolled up. It was a set up of course, Emma's idea. I was in the garden with David and the children; we were trying to clear back some of the undergrowth.

'I do believe I've just found the lawn,' said David, up to his knees in nettles. Just then they appeared, like film stars, pulling up in the BMW with the roof down, stereo blaring, sunglasses; Mitch in white silk headscarf, Dan in driving gloves, waving like royalty. The children squealed with delight.

324

'Hello all you hayseeds!' shouted Dan, jumping over the door of the car. 'Now which one of you children loves your Uncle Dan best eh? Ten quid to the winner. Good Lord is that two Deacons I see before me in the deep shrubbery, no the one in the moustache looks far too shifty, must be the gardener, tell me my good man—' And so on as he stepped gingerly across the flower-bed. I went to him; we hugged. 'Hello cocker,' he whispered in my ear. 'Bloody good to see you.' We hung on for a second, then he broke off: 'Here don't start any of that nonsense. I know all about you outdoor gardening types, gay blades to a man, David! Very good to see you, how long has it been . . .'

'Hello flyboy,' said Mitch. We clung together too. It was that sort of a day. When we finally separated and I held her at arm's length her eyes were wet. 'Thank you for coming.' It was all I could think of.

And there was more: Alice and Jack turned up in the evening. We had a dinner party, all eight of us jammed around the kitchen table munching on garlic bread and a vast lasagna that Emma had prepared. It was a master-stroke, my mother unwound for the first time in months, sandwiched between Jack Greenaway and Dan. They were marvellous; it was so good to see her laugh again. Emma and I sat opposite each other at either end. From time to time our eyes met. During the afternoon she'd suggested I stay on at the cottage for a bit after my mother and David had gone back: 'See how it goes – only if you'd like to of course.' It was what I wanted more than anything else in the world.

I looked at her, she leaned towards me, said something I couldn't catch. Dan and Jack had started to sing; David was plugging his ears with strips of paper napkin. It was turning into a traditional Deacon dinner party.

'What?' I cupped a hand to my ear.

She tried again, broke off laughing as the noise grew louder, shook her head, then cocked it to one side and smiled. 'Hello,' she mouthed.

The singing rose to a crescendo, Dan, Jack and David, heads together across the table, wailing like cartoon cats. We all joined in: 'I'm forever blowing bubbles, pretty bubbles in the air. They rise so high, they reach the sky, then like my dreams they fade and die . . .'

My desk up here in the spare room looks down on the lane. I can see straight out over the fields, along the footpath past the little spinney, across the stream at the footbridge and beyond over to the far side of the vale. The corn is tall and golden, in just a few weeks it'll be harvested, the stubble ploughed back into the soil and the cycle begun again.

It is almost exactly a year since I was made redundant from UAS. I know that I am not the same person now as I was then. I've settled in here, can't imagine any other life. I have work: I started up a one man marketing consultancy for local firms. It brings in a modest commission and keeps the business brain ticking over two days a week. One of my clients is the craft market I wandered into two villages away.

I keep house. Mandy still comes to help; her grandfather and I are putting a new roof on the garage next week. What else – the children. I can just see them now, two slow moving dots down in the bottom field. Heading for the dried-up puddle of a stream I expect. They are a constant source of frustration, revelation and delight. Jamie is so grown up, his confidence improves almost daily. Last term, for the first time ever, he began bringing a schoolfriend home for tea. A pleasant, shy boy called Matthew. Sally is Sally. She is going to marry Matthew. Saturday apparently.

Emma works like a Trojan. She's running her own

department now at Charlie's and there's heady talk of expansion into bigger premises, even of partnerships. She thrives on it, yet in the evenings seems genuinely grateful to put it aside and cook dinner or help put the children to bed, or just sit in the garden and quiz me about my day.

It's astonishing how your priorities can alter; and how futile the struggle against inevitable change is. I won't say I am happier now – I was happy then, or so I believed. But I have learned to make a peace with myself, cherish those things that are precious and be grateful for the moment.

Warner now offers an exciting range of quality titles by both established and new authors. All of the books in this series are available from:
Little, Brown and Company (UK) Limited,
P.O. Box 11,
Falmouth,
Cornwall TR10 9EN.

Alternatively you may fax your order to the above address. Fax No. 0326 376423.

Payments can be made as follows: Cheque, postal order (payable to Little, Brown and Company) or by credit cards, Visa/Access. Do not send cash or currency. UK customers: and B.F.P.O.: please send a cheque or postal order (no currency) and allow £1.00 for postage and packing for the first book, plus 50p for the second book, plus 30p for each additional book up to a maximum charge of £3.00 (7 books plus).

Overseas customers including Ireland, please allow £2.00 for postage and packing for the first book, plus £1.00 for the second book, plus 50p for each additional book.

NAME (Block Letters) ....

ADDRESS...

....

☐ I enclose my remittance for _____

☐ I wish to pay by Access/Visa Card

Number ☐☐☐☐☐☐☐☐☐☐☐☐☐☐☐☐

Card Expiry Date ☐☐☐☐